Cyber Security Technical Framework

—Trusting System Based on Identity Authentication

网际安全技术构架——基于标识鉴别的可信系统

Nan Xiang-hao

U0131712

電子工業出版社

Publishing House of Electronics Industry

北京·BEIJING

Abstract

CPK Cryptosystem changes ordinary elliptic curve public key into an identity-based public key with self-assured property. Self-assured public key can advance the authentication logic from object-authenticating "belief logic" to entity-authenticating "trust logic". Self-assured public key system and trust logic of authentication composes the key technique of cyber security. The construction of trust connecting, computing, transaction, logistics, counter-forgery and network management will be the main contents of the next generation of information security.

Readers benefited from this book will be researchers and professors, experts and students, developers and policy makers, and all other who are interested in cyber security.

图书在版编目（CIP）数据

网际安全技术构架：基于标识鉴别的可信系统：英文/南相浩著. —北京：电子工业出版社，2010.8

ISBN 978-7-121-11379-6

Ⅰ. ①网⋯　Ⅱ. ①南⋯　Ⅲ. ①计算机网络－安全技术－英文　Ⅳ. ①TP393.08

中国版本图书馆 CIP 数据核字（2010）第 136653 号

责任编辑：赵　平

印　　刷：北京市天竺颖华印刷厂

装　　订：三河市鑫金马印装有限公司

出版发行：电子工业出版社

　　　　　北京市海淀区万寿路 173 信箱　邮编：100036

开　　本：787×980　1/16　印张：16.75　字数：426 千字

印　　次：2010 年 9 月第 1 次印刷

印　　数：1 500 册　　定价：88.00 元

凡所购买电子工业出版社的图书，如有缺损问题，请向购买书店调换。若书店售缺，请与本社发行部联系，联系及邮购电话：(010) 88254888。

质量投诉请发邮件至 zlts@ phei. com. cn，盗版侵权举报请发邮件至 dbqq@ phei. com. cn。

服务热线：(010) 88258888。

About the Author

NAN Xiang-hao: Dean, South China Information Security Institute, visiting professor of Information Engineering University and Institute of Computer Science and Technology, Beijing University.

Publications:

1. *Profile to Network Security Technologies*, 2003 (Chinese)
2. *Identity Authentication Based on CPK*, 2005 (Chinese)
3. *CPK Crypto-system and Cyber Security*, 2007 (Chinese)

Forward

Providing trust in the face of anonymity is an impossibility. Since interactions on the Internet can easily be anonymous, it is imperative to find a digital authentication means that is reliable, simple to deploy, and simple to use. A method that will bring trust to the Internet and to the general population is critical. The CPK cryptosystem allows society to enjoy the benefits of eCommerce and individual privacy which is balanced with the social needs.

Anonymity, the ability to perform an act without identifying oneself, is not a new concept, but has been dramatically enhanced because of the Internet. Traditionally, the presence of an offender and a victim in the same location leaves behind physical evidence, and this evidence improves the ability of the police to identify and apprehend an offender. By comparison, the Internet has been shown to be a haven for offenders. Offenders can perform criminal acts at great distances that can transcend national boundaries in near perfect anonymity, making law enforcement dramatically more difficult.

Authentication is the natural defense of anonymity, it forms the foundation for trust by proving identity. Authentication can be used for authorization, privacy, and deterrence.

Authentication for authorization is necessary to access money in the bank or to know that the person who signed the document has the authority to commit for the organization.

Authentication for privacy is necessary to know that a conversation is private between two people. An email to your spouse should not be readable by someone who has attacked the Internet. This form of "direct encryption" has higher levels of trust if there is direct authentication by both parties.

Authentication for deterrence is necessary to be able to know who you interact with. Seeing the license of a car provides some assurance about who you are dealing with if something bad happens, there is a better chance of the police being able to track down the offender.

Cryptographic Authentication attempts to provide this proof of identity from a distance using purely digital means. This is a difficult problem that transcends the mathematics of cryptography and moves into the philosophical issues of trust and the organizational basis of society.

In Whitfield Diffie's and Martin Hellman's 1976 paper " NEW DIRECTIONS IN CRYPTOGRAPHY" the authors introducing the concept of public key cryptography and digital signatures wrote. . .

- Authentication is at the heart of any system involving contracts and billing. Without it, business cannot function. Current electronic authentication systems cannot meet the need for a purely digital, unforgetable, message dependent signature. They provide protection against third party forgeries, but do not protect against disputes between transmitter and receiver.

Since that time, there have been many digital signature schemes proposed and some standardized. In general these are now described as traditional signature schemes that have been implemented as a directed graph of public keys which are signed by a more general key until the point that there is mutual trust.

Traditional digital authentication is tied to the individual. It requires a public key distribution scheme and lacks lawful intercept abilities.

If Alice needs to send an email to Bob, she must first get Bob's public key from a repository, check the revoked key list, and authenticate this key to some root key that she trusts before she can send a message to Bob. This is a significant effort.

If Alice and Bob are conspirators in a crime, their communications cannot be investigated by law enforcement.

Identity based encryption provides simpler solutions to these problems. From Adi Shamir's 1984 paper "IDENTITY BASED CRYPTOSYSTEMS AND SIGNATURE SCHEMES" he states:

- In this paper we introduce a novel type of cryptographic scheme, which enables any pair of users to communicate securely and to verify each other's signatures without exchanging private or public keys, without keeping key directories, and without using the services of a third party.

Professor Shamir further states that...

- The scheme remains practical even on a nationwide scale with hundreds of key generation centers and millions of users, and it can be the basis for a new type of personal identification card which everyone can electronically sign checks, credit card slips, legal documents, and electronic mail.

One of the values of identity based encryption is the key generating centers can be operated by organizations who can naturally vouch for an individual's identity. For example, an university can vouch for a professor or a student, or a corporation can vouch for an employee.

Identity based encryption also provides a deterrence against the abuse of trust. In practice, a key generated by a corporation has the valuable side effect of allowing policing by that corporation of an individual's use of that key.

The CPK algorithm represents a great step forward in identity based encryption. It creates a simple to understand, easy to implement, and easy to deploy system that provides all the benefits that these visionaries imagined for public key and identity based cryptosystems.

This book delivers a complete analysis of what Identity, Authentication and Trust mean in a digital age. It shows how CPK can meet the challenges of the internet to make it a safer place.

This book may not result in world peace, but it can provide a roadmap to calm the chaos which exists on the Internet today.

James P. Hughes
Palo Alto, CA, USA

Preface

A report submitted by the US President's Information Technology Advisory Committee (PI-TAC) in 2005, entitled *Cyber Security-A Crisis of Prioritization*, marked the arrival of a new era of cyber security (cyber world). If the main task of "information security" is a passive prevention that consists mainly of plugging and patching, the main task of "cyber security" is active management that consists mainly of building trusting system. The core of active management is to establish an authentication system that sets up information security on the basis of certification system. This is so called trusting system. It is a new mission. In the past, since there were no proper evidence-showing and verifying systems, information security can only adopt the principle of "at good will", or based on the presumption that the subject was trustworthy. However, cyber security is totally different. It is established on the basis of "mutual suspicion", not allowing authentication or verification under presumption.

Such changes of main task and basic principles first affect basic theory of security. All the security protocols and standards adopting the principle of "good will" in the past shall be reconsidered with "mutual suspicion", for example, communication protocols and standards, trusted computing (including code signing) protocols and standards. This will surely lead to a revolutionary change.

At the EU crypt '07 annual meeting, James Hughes (executive chairman of Cript '04) and Guan Zhi (Ph. D student of Beijing University) delivered a presentation on identity-based Combined Public Key (CPK) system. The authoritative experts attending the meeting affirmed that CPK system is novel. Identity-based system represents new development trend of modern cryptosystem, and attracts attention from cryptography community around the world. CPK Cryptosystem has attracted great attention from China's top leaders, and also has received substantial support from the administrations of Guangdong Science and Technology Department and Beijing Municipal Science and Technology Commission. Researchers/Professors Zhou Zhong-yi, Chen Hua-ping, Lü Shu-wang, Zhai Qi-bing, Li Yi-fa and Doctors Tang Wen, Guan Zhi, Chen Yu, Tian Wen-chun, Zheng Xu have involved in this CPK project.

Another important progress is that a theory of trust logic is established based on identity authentication, to promote the conventional belief logic to trust logic. The trust logic based on identity authentication is different from the belief logic based on data authentication. The trust logic consisted of identity of entity authentication and body of entity authentication, can conduct "pre-proof". That is, identity authentication can be conducted before the body event occurs, so as to effectively prevent illegal events from happening. Large scale authentication technology is the core technology to establishing a world of trust. CPK system can solve such international puzzle well.

This book systematically introduces solutions in the main fields of trusting system. Such fields include a number of problems which cannot be solved in the past but easily dealt with now, for instance: illegal communication access, illegal software running, seal authentication systems, etc. From examples of application, readers can find that due to the core issue of identity authentication has been solved, a number of difficult problems that was impossible to solve in the past can be easily tackled. Thus, "identity authentication" is the "silver bullet" of cyber security, which will lead to the solution of all other problems. This is the base of a holistic solution of trust system. In the process of researching, Communication expert Sun Yu, Computer expert Qu Yan-wen, IT expert James Hughes and sci&tech information expert Zhao Jian-guo offered useful suggestions.

At the beginning of 2009, U. S. government has released some documents related with cyber security. The documents have stressed three points: Addressing system in internet, identity authentication and secure software engineering. The address is the identity of communication. It tells us the Identity Management, including identity definition and identity authentication, will be the basic techniques of future cyber security. How to define identity is an important subject but beyond this book. However, we have enough experience in defining identity in real life such as the mailing address, phone number, bank account number, and so on. This is the reason why we stand for real name system. From the rules of identity definition in real life we may draw an important conclusion: In trusting system, identity must have special meaning and the meaning must be commonly recognized. It is obvious that, the address is defined randomly and only explained by special DNS. in existing IPv4 and IPv6 protocols It is unfortunate that the protocols go against above mentioned basic rules. This is why Obama administration took "identity authentication" and addressing system as core task of cyber security.

The work of cyber security is in progress of developing on its track and has yielded some important results. For example, a new type of network router is designed with real name communication system. The address is the real location that bounded with the sign code, so it can prohibit any unauthorized connection. Meanwhile code signing has been developed rapidly as main part of trust computing.

CPK cryptosystem, identity authentication and trust logic is introduced in this book as the basic theory and technology of the trusting system. The construction of trust world needs a joint effort of all nations because we have a common enemy: that is the "terrorist software". I sincerely wish that this book can satisfy the demands of readers, facilitate transition of information security from network security to cyber security.

Author

In Beijing, Sep. 2009

Contents

Part One   Authentication Technique

Part Two　Crypto-systems

Part Three　CPK System

Part Four　Trust Computing

Part Five　Trust Connecting

Appendices

Part One

Authentication Technique

Chapter 1

Basic Concepts

Before the study of authentication theory, some basic concepts need to be clarified. With the development of Internet, information security has been rapidly developed. At the same time, a lot of new concepts have been raised or formed. In the forming process, new concepts may inevitably be imperfect and/or incomplete, which may easily cause misleading. If such misleading has influence on the country 's decision-making, it will lead to strategic mistake. Therefore, it is necessary to raise the disputed concepts, to discuss, research, and clarify, in order to reach consensus.

1. 1　Physical World and Digital world

Digital world is a product of IT technology development, and it is called Cyber. As a new thing, it surely has its own development rules. Only grasping the rules, can one control development of the digital world. Research on the rules just started, which shows a broad prospect.

Authentication system is first generated in the physical world, which undergoes a long development process, and forms a whole set of legal, institutional, technical, operational mechanism. While digital world is a new thing emerging recently, the research on its authentication system just began. Up until now, the physical world is still a big world, and digital world is a small world, which is a small part of the physical world. However, digital world gets bigger and bigger, more and more integrates with the physical world, and constitutes a new world with larger space.

In the authentication system, there are many similarities between the physical world and the digital world. However, there are a number of differences as well. Thus, in the study of digital world authentication system, it first pays attention to various authentication principles, authentication methods, and authentication effects of the physical world, while at the same time focuses on different characteristics between the digital world and the physical world. In general, authentication of the physical world uses physical methods, and authentication of the digital world uses logic methods. The digital world cannot entirely simulate authentication system of the physical world. Someone proposed to use logic methods to identify counterfeit banknotes. Obviously, banknotes are physical things, which cannot use logic methods to identify. A physical feature is uneasy to replicate, while a logic feature is easy to reproduce. Therefore, in real life, anti-forgery work adopts physical methods.

In the physical world, the government issues bulletin, with stamped official seal. A purpose of the official seal is to "claim" that this document is truly issued by the government, who has rights and obligations to the document. Now turning to the digital world, the government issues a bulletin, with stamped official seal (e. g., digital signature by the government). Can this play the same role as the physical seal? The answer is "Yes". Although emphasis of the physical seal is self-claiming, while focus of the logic seal is to provide non-repudiation to the other party, both can achieve the same purpose of official responsibility on the document. Thus, in most cases, the application of logic seal can simulate that of the physical seal. However, such simulation is not a formality simulation, rather a substantial simulation.

1.2　A World with Order and without Order

Both physical world and logical world are divided into a world without order and a world of order. A world of order is an organized world, a world composed of affiliation and subordination, and a world with center, such as banking system, state organs, etc. A world without order is an unorganized world, a world not composed of affiliation and subordination, and a world without center, e. g., one purchasing goods in a store belongs to the activity of a world without order, because the customer and the store do not have any organizational relationship, and do not constitute any affiliation and subordination relationship. In addition, for example, anyone to any other ones, one person to any enterprises, and any independent business to any other enterprises, all belong to the activities of a world without order.

It is relatively easy to establish authentication system in a world of order, because a world of order is a world with center and boundary. This is consistent with security property: any security has its certain function domain and effective domain. Affiliation relationship exists in the world of order, and has a general sense of trust relationship. That is, registration and jurisdiction of trust relationship is very easy to satisfy, and trust relationship can be established only by proving integration.

The main task of cyber security is to construct trusting system in the dangerous world. It does not mean that we are going to change the world without order into a completely ordered world. Instead, there will be two worlds that are going to be co-existing. Anonymity or Discussion Board will still be there, for example. To explain better, another example can be: People can freely use the road and enter the airport. However, if anyone wants to get on the plane, he/she has to follow the rule such as check in and get the boarding pass using valid identification, take the assigned seat etc. In another word, he/she enters a world with order from a world without order. Hence, Anonymity and Real Name system, Freedom system and Trusting system are separate concepts and in different definition. They are not denying each other.

It is relatively difficult to establish authentication system in a world without order. However, there may be a number of solutions. The first solution is out-of-order handling, such as: writing a receipt for a loan by oneself or handwriting signature by oneself. This solution exists in the real world, e. g., when two people know each other and have certain trust. The second solution is notarizing by a legitimate third party on the basis of disorder handling. CA certificate of PKI belongs to this. The third solution is ordered handling. For instance, if a society conducts all trades by way of writing notes, the consequences would be too ghastly to contemplate. People use banknotes issued by banks (the world of order) to conduct trades in the world without order, and use ID cards issued by Ministry of Public Security (the world of order) to conduct transaction process in the world without order. Some shopping centers adopt membership system, which is also a means of turning the world without order into the world of order.

When studying security problems or authentication problems, we must first determine which field of security problems and authentication problems needs to be solved. This is the priority of studying problems. Otherwise, the study results may be irrelevant.

1.3 Self-assured Proof and 3rd Party Proof

Trust system is comprised of prover and verifier. The prover provides evidence of authenticity, while the verifier verifies the authenticity of evidence. Thus, establishing a proof system is the key to establish the trust system. The previous security protocols and security systems did not give substantial attention to establishing a proof system. In addition, a number of works try to achieve trustworthy proof in the absence of proof system. Thus, the authentication protocol appears very complicated, while may not achieve proving purpose.

Recently, someone raised a concept of "system without certificate". If the certificate refers to third-party authentication based PKI certificate, i. e., CA certificate, nothing wrong with this concept. However, if it generally refers to any certificate, the concept is wrong. In a real society, any verification is carried out with the help of certificates, such as passport, driver's license, and resident card. The chaos of the network is because it has not established a proof system.

There are two kinds of certificates, one is third-party based certificate, and the other is self-assured ID-card. No matter which one, the certificate needs trust root. This is in common. Without trust root, the proof system cannot be established. Thus, one can say that a world without order is a system without certificate, and a world of order is a system with certificate. "Trusting system" is a "security system" established on the basis of proof system.

CPK authentication system adopts centralized management. The issued certificate is ID-card (private key), rather than CA certificate of PKI (public key).

ID-card and CA certificate are different in nature. ID-card is issued by the authority, and is a certificate that uses private key variables as the main authentication parameters. CA certificate is issued by a third party, and is a certificate that uses public key variables as the main authentication parameters. ID-card is issued by the authority, it can authorize. CA certificate is issued by a third party, it generally cannot authorize. CA certificate needs to operate online, while ID-card can be operated off-line and can directly be used to authenticate identity, to establish relatively reliable trust relationship. CA certificate of PKI indirectly establish a relatively loose trust relationship with third-party proof.

In addition to use as the essential basis for identity authentication, ID-card also uses as a basic tool for private-key distribution, to determine function domain, effective domain of a private key, classification of key variables, etc., to provide signature function while at the same time providing encryption function. CA certificate generally only provides signature function. If encryption function is needed, it must be supported by private key escrow function.

In the physical world, there are two types of proof: one is identity-based proof, i. e., self-proof, which can achieve self-justification; the other one cannot justify itself, rather it only can rely on third-party proof. Most cases in life fall into the first type. One can hardly imagine that everything has to rely on third-party proof. Indeed, a photo itself can prove that it is oneself, without proof from a third party. When shopping in a store, cash itself is a proof, and no notarization is needed from a third party. However, some cases cannot prove themselves, such as: criminal record, copyright, etc., which must be proved by a third party. Here, the third party is Intellectual Property Office, Public Security Office or Notary Public Office, etc. Lack of digital signature cannot only rely on technical means to solve. If a dispute arises, it can be judged by the Notary Public Office. Thus, it is necessary to establish notarization mechanism in the cyber world. The core issue of Notary Public Office is its fairness. Such fairness must be recognized by law, and recognized by everybody.

It is apparent that occasions that cannot justify themselves must rely on third-party notarization. In contrast, it is redundant for occasions that can justify themselves to rely on third party notarization. The current key management technology can construct identity-based key variables, i. e., the key variables themselves can prove authenticity of the identity, without proving from a third party organization. Thus, third party notarization mechanism shall not be considered as universal rules, to be used anywhere regardless of occasions.

A trusting system relies on "trust root". The trust root functions as an invisible third-party. The Ministry of Public Security issues "ID-card" to all residents. The residents can use the ID-card to transact various procedures, e. g., customs check. Here, the Ministry of Public Security is the trust root of the ID-card. Also, the bank prints banknotes for circulation. Here, the bank becomes the trust root. Same for the private key management, the key distribution center is the trust root of keys.

1.4   Certification Chain and Trust Chain

The concept of Proof chain (or certificate chain) and trust chain is easy to get confused. For instance, "DoD PKI strategy of US Department of Defense" and "FBCA Strategy of US Federal Government" clearly state that the system is established on the basis of trust transfer.

The book of "Information Assurance Technology Framework" recites: "The most important expansion of trust relationship is to merge foreign domain through cross-certification, which in fact provides the foreign domain user with the same trust property as that of the local domain user."

Thus, the theories of trust transfer and trust expansion are the two important theoretical basis of US business PKI and Department of Defense DoD PKI. "Trust transfer" theory provides basis for vertical expansion, while "cross authentication" theory provides basis for horizontal expansion.

Taking CA as an example, CA is established on the basis of certificate chain with various levels of authentication. CA treats certificate chain as trust chain, and treats the chain as trust transferring chain, without distinguishing certificate chain and trust chain. In fact, certificate chain and trust chain are of two different concepts, which belong to two different categories. The transfer relationship of certificate chain is workable, e. g., if A = B, B = C, it can be deduced that A = C. However, in a trust chain, transferability may not work, e. g., if A trusts B, B trusts C, it may not be concluded that A surely trusts C.

Trust falls into fuzzy category, which cannot come to a conclusion of correct or incorrect as that of certificate chain. Instead, it only can come to a fuzzy conclusion of trustworthy, fully trust, or distrust. This is also an important difference between certificate chain and trust chain. Thus, it is inaccurate to vaguely raise the judgment of "certificate chain transfer trust".

Trust may be transferred but diluted. Thus, the judgment of "trust expansion" that the employees of different CA can obtain the same trust of employees of same CA through cross-authentication cannot be established.

Trust theory is a complex theory. In general, the certificate is first checked, to determine its accuracy. Can this directly get the conclusion of "reliable trust relationship being established"? One can only say: The certificate is correct. This provides a proof for establishing trust relationship, but not all the proofs.

1. 5 Centralized and Decentralized Management

The implementations of authentication protocols are directly related to management system, i. e., the overall security strategy. Management system includes two types: centralized management and decentralized management.

Centralized management is a system that key management center (KMC) directly manages all user keys, i. e., a system that the private keys are uniformly generated and distributed by KMC. KMI of U. S. army, identity-based encryption IBE, and combined public key (CPK) all belong to this category.

Decentralized management is a system that the private keys are generated by individual themselves and the public key is proved by a third party CA.

From the strategic point of view: Under centralized management, the private keys are uniformly generated by means of background off-line, while the public key can be dispersedly preserved by each user. Thus, a local destruction does not affect security of the whole network. Therefore, off-line centralized generation and online dispersedly preservation system of the private-key variables has more advantages than off-line decentralized generation and online centralized preservation mechanism. Under the model of decentralized generation, the private key is generated by an individual. Thus, the public key must have centralized storage, e. g., LDAP of PKI. Since the certificate database is running online, destruction of the certificate database will paralyze the whole network. Thus, under the model of decentralized generation, centralized preservation of certificates solves the security problem, but also increases security risks.

From trust logic point of view, under the model of centralized generation, direct-level trust relationship is established between the center and the users, and, grade one inference-level trust relationship is established between the users. However, under the model of decentralized generation, only diluted trust relationship can be established between users under various levels.

From security responsibility point of view: Centralized generation is a system that an authority takes the responsibility, while decentralized generation is a system that individual takes the responsibility. Decentralized model only suits for occasions that the security responsibility is fully taken by individuals, and may not apply to the occasions that the security responsibility involves interest of a third party. For instance, loss of confidential documents not only relates to personal interests, but also involves national interest. Thus, it does not apply to confidential networks, private networks, etc.

From multi-level control point of view: Under centralized management model, it can implement level-based mandatory security policy and role-based self-assurance security policy. However, under decentralized management, it can only implement self-assurance security policy, and cannot implement mandatory security policy.

From privacy point of view: The decentralized model has tremendous advantages, but does not facilitate to manage. Under the centralized model, individual privacy can only rely on trust root. However, it facilitates management. Recently, CPK system proposes a new mechanism that under centralized management, signature key can be defined by individual. It includes both the advantages of centralized management and the advantages of decentralized management.

1.6 Physical Signature and Digital Signature

In the physical world, there are two types of signature: one is seal, and the other one is handwriting signature. The abstract subject such as organization, association, legal person, uses seal. Individual mainly uses handwriting signature, and he can also use seal. The first characteristic of physical signature is that the signing is done by the person himself as a subject; the second characteristic is that others recognize the signature. If these two characteristics cannot be satisfied, it is not the signature. In a logic world, the logic signature also needs tot meet these two characteristics. Many people use Hashed code of message digest as electronic signature. For instance, the EU Committee regulates in the "Directive on a Community Framework for Electronic Signatures", that electronic signature is a means that uses other data attached in electronic form or logically associated with electronic data for authentication. Here, apparently Hashed code is used as electronic signature. If data is the subject, this definition is not wrong. However, in the authentication system, data is always the object to be authenticated, which does not satisfy the first characteristic of signature. Thus, it cannot be used as digital signature.

Whether the digital signature is same as the physical signature? What role can digital signature play? What it can do and what it cannot do? These questions indeed need to be clarified.

Digital signature is a kind of logical seal. A characteristic of logical seal is that it is only responsible for the content, but not for the medium. This is different from the physical seal, which is first responsible for the medium, and then responsible for the content through the medium. This is better to achieve unity among medium, content and seal. However, there are situations that the content and medium are separate, for example, a blank recommendation letter. Even though the use of blank recommendation letter does not comply with relevant provisions, in the real life it does exist such situation that the blank recommendation letter is obtained in advance and the content is filled later on.

Since the logical seal cannot be responsible for the medium, and cannot 'claim' something by itself, it can only provide the other party undeniable evidence. Logical seal ensures non-modifiability of the content, and is easy to achieve authenticity. Physical seal 'claims' something by itself, and provides the other party undeniable evidence. However, it is easy to modify, and difficult to authenticate. For instance, an artist draws a painting, with signature and seal in the end, to claim or prove that this painting is his work. However, the existence of lots of fake is an example.

Electronic files can be saved in a number of physical media. The responsibility for physical media requires a common use of physical means, because only physical means can ensure the unity of media and signature. The logical mean can only be responsible for contents of the file, but cannot guarantee the unity of media and signature. Signature and content each exists in a separate place. Thus, a digital signature created by one can be removed by someone else. The digital watermark in the current research can be used in multimedia, simulating seal of the physical world, but it is very difficult to be used in the message system.

The most basic application of digital signature is non-repudiation of the participants afterwards. For example, Zhang San withdrew RMB1000 from the bank, and signed on the withdrawal form. The signature is not that he 'claims' something, rather it provides the bank undeniable evidence afterwards. That is, Zhang San cannot deny the truth of withdrawing RMB1000 from the bank afterwards, because the bank holds the evidence of Zhang San's signature.

A purpose of adducing evidence is to prove that the other side has fault, or to prove that oneself has no fault. A deficiency of logical signature is that it can only provide evidence that the other side has fault, but cannot provide evidence that oneself has no fault. For example: Zhang San wired RMB1000 to company A for orders, and had a digital signature. Now let us take a look at what role this signature can play indeed. Company A claims that they did not receive the payment for goods. Zhang San can sue company A, but he cannot provide evidence. Apparently, whether Zhang San signed or not cannot prove the fact that Zhang San wired the remittance. Only the signed acknowledging receipt by company A can provide Zhang San undeniable evidence that company A has received the payment.

In the physical world, validity of seal has certain limits. The validity is typically claimed by the verifier, and the valid range is generally limited within its jurisdiction. If the valid range needs to be expanded, it is normally through the form of protocol. For instance, a university sends offer letter to the candidate, with official seal of the university. Here, the university is verifier, and the candidates are prover. The offer letter only provides evidence admitted by the university when the students register. However, the student can purchase half-priced ticket with the offer letter, i. e., the railway station also admits the official seal of the university. Apparently, this is the result of negotiation between Ministry of Education and Ministry of Railways. In the logic world, this is same as the physical world. In the absence of specific laws and regulations, contracts, agreements, and criteria can become legal basis, as long as each party of the transaction admits.

Key exchange protocol is mainly used for data confidentiality, which is open to the involved people but confidential to irrelevant personnel. Thus, the function of key exchange solves contradiction of open and close. In a typical authentication system, it not only needs to solve the issue of digital signature, but also needs to solve the issue of key exchange. The contradiction of open digital signature and closed key exchange is difficult to manage. The key management technology depends on reasonable solution to such contradiction to a great extent.

Bio-feature belongs to physical feature, which has a characteristic of non-replicate. In daily activity, bio-feature is mainly used for "face-to-face verification", which is a very effective verification means. Can such feature apply to the cyber world?

In the cyber world, there are two kinds of occasions, one can conduct "on-spot verification", and the other one cannot carry out "on-spot verification". A customer registers in a server, and thus constituting a master-slave relationship with the server. The customer becomes prover (evidence holder), and the bank becomes evidence verifier. Under such circumstance, may it be meaningful to use bio-feature? However, this may not be the best way, which is still in dispute. Since during the process of online transmission, all the bio-features turn into logic values, same as logic features, losing the characteristic as bio-features: non-replicate. The current authentication technology has been developed to the extent that use of logic feature and bio-feature can play a role similar to "face-to-face verification".

Except for the occasion such as direct transaction between the banking system and the customer, most transactions are carried out between customers. In such occasions, there is no condition for "on-spot verification", rather it can only use logic feature to conduct indirect validation. Thus, some scholars believe that logic feature is the most economic and effective technical means for online authentication. In online communication we may realize dual direction authentication and can prevent repeating attacks.

Chapter 2

Authentication Logic

2. 1　Belief Logic

Object authentication is to verify authenticity of " something". Authentication is always implemented through certain formal proof, which is called authentication protocol. When discussing authentication logic, one naturally uses axiomatic trust, in which authentication logic is expressed as some special symbol string, known as formula. Some specific logic formula reflects rules of thinking. Thus, the axiomatic tust is used as base of authentication logic. Typically, it is used to authenticate certificates, vouchers, private keys and other important data.

In the book of *A Logic of Authentication*, Michael Burrows et al., the following principles are raised as the premise of object authentication:

1. If you have sent a number which has never been used for such purpose previously to A, and if later on you received something based on the number from A, then you have to believe that the message from A was recently generated, in fact it is a response to your message.

2. If you believe that only you and A know K, then you have to believe that all things encrypted under K-key that you have received are from A.

3. If you believe that K is the public key of A, then you have to believe that any messages that can be decrypted by K are from A.

4. If you believe that only you and A know X, then you have to believe that any encrypted messages containing X are from A.

To prove authenticity of the object O (according to BAN logic requirements), it shall at least satisfy readability, nonce and data jurisdiction.

f(O) = (integrity, nonce, jurisdiction):

On the occasion of A sending X to B, assuming that A is trustworthy, then:

(1) The rule of readability: If A encrypts and B can decrypt with the key, then B can believe

that A has same key parameters that comply with the agreement, and thus B believes that X is written by A.

(2) The rule of nonce: If B believes that X is written by A, and at the same time A provides a nonce valid proof (not valid in the past, which is an effective means for preventing replay attack (copy attack), and is also a logic method to imitate "face-to-face verification", to realize "on-spot verification" in the physical world), then B believes that A believed X.

(3) The rule of jurisdiction: If B believes that A believed X, and at the same time A provides that X is under jurisdiction of A, and then B believes X.

It is not difficult to see the characteristics of belief logic:

(1) In belief logic entities are classified into subject and object.

(2) Belief logic is to prove the authenticity of object, the conclusion of the inference is B believes X.

(3) The inference is undergone under the presupposition that A is trust, without such assumption, the inference would be difficult to establish.

(4) In most cases we draw the conclusion of 'B trust A' from 'B believes X', that is to say that authenticity of subject is derived from or after the authentication of object. Such proving method is called post-proof. The post-proof of belief logic is addressed with respect to the pre-proof of trust logic discussed below.

2.2　Standard Protocol

The belief logic based authentication protocol of International standard 509 is as follows:

One-way protocol:

1) Alice generates a random number RA

2) Alice calculates $M = \{T_A, I_B\}$; wherein T is time, and I is identity

3) Alice sends Bob $\{I_A, D_A(M)\}$; wherein I_A is the identity of Alice, and D_A is Alice's signature to M

4) Bob checks I_A, to obtain Alice's public key E_A

5) Bob verifies the signature $D_A(M)$ by using E_A

6) Bob checks I_B in M

7) Bob checks T_A in M, to confirm time of origination of the message

8) (Option) Bob take R_A from M and checks the repetition comparing with R_A in storage

Dual-way protocol:

Step 1 to step 8 are the same as one-way protocol.

9) Bob generates a random number R_B

10) Bob computes $M' = \{T_B, R_B, I_A, R_A, d\}$

11) Bob sends Alice the signature $D_B\{M'\}$

12) Alice checks the signature with E_B

13) Alice checks I_A in M'

14) Alice checks T_B in M'

15) (Option) Alice takes R_B in M' to check the repetition

Three-way protocol:

16) Alice checks the R_A comparing with the R_A sent to Bob in step 3

17) Alice sends Bob the signature $D_A\{R_B\}$

18) Bob verifies the signature with E_A

19) Bob checks R_B comparing with the R_B in step 10

2.3　Trust Relationship

2.3.1　Direct Trust

Direct trust is grade one trust, the prover (evidence holder) and the verifier forming direct relationship, they are "father and son" in genetic bond, i.e., "parent-child" relationship. Only when it is direct trust, registration and integration can be established and verified. Therefore, direct trust is the true basis for identity authentication.

In social life, there are many cases like this. The ID-card issued by Ministry of Public Security forms direct trust between the country and individuals, in which the prover and verifier constitutes direct affiliation, to prove the civil status of a person. Direct relationship is established via account number and PIN code between a bank and a customer. The customer can conduct corresponding transaction within the specified scope with the account number and PIN code. The relationship between database and client also belongs to such relationship.

2.3.2　Axiomatic Trust

Axiomatic trust is established on the basis of common sense, and does not need to prove, which can be defined as no-grade trust. The concept of this trust is very important, because it is often ignored.

When go shopping, it seems that only cash or bill is needed to make the purchase, thus the belief logic on the objects can be established, and the transaction can be done. However, in fact such transaction is actually made on the basis of axiomatic trust, under the assumption that the bearer should be a normal person. If the bearer is an incapacitated person, such as mental patient, or a child, the transaction may not be made.

Belief logic shall be conducted on the basis of assumption: The verifier (C) believes that the prover (A) is trustworthy. This is axiomatic trust. Then, authenticity of the object (X) can be proved. Thus, a strange phenomenon appears: First assuming that A is trustworthy. Upon proving authenticity of X, one can conclude again that A is trustworthy.

It can be explained as such: At the beginning, the presupposition of C trusting A is an axiomatic trust. The conclusion of C trusting A through proof of belief logic is an inference trust, which elevates the trust level from axiomatic to inference level. Axiomatic trust or inference trust is not truly identity authentication. However, they can be used as an effective means for identity authentication in the electronic transactions, as long as security policy allows, or as long as all parties involved in the transaction admit. But the belief logic is only the logic of object authentication and is not the real logic of subject authentication.

2. 3. 3 Inference Trust

Many transactions are conducted between customers. However, there is no registration relationship, administrative superior-subordinate relationship and jurisdiction relationship between the customers. Therefore, registration between customers needs to be proved by a third party. Center C issues certificate to users A and B. With C's certificate, a trust relationship can be established between A and B. Here, Center C is the third party. If Center C and users A, B have administrative superior-subordinate relationship, then C actually is the "party in charge", Center C and users A, B have "father-son" relationship, and users A, B have "full brother" relationship. If Center C and users A, B have no administrative jurisdiction relationship, then the third-party C and users A, B have "appointed" father-son relationship, just like "adoptive" relationship, and users A, B are "appointed" brothers. Trust relationship is very much like blood relationship.

1) Fuzziness of Inference Trust

Fuzziness exists in trust degree of the subject. Defining interval of trust relationship as $[1,0]$, and using T_d to represent trust degree:

- T_1: representing the subset of "full trust"
- $T_{0.8}$: representing the subset of "highly trust"
- $T_{0.6}$: representing the subset of "quite trusted"
- $T_{0.4}$: representing the subset of "general trust"
- $T_{0.2}$: representing the subset of "a little trust"

- T_0: representing the subset of "no trust"

2) Gradation and Trust Level of CA

When CA has a multi-level structure, the transfer of certificate will dilute the trust. Assuming that the probability of counterfeits is 1/100, with the increase of gradation, the probability of true will step down accordingly, for example:

First-generation CA: the probability of true is 99% ;

Second-generation CA: the probability of true is 98% ;

. . .

Seventh-generation CA: the probability of true is 51% ;

In the hierarchical structure of CA, "generation" is directly related to the degree of inference trust. The first-generation CA and second-generation CA constitutes grade one trust, the second-generation CA and second-generation CA constitutes grade two trust, the second-generation CA and third-generation CA constitutes grade three trust, etc.

2.4   Trust Logic

2.4.1   The Requirement of Trust Logic

PITAC report accurately concluded the changes of security principles, and pointed out that: The security principle used for information security is always the belief logic based on "good will", while the principle for Cyber security is the trust logic based on "mutual suspicion". In the past, all the security protocols are based on "assuming subject is trust", to prove authenticity of object, or to prove subject authenticity by inferring object authenticity. This is called post-proof, i. e., authentication can be made only after the object event occurs.

Cyber security requires proving authenticity of entity before the key event occurs. We call it the "pre-proof". It may do through "identity authentication". An entity is divided two parts: identity and its body, i. e.,

Entity = Identity + Body.

The entity can be a subject, or an object whatever. Thus, in the trust logic, entity classification of "identity and body" replaces "subject and object" in the belief logic.

Identity is a mark that one entity differs from other entities, so identity can represent entity. The classification of entity provides the possibility to prove the identity before the proof of body. Trust logic divides identity proof process and body proof process into two independent processes, so as to implement identity verification before the body process occurs. For instance, with respect to the issue of preventing illegal access during communication, with communication identity authentication, authenticity of the sender can be identified before data communication starts.

2.4.2　The Progress in Public Key

The implementation of trust logic must be supported by corresponding public key technology. The public key system has to satisfy the following conditions: adopting centralized management by Key Management Center (KMC), using the public parameter released by KMC as trust root to bind public key and identity, to make it "self-assured". The identity used by trusting system must be real name (for readers to prove by themselves). Normal public key system is not self-assured. Therefore, a self-assured public key system must be reconstructed based on the original public key system.

At the end of 20th century, a new type of public key system based on identity came out, providing technical basis for constructing self-assured public key, such as Shamir 's identity-based crypto scheme (IBC), Boneh and Franklin 's IBE, NAN and CHEN 's CPK, Saar Ron 's IB-RSA, Gene Tsudik and Xuhua Ding 's meditated RSA (mRSA), etc..

Identity-based crypto-system opened a new direction for the development of identity management and made great progress in its application in recent years. But until now, only IBC and CPK has constructed digital signature with self-assured property and CPK has the advantage of short signature. It is obvious that only CPK has been the most suitable public key system to implement identity authentication so far.

Once there is a theory of identity authentication (IA), "Trust logic" can be constructed. The implementation of Identity authentication must rely on self-assured public key in which the public key is derived from the identity itself and can be calculated by everyone. If there is a Cryptosystem that an EntityID can be mapped into a point "ENTITY" on the elliptic curve of E, and there is an integer "$entity$" satisfies $ENTITY = (entity)G$, where G is the base point, then the point ENTITY is the public key and the integer $entity$ is the private key. Because $ENTITY = \sigma_1(EntityID)$, where EntityID and σ_1 is open to public, the public key can be calculated by everyone and private key is provided by ID-card.

In this book signature and verification are respectively indicated as "SIG" and "SIG^{-1}". Encryption and Decryption are respectively indicated as "E" and "D" in the symmetric key system and "ENC" and "DEC" in the asymmetric key system.

2.4.3　Entity Authenticity

If a given public key system has "self-assured property", the following trust logic can be constructed:

The proof may composed of three parts: the proof of identity, the proof of body; and the proof of integration of identity and body. Trust logic shall prove entity authenticity through identity authentication and the requirements are as follows: Entity authentication is the function of authenticity of identity and its body:

$$\text{AUTHENTICATION (entity)} = f(\text{IdentityID}) \cap f(\text{body})$$

The function of identity authenticity of the EntityID is a signature to time by the EntityID's private key *entity*:

$$f(\text{identity}) = \text{SIG}_{entity}(\text{time}) = \text{sign}_1$$

And the verification formula is

$$f^{-1}(\text{EntityID}) = \text{SIG}_{\text{ENTITY}}^{-1}(\text{time}) = \text{sign}_1{}'$$

Where ENTITY is public key derived from EntityID, entity is the private key of the EntityID that satisfies ENTITY = (*entity*)G. If $\text{sign}_1 = \text{sign}_1{}'$ then the EntityID is true. Where $\text{sign}_1 = \text{sign}_1{}'$ means that $\text{sign}_1{}'$ conforms to sign1.

In entity authentication, it needs to provide the proof of "who I am", which can be done in two ways: one is a proof based on identity; and the other one is a proof based on third party. Either one needs trust root to prove its registration and jurisdiction.

If using third party proof, the proof chain is as follows:

$$f(\text{identity}) = \text{SIG}_{private\text{-}key1}(\text{data}) = \text{sign}_1{}'$$

The sign must contain certificate proving the authenticity of public-key_1 and the integrity of public-key_1 and the name of the user (identity). Therefore the sign composed of sign1 and certificate. And the certificate must contain the following proof:

$$\text{SIG}_{private\text{-}key2}(\text{public-key}_1), \text{public-key}_2$$

In other words the identity in the third party authentication is proved in the form of data. When verifying, a given public-key_1 is provided. The public-key_1 is proved by trust root public-key_2. When the identity is proved in the form of data the proof of integrity of "someone" and identity needs to be provided.

The function of body authenticity is a signature to the character of the body:

Proof:

$$f(\text{body}) = \text{SIG}_{entity}(\text{CHR}) = \text{sign}_2$$

Verify:

$$f^{-1}(\text{body}) = \text{SIG}_{\text{ENTITY}}^{-1}(\text{CHR}) = \text{sign}_2{}'$$

If $\text{sign}_2 = \text{sign}_2{}'$ then the body is true.

Body of entity can be represented by its character. In information system body is always in a form of data, including the bio-feature. In this case the message authentication code (MAC) can be the character of the body.

The character authentication in trust logic is the same as the object authentication in belief logic. The character authentication is a function of integrity, nonce and jurisdiction:

$$AUTHENTICATION\ (CHR) = f\ (integrity) \cap f(nonce) \cap f\ (jurisdiction)$$

Wherein, f (integrity) = MAC;

　　　　　 f (nonce) = timestamp;

　　　　　 f (jurisdiction) = SIG_{entity} (MAC);

Because the body is signed by a private key that derived from its identity the integrity of identity and body is proved at one time, so no additional proof is needed.

The behavior authenticity is a function of anticipated behavior. The anticipation of behavior may be explained as follows:

The authenticity of behavior is a function of access control and nonce.

$$AUTHENTICATION\ (behavior) = f\ (access\text{-}control) \cap f\ (nonce)$$

Anticipation of behavior is generally regulated in access control. Nonce is to prove that the behavior is not an illegal replay. Random number, time stamp, etc. can be implemented.

The authenticity of behavior is a probability of the entity authenticity, which is also called trust degree:

$$AUTHENTICITY\ (behavior) = Prob\ (authentication\ of\ behavior)$$

In trust logic, the proving side provides evidence and the verifying side verifies the evidence. In some cases there is no direct evidence and we had to use "formal proof" as it was done in the belief logic. But we must point out that such formal proof is always constructed on a modal with assumption and the proof can not be sufficient. So we may say that: "all modals are wrong, but useful".

2. 4. 4　The Characteristics of Trust Logic

(1) Trust logic is to prove the authenticity of entity that includes subject and object.

(2) Entities are divided into identity and its body in trust logic.

(3) The proof of entity can be done without assumption.

(4) The proof of identity can be done before the proof of body. It is called "pre-proof".

(5) The trust logic is to identify "friend". It is different from the logic that identifies "enemy". The friend identification is active and easy but the enemy identification is passive and hard.

(6) The proof procedure is composed of evidence-showing process and evidence-verifying process. It is clear that the implementation of trust logic must be supported by the evidence showing system and evidence verifying system.

Above characteristics illustrate that trust logic is the appropriate logic for cyber security to establish a trusting system that is not a passive defense system but is active management system.

From the view point of cyber security the information system should not be a "battle field" of information warfare but it should be a large "market" of information service where the processing information is trusted. For this purpose a new generation of Internet must be considered where the connection is trusted, the computing environment is trusted and the transaction is trusted.

2.5　CPK Protocol

CPK is a self-assured public key system in which an EntityID is mapped into a point ENTITY on the elliptic curve defined by $E: y^2 = x^3 + ax + b \pmod{p}$ with the parameter $T = \{a, b, G, n, p\}$, if an integer *entity* satisfies $ENTITY = (entity)G$ then the point ENTITY is public key and the integer 'entity' is private key. The public key can be calculated by any one and the private key is provided by ID-card.

2.5.1　One-way Protocol

One-way protocol is used in non-handshaking system such as e-Mail communication. Suppose that Alice sends data to Bob:

1) Alice signs to time or ID and MAC of the data:
$$SIG_{alice}(time \ or \ ID) = sign_1$$
$$SIG_{alice}(MAC) = sign_2$$

Alice Sends $sign_1$, data, $sign_2$, to Bob.

MSG1 Alice→Bob: $\{sign_1, data, sign_2\}$

2) Bob checks the signature:
$$SIG_{ALICE}^{-1}(time \ or \ ID) = sign_1'$$
$$SIG_{ALICE}^{-1}(MAC) = sign_2'$$

If $sign_1 = sign_1'$ then the authenticity of Alice is prove, Bob accepts the data;

If $sign_2 = sign_2'$ then the authenticity of data is proved, Bob sends the receipt. The receipt is a signature to MAC:
$$SIG_{bob}(MAC) = sign_3$$

MSG2 Bob→Alice: $\{sign_3\}$

2.5.2　Two-way Protocol

1) Alice signs to time:

$$SIG_{alice}(\text{time}) = \text{sign}_1 , \text{sends}:$$

MSG1 Alice→Bob: { AliceID, time, sign$_1$ }

2) Bob checks sign$_1$:

$$SIG_{ALICE}^{-1}(\text{time}) = \text{sign}_1'$$

If sign$_1$ = sign$_1$'then bob signs to time -1:

$$SIG_{bob}(\text{time}-1) = \text{sign}_2$$

Select a random number r and sends:

MSG2 Bob→Alice: { r, sign$_2$ }

3) Alice checks sign$_2$:

$$SIG_{BOB}^{-1}(\text{time}-1) = \text{sign}_2'$$

If sign$_2$ = sign$_2$' then Alice believes the authenticity of this session enters into transmission process. Alice signs to r, time $+i$ ($i = 1,2,\cdots$) and MAC:

$$SIG_{alice}(r) = \text{sign}_3$$
$$SIG_{alice}(\text{time}+i) = \text{sign}_4$$
$$SIG_{alice}(MAC) = \text{sign}_5$$

Where MAC = Hash(data). Alice sends:

MSG3 Alice→Bob: { data, sign$_3$, sign$_4$, sign$_5$ }

4) Bob checks the signs:

$$SIG_{ALICE}^{-1}(r) = \text{sign}_3'$$
$$SIG_{ALICE}^{-1}(\text{time}+i) = \text{sign}_4'$$
$$SIG_{ALICE}^{-1}(MAC) = \text{sign}_5'$$

If sign$_3$ = sign$_3$'then Bob believes the authenticity of Alice (the response to r must be made in a limited time or the connection will be cancelled), if sign$_4$ = sign$_4$' then Bob believes the authenticity of the i-th session and accepts the data, and if sign$_5$ = sign$_5$', then Bob believes the authenticity of data and sends receipt, the receipt is a sign to MAC:

$$SIG_{bob}(MAC) = \text{sign}_6$$

Sends to Alice:

MSG4 Bob→Alice: { sign$_6$ }.

Chapter 3

Identity Authentication

Cyber security is facing two critical problems: how to define identity and how to authenticate identity. In this book we will only discuss on the second problem.

Entity identity can be divided into user identity, communication identity, software identity, address identity, seal identity, etc. Private keys of any entity are distributed by ID-cards. Any authenticator can verify any signatures.

In a transaction, business authentication between users first occurs, which involves EntityID and data. If data contains a seal, such as corporate seal, account number seal, bank seal, special financial seal, then authentication of the identities shall be carried out respectively.

The e-Bank (ATM/POS) system takes account number as its identity. The identity provides its signature and bank can directly authenticate the account number. The bank stores only the public key used for verification, which can rule out any suspect of internal crime. Also, the user 's benefits will not be encroached in the situation of loss of bank information.

Authentication of e-check is actually authentication of various seal identities. A check may contain a number of seals, e. g., bank seal, corporate seal, special seal, etc. Each seal identity shall be respectively verified. CPK authentication is very easy, because the relying parties involved all have public key matrix (R_{ij}), which can verify any identity on spot.

If privacy is desired during the transaction, private key exchange and encryption functions can be provided.

3. 1 Communication Identity Authentication

Transaction between users is conducted through communication system (network). Hence, there is the demand for trust connecting (trust receiving). Generally speaking, business between users is of business level while business between equipments is of communication level. The communication level is different from business level and only responsible for transmission of data. Thus, in terms of communication proof system, it has nothing to do with user business.

With respect to the communication parties, the sender is always the prover, and the receiver is always the verifier. The sender sends evidence of the communication identity and data integrity. Evidence of communication identity is the signature of communication identity to the time. Evidence of data is the signature of communication identity to data. If privacy is desired, key exchange can be provided, for example:

Suppose the communication identity of terminal 1 and 2 (real names) are mapped into points TERMINAL1 and TERMINAL2 and there are an integer satisfies TERMINAL1 = (*terminal*1) G and TERMINAL2 = (*terminal*2) G, then points TERMINAL1 and TERMINAL2 are public keys and *terminal*1 and *terminal*2 are private keys. The public key is calculated by every one and the private key is provided by ID-card.

Prover:

$$SIG_{terminal1}(\text{time}) = \text{sign}_1$$

Verifier:

$$SIG_{TERMINAL1}^{-1}(\text{time}) = \text{sign}_1{}'$$

Prover:

$$SIG_{terminal1}(\text{MAC}) = \text{sign}_2$$

Verifier:

$$SIG_{TERMINAL1}^{-1}(\text{MAC}) = \text{sign}_2{}'$$

Data encryption:

$$E_{key}(\text{data}) = \text{coded-data}$$
$$ENC_{TERMINAL1}(\text{key}) = \text{coded-key}$$

Data decryption:

$$DEC_{terminal2}(\text{coded-key}) = \text{key}$$
$$D_{key}(\text{code-data}) = \text{data}$$

The first problem encountered in the communication is whether the data should be received or not, and the second problem is whether the data is received correct. As the first checkpoint for trust communication, the judgment to receive or not is very important, which can be solved only relying on authentication technology of communication identity. At this time, data has not been received yet, so its authenticity cannot be determined by data integrity signature. Rather, it can only be determined by proof of authenticity of identity. If it is an illegal identity, it will be rejected, so as to effectively prevent illegal access. If privacy is desired in the communication, key exchange and data encryption can be provided.

This trust connecting (trust receiving) technology based on communication identity authentication will bring great changes to the existing protocol of communication. For instance, the protocols such as SSL, WLAN need more than 10 steps of interaction to complete security connection. Now, with the identity authentication technology, only 1 or 2 steps is enough to implement trust connecting (trust receiving). The burden of authentication is scattered to each user terminal, and thus greatly alleviating burden of the exchange equipment, and achieving balance of load. This greatly facilitates the authentication of mobile phone communication and its privacy.

3.2 Software Identity Authentication

Transaction between users is carried out through computer. Thus, there is a demand for trust computing. There are three problems that trust computing needs to solve:

1) Whether the program shall be loaded;

2) Whether the program loaded is correct;

3) Whether the program is running as expected.

As the first checkpoint of trust computing, whether the program shall be loaded is very important, which shall be solved relying on authentication technology of software identity. If it is an illegal identity, loading is denied. In this way, malicious software such as virus will not be loaded even if they have invaded. In terms of a banking system, if no software other than those approved by the bank is allowed to run in the system, the bank president will feel comfortable to such a system. This technology is called code signing or software identity authentication.

The trust verification module (TVM) based on software identity authentication is significantly different from the conventional trust platform module (TPM) in design. The new TVM only needs three components, i. e., identity authentication, integrity measurement proxy and behavior supervision proxy, to satisfy trust computing (trust loading) environment. If confidentiality is required for some software and data, key exchange and data encryption can settle.

Software identity is defined by the manufacturer. Authentication of software identity signed by manufacturer is called first-level authentication. Proof of authenticity of software identity is the signature of the manufacturer to the SoftwareID and MAC.

If the manufacturer's identity (real name) is mapped into the point of MANUFACTURER on elliptic curve of $E(a,b)$, and an integer *manufacturer* satisfies MANUFACTURER = (*manufacturer*) G then the public key is point 'MANUFACTURER' and the private key is an integer '*manufacturer*'. The public key is calculated by every one and the private key is provided by ID-card.

Prover:

$$SIG_{manufacturer}(SoftwareID) = sign_1$$

Verifier:

$$SIG_{MANUFACTURER}^{-1}(\text{SoftwareID}) = \text{sign}_1'$$

Prover:
$$SIG_{manufacturer}(\text{MAC}) = \text{sign}_2$$

Verifier:
$$SIG_{MANUFACTURER}^{-1}(\text{MAC}) = \text{sign}_2'$$

The verification module can verify any identity on spot. Only the authenticated software is allowed to run in the computer, to ensure trust of the computing environment. The verification module only contains public variables such as public key matrix (R_{ij}), with no private variables. It can also be for general use.

3. 3 Electronic Tag Authentication

In the logistic aspect of material flowing, if counterfeits prevail, there will be no trust at all. Hence, there is a demand of anti-forgery. The electronic feature of FRID provides a good basis for anti-forgery while the physical feature can prevent being copied. Combination of the two features can provide powerful anti-forgery function. Logistic identity authentication is substantially identical to software identity authentication. Identity of the item is defined and signed by the manufacturers.

If ManufacturerID is mapped into the point of MANUFCTURER and an integer manufacturer satisfies

$$\text{MANUFACTURER} = (manufacturer)\,G$$

the public key is MANUFACTURER and private key is *manufacturer*. The public key is calculated by every one and the private key is provided by ID-card.

Prover:
$$SIG_{manufacturer}(\text{ItemID}) = \text{sign}$$

Verifier:
$$SIG_{MANUFACTURER}^{-1}(\text{ItemID}) = \text{sign}'$$

With respect to anti-forgery of identity-based authentication, the same authenticating method is used for different kind of ItemIDs in CPK authentication system and different signatures can be verified by every one because the public key can be calculated by anyone from the ManufacturerID. For example, the authentication function can be embedded in cell phones, so as to enable on spot authentication to any FRID tag, and thus effectively inhibiting widespread of counterfeits.

3. 4 Network Management

Now, information security has entered into a new era of cyber security. The theme of cyber security is to establish a trust world. It is not a passive prevention system. Instead, it is a world of active management. It is not an information system isolated from the physical world. Rather, it is an information world integrated with the physical world. The United States calls for establishing a trust world, which reflects the pulse of the new era, and represents the trend of the development. The nature of a trust world or a harmonious society is "order" in the society. To establish order, maintain order, and eventually construct a trust or harmonious society is the main task of the new generation information security.

The basic requirement of a trust world is to establish order and maintain order. Order can be established and maintained only by the technique of identity authentication. Since the founding of People's Republic of China, order of the physical world has been established over the last couple of decades. For instance, ID-card issued by Ministry of Public Security has played a critical role in establishing social order. The experience of the physical world provides valuable experience to the upcoming trust information society. If everyone has a provable unique identity on the Internet, as that in the physical world, online order will not be difficult to establish. Once online order is established, all anonymous activities will be restricted, and the object of law enforcement on the Internet will be limited to information with no legitimate identity. Today, more and more people realize that online order affects Internet's survival.

Similar to the physical world, cyber world is divided into two worlds: ordered world and disordered world. Experience of the physical world and research results indicate that an ordered world within disordered world can only be established from top to bottom, but not from bottom to top. Order in disordered world can only be guaranteed by the ordered world, but not by a world without order itself (not partial guarantee, rather overall guarantee). In the physical world, the ordered world prints banknotes, invoices, for the disordered world to use. Identity of each entity must also be under unified management, i. e., centralized and under real-name system. One will take legal responsibility to his/her signature. Thus, behavior on the Internet may be standardized and restricted. This provides powerful technical means for disposal of junk mails and obtaining evidence on the Internet.

3.5　Holistic Security

Any entity has its own identity. For instance, person has his name, user has his username, equipment has its device name (a number or a serial number), data has data name, and software (process) has software (process) name. The same user may use e-mail address as his identity in e-mail communication, use cell phone number as his identity when making phone calls, and use bank account number as his identity when making deposit or withdrawing money.

Entity identity is a characteristic that differ one entity from another, having uniqueness and independence. Similarly, the classified identity categories keep independence from one another. For example, the identity of address category is independent from the identity of phone number category, with no cross-infiltration between them. Due to the feature of independence of the identity, different security problems based on identity are independent to each other. A neat security model can be constructed as follows:

Holistic security = (security of $Category_1$ + $Category_2$ + ... + $Category_n$) ;

Category i security = (security of $Item_1$ + $Item_2$ + ... + $Item_j$) ;

Item i security = (security of $Entity_1$ + $Entity_2$ + ... + $Entity_k$) .

From above, it can be seen that security and trust issues based on identity classification eventually fall into entity level. If the security and authenticity of each entity can be proved, e. g., the authenticity of each terminal in the communication can be proved, security of the " item" can be achieved. If security of "items" is guaranteed, security of the "category" is ensured, and so on. Security of "category" ensures holistic security. Identity authentication system is established on the basis of identity-based classification, and different authentication systems are classified with the identity category. In the past, the online transaction was treated as a process, and the authenticity of the online transaction was proved by user level. Due to lack of classification, it was very complex, and the user level cannot prove authenticity of communication level. Nowadays, the online transaction is classified into two separate processes: communication authentication and transaction authentication. The communication process is authentication between terminal 1 and terminal 2, while transaction process is authentication between user A and user B. The communication process and transaction process only need to prove authenticity of their own identity. Thus, identity authentication turns complex authentication process into accumulation of separate identity authentication processes. Thus, the complex process (e. g., trust system) which PITAC considers not easy to prove can be classified into interlinked identity authentication processes that are provable, to provide strong theoretical basis for holistic security design and verification of complex system.

Authenticity of any entity starts from authentication of identity, which is the easiest and most effective means for authentication of entity authenticity. In real life, proof of a person starts from checking authenticity of his/her name. If the name proves to be true, counterfeits and impersonation can be prevented. Similarly, in the virtual world, proof of an entity starts from checking authenticity of the identity. Identity authentication is an authentication technology that applies to prove authenticity of all entities. It not only applies to online communication, but also applies to packet-switch communication, software, processes, users, and seals, etc.

Part Two

Crypto-systems

Chapter 4

Combined Public Key (CPK)

4. 1   Introduction

CPK public key is established on Elliptic Curve Cryptography(ECC). CPK follows the ECC defined by IEEE standards.

CPK cryptosystem is an identity-based public key system. The Combined-Key is a compound of Identity-Key and Separating-Key(or Accompanying-Key). The Combined-Key pair is denoted as (csk,CPK).

The Identity-Key is generated from identity via the Combining Matrix. The Combining Matrix defined by the Key Management Center (KMC) divided into Secret Matrix and Public Matrix. The Secret Matrix is used to produce secret keys and kept secret in KMC,while the Public Matrix is used to compute public keys and open to the public. The Combining Matrix will bind the key to its identity. The pair of Identity-Key is denoted as (isk,IPK).

An Accompanying-Key is randomly generated by individuals and compound with the Identity-Key to generate unlimited pairs of Combined-Key (csk1,CPK1), and the pair of Accompanying-Key pair is denoted as (ask,APK). (optional)

A Separating-Key stream is generated by KMC and compound with the Identity-Key to produce a Combined-Key pair stream(csk2,CPK2). Separating-Key pair is denoted as (ssk,SPK).

Accompanying-Key will be selected in the trusting system according to the security requirement.

4. 2   ECC Compounding Feature

CPK is constructed on ECC over field Fp, $E: y^2 = x^3 + ax + b \mod p$, the parameters are denoted as (a,b,G,n,p), in which a,b is the coefficient, $a,b,x,y \in p$, p is prime, G is the base point of the addition group, n is the order of cyclic group generated by base point G. Let an arbitrary integer r less then n be a private key then the point ($rG = R$) is the corresponding public key.

The ECC compounding feature is described as follows:

In ECC, the sum of public keys and the sum of corresponding private keys are still the valid ECC key pair. For example, if the sum of private keys is:

$$r = (r_1 + r_2 + \ldots + r_m)$$

Then the sum of corresponding public keys will be

$$R = R_1 + R_2 + \ldots + R_m$$

In which the + operation of public keys is point addition.

Then (r, R) will be a new valid ECC key pair.

This is because

$$R = R_1 + R_2 + \ldots + R_m = r_1 G + r_2 G + \ldots + r_m G = (r_1 + r_2 + \ldots + r_m) G = rG.$$

4.3 Identity-Key

4.3.1 Combining Matrix

There are two combining matrices: the secret and the public. The size is $h \times 32$. The secret matrix is composed of different random numbers $r_{i,j}$ ($0 > r_{i,j} > n$), the matrix is denoted as skm.

$$skm = \begin{pmatrix} r_{1,1} & r_{1,2} & \cdots & r_{1,32} \\ r_{2,1} & r_{2,2} & \cdots & r_{2,32} \\ & & \cdots & \\ r_{32,1} & r_{32,2} & \cdots & r_{h,32} \end{pmatrix}$$

The public matrix is derived from the secret matrix, i. e. $r_{ij} G = (x_{i,j}, y_{i,j}) = R_{i,j}$, the public matrix is denoted as PKM.

$$PKM = \begin{pmatrix} R_{1,1} & R_{1,2} & \cdots & R_{1,32} \\ R_{2,1} & R_{2,2} & \cdots & R_{2,32} \\ & & \cdots & \\ R_{32,1} & R_{32,2} & \cdots & R_{h,32} \end{pmatrix}$$

4.3.2 Mapping from Identity to Matrix Coordinates

The mapping from identity to the coordinates of the matrix is implemented through a hash function. Suppose $h = 2^k$ then the sequence of the output composes k-bit integer string w_i.

$$YS = \text{Hash}(ID) = w_1, \ldots, w_{34}$$

w_1 to w_{32} is used to indicate the raw coordinates, and w_{33} and w_{34} is used to indicate the Separating-Key coordinate. Column coordinates are used successively from 1 to 32.

4.3.3 Computation of Identity-Key

The secret Identity-Key isk is generated in the KMC. Given i-th raw coordinate is noted as w_i, and column coordinate is i-th. Then the secret key generation is implemented through the addition on finite field Fn. Entity A's secret key is:

$$\text{isk}_A = \sum_{i=1}^{32} r_{w_i, i} \bmod n$$

The generation of public key is implemented by relying party through point addition on elliptic curve $Ep(a,b)$:

$$\text{IPK}_A = \sum_{i=1}^{32} R_{w_i, i}$$

4.4 Key Compounding

4.4.1 The Compounding of Identity-Key and Accompanying-Key (Optional)

A pair of Accompanying-Key $(\text{ask}_A, \text{APK}_A)$ is defined by every individual (namely A), and the secret combined key csk1 is calculated by KMC:

$$\text{csk}_A 1 = (\text{isk}_A + \text{ask}_A) \bmod n$$

The secret Accompanying-Key ask_A is deleted and the public Accompanying-Key APK_A is signed by its Identity-Key;

$$\text{SIG}_{\text{isk}_A}(\text{APK}_A) = \text{sign}_1$$

The secret Combined-Key csk1_A, public Accompanying-Key APK_A and the sign_1 is written into A's ID-card.

The public Combined-Key CPK1_A will be calculated by relying party:

$$\text{CPK1}_A = \text{IPK}_A + \text{APK}_A$$

APK_A is sent by signer A

4.4.2 The Compounding of Identity-Key and Separating-Key

A set of Separating-Key pair (ssk, SPK) is generated and the secret Combined-Key csk2 is calculated by KMC for entity A and written into ID-card: The set of public Separating-Key will be published in a form of file.

$$csk2_A = (isk_A + ssk_A) \mod n$$

The public Combined-Key CPK_{2A} will be calculated by relying party:

$$CPK2_A = IPK_A + SPK_A$$

SPK_A could be selected according to the indication of $w_{33} \ldots w_{37}$ in YS sequence.

4.5   CPK Digital Signature

4.5.1   Signing with Accompanying-Key (Optional)

Signing: Takes combined private key csk1 from the card, and sign for M:

$$SIG_{csk1}(M) = sign$$

Takes the Accompanying-Key APK and sign1 from the card,

Sends the signature "sign", APK and sign1.

Verifying: Calculates the public Identity-Key IPK;

Verifies sign1:

$$SIG_{IPK_A}^{-1}(APK) = sign1'$$

Calculates the public key:

$$CPK1 = IPK + APK$$

Verifies sign:

$$SIG_{CPK1}^{-1}(M) = sign'$$

4.5.2   Signing with Separating-Key

Signing: Takes private key csk2 from the card to sign for M:

$$SIG_{csk2}(M) = sign$$

Sends the "sign" only

Verifying: Calculates the Identity-Ksey IPK

The Separating-Key SPK is taken out from published file

Calculates the public Combined-Key:

$$CPK2 = IPK + SPK$$

Verifies the signature:

$$SIG_{CPK2}^{-1}(M) = sign'$$

4.6   CPK Key Exchange

4.6.1   Key Exchange with Separating-Key

CPK key exchange follows, Diffie-Helman protocol.

Encryption: Calculates the other side's public Identity-Key IPK

Takes the other side's public Separating-Key SPK

Calculates the other side's public Combined-Key:

$$CPK2 = IPK + SPK$$

Encrypts data:

$$E_{CPK2}(data) = code$$

Decryption: Decrypts with the private Combined-Key in the card:

$$D_{csk2}(code) = data$$

4.6.2   Key Exchange with Accompanying-Key
(Optional)

In on-line communication the two sides are needed to authenticate each other before connecting.

requests: the client side sends authentication information

$$SIG_{csk1_c}(ID_c) = sign_c, APK_c, sign_{1,c}$$

Response: the server side sends authentication information

$$SIG_{csk1_s}(ID_s) = sign_s, APK_s, sign_{1,s}$$

Thus, both sides have each other's public key.

4.7   Security Analysis

Accompany-Key(AK) may be defined randomly by individuals and encrypts Identity-Key(IK) with one-time-pad key stream. There is no concern for security because there is no repeat in the key stream. The AK is signed with IK, so it still keeps the bounding relationship between the identity and key.

Separating-Key(SK) is defined randomly by the KMC and encrypts IK with a limited key stream. So there may be repeats in the key stream. In such case the repeated SKs can be counteracted and further exposes the linear equation of IK.

The address of the SK is binary stream provided by $w_{33} - w_{34}$ in YS sequence. A system may select one of address lengths, we take the address length of 2^{10} for example, the capacity of the address is 1024. Suppose that the key length of the ECC is 20 bytes, the storing space of 40KB (store both x and y) will be needed to publish all of the SKs.

One can fined the same address used by different users through YS sequence. Because the size of the combining matrix is 32 x 5 ($h = 2^5 = 32$) in this example, the rank of linear independent equation is $2^{10} - 1 = 1023$. Therefore, when the average occurrence of repeat is less than 1024, there will be no unique solution for the equation and the system is still secure. For example: When the number of the users is about the same as $2^{10} \approx 1000$ times of the number of SK, the number of the users will be up to 1,000,000. Then different users will use the same SK 1024 times in average. In all of $(1,000)^2$ capable pairs, the probability of the repeated pair is 1/1024. That is to say, there will be $(1024)^2/1024 = 1024$ repeated pairs in the SK stream. The 1024 repeated pairs is not a threat to the system. This is because:

a) Within those repeated pairs only the ones in conspiracy are in concern and the rest is meaningless. Let's assume that half of the users participate in conspiracy, in another word, 500,000 users are in conspiracy, and half of the 1024 repeated pairs are meaningless, then only 512 repeated pairs are useful;

b) In the linear equation of IK after counteracting the impact of SK, only linearly independent equations are useful and linearly dependent equations are meaningless. So the number of useful equations will be smaller than 512. Therefore when the rank or equations is 2^{10}, the number of the users may be up to 2^{10} times of the number of SK. The scale of collusion doesnt need to be considered.

SK is defined by KMC of the system (trust root) and good for digital signature and key exchange in one – way and two – way authentication mode. It is easy to be applied to construct trusting system and supports horizontal key management in a massive scale of authentication network. However, it takes some storage space to publish the public keys. The public matrix and SKs are stored by amount addition and the key management scale is enlarged by amount multiplication. It is obvious that one can obtain the largest scale by adopting the same amount of Variables in matrix and SK. The security and scale is depended by the capacity of storage. Some examples are listed in table 4. 1

Table 4. 1   Key storage and key management scale

matrix size	2^{10} (4040KB)	2^{13} (327KB)	2^{16} (2.6MB)	2^{17} (5.2MB)	2^{18} (11MB)	2^{22} (167MB)
SK size	2^{10} (40KB)	2^{13} (327KB)	2^{1} (2.6MB)	2^{17} (5.2MB)	2^{18} (11MB)	2^{22} (167MB)
Storage	80KB	654KB	5.2MB	10.4MB	22MB	334MB
Scale	$2^{10+10}=1 \times 10^{6}$	$2^{13+13}=6.7 \times 10^{7}$	$2^{16+16}=4.2 \times 10^{9}$	$2^{17+17}=1.7 \times 10^{10}$	$2^{18+18}=6.8 \times 10^{10}$	$2^{22+22}=1.7 \times 10^{13}$

Chapter 5

Self-assured and 3rd Party Public Key

5.1 New Requirements of the Crypto-System

Information security mainly involves data authentication and data confidentiality. Authentication technology mainly depends on authentication protocol and digital signature technology; while data confidentiality mainly depends on key exchange protocol and encryption technology. A common international practice is that digital signature adopts the way of self-definition by users, called distributed model; and key exchange adopts the way of unified definition by the Key Management Center, called centralized model.

Digital signature is the core technology in authentication system. Any authentication system is constituted by evidence-holder and evidence-verifier. In general, evidence is shown by the way of signing, and authentication is realized by the way of verifying the signature. When the digital signature is used for identity authentication, no matter it is for proof or verification, the following issues shall be considered:

1) Scale of digital signature: the signature space shall correspond to the identity space. If the identity is a bank account number, when the length of the account number is 22 in decimal, the identity space is 10^{22}. It is required to provide signatures to all the identities.

2) Length of digital signature: the length of the sign code cannot be too long, the shorter the better. For instance, in the label authentication, the length of the label itself is only a few bytes to tens of bytes, while the length of the signature is more than 100 bytes to hundreds of bytes, then there is a suspicion of "spending 10 dollar to save 5 dollar" logically, which greatly restricts the application.

3) Directness of verification: once receiving the proof, it can conduct on-spot verification, to avoid waiting.

4) Promptness of verification: calculation of verification shall be prompt, to avoid verification becoming the system bottleneck.

The most outstanding problems that need to be solved in key exchange are:

1) Scale of key exchange: Modern communications are individual communications. Taking Internet and cell phone net for example, it needs to perform private communications among users. The demand for public and private keys shall at least equal to number of users. This requires a scale of billions.

2) Directness of key exchange: In the on-line communications, key exchange is carried out by hand-shaking between the two communication parties. This is the well-known Diffie-Hellman key exchange protocol. However, in Internet communication, it requires one-way (no round way) key exchange, i. e. , the sender encrypts, and the receiver is able to decrypt. In the key exchange, the main conflict focuses on the encrypting party, who may first need to know the other side's public key before encrypting. This is different from digital signature, in which the signer is active and he can send his public key to the relying party. But in the key exchange, the encrypting party is the passive so the issue is how to obtain the relying party's public key.

5.2   Development of Crypto-Systems

In order to seek a cryptographic system with immediacy and scalability, the research has undergone more than 20 years. Following is a brief of the progress.

In 1976, Diffie and Hellman proposed the D-H key exchange protocol, which becomes the basis for all the current key exchange protocols and opens up a new direction for modern cryptography developments. However, the protocol is of two-way handshaking (on-line exchange), not of one-way direct exchange (off-line exchange).

In 1984, Shamir proposed identity-based public key Crypto-System IBC for the first time. In IBC the identity itself is the public key and private key is defined by the center. IBC is self-assure and no need to be certified by third party. But IBC only implements digital signature.

In 1996, PKI is emerged, in which the key is defined by individual. The public key must be certified by third party, so PKI is 3rd party-assured. The digital signature satisfies the demand of individual privacy. However, the key exchange protocols must be supported by a bulky directory database (LDAP), and does not satisfy the requirement for immediacy.

In 2001, Dan Boneh and Matthew Franklin proposed identity-based encryption IBE. BF-IBE is self-assured and abolishes CA certificate however it cannot realizes no-handshaking one-time key exchange.

In 2003, NAN Xiang-hao and CHEN Zhong released CPK public key Crypto-system based on elliptic curve. CPK is self-assured. In 2007, CHEN Hua-ping and LI Yi-fa formed two-factor CPK-acp with Accompanying-Key. In 2008, YU Ming-yuan at al constructed CPK-ccc on conic curve, in 2009, CHEN Yu and GUAN Zhi constructed CPK-bpc with bilinear pair.

In 2008, Saar Ron constructed identity based IB-RSA, Gene Tsudik and Xu-hua Ding released a meditated RSA Scheme (mRSA).

5.3 Digital Signature Mechanism

Currently, the digital signature systems of interests is whether can be used in identity authentication. Here is the list of some typical schemes including Shamir's IBC, CPK, third-party PKI, identity-based RSA, etc. Below is a simple comparison to the five signature schemes in identity authentication.

5.3.1 IBC Signature Scheme

IBC is identity based scheme and self-assured.

The center has two secret prime p and q. To publish the parameter $T = \{e, n\}$ where $n = p \times q$, e is a fixed number.

Assume that Alice's public key is $ID_A = g^e$, private key is $g = (ID_A)^d \mod n$; where $e * d \equiv 1 \mod \varphi(n)$

The signature is $SIG_g(TAG) = sign$, where TAG = Time Domain;

Alice Choose a random number r, calculating $t = r^e \mod n$

Calculates his signature: $s = g \, r^{f(t,m)} \mod n$

The signature is (s, t) and signature length is $2n$.

Bob verify the signature: $SIG_{ID_A}^{-1}(TAG) = sign'$

Calculates $s^e = ID_A \, t^{f(t,m)} \mod n$

$(\because s^e = g^e \, r^{ef(t,m)} \mod n, s = g \, r^{f(t,m)} \mod n)$

5.3.2 CPK Signature with Separating-Key

Assumption: private key: alice = isk + ssk, provided by ID-card;

Signature:

$$SIG_{alice}(TAG) = sign = (s, r)$$

where TAG = Time domain;

Signature length, sign = (s, r)

The sign lenth is 2n, But r can set half, and the signature length would be 1.5n

Verification: Calculate the public:

$$ALICE = IPK + SPK$$

(SPK is automatically selected on the public file.)

Verify the sign:

$$SIG_{ALICE}^{-1}(TAG) = sign'$$

5. 3. 3　CPK Signature with Accompanying-Key

Assumption: Alice's private key:

$$alice = isk + ask$$

The private key alice is provided by ID-card;

Signature:

$$SIG_{alice}(TAG) = (s,r) = sign$$

Sends $\{sign, APK_{Alice}, sign_1\}$

Where $sign_1$ and APK_{Alice} is provided by ID-card and $sign_1 = SIG_{isk_{Alice}}(APK_{Alice})$.

The signature length, $(s,r) = 1.5n, APK = 1n, sign_1 = 1.5n$, total $4n$

Verification: Verifier receives the signature: $\{sign, APK_{Alice}, sign_1\}$

Verifies APK:

$$SIG_{IPK_{Alice}}^{-1}(APK) = sign_1'$$

Calculates public key:

$$ALICE = IPK + APK$$

Verifies sign:

$$SIG_{ALICE}^{-1}(TAG) = sign' = (s,r)$$

5. 3. 4　PKI Signature Scheme

PKI is a system assured by third party. In order to the convenience of verification the signature may be sent together with the certificate. If the CA is the trust root and known to all relying parties,

1) Identity authentication implemented with PKI_{-RSA}

Assume: the private key of Alice is SK_{Alice} and the public key is PK_{Alice}, the third party is CA

Signature:

$$SIG_{sk_{alice}}(AliceID) = sign$$

Sends: $\{sign, sign_1, sign_2\}$

Where AliceID is the identity of Alice,

$$sign_1 = SIG_{sk_{CA}}(PK_{Alice})$$
$$sign_2 = SIG_{sk_{CA}}(AliceID)$$

Verification:

$$SIG_{PK_{CA}}^{-1}(sign_1) = PK_{Alice}$$

$$SIG_{PK_{Alice}}^{-1}(sign) = AliceID'$$

$$SIG_{PK_{CA}}^{-1}(sign_2) = AliceID''$$

If AliceID' = AliceID'' then the identity AliceID is proven to be true.

2) Identity authentication implemented with PKI_{-ECC}

Assume: the private key of Alice is SK_A and the public key is PK_A, the third party is CA

Signature:

$$SIG_{sk_{alice}}(AliceID) = sign$$

Sends: $\{sign, PK_{Alice}, sign_1, AliceID, sign_2\}$

Where AliceID is the identity of Alice,

$$sign_1 = SIG_{sk_{CA}}(PK_{Alice})$$

$$sign_2 = SIG_{sk_{CA}}(AliceID)$$

Verification:

$$SIG_{PK_{CA}}^{-1}(PK_{Alice}) = sign_1'$$

$$SIG_{PK_{CA}}^{-1}(AliceID) = sign_2'$$

$$SIG_{PK_{Alice}}^{-1}(AliceID) = sign'$$

If sign = sign' then AliceID is proven to be true.

5.3.5 IB-RSA Signature Scheme

Assume: Alice has his secret prime p and q, his public key is Hash(ID) $\rightarrow$ e, private key is d, $(d \times e = 1 \mod (p-1)(q-1))$

● Signature:

$$SIG_d(AliceID) = sign$$

$$SIG_{sk_{CA}}(n) = sign_1$$

Signature length, $sign + sign_1 = 2n$.

● Verification:

$$SIG_{PK_{CA}}^{-1}(sign_1) = n$$

$$Hash(ID) \rightarrow e$$

$$SIG_e^{-1}(sign) = AliceID'$$

In RSA scheme modular n take the real role of public key so the modular n must be certificated by 3rd party CA. because the public key e is identity based and the identity authentication is self-assured there is no need to prove the bounding of public key and identity.

5.3.6 mRSA Signature Scheme

Let (n,e) be an Alice's RSA public key, d be the private key, CA split d,

$$\mathbf{d}_{alice} + \mathbf{d}_{SEM} = \mathbf{d} \bmod \varphi(n)$$

thus Alice has $(n, \mathbf{d}_{alice})$. SEM has $(n, \mathbf{d}_{SEM})$.

The split of private key does not affect encryption. Bob encrypts as usual:

$$C = M^e \bmod n$$

But when signing or decrypting it cannot be complete in one time, Alice signs or decrypts half and SEM completes the sign or decryption.

5.3.7 Comparison of Schemes

The composition and signature length for identity authentication is listed in Table 5.1.

Table 5.1 Comparison of signature length for Identity Authentication

Scheme	Signature Length	Key Length	Composition
IBS	$2n = 256B$	128B	Sign
CPK$_{-sep}$	$2n = 40B$	20B	Sign
CPK$_{-acp}$	$4n = 80B$	20B	Sign, APK, $sign_1$
PKI$_{-RSA}$	$3n = 384B$	128B	Sign, $sign_1$, $sign_2$
PKI$_{-ECC}$	$9n = 216B$	20B	Sign, $sign_1$, $sign_2$, PK, ID
IB$_{-RSA}$	$2n = 256B$	128B	Sign, $sign_1$
mRSA	$1n = 128B$	128B	Sign

From the above table, it can be seen that the most outstanding systems in digital signature are IBC and CPK. IBC signature does not become a standard, and its signature is very long. CPK signatures comply with international standard no matter it is centralized or distributed. Its signature code is relatively short, making it more practical. Thus, it is believed that the CPK is currently most outstanding digital signature system.

5.4 Key Exchange Scheme

Currently, the key exchange schemes of interest include IBE, CPK, and 3rd PKI, etc.

5. 4. 1   IBE Key Exchange

The center defines system-key s, publishes points P, sP;

The IBE key distributing and key exchanging procedure is shown in Fig. 5. 1.

Alice sends his AliceID to the center, center verifies the authenticity of AliceID and return s (AliceID) to Alice.

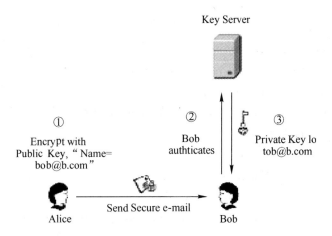

Fig. 5. 1   IBE key distribution and exchange

If Bob wants to send a encrypt message to Alice, then

Bob chooses a random number r, and calculates $r(ID_A)$ and rP;

Bob defines key $= Pair(r(ID_A), sP)$,

Bob encrypts data with the key:

$$E_{key}(data) = code$$

Bob sends code and rP to Alice.

Alice calculates the key with his'private key's(AliceID):

$$key = Pair(s(AliceID), rP) = Pair(r(AliceID), sP)$$

Alice decrypts the data: $D_{key}(code) = data$

5. 4. 2   CPK Key Exchange

Suppose Alice encrypts for Bob, and Bob decrypts:

The CPK key distributing and key exchanging procedure is shown in Fig. 5. 2.

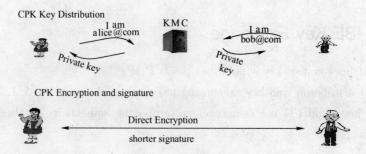

Fig. 5. 2　CPK key distribution and exchang

Alice calculates Bob's public key:

$$\sigma(\text{BobID}) = \text{BOB}$$

Alice chooses a random number r, calculates r(BOB);

Alice calculates rG as key; where G is the basic point of ECC;

Alice encrypts with the key

$$E_{key}(\text{data}) = \text{code}$$

Alice sends the code and r(BOB) to Bob;

Bob calculates the key with his private key bob:

$$\text{bob}^{-1} \, r \, (\text{BOB}) = \text{bob}^{-1} \, r \, (\text{bobG}) = \, rG = key$$

Bob decrypts with the key:

$$D_{key}(\text{code}) = \text{data}$$

5. 4. 3　Other Key Exchange Schemes

In 3rd PKI, IB-RSA schemes, Alice can only obtain Bob's public key from the parameter database or LDPA, as shown in Fig. 5. 3.

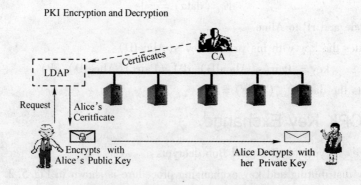

Fig. 5. 3　PKI Encryption and Decryption

In mRSA scheme, the encryption is convenient but the decryption cannot complete in one time, as shown in Fig. 5. 4.

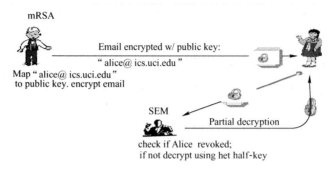

Fig. 5. 4   mRSA Decryption

5. 4. 4   Performance Comparison

The performance of above schemes is compared in two aspects: one-direction exchange and two-direction exchange. In modern communication security the one-direction key exchange takes more important role. The results are shown in Table 5. 2 below.

Table 5. 2   Comparison of Key Exchange Schemes

	One-direction exchange	Two-direction exchange
IBE	√ by local calculation	√ by local calculation
CPK$_{-SEP}$	√ by local calculation	√ by local calculation
CPK$_{-ACP}$	×	√ by dual direction signatures
PKI	×	√ by dual direction signatures
IB-RSA	×	√ by dual direction signatures
mRSA	√ via meditate center	√ via meditate center

From Table 5. 2, it can be seen that there are not many successful key exchange schemes so far. The better schemes are BF-IBE and CPK$_{-SEP}$. Comparing IBE with CPK$_{-SEP}$, IBE does not occupy system resource, while CPK$_{-SEP}$ occupies system resource by several tens of megabytes. The security of IBE depends on only one secret Separating-Key s, and the decryption process must be completed via the center, while the security of CPK$_{-SEP}$ depends on combining matrix and the encryption and decryption processes can undergo directly between the two terminals. IBE cannot be used for digital signature, while CPK$_{-SEP}$ can be used for digital signature.

5.5　Discussion on Trust Root

In the authentication system, the authenticity of trust root is of most significance. If there is no trust root or the authenticity of trust root cannot be proved then the entire authentication system does not hold water, the proof lacks of basis.

Under the situation that the private key is uniformly defined by the Key Management Center (KMC) of the system, the trust root is KMC. This is called centralized management. Its authenticity proof is very simple and clear. Especially for identity-based public key system, just like biometrics, it can be self-assured.

To provide privacy for individuals, some schemes allow individuals to produce private key themselves. This is called decentralized management. Under such management, proof of trust root has become a hard problem.

Proof of trust root has two ways: self-assured and CA-assured. If CA-assured proof changes its original proving logic to adapt an on-spot like verification, i. e. , the certificate is not provided by LDAP but by user himself. That is to say, 3rd party-assured mechanism turns to self-assured mechanism. This results in a series of complex logic problems, which need careful inference.

If the public key PK_M of identity M is provided by LDAP, then the authentication logic is tenable. However, the authenticity of CA is still not proven yet. It also has the above problems.

If such mechanism is used in e-tag anti-forgery system, electric seal system, communication system, code signing system, email system etc. the verifier first needs to prove authenticity of the certificate. The root certificate must be guaranteed not to be counterfeited or replaced. This is an issue that should be noted in the offline proof of the third-party system.

Chapter 6

Bytes Encryption

Block cipher, as the first open system cipher, has been developed for over 30 years. There are many outstanding cipher systems that came out one after another, such as DES, AES, etc. However, the cipher width of these systems is fixed. Thus, when encrypting data that has a length less than the cipher width, it may cause expansion of the data, which changes the original data structure. This solution provides encryption methods to any number of byte from single-byte to 8-byte data without change of cipher length, to allow the data of relational database keep the original data structure upon encryption. Besides encryption of 8-bit code data, an encryption method of 7-bit code data is also raised, so that ASCII code can still keep the attributes of ASCII code upon encryption. In this solution, key granularity from database level, directory level, file level to record or segment level, is suitable for protection of data in relational database.

6.1　Technical Background

In block cipher a block of plain text is changed to a block of ciphered code under a key. It breaks through the conventional operation mode of stream cipher. That is, it does not conduct encryption operation by bits or characters, rather it uses a group of bits as the essential encryption unit. A block length can be 64 bits or 256 bits, which is called block width.

Another characteristic of block cipher is that same key encryption can be used to different plain text, and thus the key management is very convenient. This is not possible in sequence cipher, which requires to using different keys for each encryption, and brings a lot of inconvenience to key management.

Since block cipher operates by "group", one bit error may cause one group error. This is called error extension. In sequence cipher, one bit error may only lead to one bit error, and will not cause error diffusion. However, out of bit may cause failure of the whole communication.

In 1970s, block cipher came out and attracted a lot of attention, and received widespread application. As a result, a variety of block encryption systems have appeared, in which the most well-known systems include DES, AES, etc., which have become the international standards.

There are two different situations for data encryption: one is encryption of transmitting data, and the other one is encryption of stored data. Sequence cipher can only be used for encryption of communication data, but not for recorded data in relational database. This is because different key encryption shall be used to different files in the database, while key is a secret variable and very hard to handle. Thus, block cipher encryption is typically used to storage data in the database.

Based on different storage data, the database is divided into document database and relational database, in which the document database is a data warehouse, and the data stored in relational database is table-type. The table is composed of rows and columns, in which rows are called records and columns are called segments. Thus, a record is composed of a plurality of segments. The each segment may have different length. If using block encryption system to encrypt each segment, then the encrypted segment length will change when the segment length is less than the block width or the segment length is not the multiples of the block width. A segment length at least is one block width or its multiples.

Thus, there are special needs:

1) Upon the data is encrypted, the segment length keeps unchanged. Taking segment "sex" for example, a bite can represent male or female, or two bytes can represent "male" or "female" in Chinese. Upon being encrypted, the segment length still keeps one byte or two bytes. This also involves basic unit of encryption, i. e. , the minimum basic unit can be byte encryption.

2) Upon encryption, ASCII code can still be ASCII code, because some systems do not recognize access of binary data.

This solution designs two kinds of operation: one is 8-bit code operation, which obtains 8-bit binary data upon encryption; the other one is 7-bit code operation, which first retains the sign bit of each byte, and the 7-bit binary code still can obtain 7-bit binary code upon encryption, then the retained sign bit restores to each byte, making it 8-bit ASCII code. Internationally, there has been no block cipher with 7-bit operation.

This solution designs 8 encryption methods of 1-byte, 2-byte, 3-byte, 4-byte, 5-byte, 6-byte, 7-byte and 8-byte, with the key length fixed. The segment length keeps unchanged upon encryption.

8-byte and oddment processing principles:

1) 8-byte operation is the basic operation. When the length of data is greater than 8-byte or multiples of 8-byte, the 8-byte operation will be processed first.

2) Processing principles of the length great than 8-byte:

9-byte data = 8-byte operation + 1-byte operation;

10-byte data = 8-byte operation + 2-byte operation;

11-byte data = 8-byte operation + 3-byte operation, and so on.

6.2   Coding Structure

The main coding components include transposition table (disk) and substitution table (subst).

6.2.1   Transposition Table (disk)

Transposition table is a table that indicates position change relationship. Disk table has two types: one is disk8[i], for encryption of 8-bit binary code; and the other one is disk7[i], for encryption of 7-bit ASCII code. Transposition table is divided into forward table and backward table, in which forward table is used for encryption, and backward table is used for decryption. The forward table is indicated by disk8e and disk7e, and the backward table is indicated by disk8d and disk7d.

Transposition table has 4 sheets in total, marked with 0..3. Taking disk8e[0] for example, 8 rows constitutes 8 transposition rounds. Each transposition round has 8 start points. Different rounds and different start points constitute different transposition relationship.

disk8e[0]

	0	1	2	3	4	5	6	7
[0]	7	4	2	3	5	1	6	7
[1]	4	6	4	5	0	7	2	3
[2]	6	0	7	6	4	3	7	5
[3]	1	2	6	1	7	0	5	6
[4]	2	7	0	2	3	5	1	0
[5]	0	1	3	7	6	2	4	4
[6]	5	3	1	0	2	4	3	2
[7]	3	5	5	4	1	6	0	1

disk7e[0]

	0	1	2	3	4	5	6
[0]	2	4	8	1	5	5	0
[1]	5	2	0	4	3	1	6
[2]	1	6	4	0	6	3	2
[3]	3	0	6	2	1	4	5
[4]	0	3	1	5	4	6	1
[5]	6	1	5	3	0	2	4
[6]	4	5	2	6	2	0	3

disk8e[1]

	0	1	2	3	4	5	6	7
[0]	3	4	7	2	1	0	5	6
[1]	5	2	1	6	7	4	0	3

disk7e[1]

	0	1	2	3	4	5	6
[0]	6	1	5	2	9	4	3
[1]	3	0	2	6	4	5	6

[2] 1 0 4 5 3 6 2 5
[3] 4 6 0 1 5 3 7 2
[4] 0 1 6 3 2 5 1 4
[5] 7 5 2 0 4 1 3 7
[6] 2 3 5 7 6 7 4 0
[7] 6 7 3 4 0 2 6 1

[2] 1 3 4 5 1 6 0
[3] 0 2 3 4 5 1 2
[4] 5 6 0 1 3 2 4
[5] 2 4 1 3 6 0 5
[6] 4 5 6 0 2 3 1

disk8e[2]
  0 1 2 3 4 5 6 7
[0] 5 2 7 3 6 7 6 0
[1] 2 0 5 7 1 3 4 7
[2] 0 7 2 4 3 5 1 6
[3] 7 4 6 0 2 1 5 1
[4] 1 6 3 2 0 4 2 3
[5] 4 1 0 6 5 2 3 4
[6] 3 5 4 1 7 6 0 2
[7] 6 3 1 5 4 0 7 5

disk7e[2]
  0 1 2 3 4 5 6
[0] 2 5 4 5 1 0 2
[1] 0 2 5 1 3 4 6
[2] 5 6 1 2 0 3 4
[3] 1 3 6 4 6 5 0
[4] 3 1 2 0 4 6 3
[5] 6 4 0 3 2 1 5
[6] 4 0 3 6 5 2 1

disk8e[3]
  0 1 2 3 4 5 6 7
[0] 7 3 0 7 4 2 5 6
[1] 2 0 7 3 5 7 4 1
[2] 6 7 4 0 3 1 7 2
[3] 3 1 1 4 0 5 2 5
[4] 5 4 6 1 2 3 6 0
[5] 0 6 2 5 7 6 1 3
[6] 4 2 5 6 1 0 3 7
[7] 1 5 3 2 6 4 0 4

disk7e[3]
  0 1 2 3 4 5 6
[0] 2 0 3 1 6 4 6
[1] 6 2 5 0 3 6 1
[2] 0 5 4 5 1 3 2
[3] 3 1 0 2 4 5 4
[4] 1 3 6 4 2 0 5
[5] 4 6 1 3 5 2 0
[6] 5 4 2 6 0 1 3

6. 2. 2 Substitution Table (subst)

Substitution table sub8e is a 16 × 16 single substitution table, for 8-bit operation. Substitution table sub7e is an 8 × 16 single substitution table, for 7-bit operation.

Subst8e

	0	1	2	3	4	5	6	7	8	9	A	B	C	D	E	F
0	0B	9A	43	CD	17	B4	2A	84	77	FF	52	8E	70	03	A7	34
1	D6	3C	93	1D	DD	4B	C6	A6	42	9F	C5	11	B3	83	5C	07
2	82	F4	0A	E3	64	C4	16	8D	D5	25	CC	7C	33	29	9E	4D
3	6D	DE	4A	BE	81	10	A5	6F	3D	B5	6A	1F	5B	BD	12	7B
4	9B	AB	24	2B	D7	B2	41	92	EF	51	00	89	D4	4C	99	38
5	18	FC	53	C3	3B	78	F5	06	5A	CB	44	E2	15	94	2F	6C
6	49	B1	1E	D3	01	E0	57	32	EE	63	9D	28	BC	66	AA	56
7	58	BA	80	9C	F3	37	E7	7D	1C	D2	02	A2	5D	E8	20	DC
8	C8	6E	FE	0F	AF	48	A1	88	50	76	F0	71	B7	0C	ED	62
9	05	2C	91	E6	69	FD	79	13	8F	A9	39	40	95	75	A8	3F
A	8C	F6	59	BB	CA	23	AD	65	D8	08	C7	AE	1B	F9	47	8B
B	36	14	D1	87	26	E1	72	BF	45	B6	6B	CE	7A	2D	DB	67
C	DF	60	A0	68	E9	7E	0E	B8	4E	E4	5E	21	F2	54	8A	C1
D	4F	C9	AC	09	D9	5F	EC	97	F7	1A	A3	EA	55	FB	96	30
E	27	C2	73	B9	46	F8	31	E5	3A	CF	F1	2E	DA	85	0D	EB
F	74	B0	19	90	A4	04	D0	35	FA	22	C0	7F	3E	98	61	86

Subst7e

	0	1	2	3	4	5	6	7	8	9	A	B	C	D	E	F
0	2A	61	10	5A	2F	4C	09	24	67	1B	04	37	33	0A	64	14
1	0F	55	44	18	78	01	29	76	03	6F	3F	13	59	22	49	5E
2	79	1E	6B	43	3C	7E	23	36	74	2E	68	0B	38	28	75	34
3	3D	7F	1F	54	00	45	19	62	12	21	4E	32	51	40	3B	71
4	5B	02	4A	7A	2B	4F	69	1A	42	6C	15	57	70	1D	5D	0C
5	17	72	30	16	60	39	08	66	2C	52	7D	27	35	50	65	58
6	4B	07	6E	26	73	11	53	20	7C	5C	48	05	6D	63	0D	46
7	31	6A	56	06	3A	25	7B	3E	4D	0E	5F	41	1C	47	77	2D

6.2.3 Key Structure

Given 8 mod 256 shift registers, and the linking polynomial is $(8,1,0)$. The output of port 8 feeds back to port 1 through mmm substitution.

Substitution table mmm is a 16×16 single substitution table, for using in derivation of key variables.

The feedback relationship is as follows:

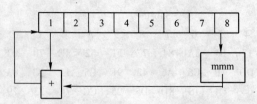

Where ' + ' means arithmetic addition, and 'mmm' is a substitution table. The content of the table in as follows.

mmm substitution table

	0	1	2	3	4	5	6	7	8	9	A	B	C	D	E	F
0	CC	87	F0	75	BC	1F	F8	52	00	3A	8E	57	AC	6E	F5	23
1	17	2B	89	D5	12	FC	A3	EF	67	94	5C	C7	9E	DF	56	DA
2	C2	FF	47	83	E6	2C	39	02	AD	1E	E4	07	51	1D	A6	0A
3	3B	A8	11	20	62	CB	B3	B5	22	D2	2A	EE	D8	F4	9F	86
4	FB	63	AE	58	FE	10	7E	35	E5	4F	7F	55	5B	8D	4B	7A
5	90	E1	53	E0	95	48	4E	66	31	F6	C8	6D	06	3E	C6	BF
6	46	04	F7	38	01	C0	0B	A1	8F	0F	43	85	AB	F9	68	93
7	A2	AF	73	DB	6F	16	9A	6C	72	A7	D1	1B	65	1C	79	3F
8	21	33	0C	45	B8	5D	76	29	BB	2E	61	DE	99	B6	5F	E3
9	9B	82	7B	E7	27	54	9D	DD	81	E9	E2	78	BD	37	ED	30
A	74	59	D4	32	8B	BA	0D	26	13	7D	05	C5	15	71	B2	CF
B	34	E8	18	C1	F1	40	92	AA	8A	C9	B1	44	A5	EC	24	69
C	88	28	CD	03	6A	64	D7	42	FA	5E	3D	F2	8C	08	D9	B7
D	6B	D6	3C	CA	DC	FD	2D	EA	19	96	CE	14	25	D0	80	4A
E	B9	A9	C3	7C	A4	4C	B0	84	C4	77	EB	A0	D3	49	BE	98
F	41	9C	4D	B4	1A	91	70	0E	5A	F3	36	50	2F	97	60	09

The key occupies one block, and the block length is 64-bit (8-byte). Using the given key (original key) as the initial value and conducting feedback operation, the status upon 16 times of feedback is the first set of derived keys (keyb[0]); upon another 24 times of feedback, the second set of derived keys (keyb[1]) is obtained, and so on. With 16 times of feedback and 24 times of feedback in circulation, totally 18 sets of derived keys, keyb[0]...keyb[17], can be derived in turn. Wherein, keyb[0], keyb[9] are for indicator variables, and keyb[1...8], keyb[10...17] are for constant variables in each level of operation.

Indication function: Low 4 bits of each byte of keyb[0,i] and keyb[9,i] indicate the transposition table it uses; high 4 bits of each byte of the keys indicate start point of the transposition table.

Constant function: Except for keyb[0,i] and keyb[9,i], other 16 sets of keyb key variables are all used as constant variables to add with data block, used in turn during iterative change in each round.

6. 2. 4 Operation Flowchart

The operation flowchart is shown in Fig. 6. 1.

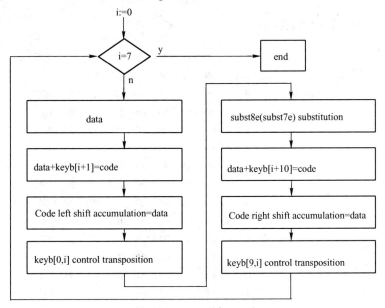

Fig. 6. 1   Operation flowchart

6. 3   8- bit Operation

6. 3. 1   Assumptions

Assume:	[7]	[6]	[5]	[4]	[3]	[2]	[1]	[0]
key :	08	07	06	05	04	03	02	01

data:								
byte = 1								01
byte = 2							02	01
byte = 3						03	02	01
byte = 4					04	03	02	01
byte = 8	08	07	06	05	04	03	02	01

byte: field length, byte = 1, 2, 3, 4, 8

bits: number of bits in one byte, bits = 8

i : operation of no. i round

6.3.2 Key Derivation

	[7]	[6]	[5]	[4]	[3]	[2]	[1]	[0]
Assuming original key:	08	07	06	05	04	03	02	01
derived keys keyb[0] :	4C	A4	7F	5D	08	18	94	B7
[1] :	92	5F	60	D6	DC	38	95	62
[2] :	6F	E0	38	B7	89	52	F8	6F
[3] :	F8	64	03	7C	DC	6F	C7	CF
[4] :	1E	61	87	48	2F	69	42	85
[5] :	09	E2	D3	0B	CD	B4	B4	A3
[6] :	F7	2D	36	22	BC	BB	49	AB
[7] :	E8	6B	9E	81	BA	48	C2	DC
[8] :	BF	02	74	36	94	B8	9C	57
[9] :	BD	C9	6D	4C	2A	FF	DB	99
[10] :	EF	90	6F	5F	0E	48	94	1A
[11] :	8F	23	FB	41	2E	97	9E	0C
[12] :	F1	CD	13	08	1E	AD	41	66
[13] :	15	52	FF	92	67	D4	06	AA
[14] :	BA	34	D3	80	DF	40	FD	D7
[15] :	3D	BD	27	6E	54	00	12	D7
[16] :	EA	6A	2E	C3	34	30	A0	F1
[17] :	27	7A	AF	82	7E	E6	A0	AC

6.3.3 Combination of Data and Keys

Data adds with corresponding keyb[i + 1, j]

for j: = 0 to byte − 1 do

    if bits = 8 then data[j] := (data[j] + keyb[i + 1, j]) mod 256

During operation of no. 0 round, i = 0

    byte = 1: data[0] := (data[0] + keyb[i + 1, 0]) mod 256;   (63)

    byte = 2: data[1] := (data[1] + keyb[i + 1, 1]) mod 256;   (96)

            data[0] := (data[0] + keyb[i + 1, 0]) mod 256;   (64)

         ...   ...

    byte = 8: data[7] := (data[7] + keyb[i + 1, 7]) mod 256;   (93)

$$\text{data}[6]:=(\text{data}[6]+\text{keyb}[i+1,6])\bmod 256;\qquad(61)$$
$$\text{data}[5]:=(\text{data}[5]+\text{keyb}[i+1,5])\bmod 256;\qquad(63)$$
$$\text{data}[4]:=(\text{data}[4]+\text{keyb}[i+1,4])\bmod 256;\qquad(\text{DA})$$
$$\text{data}[3]:=(\text{data}[3]+\text{keyb}[i+1,3])\bmod 256;\qquad(\text{E1})$$
$$\text{data}[2]:=(\text{data}[2]+\text{keyb}[i+1,2])\bmod 256;\qquad(\text{3E})$$
$$\text{data}[1]:=(\text{data}[1]+\text{keyb}[i+1,1])\bmod 256;\qquad(\text{9C})$$
$$\text{data}[0]:=(\text{data}[0]+\text{keyb}[i+1,0])\bmod 256;\qquad(\text{6A})$$

6.3.4 Left Shift Accumulation

Data in data[i] expands based on number of bytes, and puts into dd[j]:

1byte:63 expanding based on 1-bit

0	1	1	0	0	0	1	1

2byte:96 64 expanding based on 2-bit

10	01	01	10	01	10	01	00

. . .

8byte:93 61 63 DA E1 3E 9C 6A remain unchanged

10010011	01100001	01100011	11011010	11100001	00111110	10011100	01101010

expanded   centralized

dd:[7][6][5][4][3][2][1][0]

byte=1: 0 1 1 0 0 0 1 1 (63)

byte=2: 2 1 1 2 1 2 1 0 (96 64)

. . .

byte=8: 93 61 63 DA E1 3E 9C 6A (93 61 63 DA E1 3E 9C 6A)

data in dd accumulates in left shift, and puts into ee upon accumulation, then:

ee[0]:=dd[0];

for j:=1 to bits−1 do ee[j]:=(ee[j−1]+dd[j]) mod (2**byte);

Upon left shift accumulation, variables of each EE[i] are:

ee:[7][6][5][4][3][2][1][0]

byte=1: 0 0 1 0 0 0 0 1 (21)

byte=2: 2 0 3 2 0 3 1 0 (8E 34)

. . .

byte=8: 56 C3 62 FF 25 44 06 6A (56 C3 62 FF 25 44 06 6A)

6. 3. 5   Transposition Conversion

Data in ee is controlled by keyb[0,i], for disk8e transposition conversion. bits 6,7 of keyb[i] indicate table no. of disk8e, bits 5,4,3 indicate the operation round, and bits 2,1,0 indicate the start point, e. g. :

The control number for no. i round:

c := (keyb[0,i] and 192) div 64;

b := (keyb[0,i] and 56) div 8;

a := (keyb[0,i] and 7;

In this example, keyb[0,0] = b7, c = 2, b = 6, a = 7, then: 2 table, 6 round, 7 start point:

ee:[7][6][5][4][3][2][1][0]

byte = 1: 0 0 1 0 0 0 0 1   (21)

byte = 2: 2 0 3 2 0 3 1 0   (8E 34)

...

byte = 8: 56 C3 62 FF 25 44 06 6A   (56 C3 62 FF 25 44 06 6A)

Trans

0	3	2	5	1	4	6	7
6	5	4	3	2	1	0	7

byte = 8: 06 FF 44 C3 62 25 56 6A   (06 FF 44 C3 62 25 56 6A)

...

byte = 2: 1 2 3 0 3 0 2 0   (6C C8)

byte = 1: 0 0 0 0 1 0 0 1   (09)

[7][6][5][4][3][2][1][0]

6. 3. 6   Single Substitution Conversion

ee combines into byte that constitutes new data, and conducts single substitution conversion through subst8e.

byte = 1: subst8e(09) = FF

byte = 2: subst8e(6C) = BC subst8e(C8) = 4E

...

byte = 8: subst8e(06) = 2A subst8e(FF) = 86 subst8e(44) = D7

subst8e(C3) = 68 subst8e(62) = 1E subst8e(25) = C4

subst8e(56) = F5 subst8e(6A) = 9D

6.3.7 Re-combination of Data and Keys

ee combines into byte that puts in data, and adds with keyb$[i+10,j]$

for $j:=0$ to byte -1 do

data$[j]:=($ data$[j]+$ keyb$[i+10,j])$ mod 256;

during operation of no. 0 round $i=0$

$$byte=1: \text{data}[0]:=(\text{data}[0]+\text{keyb}[i+10,0]) \bmod 256; \quad (19)$$
$$byte=2: \text{data}[1]:=(\text{data}[1]+\text{keyb}[i+10,1]) \bmod 256; \quad (50)$$
$$\text{data}[0]:=(\text{data}[0]+\text{keyb}[i+10,0]) \bmod 256; \quad (68)$$

$\cdots$

$$byte=8: \text{data}[7]:=(\text{data}[7]+\text{keyb}[i+10,7]) \bmod 256; \quad (19)$$
$$\text{data}[6]:=(\text{data}[6]+\text{keyb}[i+10,6]) \bmod 256; \quad (16)$$
$$\text{data}[5]:=(\text{data}[5]+\text{keyb}[i+10,5]) \bmod 256; \quad (46)$$
$$\text{data}[4]:=(\text{data}[4]+\text{keyb}[i+10,4]) \bmod 256; \quad (C7)$$
$$\text{data}[3]:=(\text{data}[3]+\text{keyb}[i+10,3]) \bmod 256; \quad (2C)$$
$$\text{data}[2]:=(\text{data}[2]+\text{keyb}[i+10,2]) \bmod 256; \quad (0C)$$
$$\text{data}[1]:=(\text{data}[1]+\text{keyb}[i+10,1]) \bmod 256; \quad (89)$$
$$\text{data}[0]:=(\text{data}[0]+\text{keyb}[i+10,0]) \bmod 256; \quad (B7)$$

6.3.8 Right Shift Accumulation

Data performs n-bit expansion with given byte, and stores in dd$[i]$:

ee$[7]:=$ dd$[7]$;

for $j:=6$ down to 0 do ee$[j]:=($ ee$[j+1]+$ dd$[j])$ mod $2**$byte;

	expanded							centralized
dd:[7]	[6]	[5]	[4]	[3]	[2]	[1]	[0]	
byte=1: 0	0	0	1	1	0	0	1	(19)
byte=2: 1	1	0	0	1	2	2	0	(50 68)

$\cdots$

byte=8: 19 16 46 C7 2C 0C 89 B7   (19 16 46 C7 2C 0C 89 B7)

Upon right shift accumulation, variables of each ee$[i]$:

ee:[7]	[6]	[5]	[4]	[3]	[2]	[1]	[0]	
byte=1: 0	0	0	1	0	0	0	1	(11)
byte=2: 1	2	2	2	3	1	3	3	(6A DF)

$\cdots$

byte = 8 : 19 2F 75 3C 68 74 FD B4   (19 2F 75 3C 68 74 FD B4)

6.3.9 Re-transposition

Controlled by keyb[9,i], data conducts disk8e transposition conversion. In this example, keyb[9,0] = 99, c = 2, b = 3, a = 1, i. e. , 2 : table, 3 : round ; 1 : start point :

ee:[7][6][5][4][3][2][1][0]

byte = 1 : 0 0 0 1 0 0 0 1   (11)

byte = 2 : 1 2 2 2 3 1 3 3   (6A DF)

...

byte = 8 : 19 2F 75 3C 68 74 FD B4   (19 2F 75 3C 68 74 FD B4)

3	5	1	6	2	0	4	7
0	7	6	5	4	3	2	1

byte = 8 : 74 B4 3C 2F FD 19 68 75   (74 B4 3C 2F FD 19 68 75)

...

byte = 2 : 1 3 2 2 3 1 3 2   (7A DE)

byte = 1 : 0 1 1 0 0 0 0 0   (60)

[7][6][5][4][3][2][1][0]

Until now, operation of no. 0 round ends, and operation of no. 1 round starts. Totally operation of 8 rounds is conducted. The encrypted results are as follows :

	byte = 1	byte = 2	...	byte = 8						
[0]	60	7A DE	74	B4	3C	2F	FD	19	68	75
[1]	09	4A AB	FE	FE	D5	E6	3D	FE	95	DB
[2]	82	CB EF	A0	09	DB	68	EE	A8	A5	FF
[3]	4D	F6 90	E0	0C	66	E8	58	29	13	DB
[4]	98	10 72	7F	5D	59	F8	8D	C4	E6	8E
[5]	7A	90 01	E9	55	F2	C8	3D	1E	96	2B
[6]	81	8E EE	61	F6	54	E2	06	62	0D	EA
[7]	47	6E BA	CF	3E	B1	D8	C1	9B	32	20

6.4 7-bit Operation

6.4.1 Given Conditions

byte : block length, byte = 1, 2, 3, 4, 8

bits: number of bits in one byte, bits = 7

i : operation of no. i round

		[7]	[6]	[5]	[4]	[3]	[2]	[1]	[0]
Assuming:									
Key:		08	07	06	05	04	03	02	01
data:	byte = 1								01
	byte = 2							02	01
	byte = 3						03	02	01
	byte = 4					04	03	02	01
	byte = 8	08	07	06	05	04	03	02	01

6. 4. 2   Key Derivation

keyb is derived from key

	[7]	[6]	[5]	[4]	[3]	[2]	[1]	[0]
original key :	08	07	06	05	04	03	02	01
derived keyb [0]:	4C	A4	7F	5D	08	18	94	B7
[1]:	92	5F	60	D6	DC	38	95	62
[2]:	6F	E0	38	B7	89	52	F8	6F
[3]:	F8	64	03	7C	DC	6F	C7	CF
[4]:	1E	61	87	48	2F	69	42	85
[5]:	09	E2	D3	0B	CD	B4	B4	A3
[6]:	F7	2D	36	22	BC	BB	49	AB
[7]:	E8	6B	9E	81	BA	48	C2	DC
[8]:	BF	02	74	36	94	B8	9C	57
[9]:	BD	C9	6D	4C	2A	FF	DB	99
[10]:	EF	90	6F	5F	0E	48	94	1A
[11]:	8F	23	FB	41	2E	97	9E	0C
[12]:	F1	CD	13	08	1E	AD	41	66
[13]:	15	52	FF	92	67	D4	06	AA
[14]:	BA	34	D3	80	DF	40	FD	D7
[15]:	3D	BD	27	6E	54	00	12	D7
[16]:	EA	6A	2E	C3	34	30	A0	F1
[17]:	27	7A	AF	82	7E	E6	A0	AC

6.4.3 Combination of Data and Key

Data adds with corresponding $keyb[i+1,j]$.

for $j := 0$ to byte -1 do

$\quad data[j] := (data[j] + keyb[i+1,j])$ mod 128;

During operation of no. 0 round $i = 0$

$\quad$ byte $= 1$: $data[0] := (data[0] + keyb[i+1,0])$ mod 128; $\qquad$ (63)

$\quad$ byte $= 2$: $data[1] := (data[1] + keyb[i+1,1])$ mod 128; $\qquad$ (16)

$\qquad\qquad\quad data[0] := (data[0] + keyb[i+1,0])$ mod 128; $\qquad$ (64)

$\quad \ldots$

$\quad$ byte $= 8$: $data[7] := (data[7] + keyb[i+1,7])$ mod 128; $\qquad$ (13)

$\qquad\qquad\quad data[6] := (data[6] + keyb[i+1,6])$ mod 128; $\qquad$ (61)

$\qquad\qquad\quad data[5] := (data[5] + keyb[i+1,5])$ mod 128; $\qquad$ (63)

$\qquad\qquad\quad data[4] := (data[4] + keyb[i+1,4])$ mod 128; $\qquad$ (5A)

$\qquad\qquad\quad data[3] := (data[3] + keyb[i+1,3])$ mod 128; $\qquad$ (61)

$\qquad\qquad\quad data[2] := (data[2] + keyb[i+1,2])$ mod 128; $\qquad$ (3E)

$\qquad\qquad\quad data[1] := (data[1] + keyb[i+1,1])$ mod 128; $\qquad$ (1C)

$\qquad\qquad\quad data[0] := (data[0] + keyb[i+1,0])$ mod 128; $\qquad$ (6A)

6.4.4 Left Shift Accumulation

Data in $data[i]$ expands based on number of byte, and puts into $dd[j]$:

1byte: 7bit 63 expanding based on 1 bit

	1	1	0	0	0	1	1

2byte: 7bit 16 64 expanding based on 2 bit

	00	10	11	01	10	01	00

$\ldots$

8byte: 7bit 13 61 63 5A 61 3E 1C 6A remain unchanged

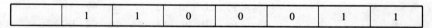

0010011	1100011	1100001	101010	1100001	0111110	0011100	1101010

$\qquad\qquad$ expanded $\qquad\qquad\qquad\qquad$ 7bit centralized

$\qquad dd:[7][6][5][4][3][2][1][0]$

byte $= 1$: $\quad$ 1 $\ $ 1 $\ $ 0 $\ $ 0 $\ $ 0 $\ $ 1 $\ $ 1 $\qquad$ (63)

byte $= 2$: $\quad$ 0 $\ $ 2 $\ $ 3 $\ $ 1 $\ $ 2 $\ $ 1 $\ $ 0 $\qquad$ (16 64)

...

byte = 8: 13 61 63 5A 61 3E 1C 6A   (13 61 63 5A 61 3E 1C 6A)

data in dd accumulates in left shift, and puts into ee[i] upon accumulation:

ee[0] := dd[0];

for j := 1 to bits − 1 do ee[j] := (ee[j − 1] + dd[j]) mod (2 ∗ ∗ byte);

when byte = 8

for j := 1 to bits − 1 do ee[j] := (ee[j − 1] + dd[j]) mod (2 ∗ ∗ (byte − 1));

    ee: [7][6][5][4][3][2][1][0]
byte = 1:   0   1   0   0   0   0   1   (21)
byte = 2:   1   1   3   0   3   1   0   (2E 34)

...

byte = 8: 56 43 62 7F 25 44 06 6A   (56 43 62 7F 25 44 06 6A)

6. 4. 5 Transposition Conversion

Data in ee is controlled by keyb[0,i], and conducts disk7e transposition conversion. However, when byte = 8, it conducts same disk8e operation as when bits = 8. When byte < > 8, bits 6,5 of keyb[i] indicate disk7e table no. , bits 5,4,3 indicate operation round, bits 2,1,0 indicate start point, e. g. :

The control numbers of no. i round:

c := (keyb[0,i] and 96) div 32;

b := (keyb[0,i] and 56) div 8;

a := (keyb[0,i] and 7;

In this example, keyb[0,0] = b7, c = 1, b = 6, a = 7 mod 7 = 0, i. e. , 1 : table, 6 : round, 0 : start point:

    ee: [6][5][4][3][2][1][0]
byte = 1: 0   1   0   0   0   0   1   (21)
byte = 2: 1   1   3   0   3   1   0   (2E 34)

| 1 | 5 | 4 | 2 | 0 | 6 | 3 |
| 6 | 5 | 4 | 3 | 2 | 1 | 0 |

byte = 2: 1   1   3   0   0   1   3   (2E 07)
byte = 1: 0   1   0   1   0   0   0   (28)
    dd: [6][5][4][3][2][1][0]

When bits = 8, c = 1, b = 6, a = 7, with disk8e conversion, then:

[7][6][5][4][3][2][1][0]
56 43 62 7F 25 44 06 6A

4	3	1	7	2	0	5	6
6	5	4	3	2	1	0	7

6A 06 56 43 25 62 44 7F

6.4.6　Single Substitution Conversion

ee combines into byte which constitutes new data, and conducts single substitution conversion through subst7e

byte = 1: subst7e(28) = 74

byte = 2: subst7e(2E) = 75 subst7e(07) = 24

$\cdots$

byte = 8: subst7e(6A) = 48 subst7e(06) = 09 subst7e(56) = 08

　　　　　subst7e(43) = 7A subst7e(25) = 7E subst7e(62) = 6E

　　　　　subst7e(44) = 2B subst7e(7F) = 2D

6.4.7　Re-combination of Data and Key

ee combines into byte which puts in data, and adds with keyb[i + 10, j]

for j := 0 to byte − 1 do

data[j] := (data[j] + keyb[i + 10, j]) mod 128;

During operation of no. 0 round i = 0

byte = 1: data[0] := (data[0] + keyb[i + 10, 0]) mod 128;　　(0E)

byte = 2: data[1] := (data[1] + keyb[i + 10, 1]) mod 128;　　(09)

　　　　　data[0] := (data[0] + keyb[i + 10, 0]) mod 128;　　(31)

　　　　$\cdots$

byte = 8: data[7] := (data[7] + keyb[i + 10, 7]) mod 128;　　(37)

　　　　　data[6] := (data[6] + keyb[i + 10, 6]) mod 128;　　(19)

　　　　　data[5] := (data[5] + keyb[i + 10, 5]) mod 128;　　(77)

　　　　　data[4] := (data[4] + keyb[i + 10, 4]) mod 128;　　(59)

　　　　　data[3] := (data[4] + keyb[i + 10, 3]) mod 128;　　(0C)

　　　　　data[2] := (data[5] + keyb[i + 10, 2]) mod 128;　　(36)

　　　　　data[1] := (data[6] + keyb[i + 10, 1]) mod 128;　　(3F)

$$\text{data}[0] := (\text{data}[7] + \text{keyb}[i+10,0]) \bmod 128; \qquad (47)$$

6. 4. 8 Right Shift Accumulation

Data conducts n-bit expansion with given byte, and stores in dd[i],

```
            expanded           centralized
      dd: [7][6][5][4][3][2][1][0]
byte =1:      0   0   0   1   1   1   0      (0E)
byte =2:      0   1   0   2   3   3   2      (09 3E)
      . . .
byte =8:  37  19  77  59  0C  36  3F  47     (37 19 77 59 0C 36 3F 47)
```

Variables of each ee[i] upon left shift accumulation:

$ee[7] := dd[7]$;

for $j := 6$ down to 0 do $ee[j] := (ee[j+1] + dd[j]) \bmod 2 * * \text{byte}$;

when byte $= 8$

for $j := 6$ down to 0 do $ee[j] := (ee[j+1] + dd[j]) \bmod 2 * * (\text{byte} - 1)$;

```
      ee:[7][6][5][4][3][2][1][0]
byte =1:      0   0   0   1   0   1   1  (0B)
byte =2:      0   1   1   3   2   1   3  (0B 67)
      . . .
byte =8:  37  50  21  68  50  37  2C  62  (37 50 21 68 50 37 2C 62)
```

6. 4. 9 Re-composition

Controlled by keyb[9,i], data conducts disk7e and disk8e composition conversion. In this example, keyb[9,0] = 99, c = 0, b = 3, a = 1, i. e. , 0: table, 3: round, 1: start point:

```
          [6][5][4][3][2][1][0]
byte =1:   0   0   0   1   0   1   1      (0B)
byte =2:   0   1   1   3   2   1   3      (0B 67)
```

```
┌                       ┐
│ 1   6   3   5   2   0   4 │
│ 0   6   5   4   3   2   1 │
└                       ┘
```

```
byte =2:   1   1   3   3   1   2   0      (2F 58)
byte =1:   1   0   1   1   0   0   0      (58)
          [6][5][4][3][2][1][0]
```

When byte = 8, composition conversion is as follows:

[7][6][5][4][3][2][1][0]
37 50 47 20 2C 62 21 68

| 3 | 4 | 0 | 7 | 2 | | 1 | 6 | 5 |
| 0 | 7 | 6 | 5 | 4 | | 3 | 2 | 1 |

47 20 21 68 50 37 2C 62
[7][6][5][4][3][2][1][0]

Until now, operation of no. 0 round ends, and operation of no. 1 round starts. When bits < 8, operation of 7 rounds is conducted. When bits = 8, operation of 8 rounds I conducted. The encrypted results are as follows:

	byte = 1	byte = 2	...	byte = 8
[0]	58	2F 58		47 20 21 68 50 37 2C 62
[1]	16	27 79		18 31 30 52 14 77 34 44
[2]	1E	3D 5E		42 0C 07 09 42 0E 00 02
[3]	1E	52 45		16 63 68 03 69 25 7E 32
[4]	20	25 59		7B 60 2D 3C 6F 4F 77 12
[5]	7B	07 3E		66 04 42 37 7E 4F 2B 50
[6]	65	31 48		43 63 16 79 03 52 30 38
[7]	7E	13 2F		43 65 48 1C 4D 52 22 1E

6.5 Security Evaluation

This solution is specialized for encryption of storage data such as database, especially for encryption of relational database. Database system typically has strict access control mechanism, which protects the database safety.

The main purpose of relational database encryption is to protect the data contents. However, encryption certainly will affect database function. Thus, encryption shall not affect database search efficiency as much as possible, and shall not damage data structure of the database.

6.5.1 Key Granularity

Database has structural keys. Structural keys are used for segmentation of database. One database can set one type of structural keys, or one database system can set same type of structural keys.

(1) mmm, subst8e or subst7e substitution table.

(2) disk8e or disk7e transposition.

Database has database key.

Catalog has catalog keys. Different catalogs define different keys.

File has file keys. Each file (table) has a file key (fik), with a length of 64 bits, which is automatically generated when creating the file, and is stored in the file key file under the encrypted protection of root directory key mum. For example:

$$E_{mum}(fik_i)$$

The access right of the file key file is same as the one of the file. The file key is used for encryption/decryption of data. For example:

$$E_{FIki}(data)$$

With the file key, the record key and field key are automatically defined.

6.5.2   Confusion and Diffusion

In each round conversion, data variable and key variable combine, with twice transposition conversion and once substitution conversion, to achieve good confusion effects.

In each round conversion, good diffusion effects can be achieved through twice n-bit expansion and centralization, twice left/right shift accumulation conversion and once substitution conversion.

6.5.3   Multiple-level Product Conversion

The level is set to be 8-level iteration, with each level uses unique key. The key is derived from non-linear mod q shift register, and is extracted at an interval of 16 rounds and 24 rounds, which damages continuity of the sequence.

From the above analysis, it can be seen that this solution solves the issue of convenient database search while remaining data structure under the precondition of ensuring encryption.

Part Three

CPK System

Chapter 7

CPK Key Management

An authentication system based on combined public key (CPK) crypto-system will be introduced in this chapter. The main work in an authentication system is digital signature. However, sometime there will be a need for both digital signature and key exchange. The key exchange requirement is to achieve other party's public key with no-handshaking (one-way), which is more difficult and complicated than digital signature.

The system design takes the most complicated situation, i. e. , key exchange, into consideration. If the system only needs digital signature, then the functions associated with key exchange can be deleted.

7.1 CPK Key Distribution

7. 1. 1 Authentication Network

CPK authentication network concerned is a horizontal single-layered grid network (see Fig. 7. 1). The grid authentication network has no center, and all the transactions are implemented among customers. The network with center can be seen as a special case of grid network. KMC is an off-line independent organization, and has no business relations with user transaction. Under the centralized management mode, KMC is the trust root.

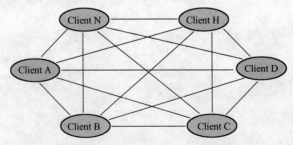

Fig. 7. 1 Horizontal Authentication Network

Development and spread of horizontally structured networking and end to end transmission technology such as store-forward communication and packet switching raise many new issues to the authentication system. The issues can be summarized as follows: scalability of proof and immediacy of verification in digital signature. Different domains and classifications were defined in the networks in the past but now the horizontal management i. e. the management over the Grid authentication network has become the new trends. To meet the new requirement it must be supported by new technology and theory.

7. 1. 2   Communication Key

Since the authentication network is a grid network with no center, and the modern communication is individualized and end to end communication, on the open public network (such as Internet, telephone network), it is redundant to divide the network or data into function domains (e. g. longitudinal multi-layered division, horizontal internal-external network division), and to divide personnel and data into different classifications (except for private network).

Despite all that, in view of the actual situation of coexistence of private network and public network, it is acceptable to remain function domain division of keys and registration classification of personnel.

Communication key is a main parameter variable that ensures communication between the communicating parties. The keys are divided into symmetric keys and asymmetric keys.

① Symmetric Key: A common key shared by both communicating parties.

② Asymmetric Key: The decryption key is owned by the designated party.

7. 1. 3   Classification of Keys

In generally, there is no need to define different classifications for the communication network and computer facilities in public network. It is the same as above mentioned authentication network. But if the keys are used in file management then files may be classified different levels to realize different encryption.

The keys are classified by roles and domain. Role is divided into:

1. System administrator

2. Senior employees

3. Mid-level employees

4. General employees

5. Customers

Domain is divided into:

1. Global domain.

2. District domain.

Different keys are distributed to different classes and domain for enabling different access control.

The classes shall be downward-compatible. For example, senior employees shall have the processing capability of senior employees, mid-level employees, general employees, and customers; mid-level employees shall have the processing capability of mid-level employees, general employees, and customers; general employees shall have the processing capability of general employees and customers; customers shall only have the processing capability of customers.

7.2 CPK Signature

The study of authentication protocol has made considerable progress internationally, and it is relatively matured from theory to technology. So far there are two kinds of authentication protocols: international standard and CPK protocol.

7.2.1 Digital Signature and Verification

Digital signature protocol: ECDSA;

1) Signing Procedure:

1. Choose an integer $k, 0 < k < n$

2. Calculate $kG = (x_1, y_1)$, $r = x_1 \bmod n$; if $r = 0$, go to step 1

3. Calculate $k^{-1} \bmod n$

4. Calculate $s = k^{-1}\{h + d_A r\} \bmod n$; h is the hash code of the document

5. If $s = 0$, go to step 1

6. The signature to hashed code h is a pair of integers (r, s)

2) Verification Procedure:

1. Check r and s, to see whether $0 < r, s < n$

2. Calculate $w = s^{-1} \bmod n$, and find hash code h

3. Calculate $\eta_1 = hw \bmod n$; $\eta_2 = rw \bmod n$

4. Calculate $\eta_1 G + \eta_2 Q_A = (x_0, y_0)$; $v = x_0 \bmod n$

5. If $v = r$, the signature is verified

7.2.2 Signature Format

The signature format (Table 7.1) is implemented in accordance with the international standards. The signature format mainly includes the number of signatures, identities used for signatures and signature codes.

Table 7.1 Digital Signature Format

SERIAL NO.	BYTES	MEANING	CONTENTS
1	2	Identity of Signature Field	QM
2	1	Number of Signatures	
3	25	Identity$_1$	'...'
4	48	Signature Code$_1$	Sign$_1$
7	25	Identity$_2$	'...'
8	48	Signature Code$_2$	Sign$_2$
...	...	...	...
4n + 3	25	Identity$_n$	'...'
4n + 4	48	Signature Code$_n$	Sign$_n$

7.3 CPK Key Exchange

1) 'One-to-one' Key Exchange

A: Choose a random number r, calculate: r (bG), sending to B;

calculate: rG as key k

B: Calculate with its own private key: b^{-1} r bG = rG = k

2) 'One-to-multi' Key Exchange

'One-to-multi' key exchange is implemented by 'one-to-one' key exchange. Suppose A sends message m to users B, C, D, etc.

1. A generates a random number r;

2. Calculate rG as data encrypting key KEY and encrypt data with the KEY;

$$E_{KEY}(data) = code$$

3. Send to B, supposing B's public key is bG = β, then send rβ and code;

4. Send to C, supposing C's public key is cG = γ, then send rγ and code;

5. Send to D, supposing D's public key is dG = δ, then send rδ and code;

and so on.

3) ElGamal key exchange

Suppose Bob's private key is b and public key is bG. Now Alice sends P to Bob.

Alice: selects a random number k and calculates k(bG) with Bob's public key and sends (kG,

$P + k(bG))$ to Bob.

Bob: calculates $b(kG)$ with his private key b and $P + k(bG) - b(kG) = P$

7.4   CPK Data Encryption

In view of the actual situation of coexistence of private network and public network, personnel and data clearance can be remained.

The definition of Role keys:

1. Key variable for system administrator: $role_1$-key;
2. Key variable for senior employees: $role_2$-key;
3. Key variable for mid-level employees: $role_3$-key;
4. Key variable for general employees: $role_4$-key;
5. Key variable for customers: $role_5$-key;

Role-keys are defined in the ID-card, and the higher level is downward compatible with the lower level.

The definition of Domain keys

1. Domain global key: domain1-key;
2. Domain district key: domain3-key

The composition of data encrypting keys:

$$ran\text{-}key \oplus role_n\text{-}key \oplus domain_i\text{-}key$$

Data encryption procedure:

Generate random number: ran-key;

$$E_{ran\text{-}key \oplus role_n\text{-}key \oplus domain_i\text{-}key}(data) = coded\text{-}text;$$
$$E_{PK}(ran\text{-}key) = coded\text{-}key$$

Data decryption procedure:

$$D_{SK}(code\text{-}key) = ran\text{-}key$$
$$D_{ran\text{-}key \oplus role_n\text{-}key \oplus domain_i\text{-}key}(coded\text{-}text) = data$$

7.5   Key Protection

All stored keys are protected by physically and logically. The main logical protection method is encryption under password.

7.5.1   Password Verification

Upon turning on the authentication device the device automatically enter into password verification procedure.

Password (PWD): xxxxxxxx

Password is used to protect private key variable. The protection relationship is as follows.

Private keys are encrypted under random key R_1, R_1 is defined by the manufacturer.

$$E_{R1}(csk_1) = Y_1$$
$$E_{R1}(csk_2) = Y_2$$

R_1 is protected by password:

$$E_{PWD}(R_1) = Z_1$$

Thus, upon entering the password, first finds R_1

$$D_{PWD}(Z_1) = R_1$$

Then, checks the legitimacy of the password:

$$E_{R1}(R_1) \oplus R_1 = Z_2'$$

Compares Z_2' to Z_2 in the ID-card and judges whether the password is correct or not. If correct, then go to the next step.

Once the password is entered, it will remain in the password field before exiting the authentication procedure, and no-reentry is needed. In addition, before exiting the authentication procedure, it will be in a status of ready to call for all sorts of key-variables.

If the password failed for five consecutive times, it counts as a security incident, and parameter Z_2 will be set to "0", which can only be restored at the KMC center.

7.5.2 Password Change

When entering into password change procedure, begin with the password authentication

Password (PWD): xxxxxxxx

Check the legitimacy of password: if passed then

New password (PWD$_1$): xxxxxxxx

Decrypt Z_1 with the original password PWD:

$$D_{PWD}(Z_1) = R_1$$

Re-encrypt R_1 with the new PWD_1:

$$E_{PWD1}(R_1) = Z_1'$$

Change the original variable Z_1 to Z_1'.

Chapter 8

CPK-chip Design

8.1 Background

With development and application of public network, new requirements for constructing trusting system are raised. Authentication system is the core technology of the trusting system, while key management technology is the core technology of authentication system. There are two main difficulties in key management: the scalability and direct distribution. CPK key management solves these two difficulties, and creates conditions for realizing trusting system on scaled public network.

CPK is implemented in a chip without on-line support of database. It has incomparable advantages comparing with the above-mentioned two systems (PKI and IBE), in terms of scalability, economy, feasibility, and operation efficiency.

8.2 Main Technology

The CPK system must provide an authentication system and encryption system based on specialized hardware device. The CPK system not only can effectively withstand attacks from users to ensure security of the CPK system, but also is easy to manage so that the CPK system can be widely applied.

The CPK system uses specialized hardware device to store, manage and protect confidential/sensitive data, such as private keys in the system. Comparing with software-only realization, the private keys only take part in internal operation, and even the system legal users cannot read out the private key from the system. This makes the attackers impossible to obtain the private keys, so as to ultimately eliminate the possibility of any attack.

The CPK system is an authentication system that uses chip to realize functions of encryption and decryption, digital signature and verification, key storage and management, the special software system (COS), ID-card, signature protocol and key exchange protocol, encryption algorithm and HASH function are all realized by way of modular design. The system includes:

- Processor, for handling various data, so as to control and manage the whole system;
- Secure memory, the data of which can only be accessed by special instruction of the process or special peripheral device; wherein the attackers cannot access the data bypassing the interface, or by logical/physical ways of chip attack;
- Public key engine, for providing instructions used for public key operation, and for supporting elliptic curve key operation;
- Symmetrical cryptography engine, for providing operation instructions used for symmetric encryption and hash function;
- Random number generator, for generating random numbers;
- System protection, including protective devices against attacks to safety package of chip and anti-chip attack analysis;
- Communication interface, including USB controller, serial interface or intelligent card interface, for communicating with peripheral equipment.

The system software includes the following:

- Private key management module is used for the storing, managing, handling and protecting private keys, all the operations to the private keys are done by this module. The module calls elliptic curve key module to conduct elliptic curve signature and key exchange operation of elliptic curve public key;
- Public key management module is used for the mapping of identity to combination matrix, and calculating the corresponding public key;
- Access control module is used for protecting the system through password and cryptography function;
- Elliptic curve cryptography module is used for conducting elliptic curve signature, verification, and key exchange, etc.;
- Symmetric cryptography module is used for providing symmetric encryption, hash function, etc;
- Random number generating module is used for generating random numbers;
- Encoding/decoding data format module is used for encoding/decoding the data with CPK format;
- Communication protocol module is used for implementing communication protocol with CPK agents, and providing service to CPK agents by way of "request-response" instruction.

According to a preferred embodiment of the solution, if the system does not include the public key engine, symmetric cryptography engine and random number generator, then the system may invoke corresponding elliptic curve key module, symmetric cryptography module and random number generator, to implement the functions. The data includes public key matrix, current user's identity and corresponding private key, which are stored in the form of ID-cards. The main functions include ID attributes management, encryption, signature, protocol execution, key storage and management, which can be plug-and-play. The system includes at least one of intelligent card chip integrated with processor and memory, independent memory device and safety computer. Based on the package and interface, the chip can be at least one of intelligent card, USB memory, Flash memory, and cell phone SIM card.

8.3 Chip Structure

CPK authentication system is realized with CPK-chip. The chip includes special COS, CPK cryptosystem, ID-card, signature protocol and key exchange protocol, encryption algorithm and HASH function, etc. Based on different package and interface, the chips can be divided into the forms of ID-card, Flash memory card, and cell phone SIM card. If desired, the public key matrix can be written into the chip. An authentication system can be easily constructed by a chip having the functions of cryptography, signature and verification, key storage.

In authentication system, most functions are implemented within the chip to ensure the security of authentication procedure, and to provide the simplest way for authentication.

Fig. 8.1 shows the basic structure of a CPK-chip, the system includes CPK special hardware device.

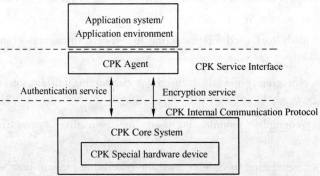

Fig. 8.1   Basic structure of a CPK-chip

Logically, the system includes two main parts, core and agent. Core is to provide the functions of authentication and encryption through hardware interface or software interface. Agent is usually embedded into the application system to provide CPK authentication and encryption service. There may be various forms of the service interface, including, API, middleware, system service, network service, etc. Agent itself does not implement CPK basic functions. Rather, it invokes the functions by using the special communication protocol, and provides such services to the application environment. Agent may also implement certain level of package or enhancement to the functions of the core, so as to satisfy the requirements of the application system.

Fig. 8.2 shows a detailed structure of CPK-chip. It is composed of software in combination with hardware, in which the software is running on the specialized hardware device, common network and computer platform, respectively.

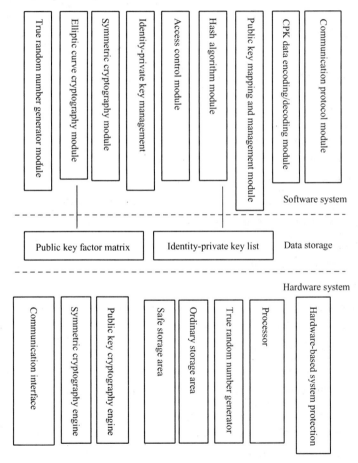

Fig. 8.2　Detailed structure of CPK-chip

CPK-chip includes hardware, software (i. e., CPK-COS) and internal relevant data therein. Detailed explanation of CPKCOS is given below.

① CPKCOS provides identity-based, no third party needed, off-line authentication. CPKCOS realizes CPK system by way of chip, to provide one or multiple unique identities for each entity. Each entity can identify each other with the identity. CPKCOS can support multiple identities in one chip, allow the chip to support a number of applications with changeable mapping algorithms, and flexibly cancel/update the identity.

② CPKCOS sets a security level indication for each identity. CPKCOS only implements operation that complies with the security level restriction, so as to support multiple-security-level safety required in system such as army system.

③ CPKCOS provides ECDSA digital signature, ECDH key exchange, AES and Triple-DES symmetric data encryption, and SHA series hash algorithm. In addition, CPKCOS can conduct a variety of security applications such as authentication and encryption, and can be used as auxiliary security algorithm module.

④ CPKCOS supports system software upgrading, to add other cryptography algorithm and to add expansion function.

In order to ensure the system security, the software system is specially designed to fit with the specialized hardware. CPKCOS is used to represent the software system below. Logically, CPKCOS ensures security of data such as private keys.

① CPKCOS divides the memory into secure storage area and insecure storage area. The secure area is composed of security enhanced EEPROM memories, and the insecure area is composed of ordinary Flash memories. CPKCOS stores the important programs and data such as the system programs, the confidential data such as private keys, the program segments of operation confidential data in the secure area; and stores the public data such as public key matrix in the insecure area. The CPKCOS system program segment ensures that the data has not been changed by verifying signature and integrity of data and program in insecure area, and ensures confidentiality of data in the storage area by way of encryption. The design of insecurity storage area allows CPKCOS to support Flash memory outside the chip, to ensure its security.

② CPKCOS system does not provide read/write interfaces to outside for confidential data such as private keys. The interfaces can only be used for normal signature and decryption, but not for obtaining confidential data. Even the legal user cannot read out the private key data.

③ CPKCOS protects chip and its internal sensitive data through password. The user can use CPK security chip only after inputting the verification password. CPKCOS system adds time delay during password verification, so as to greatly increase the time spent by the attackers for password attempts. In addition, there is a verification failure counter within the chip. If the failure times of the password verification exceed the highest limit, the sensitive information within the chip will be self-destroyed.

8. 4 Main Functions

8. 4. 1 Digital Signature

The system includes four basic CPK operation functions: CPK system based signature, verification, data encryption and decryption.

Fig. 8. 3 shows the flowchart of CPK digital signature.

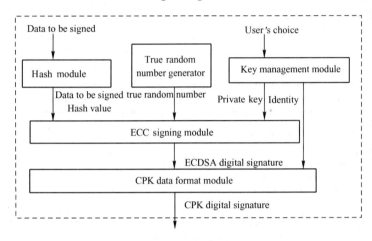

Fig. 8. 3   CPK digital signature flowchart

1) To choose one identity for digital signature.

2) To inputs the data to be signed.

3) Hash module calculates the hash value of the data.

4) The random number generator generates random number.

5) The private key management module reads corresponding private key with the identity.

6) The ECC signing module generates ECDSA digital signature with the hash value, the random number and the private key.

7) The data format module output the digital signature as CPK format.

The signature verification process is as follows:

1) To reads in digital signature and data from outside.

2) Hash module calculates the hash value of the data.

3) CPK data format module obtains the signer's identity and digital signature data from the CPK formatted data.

4) Identity mapping module maps the identity to a public key.

5) ECC signing module verifies whether the signature is valid or not with the hash value, ECD-SA digital signature and signer's public key, and send the result back to the user.

8.4.2 Data Encryption

Fig. 8.4 shows a workflow of CPK data encryption. With CPK data encryption, one user can send encrypted data to any other users. The data is encrypted with standard encryption algorithm. The key exchange protocol provides the recipient with decryption function by using its own private key. Detailed process is as follows:

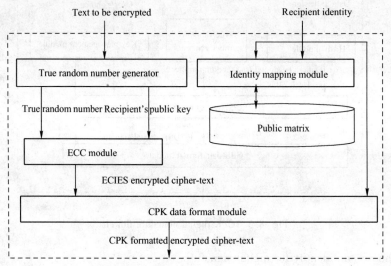

Fig. 8.4   CPK encryption workflow

1) CPK-chip reads in recipient 's identity and encrypted data from outside.

2) The mapping module calculates the recipient's public key with the identity and public matrix.

3) Random number generator generates random numbers for key exchange.

4) ECC module provides key exchange protocol, that encrypts the data with symmetric key, and encrypt the symmetric key with public key of the recipient, and finally generates ECIES encrypted cipher-text.

5) CPK data format module output the CPK formatted cipher-text.

The decryption process is as follows:

1) CPK-chip reads in encrypted data from outside.

2) CPK data format module reads out identity and ECIES encrypted data.

3) key management module obtains corresponding private key.

4) ECC module provides key exchange protocol, seek symmetric key of the encrypted data with the private key, then decrypt the ciphered text to plain text with the symmetric key, and output the plain text.

Due to various hardware devices have different storage and handling capacity, plus different particular application environments, different function modules of the system will evenly distribute between CPK core system and CPK Agents. If the function of the specialized hardware device is more powerful, then more of system function modules are realized on the specialized hardware devices. If the hardware device function of the specialized device is more powerful, then more of the system function modules are realized on the CPK agents in the application environment.

Three representative specialized hardware devices are intelligent card chip, safety computer, and memory card without handling capacity.

The Implementation has following advantages and benefits:

(1) Previous authentication all adopts "belief logic" starting from pre- assumption and by formalized inference and proof, and the proof is limited only to the object. This system adopts "trust logic" to prove the authenticity of an entity without pre-assumption.

(2) Previous authentication only solves authentication of non-large scale (scale of thousands or tens of thousands). This system applies for authentication of ultra-large scale such as email address, personal phone number and personal account no. The scale is counted by thousands of billions.

(3) Previous authentication uses 3rd party mechanism and database as the necessary means for authentication. The cost is high, and the system maintenance is complicated. This system uses one chip to realize the authentication system, and cancels the CA mechanism and database, so as to greatly simplify the authentication process, improve authentication efficiency, greatly reduce the cost, and save the operation and maintenance expenses.

Chapter 9

CPK ID-card

9.1 Background

Identity certificates of CPK are uniformly issued by the key management center (KMC), and the certificates are obtained with ID-card of intelligent ID-card. The user (terminal or any entity) in the authentication network uses the ID-card to implement authentication function between any two points (including key exchange and digital signature) in the thousands of billion ultra-large scale range.

Comparing with CA certificate of PKI, CPK ID-card has many differences. In CPK authentication system, ID-card is the identity certificate, recording the attributes of an entity, private key and other relevant information, for proving the authenticity of the entity. Relevant contents write into ID-card, CPK-key, and other hardware devices.

Entity attributes (entity identity, clearance grade, function domain, etc.) are defined and the corresponding private key variables and other relevant information are involved in the ID-card. Therefore the ID-card will be the main tool of key distribution.

ID-card, as the core part of CPK authentication, applies for ultra-large scale authentication system. The key management system includes registration department, key producing department and issuing department. The registration department receives application from the user, sends the ID-card data to producing department. The producing department sends the ID-card to issuing department and the issuing department distributes it to users.

ID-card is the key data structure in CPK system. The terminal entity of the CPK authentication network uses the ID-card to implement encryption, and signature. ID-card is generated by the key management center and encapsulated into ID-card. The most important elements in ID-card are the identity definition of an entity and its private key. The identity is the name of an entity and noted as ID, is the only representation of an entity. In the CPK system, each identity can map to the only one public key. ID-card also includes the private key corresponding to the identity. Each identity can belong to different function domains. The function domain is divided into two degree: global and district. The function domain maybe composed of different combination matrices. The public matrix can be option, which can be included in the chip of ID-card or can be stored in the external memory medium. Table 9. 1 illustrates relevant international standards of CPK authentication system.

Table 9. 1　Relevant international standards of CPK authentication system

X. 208	ASN. 1 language	
X. 209	ASN. 1 code scheme	
X. 509	Adopts partial certificate attributes therein	
SEC1v1. 0	Algorithm and scheme of elliptic curve	ASN. 1 is not complete, lacking of ECIES, etc.
SEC2	Elliptic curve parameters	
ECCX509	Maintain ECC compatible with X. 509	Still under development draft stage
PKCS#5	Password-based encryption standard	For protecting private key of the certificate
PKCS#7	Public key encryption and digital signature	Modifying it to adapt for identity-based encryption signature
PKCS#8	Private key protection	Modifying it to adapt for identity-based encryption signature

CPK authentication system relies on existing relevant international standards, and CPK authentication system is based on the international standards listed in Table 9. 1. In order to apply for CPK system, some of the standards are expanded and modified in addition to maintain compatibility.

This standard adopts international standard of ASN. 1 language to describe ID-card format. When existing standards are needed, this standard gives reference to the relevant standards.

ID-card adopts ASN. 1 of X. 208 standard to define abstract data structure of the certificate, and uses X. 209 to encode into binary file or data. The data type of the card is compatible with current international standards. Currently relied international standards include [RFC2459], [SEC1], [SEC2], [PKCS#5], [PKCS#7], [PKCS#12].

9. 2　ID-card Structure

ID-card is a core element in CPK system. The most important element of the ID-card is the identity of entities and its private key. The identity must be unique. In CPK system, each identity can be mapped onto a unique key pair. The private keys of the identity are provided by ID-card and the public keys are provided by public file in key exchange or by signing party in digital signature.

The contents of an ID-card are consisted of two parts: the main body and the variables. The part of main body is constant that defines properties of the entity. The part of variables defines the keys and other parameters.

9.2.1 The Part of Main Body

1	ID-card Title	Bill Seal System of Minsheng Bank
2	Name of the holder	e. g. :Zhang San
3	Clearance	1 – 5
4	Identity1 (global)	
5	Identity2 (district)	
6	Valid term	2007 – 2010
7	The name of issuer	

9.2.2 The Part of Variables

The variables are the core of ID-card. It configures the key and the parameter variables. Following is an example of a common ID-card that is applicable for both public network and private network.

1. Verification Item

It is used to verify authenticity of the password, to confirm the rights to power on.

Z_1 : Verification Parameter $\qquad Z_1 = E_{PWD}(R_1)$

Z_2 : Verification Parameter $\qquad Z_2 = E_{R1}(R_1) \oplus R_1$

2. classification key

0	System administrator	$C_1 = E_{R1}(Class_1)$
1	Senior employees	$C_2 = E_{R1}(Class_2)$
2	Mid-level employees	$C_3 = E_{R1}(Class_3)$
3	General employees	$C_4 = E_{R1}(Class_4)$
4	Customers	$C_5 = E_{R1}(Class_5)$

3. Private Keys

Domain : global

0	Private key$_1$	$E_{R1}(csk_1)$
1	Private key$_2$	$E_{R1}(csk_2)$

Domain : district

0	Private key$_1$	$E_{R1}(csk_1)$
1	Private key$_2$	$E_{R1}(csk_2)$

4. Key Issuing Item

0	Issuing Authority	Key Management Center
1	Sign	SIG_{KMC-1} (MAC of ID-card) = sign

9.3 ID-card Data Format

Data format of ID-card adopts ASN. 1 language to define. The method of OSI defining abstract objects is referred to as ASN. 1 (Abstract Syntax Notation One, X. 208). A set of rules for transferring the objects to bit stream of " 0" and " 1" are referred to as BER (Basic Encoding Rules, X. 209). DER encoding rules are one subset of BER, which have the only one encoding style for each ASN. 1 value.

```
CPKIdentifier :: = CHOICE {              -- Need change and expansion
    octetString    [0] OCTET STRING,
    emailAddress   [1] EmailAddress,      -- Need definition
    number         [2] INTEGER
}
```

The particular format of CPK identity will be further defined in the formal standard.

```
CPKDomainParameters :: = SEQUENCE {
    version               Version,
    mapAlgorithmAlgorithmIdentifier, -- Not sure, use PKCS standard
    columnSize            INTEGER,
    rowSize               INTEGER,
    ellipticCurve         CurveParameters,
    publicMatrix          PublicMatrix
}
Version: = INTEGER
```
INTEGER is ASN. 1 standard data type, indicating an integer with random length.
```
CurveParameters :: = Parameters
```
Parameters data type indicates the parameters of elliptic curve, defined by [SEC1].
```
PublicMatrix ::- = SEQUENCE OF ECPoint;
```

PublicMatrix is a sequence constructed by elliptic curve points with the number of columnSize * rowSize. ECPoint is defined by [SEC1].

```
CPKDomain :: = SEQUENCE {
    identity              CPKIdentity,
```

```
        parameters      CPKDomainParameters OPTIONAL,
    }
```

CPK function domain parameters mainly include identity domain and public matrix domain, in which public matrix is optional.

```
    CPKCertificate : = SEQUENCE {
        version       Version DEFAULT v1(1),
        domain        CPKDomain,
        identifier    CPKIdentity,
        privateKey CPKPrivateKeyInfo, -- Not sure, use PKCS#8 standard
        keyUsage  KeyUsage,          -- X.509 KeyUsage
        validity      Validity,          -- X.509 Validity
        extensions Extensions        -- X.509 Extensions
    }
    CPKPrivateKeyInfo ::= EncryptedPrivateKeyInfo -- PKCS#8
```

Private key information protected by encryption is defined by relevant standard of PKCS#8.

KeyUsage refers to key usage, Validity refers to period of validity, and Extension refers to expansion, all defined by X.509 standard.

The objects defined by ASN.1 will be further explained below.

(1) CPKIdentity

Identity in the CPK authentication system is represented by CPKIdentity and CPKIdentity will be mapped to its public key.

For example, in Email application, EmailAddress will be taken as CPKIdentity. both Alice@ example. com and ALICE@ Example. com will be converted to the same alice@ example. com, because even though the two have differences in character, they belong to same identity.

(2) CPK Domain

Function domain is represented by CPKDomain. Different function domain may use different combination matrices or the same combination matrix. Encryption or decryption, digital signature or verification can be implemented among the entities through the ID-card.

CPK ID-card can support multi-identities.

(ⅰ) Supporting multi-identities: Each CPKCertificate defines one identity, which belongs to the only one function domain defined by CPKDomain. The certificate data issued to the user can include multiple CPKCertificate belonging to the same domain, so as to support multi-identities.

(ⅱ) Supporting function domains: Each CPKDomain defines one domain. The certificate data issued to the user can include a plurality of CPKDomain, so as to provide mutual authentication ability among different domains.

(iii) Effective use of storage space: If a plurality of CPKCertificate belong to one domain, then the attribute Domain of the CPKDomain type can adopt simplified storage mode, i. e. , the optional attribute CPKDomainParameters of CPKDomain will not be encoded.

```
CPKinsideSample1 :: = SEQUENCE {
emailCertificateCPKCertificate,
    idcardCertificate      CPKCertificate,
    phoneCertificate       CPKCertificate,
    internetDomain         CPKDomain,
    phoneDomain            CPKDomain
}
```

In this embodiment, the chip includes three CPKCertificate portions of ID-card, i. e. , including three pairs of identity-private keys. However, the common public key matrix is not repeatedly stored. Instead, it is separately stored as internetDomain. Because the key lengths required by phone authentication and internet authentication are different, the ID-card supports two different matrices, i. e. , two different function domains CPKDomain.

According to the second embodiment, multi-security grades are supported. In one application, different-level organizations need to support different security grades and function domains. Mutual communication can be realized within the same domain, to share keys. In order to support the application, a new part - security grade is introduced into the ID-card .

A user 's identity format is: Username = alice@ security. net; SecureLevel = 3; the user 's public key/private key pair is mapped to multiple fields.

Within the same domain, a common key can be used. In other words, a common key is added in the ID-card, and shared by all users.

9. 4   ID-card Management

9. 4. 1   Administrative Organization

Key Management Center (KMC) is responsible for registration and ID-card issuing. KMC works completely off-line.

KMC is comprised of Registration Department, Product Department and Issue Department, as shown in Fig. 9. 1.

The top Key Management Center may set up some issuing agencies in different regions as re-

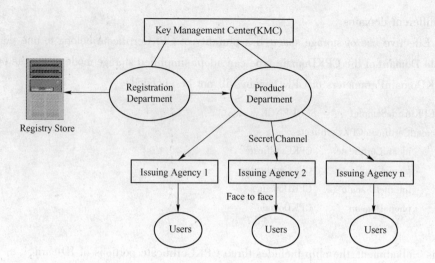

Fig. 9. 1   Organization of Key Management Center (KMC)

quired. The agency assists the KMC to handle ID-card (or ID certificate) application, production and issuance. There must be a secret channel built between the agencies and the Center to ensure confidentiality. It can be seen that the transmission of ID-card contents must be processed in a secure network. The network is completely the same as ordinary secure business network.

9. 4. 2   Application for ID-card

The principle of key distribution is to use real-name system. One identity has one key. Typically, face-to-face distribution method is used.

The applicant provides relevant evidence or proof:

1) Applying for name signature: Providing real name.

2) Applying for address signature: Providing real address.

3) Applying for phone signature: Providing phone number.

4) Applying for corporation signature: Providing the name of corporation.

5) Applying for account No. signature: Providing bank account No.

Application for account No. key: According to the requirements of the bank, it can be done upon satisfying the conditions of setting up an account; such as providing his/her ID number, phone number, address, etc. A bank card only has one account No., and one person may hold multiple cards.

Application for Name key: Legal person proof documents or bank's position proof documents shall be provided. The name-key of 3rd-layered net shall be handled at KMC of 3rd-layered net, and the name-key of 2nd-layered net shall be handled at KMC of 2nd-layered net.

Application for Unit-key: Unit proof documents shall be provided by the one in charge of financial seal and unit seal. The unit-key of 3rd-layered net shall be handled at KMC of 3rd-layered net, and the unit-key of 2nd-layered net shall be handled at KMC of 2nd-layered net.

Application for Phone no. key: The bank proof document is needed. The phone number key of 3rd-layered net shall be handled at KMC of the 3rd-layered net, and the phone number key of 2nd-layered net shall be handled at KMC of the 2nd-layered net with proof documents from more than two banks.

Application for email address key: The bank proof document is needed. The email address key of 3rd-layered net shall be handled at KMC of 3rd-layered net, and the email address key of 2nd-layered net shall be handled at KMC of 2nd-layered net with proof documents from two banks.

In the banking business, the signatures playing a key role are account number, name, unit, position, etc. The phone number and e-mail address are mainly used for security of data transmission.

Customers go to the Registration Department for ID-card application. Registration Department is mainly in charge of the body part of ID-card. Registration contents and definition procedure of Registration Department are as follows.

The applicant submits an application form for registration to Registration Management Center (RMC), who checks the application form. CPK system adopts the real-name mechanism. Taking the bill-seal system of Minsheng Bank for example, the application form is shown as in Fig. 9.2.

Filing	Name	Ding Yi	Applied for	Bill
	Type of card	ID card	ID No.	256701800101234
	Address	XXXX	Phone No.	010-12345678

Signature of Applicant   Signature of Administrator

Date

Fig. 9.2 Application form

9.4.3 Registration Department

Registration Department is responsible for applicant name, ID card number, and conduct inquiries to judge whether there is duplication. If there is duplication, then it needs to be redefined. A registration device retains the former names (report loss) and the name being used currently; to check whether the user applies for the first time. If so, the relevant parameters are recorded, and cards (bank card, business card, phone card, access card, ATM card, etc.) are classified based on the usage. All the parameters necessary for production are transferred to the production department.

Registration Department makes clear definition to identity, role, key, matrix no. and configuration, etc.

Identity: personal name, mail address, organization name, position, phone number, accounts number ($Account_1$, $Account_2$, $\cdots$, $Account_n$). If it is an account number, whether it is an account no. of credit, debit, industry and commerce, pension, or medical insurance shall be distinguished. The number of identities can be either one or multiple.

Role: one of customers, general employees, mid-level employees, and senior employees.

Registration Department hands over the determined data, upon signed, together with the new card to Production Department. So far the new card has been recorded all parameters which would be used in key production.

9. 4. 4 Production Department

Production Department is responsible for the private keys and parameters in the ID-card. Producing procedures are automatically performed by the background process.

1) Turn-on operation

Insert the ID-card of the device.

The $administrator_1$ turns on the device:

Enter $password_1$ (PWD_1):

xxxxxxxx

The $administrator_2$ turns on the device:

Enter $password_2$ (PWD_2):

xxxxxxxx

PWD is double-locked password, and can only be opened by two administrators.

$$PWD = PWD_1 \oplus PWD_2$$

Thus, when the password is entered, first finds R_1:

$$DPWD(Z_1) = R_1$$

Checks the legitimacy of the password:

$$E_{R1}(R_1) \oplus R_1 = Z_2'$$

Compares Z_2' with Z_2 in ID-card and judges the password. If correct, open the device.

2) Key producing Procedures

The ID-card generating device composes two parts: the private key combining matrix ($r_{i,j}$) (i, j = 0. 31) and CPK-chip.

The diagram of key generating device is shown in Fig. 9. 3.

The administrator defines a unique serial number first and prints it on the face of new ID-card,

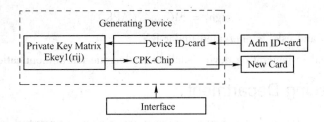

Fig. 9.3　Key generating device

to facilitate future management.

Receiving the formatted data from the registration department the device produces all relevant data. Now the device has produced all relevant functions and parameters.

3) Key Protection

Produces the random number R1 and encrypts the private keys :

$$E_{R1}(\text{private key / key parameter}) = Y;$$

Finds Z_1,

$$Z_1 = E_{PWD}(R_1)$$

If the user does not define PWD, it shall be defined by the manufacturer. The PWD defined by the manufacturer is a fixed number which requires to be changed before formal use.

Finds the verification parameter Z_2,

$$Z_2 = ER_1(R_1) \oplus R_1$$

Finally, finds MAC of the ID-card contents for the signature of the issuing authority.

4) Writing Data to Card

Mark the generating device as A, the private key for A is e_A, the public key is $e_A G$, and the new card as B

A: Send its own public key $e_A G$ (or spare key_2) to B;

B: Generate a random number k_1, and calculate $k_1 G = Pm = (x,y)$,

Generate a random number k_2, $k_2 G$ and $k_2(e_B G)$;

Send two points $(k_2 G, Pm + k_2(e_B G))$ to A

A: Use $k_2 G$ and private key e_A to calculate:

$$e_A(k_2 G)$$
$$Pm + k_2(e_A G) - e_A(k_2 G) = Pm = (x,y)$$

Take x as key $E_{key}(\text{csk/ APK})$, send it to B.

B: Decrypt with x, and write csk_1, csk_2, APK and $sign_1$ into new card, where

$$csk_1 = isk + ask$$
$$csk_2 = isk + ssk$$

$$\text{sign}_1 = \text{SIG}_{\text{KMC}-1}(\text{APK})$$

Private key csk_1 and csk_2 is encrypted under RN_1.

The software used in generating device shall be undergone tag authentication.

9.4.5 Issuing Department

Upon obtaining the ID-card, it is better for the users to change password in advance.

The ID-cards are implemented by chip technology.

1. CPK-key is implemented by USB memory, mainly used in PC.

2. CPK-card is implemented by IC card, mainly used as credit card.

3. CPK SIM card is used in cell-phone.

4. CPK-chip is mainly used in printed board.

Contents in the chip can be different according to various uses.

1. The chip may include all the required parameters and protocols for executing.

2. The chip may only retain the private key and the remaining operation is accomplished by the card reading device.

3. The chip may retain symmetric key to be used in fixed communication.

Part Four

Trust Computing

Chapter 10

SoftwareID Authentication

10. 1   Technical Background

This program involves signature technology, authentication technology, and in particular deals with the CPK-based software label authentication technology.

Computing environment can be a stand-alone, and also can be networking of a number of computers. But the latter case mixes up the two technical issues in different areas, so it further complicates the simple problem. Trusted computing platform (TCP) of the current international research has chosen the latter technology route.

To resolve trusted computing it is necessary to deal with two major issues of the scale of key management and identity-based key distribution, but at the present, the key issue of identity authentication in the software world has yet not been resolved internationally. In the authentication system, the verification technology is more important than the proving technology. Some systems can provide proof of identities, but fail to provide the means to verify the identity. The reason for why Trusted Platform Module (TPM) of TCP is designed so complicated is that it does not solve the key technologies of identity authentication, but is about to resolve the issues of trusted computing in PC and trusted connection with outside PCs at the same time. However, the only key objective that the trusted computing is executing, so that to bring out trusted computing environment.

This technology sets up the subject of trusted computing based on the scaled identity authentication, and separate the subjects of trusted computing and trusted connecting because simple and effective solutions of trusted connecting has emerged so it is only required to be focused on solving the trusted computing of a single computer. The core of its technical route is to set up an orderly software market for the control of non-authorized software, especially the loading and execution of malicious software.

In the real world, as any merchandise has a trademark, the 'no trademark' products are often counterfeit products disrupting the social and economic order. Similarly, in software market it is helpful to improve computing environments and the credibility of the calculation if the software label management is implemented for effectively preventing malicious software interference.

10. 2　Main Technology

The CPK-Based code signing technique is consisted of two parts: the signing module and the verifying module, and any executing program code is consisted of two parts: label of the code and body of the code. Here the 'label 'stands for the identity or the name of program code and the 'body 'stands for the program code itself.

Signing Module: placed only signing machine, the machine is inserted with ID-card and has CPK signing function. There is three level of code signing:

- The manufacturer level: The codes are signed by the manufacturer, and the manufacturer of the source codes provides the responsibility for the codes.
- The enterprise level: The codes are signed by the enterprise, and the enterprise of the source codes provides the responsibility for the codes.
- The individual level: The codes are signed by individuals, and individuals are responsible for the codes that they select to use.

Verifying Module: If a PC is equipped with Verifying Module then it only has verifying function. If a PC needs to have signing function (individual signing) then the PC must be inserted with ID-card. The Verifying Module may have different security policy, such as:

1. To allow the execution of the codes signed by the manufacturer.
2. To allow the execution of the codes signed by enterprise.
3. To allow the execution of the codes signed by individual.

CPK is a self-assured public key system in which an EntityID is mapped into a point ENTITY on the elliptic curve defined by $E: y^2 = x^3 + ax + b \pmod p$ with the parameter $T = \{a, b, G, n, p\}$, if an integer *entity* satisfies ENTITY = (*entity*) G then ENTITY is public key and *entity* is private key. Because ENTITY = σ_1 (EntityID) and σ_1 is open to public, the public key can be calculated by any one and the private key is provided by ID-card.

The ID-card of manufacturer is shown as Table 10. 1.

Table 10. 1　manufacturer 's ID-card

1	Z1: verification parameter	16B	$E_{PWD}(R1) = Z1$
2	Z2: verification parameter	16B	$E_{R1}(R1) \oplus R1 = Z2$
3	Identity definition	25B	ManufacturerID
4	Private key	32B	$E_{R1}(\text{manufacturer}) = Y1$
5	Name of issuing unit	25B	KMC
6	Signature of issuing unit	48B	$SIG_{kmc}(\text{mac})$

The ID-card is distributed by key management center (KMC).

10. 3   Signing Module

Signing Module and Verifying Module may be directly implemented with ID-card. All signing and verifying function is done within ID-card. However, if a device does not need any signing function then the Verifying Module may be implemented by outside software. For example the software in switching device of communication, the software in banking system, the software in cell phone, the software in Automate Telling Machine, etc. are only allowed to execute the formally equipped software and there is no private parameter in the Verifying Module, it may realized in open program outside ID-card.

The software labels are defined by the signing party, and the signing party will provide the responsibility for the software codes. The Signing Module signs to software label and software body. The signing protocol is ECDSA. The structure of Signing Module within ID-card is shown in Fig. 10. 1.

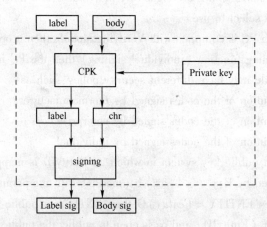

Fig. 10. 1   Signing Module

Suppose that the software identity is 'name' and the software body is 'data', and the Signing Module signs to the 'name' and 'data'. The sign to identity provides the evidence of signing party's responsibility for the software, and the sign to 'body' proves that the software of 'identity' and 'body' is the unbreakable pair. The signing procedure is as follows.

1. If an operation system is produced by a manufacturer then the manufacturer signs to all software identities and software bodies in the operation system respectively.

Suppose the ManufacturerID's public key is MANUFACTURER and private key is 'manufac-

· 94 ·

turer 'then the authentication procedure is as follows:

Prover: $$\text{SIG}_{manufacturer}(\text{SoftwareID}) = \text{Sign}_1$$
$$\text{SIG}_{manufacturer}(\text{MAC}) = \text{sign}_2$$

Sign_1 means a manufacturer's sign_1 to the identity, and sign_2 to the body of the software. Because the software body is a long data string the signature is only made to its characteristics. The MAC of Hash function may be the characteristic of the software body but it is too complicated. In common case it is recommended that the characteristic is computed simply and quickly. The main object of body signing is to prove the unity of identity and body while not to prove the integrity of the data of the body.

2. If an enterprise produces application software then the enterprise signs to all identities and bodies of the application software respectively.

Suppose the EnterpriseID 's public key is ENTERPRISE and the private key is 'enterprise ', then the authentication process is as follows:

$$\text{SIG}_{enterprise}(\text{SoftwareID}) = \text{sign}_3$$
$$\text{SIG}_{enterprise}(\text{MAC}) = \text{sign}_4$$

Here, sign_3 means an enterprise 's sign to the identity, and sign_4 to the body of the software.

In a case that the operation system has not the signature of manufacturer, the enterprise can sign it in substitution of manufacturer.

3. If a person selects some application software to use then he would sign to all identities and bodies of the application software respectively.

Suppose an IndividualID 's public key is INDIVIDUAL and the private key is 'individual ', then the authentication process is as follows:

$$\text{SIG}_{individual}(\text{SoftwareID}) = \text{sign}_5$$
$$\text{SIG}_{individual}(\text{MAC}) = \text{sign}_6$$

Here, sign_5 means an individual's sign to the SoftwareID, and sign_6 to the body of the SoftwareID.

10. 4 Verifying Module

Every set of computer is equipped with the Verifying Module. Verifying Module is composed of CPK module and public matrix. The public matrix ($R_{i,j}$) is used to calculate the relying party 's public key. It may be implemented by ID-card without private key, or by the software written outside ID-card. The construction of Verifying Module is shown in Fig. 10. 2.

The verification process in this module is carried out in two steps.

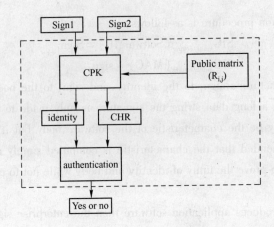

Fig. 10. 2   Verifying Module

In the first step, check the signature of sign$_1$ to identity first before loading the body of software, to determine whether the software body shall be downloaded. Sign$_1$ provides the proof of the authenticity of the identity, with which if it is not consistent, it will be not download, and in return it will be downloaded.

Checking manufacturer's signature to SoftwareID

$$SIG_{MANUFACTURER}^{-1}(SoftwareID) = sign_1'$$

If sign$_1$ = sign$_1'$ then the check is passed or the calling and loading is cancelled.

Checking enterprise's signature to SoftwareID

$$SIG_{ENTERPRISE}^{-1}(SoftwareID) = sign_3'$$

If sign$_3$ = sign$_3'$ then the check is passed or the calling and loading is cancelled.

Checking enterprise's signature to identity

$$SIG_{INDIVIDUAL}^{-1}(SoftwareID) = sign_5'$$

If sign$_5$ = sign$_5'$ then the check is passed or the calling and loading is cancelled.

The check is processed according to the security policy.

In the second step when the software is being downloaded, the Verifying Module is computing the characteristic or integrity code MAC, and checking sign$_2$, which provides unity proof of the identity and the body, if met, then implements it, if not, terminates the process.

Checking manufacturer's signature to body

$$SIG_{MANUFACTURER}^{-1}(MAC) = sign_2'$$

If sign$_2$ = sign$_2'$ then the check is passed or the calling and loading is cancelled.

Checking enterprise's signature to body

$$SIG_{ENTERPRISE}^{-1}(MAC) = sign_4'$$

If $sign_4 = sign'_4$ then the check is passed or the calling and loading is cancelled.

Checking enterprise 's signature to body

$$SIG^{-1}_{INDIVIDUAL}(MAC) = sign'_6$$

If $sign_6 = sign'_6$ then the check is passed or the calling and loading is cancelled.

10. 5 The Feature of Code Signing

The code authentication in this scheme is divided into two steps wherein the key of the authenticity lies in the first step of identity authentication, which verifies the identity before the loading event arises. This technique has not realized yet in any other trust computing such as the popular TPM.

Verifying Module follows a security policy of "only recognizes our side, while excludes all other sides". So that any virus and malicious code can not take any role within the computer even if they have intruded, because they have not legal signature of manufacturers or enterprises.

Verifying Module (VM) is very simple, the main task of which is just to guarantee the trusted computing environment within the computer and irrelevance between the verification modules, so there is no need for the Verifying Module to set their own special labels, but it is universal, which brings great convenience for the universal use of Verifying Module; the module does not contain any secret variable, so it can be publicized; it makes everyone to be able to calculate any public key from any identity and verify any signature. The workflow of the module is only "use and judge" so it is not necessary to retain any history record, thus greatly reducing the burden of modules.

In this scheme, the trust root is the key management center, who manages all keys used in this scheme. The sub trust roots are on the Signing Module. Signing Module is only set up at the management agencies, which may be organizations of national trademark management, software associations or software evaluation centers and may also be a corporate league. From the point view of setting up an orderly software market to protect the trusted computing environment of each computer, it is more beneficial to be managed by the relevant national departments. Branches can be built in each province, responsible for the admissibility of the various signing businesses.

The scheme contributes to the orderly management of the software market and is conducive to the loading and operation control of all kinds of application software, which further benefits the establishment of the trusted computing environment. For computer users, it is workable to configure each machine only with the Verifying Module, thus generalization of Verifying Module is especially in favor of universal use.

Chapter 11
Code Signing of Windows

11.1 Introduction

In this chapter, we mainly describe the theory realized in Code authentication of Windows operating system. By means of the file mini-filter which intercepts the opening operation of executable file, code authentication of Windows operating system identifies the executive program code by authentication code. Only when the code checking is passed, it can be executed. Any authorized software has its own authentication codes so that it is very easy to distinguish the authorized software and unauthorized software. Any unauthorized software such as malicious code and virus has no authentication code and easily to be prevented from loading and executing.

This chapter is organized as follow: To begin with, in order to explain the characteristic of Windows' executive code, we introduce such term—the formation of PE files; in addition, we introduce Microsoft 's new interface of file filter—mini-filter, so as to illustrate how to achieve code authentication.

11.2 PE File

Executive code of Windows is mainly based on the formats of PE files.

The format of PE (short for "portable executable") file is an executable binary system format under each edition of Windows Operating Systems which are published after Windows NT and Windows 95. Those executable files whose suffix is exe, dll, or sys, are of this format.

The format of PE file is organized as a liner data stream, which begins with a MS-DOS Header, then a vestigial system of real model and a symbol of PE file, followed by PE file header and optional header. All these sections are followed by session header, then by session entity. The ending of such file contains some other area, some of which are relocated information, symbol information, line information and string table. All these components are illustrated in Fig. 11. 1.

MS-DOS MZ Header
MS-DOS stub
PE file symbol
PE file header
PE optional header
All session header
Session 1
Session 2
...
Session n

Fig. 11. 1   components in Windows

11. 3   Mini-filter

File filter in Windows Operating system can intercept the demand that file operation of operating system operated by application program. Mini-filter is a new file filter developing interface offered by Microsoft. This set of new interface is both simple and clear. It can obtain more reliable and simple by less effort. Code authentication is realized by means of mini-filter.

11. 3. 1   NT I/O Subsystem

I/O Subsystem of Windows NT or after-edition (in the following part, we called " NT" for short.) is a frame, in which all kernel driving programs interact with its external devices. Such I/O subsystem is constructed by the following components.

- NT I/O Manager: defines and manages the whole frame;
- File system driving: responsible for file system based on local disc;
- Network redirector: responsible for I/O access request for network;
- Network file server: responsible for I/O access request for network to locality;
- NDIS: offers universalized functions to a collection of devices, such as SCSI driving; or offer additional functions, such as software image driver, etc.
- Filter driving: insert into driving storey to realize the function that can't achieve by existing driver directly.

Windows NT excutive componerts is shown in Fig. 11. 2.

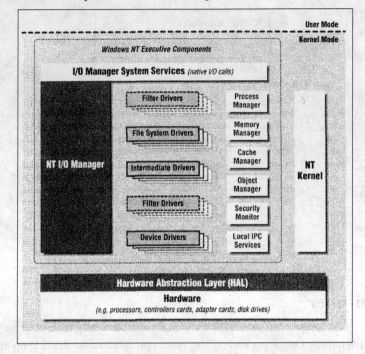

Fig. 11. 2　Windows NT Executive Components

I/O subsystem is based on packet, i. e. all I/O requests are submitted by I/O Request Packet (IRP). Usually, IRP is the target kernel program constructed and conveyed by I/O manager when the user requests.

11. 3. 2　File Filter Driving

NT I/O subsystem is designed as expandable. One form of such expandability is file filter driving program, which can intercept file operating request of operating system by application software, since it intercepts the request before which approaches the target, so file filter has the opportunity to expand or modify the functions offered by the original receiver. Normally, file filter is applied to realize file encryption system, anti-virus system, and file monitor system, etc.

In the perception of Programming, file filter takes advantages of the interface offered by Windows driver SDK, defines a series of callbacks, which correspond with relevant IRP. After applying registered function offered by driving SDK of Windows, IRP request sent by I/O manager can be intercepted, so as to operate relevant process, for instance: when it comes to encrypting file system, it will intercept writing request to encrypt, while intercept reading request to decipher.

The Kernel Mode is shown in Fig. 11.3.

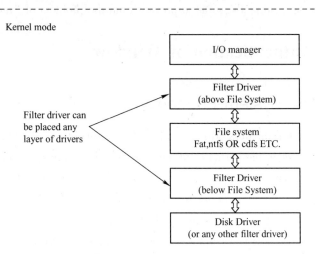

Fig. 11.3   Kernel Mode

11.3.3 Mini-filter

Usually, based on the filter's instance of Windows operating SDK, traditional file filter applies IRP and devices to filter the object, which proves to be the "old filter model" at the most. Later, Microsoft developed a filter based on the "old filter model"—Filter Manager (included in Windows 2000 SP4, Windows XP SP1, Windows2003 SP1; while in other after-edition Windows, filter manager is set up by implication.) Filter manager is able to supply a series of new interfaces to exploit new filter driver program—mini-filter. Compared with the interface of the "old filter model", the interface of mini-filter has several advantages, take the nelation among driver and modules shown in Fig. 11.4 as an instance:

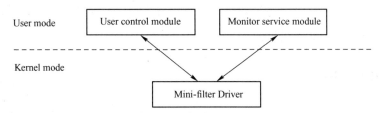

Fig. 11.4   The relation between driver and module

1) This set of new interface is both simple and clear. It can obtain more reliable and simple by less effort;

2) Dynamic loading, unloading, attaching and un-attaching;

3) Supports non-circulatory I/O, i. e. I/O conveyed by mini-filter can only approve that pass the filter stack and pass on directly, so as to prevent from the problem of "reentry".

11. 4　Code Authentication of Windows

11. 4. 1　The System Framework

Applying the system framework which was based on mini-filter, code authentication of Windows mainly includes mini-filter in the kernel condition, the user control module, and monitor service module in the user state. Among them, the mini-filter is responsible for file filtering, while the user control module receives users'input, modifies the system setting and status. The monitor service module is responsible for operation in the user state of file filtering.

1) Kernel driver: in the kernel condition, mini-filter takes charge of file filtering, including the interception of executable file opening operation, collecting of file's characteristics, and gain of signature.

2) Monitor service: in the user state it deals with data conveyed by kernel filtering program.

3) User control: in the user state, this module approves users to receive their input, modifies the system setting and status.

11. 4. 2　Characteristics Collecting

As mentioned, executive codes of Windows are based on the formats of PE files; however, code session's location of PE file depends on the deviant of both MS-DOS MZ header and PE header. Usually, PE file is modified by way of additional code session, meanwhile, the size of file, and the deviant of both MS-DOS MZ header and PE header can be modified according demand. Therefore, PE file's characteristics compose of the header of PE file and the size of file as main characteristic, and others part of the file as supplement.

11. 5　Conclusion

The code signing on Windows system has been exploited successfully by South China Information Security Industry Park, and would be launch a pilot project in the Counter System of China Minsheng Bank.

Chapter 12

Code Signing of Linux

12. 1　General Description

Linux code authentication intercepts load of executable file with Linux security module (LSM). Before the executable file being loaded the file identity is first authenticated and after loading then the body of file is authenticated. Only the file passes authentications can be executed, so as to prevent loading and executing non-authorized software, especially malicious software.

First, we are going to explain the structure of ELF Linux executing code file and the implementation of the code authentication, and then Linux security module (LSM) framework.

12. 2　ELF File

Executable and Linking Format (ELF) file is the primary object file format under x86 Linux system. It has three main types.

(1) Re-locatable file that suits for connection, i. e. , normally called object file, with suffix as . o. It, together with other object files, can create executable file and shared object file.

(2) Executable file that suits for executing, for providing process image of the procedure, and memory executing of load.

(3) Shared object file. A connector can connect it with other re-locatable file and shared object file to other object file. A dynamic connector can also incorporate it with executable file and other shared object file to create a process image.

First, see general layout of ELF file below:

ELF header

Program header table

Segment 1

Segment 2

…

Segment n

Section header table (optional)

Segment is composed of several sections, and section header table has relevant description to information of each section. Signature information, just as a section, is stored in the file.

12. 3　Linux Security Module (LSM) Framework

Linux security module(LSM) is a lightweight common access control framework of Linux kernel. It enables various security access control model to implement in the form of Linux loadable kernel module, and the user can choose proper security module to load to Linux kernel if desired, so as to greatly improve flexibility and usability of Linux security access control mechanism.

Linux security module(LSM) adopts the method of placing hooks in the kernel source code, to mediate the access to the kernel inner objects. The objects include: task nodes, opened files, etc. Before the Linux kernel attempts to access to the inner object, a hook of Linux security module (LSM) invokes a function that the security module must provide, so as to raise such question as " whether the access is permitted to execute?" to the security module. Based on its security strategy, the security module makes the decision and responds: allowed, or refuse to return with an error.

During the process of kernel direction, Linux security module(LSM) framework is initiated as a series of virtual hook functions, to realize conventional UNIX super-user mechanism. When loading a security module, function register_security( ) shall be used to register this security module to the Linux security module(LSM) framework. This function will set the global table security_ops, to direct it to the hook function pointer of this security module, so as to allow the kernel to inquire the access control strategy to this security module. Once a security module is loaded, it becomes the security strategy decision-making center of the system, and will not be covered by the following function register_security( ), until this security module is unregistered to the framework by using function unregister_security( ). This simply replaces the hook function with the default, and the system returns back to UNIX super-user mechanism. In addition, Linux security module (LSM) framework further provides function mod_reg_security( ) and function mod_unreg_security( ), to enable following security modules to register and unregister with the first registered main module, but the strategy implementation is decided by the main module: whether to provide certain strategy to implement module stack so as to support module function incorporation, or to simply return error to ignore the following security modules. These functions are all provided in the kernel source code file security/

security. c.

Drawing the authenticated file data and signature information is conducted in the hook function, and the final result is also returned by the hook function, so as to allow or prohibit loading of the file.

12.4 Implementation

Linux code authentication is based on Linux security module (LSM) common structure, including kernel security module, data transmission module for transmitting data, and daemon process in charge of verification. The logical structure is shown in Fig. 12.1.

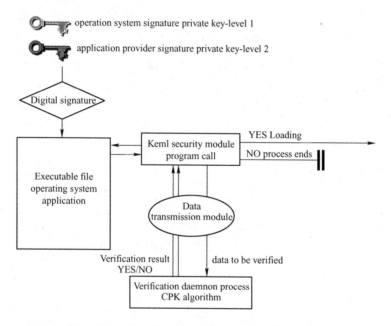

Fig. 12. 1 Logic diagram of Linux code authentication

（1）Kernel security module: in charge of intercepting ELF file to be loaded, taking out data to be verified; transmitting the processed data together with the signature information to the data transmission module; and then returning the verification result, so as to allow or prohibit loading the ELF file.

（2）Data transmission module: in charge of transmitting the data of the kernel security module to the verification daemon process, receiving verification result from the verification daemon process, and returning the verification result to the kernel security module.

（3）Verification daemon process: verifying the data transmitted by the data transmission module, and returning the result to the data transmission module.

Part Five

Trust Connecting

Chapter 13

Phone Trust Connecting

In phone authentication system the phone number is taken as the identity. Phone communication is may originated from any phone number and terminated to any phone number via public network which constitutes a typical grid authentication network.

Cell phone communication has many various usages: it can transmit digital data and digital voice. The data communication over the Internet is the same as email communication and has been discussed in above Chapter thus will not be discussed here.

In personalized voice communication, there are two main problems to be solved. The first problem is to verify whether the connection is true, i. e. the connection it is not illegal; the second problem is to provide privacy, i. e. the contents cannot be read by any irrelevant personnel.

Cell phone authentication between individual users is implemented by ID-card. In cell phone system the ID-card is implemented in SIM-card. The ID-card is issued by key manage center (KMC).

Cell phone authentication between individual users is implemented by ID-card. In cell phone system the ID-card is implemented in SIM-card.

13. 1　Main Technologies

The phone authentication is realized by CPK Cryptosystem. CPK is a self-assured public key system in which an EntityID is mapped into a point ENTITY on the elliptic curve defined by $E: y^2 = x^3 + ax + b \pmod p$ with the parameter $T = \{a, b, G, n, p\}$, if an integer '*entity*' satisfies $ENTITY = (entity)G$ then the point ENTITY is public key and the integer '*entity*' is private key. Because $ENTITY = \sigma_1(EntityID)$ and σ_1 is open to public, the public key can be calculated by any one and the private key is provided by ID-card. The main contents in SIM-card are listed in Table 13. 1.

Table 13. 1　ID-card for SIM-card

1	Z1 : verification parameter	16B	$E_{PWD}(R1) = Z1$
2	Z2 : verification parameter	16B	$E_{R1}(R1) \oplus R1 = Z2$
3	Identity definition	25B	01062871133
4	Role level	1B	5
5	Private key1	32B	$E_{R1}(\text{phone-no}) = Y1$
6	Role level 5 key	48B	$E_{R1}(\text{key1}) = Y3$
7	Name of issuing unit	25B	KMC
8	Signature of issuing unit	48B	$SIG_{KMC-1}(\text{mac})$

Upon power-on the phone user enters password. If password authentication is passed users can operate the CPK authentication system.

Assuming: The communication parties are Alice and Bob, each having its own phone number;. and the identities are briefly noted AliceID = 12345678 and BobID = 87654321 instead of the long numbers. In identity-based CPK crypto-system identity can be mapped into public key and private key respectively. Suppose "ALICE" is the public key and "*alice*" is the private key.

13. 2　Connecting Procedure

The Connecting procedure is as follows.

Suppose Alice calls Bob and sends connection request:

$$SIG_{alice}(\text{time}) = \text{sign}_1$$

Msg1 : Alice→Bob, { AliceID, time, sign$_1$ }

Bob verifies the signature:

$$SIG_{ALICE}^{-1}(\text{time}) = \text{sign}_1'$$

If sign$_1$ = sign$_1'$ then Bob signs to (time − 1):

$$SIG_{bob}(\text{time} - 1) = \text{sign}_2$$

Bob sends sign$_2$ and a random number r to Alice.

Msg2 : Bob→Alice, { r, sign$_2$ }

Alice verifies sign$_2$:

$$SIG_{BOB}^{-1}(\text{time} - 1) = \text{sign}_2'$$

If sign$_2$ = sign$_2'$ then it proves the receiver is Bob and signs to r, Alice signs to (time + 1) and return to Bob data and sign to checksum. The signs are:

$$SIG_{alice}(r) = \text{sign}_3$$

$$\mathrm{SIG}_{alice}(\,\mathrm{time}+1\,)=\mathrm{sign}_4$$

$$\mathrm{SIG}_{alice}(\,\mathrm{checksum}\,)=\mathrm{sign}_5$$

Msg3 : Alice→Bob, $\{\,\mathrm{sign}_3\,,\mathrm{data}\,,\mathrm{sign}_4\,,\mathrm{sign}_5\,\}$

Bob verifies signs :

$$\mathrm{SIG}_{ALICE}^{-1}(\,r\,)=\mathrm{sign}_3'$$

$$\mathrm{SIG}_{ALICE}^{-1}(\,\mathrm{time}+1\,)=\mathrm{sign}_4'$$

$$\mathrm{SIG}_{ALICE}^{-1}(\,\mathrm{checksum}\,)=\mathrm{sign}_5$$

If $\mathrm{sign}_3=\mathrm{sign}_3'$, it is correct response to the challenge, if $\mathrm{sign}_4=\mathrm{sign}_4'$, then allows to receive the data, and if $\mathrm{sign}_5=\mathrm{sign}_5'$ then return receipt. The receipt is :

$$\mathrm{SIG}_{bob}(\,\mathrm{checksum}\,)=\mathrm{sign}_6$$

Msg4 : Bob→Alice, $\{\,\mathrm{sign}_6\,\}$

Alice verifies sign_6 :

$$\mathrm{SIG}_{BOB}^{-1}(\,\mathrm{checksum}\,)=\mathrm{sign}_6'$$

If $\mathrm{sign}_6=\mathrm{sign}_6'$, then proves the data is sent to Bob correctly.

The authentication of connecting procedure is implemented by separating-key or accompanying-key. The public key is provided respectively by key pool or signer.

13.3 Data Encryption

If the data is encrypted, the data structure will be as follows :

Data = $\{\,\mathrm{sender}\,,\mathrm{receiver}\,,\mathrm{encrypted\text{-}key}\,,\mathrm{encrypted\text{-}data}\,\}$

Encrypting procedure :

1) Alice generates a random number r and calculates $\mathrm{key}_1=r\times(\,G\,)$;

2) Alice encrypts the key with Bob's public key :

$$\mathrm{ENC}_{BOB}(\,\mathrm{key}\,)=\mathrm{coded\text{-}key}_1$$

Where, ENC is encryption function with asymmetric key.

In the same way,

3) Bob generates a random number r and calculates $\mathrm{key}_2=r\times(\,G\,)$;

4) Bob encrypts the key with Alice's public key :

$$\mathrm{ENC}_{ALICE}(\,\mathrm{key}\,)=\mathrm{coded\text{-}key}_2$$

The communication from Alice to Bob uses the key of coded-key_1 and the communication from Bob to Alice uses the key of coded-key_2.

5) Key_1 is modulo 2 added to the role-key :

$$\mathrm{key}_1\oplus\mathrm{role\text{-}key}=\mathrm{new\text{-}key}_1$$

6) Encrypts voice1 with new-key$_1$:

$$E_{new-key1}(voice_1) = cipher\text{-}text_1$$

In the same way

7) Key$_2$ is modulo 2 added to the role-key:

$$Key_2 \oplus role\text{-}key = new\text{-}key_2$$

8) Encrypts voice$_2$ with new-key$_2$:

$$E_{new-key2}(voice_2) = cipher\text{-}text_2$$

Where, E is encryption function with symmetric key.

13. 4   Data Decryption

1) Bob decrypts the key with private key provided by Bob's ID-card.

$$DEC_{bob}(coded\text{-}key_1) = key_1$$

Where, DEC is decryption function with asymmetric key.

2) Alice decrypts the key with private key provided by ID-card.

$$DEC_{alice}(coded\text{-}key_2) = key_2$$

3) Key$_1$ is modulo 2 added to role-key:

$$Key_1 \oplus role\text{-}key = new\text{-}key_1$$

4) Key$_2$ is modulo 2 added to role-key:

$$Key_2 \oplus role\text{-}key = new\text{-}key_2$$

5) Recover voice$_1$ with new-key$_1$:

$$D_{new-key1}(cipher\text{-}text1) = voice_1$$

6) Recover voice$_2$ with new-key$_2$:

$$D_{new-key2}(cipher\text{-}text2) = voice_2$$

Where, D is decryption function with symmetric function.

Upon Alice and Bob receives coded-key$_1$ or coded-key$_2$ respectively, the conversation key new-key$_1$ for A-B communication, i. e. $E_{new-key1}(voice_1)$, and the conversation key new-key$_2$ for B-A communication, i. e. $E_{new-key2}(voice_2)$ are calculated.

Each time when the conversation ends, the system needs to select whether the conversation is to continue or not. If select to end the conversation, the system will change to plain text mode. If select to continue, the system returns to the key exchange process.

Chapter 14

Socket Layer Trust Connecting

14.1 Layers of Communication

Information network protocol is usually divided into a number of layers, with each layer responsible for different functions. The communication protocol in different layers (link layer, network layer, transport layer and application layer) has special considerations on security, to deal with various security issues which draws more and more attention now.

Taking TCP/IP protocol for example, it is usually composed of five-layer protocols: physical layer, link layer, network layer, transport layer, and application layer.

- Physical layer: The purpose of physical layer is to transmit the original bit stream from one computer to another computer.

- Link layer: The functions of link layer include providing well-designed service interfaces for the network layer, determining how to form the bits on the physical layer into a frame, handling transmission errors, and adjusting the flow rate of the frame.

- Network layer: The network layer is responsible for handling the activity of subgroup in the network, and sending the subgroups from the source port to the destination port through various ways.

- Transport layer: The transport layer mainly provides port-to-port communications for the application programs on the source-port computer and destination port computer.

- Application layer: The application layer is responsible for handling the specific application program details.

Except for the physical layer, each layer of TCP/IP protocol stack contains multiple communication protocols, such as wireless local area network (Wireless LAN, WLAN) protocol of the link layer, IP (Internet Protocol) protocol of the network layer, TCP/UDP (Transport Control Protocol/User Datagram Protocol) protocol of the transport layer, and SMTP (Simple Mail Transfer Protocol) protocol of the application layer. In the existing important communication protocols, special consideration is taken to the security, such as EAP_TLS (Extensible Authentication Protocol_Transport Level Security) authentication in IEEE 802. 11i wireless LAN protocol of the link layer, IKE (Internet Key Exchange) protocol of the network layer, and SSL/TLS (Secure Socket Layer/Transport Layer Security) protocol of the transport layer.

Below is a process that takes SSL/TLS protocol as an example, to implement authentication in the communication connection process(See Fig. 14. 1):

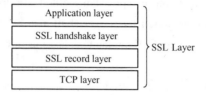

Fig. 14. 1   SSL Layer

SSL uses two layers. The lower layer is Record Protocol Layer and the upper layer is Handshake Protocol Layer as shown in the picture below. Before data transmission between Client and service the mutual authentication and key exchange takes place in handshake layer. The record protocol layer includes data compression and encryption. Sensitive data can be sent via record protocol layer.

14. 2   Secure Socket Layer (SSL)

Secure Socket Layer (Secure Socket Layer, SSL) is a currently most popular protocol that establishes security link. It goes through a number of revisions, from Version 1 at the beginning to Transport Layer Security (TLS) finally adopted by IETF. SSL/TLS protocol is positioned between TCP and the application layer, and uses TCP to provide a port-to-port security service. Its main purpose is to ensure data security and integrity between two communication applications. SSL/TLS protocol is composed of two layers: recording layer and handshaking layer. The recording layer is on top of TCP, to provide basic security service for various higher-level protocols, in particular, implementing operations of compression/decompression, encryption/decryption, calculating MAC/verifying MAC. The handshaking layer allows the server and the client-side to conduct mutual authentication, and to negotiate encryption algorithm and generate key, before the application layer protocol transmits data.

The existing SSL/TLS handshaking protocol requires 13 steps to complete the whole handshaking process. The protocol is very complicated, and apparently consumes bulky resources. The whole handshaking process is generally divided into four phases:

Phase 1: Establishing Security Capability

The client-side sends a "ClientHello" message to the server, and the server must respond with a "ServerHello" message, or a fatal error causes the connection failure. The "ClientHello" and "ServerHello" messages are used to establish enhanced security capability between the client-side and the server. "ClientHello" and "ServerHello" establish the following attributes: protocol version number, conversation ID, cipher text, and compression method. In addition, the random numbers respectively generated by the two clients and the server shall also be exchanged.

Msg1 (ClientHello) C→S: versionC | randomC | session_idC | cipher_suites | compression _methods

Msg2 (ServerHello) S→C: versionS | randomS | session_idS | cipher_suite | compression _method

Phase 2: Server Authentication and Key Exchange

If authentication is to be implemented, after the Hello message, the server will send out its certificate. In addition, if desired, a "ServerKeyExchange" message can also be sent out (e.g., server has no certificate or the certificate is used for signature only). If authentication has already been conducted to the server, and it is suitable to the selected cipher text, then a request can be sent for a certificate from a client. Now the server can send out "ServerHelloDone" message, to indicate that the first two phases of handshaking protocol have been accomplished. Then, the server will wait for the client's response.

Msg3 (Certificate) S→C: certificate_listS

Msg4 (ServerKeyExchange) S→C: exchange_keys

Msg5 (CetificateRequest) S→C: certificate_typesC | certificate_authorities

Msg6 (ServerHelloDone) S→C: NULL

Phase 3: Client Authentication and Key Exchange

If the server has already sent out a CertificateRequest message, then the client must respond with a Certificate message. Next, the ClientKeyExchange message is sent out, the content of which depends on the public-key cryptographic algorithm selected from ServerHello and ClientHello. If the client has sent out a certificate having signature capacity, then a CertificateVerify message having digital signature will be sent out and implement explicit verification to the certificate.

Msg7 (Certificate) C→S: certificate_listC

Msg8 (ClientKeyExchange) C→S: exchange_keys

Msg9 (CertificateVerify) C→S: signature

Phase 4: Conversation Ends

Now, a "ChangeCipherSpec" message is sent out from the client, and at the same time the client duplicates this predetermined cryptography protocol to the current cryptography protocol. Next, the client immediately adopts the new algorithm, key and password to send out finished message. In response, the server will send out its own "ChangeCipherSpec" message, convert the predetermined cryptography protocol to the current cryptography protocol, and use the new cryptography protocol to send out its own finished message. Up until now, the handshaking is complete. The client and server can begin to exchange application data.

Msg10 (ChangeCipherSpec) C→S: change_cipher_spec_type

Msg11 (Finished) C→S: verify_dataC

Msg12 (ChangeCipherSpec) S→C: change_cipher_spec_type

Msg13 (Finished) S→C: verify_dataS

However, these security protocols fail to solve the authentication problem of super-large scale communication identities, and thus have not given out a proof that this connection is trusted.

In particular, even though the existing network protocols all considered security issues, yet problems concerning the following aspects still typically exist.

1) The authentication & negotiation process needs to obtain public key certificate, which certainly will consume a large amount of bandwidth resources.

2) Management and distribution of large amount of certificates greatly increase complexity of the system.

3) It is very difficult to ensure the integrity of the interactive messages before obtaining the certificates, and the specific message is needed to ensure integrity of the entire interactive process.

4) Excessive interactions, more complicated process, and costly implementation.

5) Unresolved problem relating to illegal access.

14. 3 Trusted Socket Layer (TSL)

The object of this solution is to overcome the above-mentioned deficiencies, providing a CPK-based communication identity authentication system and method. It directly realized verification of client-to-client in the CPK trust connection (trust access), characterized by less expense of system resources, easy management of certificates, and greatly simplified process of establishing communication, etc.

In order to achieve the objection of this solution, a communication identity authentication system is provided. The communication system includes CPK authentication unit, for authenticating identity and integrity code of various terminals by using CPK system during connection of different terminals in the communication system and at various layers of the information network.

A communication identity authentication method is comprised of the following steps.

Step A) The first terminal sends its identity and identity authentication codes to the second terminal.

Step B) The second terminal uses CPK system to analyze the data transmitted from the first terminal, and verifies the signature with the identity and public key of the first terminal, to directly determine authenticity and legality of the first terminal identity. If legal, then the second terminal accepts. Otherwise, the second terminal refuses to accept.

Step C) The second terminal sends acknowledgement of receipt to the first terminal. The receipt can be a time stamp or data integrity code. Interaction is over.

The beneficial effects are to authenticate the communication identity and provide authenticity proof. Above CPK authentication protocol simplifies the complicated multiple interactions in the connecting process to one-step process, which directly achieves trusted connection of any two client terminals, and satisfies the demand of various layers to the trusted connection (trusted access) in the communication connecting. The communication identity authentication process is characterized by less expense of system resources, and simplified management of certificates, so as to greatly simplify the establishment of the trusted communication connection, and significantly improve the operation efficiency.

The combined public key (CPK) can generate a large amount of public key and private key pairs, to achieve identity-based ultra large scale key generation and distribution, which provides technical basis for the proof of the communication identity.

14.4 TSL Working Principle

The socket layer identity authentication is running in the bottom layer of the communication system, in which the identities of both parties in communication are defined by the communication system, and operations of encryption/decryption, signature/verification are accomplished by invoking the CPK communication identity authentication system at the bottom layer. Different realization ways can be flexibly selected based on characteristics of the actual application system. Below is a CPK-based identity authentication method of the transport layer. For illustration purpose, it uses SSL/TLS protocol as an example.

We shall have a detailed description to the CPK-based communication identity authentication. An excellent communication identity authentication not only needs to provide reliable proving means, but also needs to provide easy verifying means. The CPK trusted connection (trusted access) is established on the basis of identity authentication, which is a key step of the trusted connection (trusted access). Also, to achieve simple verification, two major issues of scalability and identity proof shall be solved technically.

In the socket layer the terminal name, IP address, device name, etc. can be taken as the identity. In this example we will take the terminal name as the identity. Suppose that we are establishing a trust connection between Client and Server.

The socket layer authentication is realized by CPK Cryptosystem. CPK is a self-assured public key system in which an EntityID is mapped into a point ENTITY on the elliptic curve defined by E: $y^2 = x^3 + ax + b$ (mod p) with the parameter $T = \{a, b, G, n, p\}$, if an integer '$entity$' satisfies ENTITY = ($entity$)G then the point ENTITY is public key and entity is private key. Because ENTITY $= \sigma_1$ (EntityID) and σ_1 is open to public, the public key can be calculated by any one and the private key is provided by ID-card.

Client and Server is inserted with CPK-card, and has CPK functions. In CPK-crypto-system the identity is mapped into the public key, for example, point "CLIENT" is public key and integer "$client$" is private key. The public key can be calculated by relying parties and private key is provided by ID-card. The contents of Socket layer ID-card of client are listed in Table 14.1.

Table 14.1　ID-card of Client for Socket Layer

1	Z1: verification parameter	16B	$E_{PWD}(R1) = Z1$
2	Z2: verification parameter	16B	$E_{R1}(R1) \oplus R1 = Z2$
3	Identity definition	25B	ClientID
	Role level	1B	5
5	Private key1	32B	$E_{R1}(client) = Y1$
6	Role level 5 key	48B	$E_{R1}(key1) = Y3$
7	Name of issuing unit	25B	KMC
8	Signature of issuing unit	48B	$SIG_{kmc}(mac)$

The trusted connection flow is as follows:

Flow of Sending	Flow of Receiving
1. Start	Receive
2. Generate digital signature	Verify signature and send r
3. Sign r	Verify the sign to r
4. Continue	Whether to continue
5. Calculate encrypting key	Calculate decrypting key

6. Encrypts data   Decrypts data

7. Send the signature and the cipher text   Send the receipt

8. The end

14. 5   TSL Address Authentication

The Connecting between Client and Server:

Client sends connection request to Server, the request is the sign to time:

$$SIG_{client}(time) = sign_1$$

In which SIG is the signing protocol, 'client' is the private key provided by ID-card, and the Time indicates freshness of the identity message, i. e. indicates that the communication connection is fresh.

Msg1: Client→Server: {time, sign_1}

Upon receiving the request Server verifies the signature:

$$SIG_{CLIENT}^{-1}(time) = sign_1'$$

Where SIG^{-1} is the verifying protocol and the public key CLIENT is calculated from ClientID.

If $sign_1 = sign_1'$ then the Server sends a sign to $(time - 1)$:

$$SIG_{sever}(time - 1) = sign_2$$

Msg2: Server→Client: {sign_2}

Client verifies $sign_2$:

$$SIG_{SERVER}^{-1}(time - 1) = sign_2'$$

If $sign_2 = sign_2'$ then Client signs to $(time + 1)$:

$$SIG_{client}(time + 1) = sign_3$$

Client sends $sign_3$ together with data and the sign to checksum:

$$SIG_{client}(checksum) = sign_4$$

Msg3: Client →Server, {sign_3, data, sign_4}

Bob verifies $sign_3$,

$$SIG_{CLIENT}^{-1}(time + 1) = sign_3'$$

If $sign_3 = sign_3'$, it proves the sender is Client and allows the connection. If $sign_3 \neq sign_3'$ or there is no reply to $sign_3$ for a certain time then the connection will be rejected. Further verifies $sign_4$:

$$SIG_{CLIENT}^{-1}(checksum) = sign_4'$$

If $sign_4 = sign_4'$, then it proves the data is coming from Client and received correctly. Server send the receipt:

$$SIG_{server}(\text{checksum}) = \text{sign}_5$$

Msg4 : Server→Client , $\{\text{sign}_5\}$

Client verifies sign5 :

$$SIG_{SERVER}^{-1}(\text{checksum}) = \text{sign}_5'$$

If $\text{sign}_5 = \text{sign}_5'$, then proves the data is sent to Server.

The authentication of connecting procedure may be implemented by separating-key or accompanying-key. The public key is provided respectively by key pool or signer.

If the data is encrypted the data construction will be as follows :

$$\text{data} = \{\text{sender}, \text{receiver}, \text{coded-key}, \text{coded-text}\}$$

The data encrypting procedure goes through the following steps.

1) Generates a random number r, and calculates key; key = r (G); where G is base point of elliptic curve; the key will be used in data encryption.

2) Encrypts the key with public key :

$$ENC_{SERVER}(\text{key}) = \text{coded-key}$$

Where Server is public key and ENC is encryption function with asymmetric key. The coded-key will be sent to Server.

3) Key is modulo 2 added to role-key :

$$\text{key} \oplus \text{role-key} = \text{new-key}$$

4) Data can be encrypted under the new-key :

$$E_{\text{new-key}}(\text{data}) = \text{coded-data}$$

The decryption procedure :

1) Server decrypts the key with private key :

$$DEC_{server}(\text{coded-key}) = \text{key}$$

Where private key is provided by ID-card.

2) Key is modulo 2 added to role-key :

$$\text{key} \oplus \text{role-key} = \text{new-key}$$

3) Data can be decrypted under new-key :

$$D_{\text{new-key}}(\text{coded-data}) = \text{data}$$

Where, D is decryption function with symmetric key.

Server sends the receipt of the data Msg4 to Client; the receipt of data is the sign to mac :

$$SIG_{server}(\text{MAC}) = \text{sign}_6$$

Msg5 : Server→Client : $\{\text{sign}_6\}$

Mac is message integrity authentication code. It proves that the data was received by Server.

14. 6　Comparison

The original SSL/TLS protocol is completed in the circumstances of not solving scalability and identity authentication, from the aspect of CPK-based communication identity authentication method, a comparative analysis of SSL/TLS protocol is given as below.

Phase I: At the beginning of this phase, in the SSL/TLS protocol, the server and the client do not have each other's certificate, and thus the message of this phase are transmitted in the form of plain text. However, in the CPK trust connection (trust access), directly uses the identity signature to prove trustworthy of the connection at the beginning.

Phase II and Phase III: In SSL/TLS protocol, the server and the client conduct key exchange through complicated processes. However, in the CPK trust connection (trust access) protocol, the key exchange is accomplished simultaneously in the first phase of "identity authentication". Thus, the second and third phases are redundant.

Phase IV: In CPK Trust connection protocol the server and the client can obtain each other's public key by calculating, the integrity of interaction can be ensured from beginning of the interaction. Thus, the fourth phase is also redundant.

This communication identity authentication method gives out standardized framework of identity authentication protocol in the TCP/IP protocol stack. The communication identity authentication method also applies to demand for trust connection (trust access) from each layer (link layer, network layer, transport layer and application layer) of the protocol stack, and is characterized by inexpensive system resources, easy management of certificates, greatly simplified process of establishing links, and high operation efficiency.

Chapter 15

Router Trust Connecting

Routers in the information networks are the basic component of the internet. This solution, for the first time, adopts identity authentication technology in the design of routers, to provide address authenticity proof and prevent illegal access; for the first time, adopts software identity authentication technology, to provide trustworthy of router operation environment and prevent intrusion of malicious software such as trogons. If dual direction communication is possible in future router then we can realize random challenge and signed response to resist DOS attacks This design also provides encryption and decryption function, to ensure privacy. This is the key security requirement of the new generation internet protocol. This design combines with novel addressing technology addressed with geographical positions, to constitute router for the next generation internet. This technology also can be used for design of novel switchboards in telecommunication networks.

Routers work in the network layer of OSI 7-layer protocols. Its main function is to connect network with network, to transmit data packets among the networks. Router has become the most important network equipment. Thus, research of the new generation router will become the core technology of the next generation internet research. The IPv4, IPv6 protocols for the previous internet running cannot satisfy the new requirement of cyber security trust connection. TCP/IP protocol fails to consider security issue. It cannot provide address authenticity proof, cannot prevent illegal access, and cannot resist DOS attacks. Currently, various malicious software and junk information prevail in the internet, severely contaminate operating environment of the internet, and directly affect survival of the internet. Thus, various countries launched the research for new generation green internet. In 2008, 65 European institutions jointly issued Bled Declaration, calling for developing new generation internet. EU raised Euro 9.1 billion, to support research and development of future internet. US Obama administration proposed identity authentication and addressing system as the main scientific research mission this year, and emphasized international cooperation. ISO proposed future network plan in 2007.

In China, we have not officially proposed next generation internet plan yet. However, various projects are underway. We have realized real name addressing system in IPv9 based on geographical positions, which solves the key technical issue of the next generation internet. Afterwards, Korea also proposed the concept of geographical location addressing, and becomes the second country that proposed new addressing way. CPK identity authentication technology is matured, and can be used in internet protocols, to prevent illegal access such as forgery and to prevent attacks such as DOS, Trojan and virus. In combination with addressing technology of IPv9, routers under novel mechanism are realized. Thus, we have the technical basis to develop the next generation internet protocol.

15. 1　**Principle of Router**

Router accepts data packets from one network interface, and transfers to next destination address. The destination address is provided by routing table. If the destination address is found, the next MAC address is added in front of the data packet; and TTL (time to live) field of IP packet starts to subtract, and re-calculates check sum. When the data packets are sent to the output port, they need to wait in order, so as to be transferred to output link. The routers divide the relatively large data into proper sized data packets based on pre-determined rules, and then send the data packets via same or different routes, respectively. Upon the data packets reach destination in sequence, they may return to original data form based on certain order.

The process of storing and transferring data packets is as follows.

When the data packets reach the router, based on network physical interface type, the router invokes corresponding link layer function module, interprets the link layer protocol header of the data packets, and verifies data integrity, including CRC check and frame length check.

Based on the destination IP address of the IP packet in the frame, the next IP address is sought in the routing table, and the TTL field of the IP data packet starts to subtract, and re-calculates checksum.

Based on the next IP address, the IP data packets are sent to the corresponding output link layer, to package into corresponding link layer packet, which is sent out via network physical interface.

The above is a simple workflow of the router, without elaborating other additional functions, e. g. , access control, network address change, queue priority, etc. , since some work has no relation to the authentication system, or will be included in the ID-based router trusted connection discussed below.

15. 2　Requirements of Trusted Connection

In order to realize trusted connection among the routers, IP address is used as the identity of the router, to ensure its uniqueness. Assuming Alfa is the IP address of a router, and Beta is the IP address of another router. If CPK-card defined as Alfa is inserted in any router, then this router becomes a router having an identity as Alfa. Likewise, if CPK-card defined as Beta is inserted in any router, then the router becomes a router having an identity as Beta. As an example, Alfa = " China - Beijing - Haidian - Peking University" , and Beta = " China - Beijing - Haidian - Tsinghua University" .

Now assuming the origin address is Alfa, and the destination address is Beta. Its connection is shown in Fig. 15. 1.

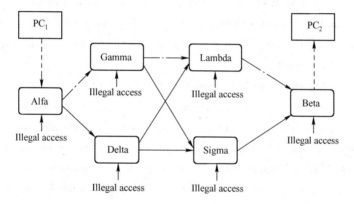

Fig. 15. 1　Origin and Destination

IP packet of the origin router finally reaches the destination router via a number of switching routers. It is very easily occurs illegal access in the switching routers, and Beta very likely does not know the data packets received coming from where. Thus, there comes an issue of authenticating origin address. Origin address can be verified by any passing routers. However, such verification may be an option, but it is necessary in the destination router. From the above basic knowledge about working process of router, it can be seen that the previous router only concerns the next routing, but not where the data packets come from. Thus, if verification of the origin address cannot be solved, illegal access cannot be overcome.

Someone tried to use encryption to solve illegal access. However, under the circumstances of public-key system, this is fruitless effort. For example, Beta is the receiver, but its public key is open to public, and anyone can encrypt for Beta. Thus, Beta still cannot know who the sender is.

In order to realize trusted connection, the router must satisfy the below three requirements:

1) The origin IP address must give a origin address evidence that can be verified by any routers.

2) The switching router must verify the origin address and may give a routing evidence (option).

3) The router can prevent illegal access, and resist DOS attacks (in case of full duplex communication).

15. 3　Fundamental Technology

In the CPK cryptosystem, Entity identity EntityID is mapped to the point ENTITY on elliptic curve $E: y^2 = x^3 + ax + b \pmod{p}$ with parameters as $T = \{a, b, G, n, p\}$, and there is an integer that satisfies ENTITY = $(entity)$ G. ENTITY is a public key, and $entity$ is a private key. Because ENTITY = σ_1(EntityID) and σ_1 is open to public, the public key can be calculated by anyone, and the private key is provided by ID-card. Thus, typically any IdentityID can be mapped to public/private key pair IDENTITY and $identity$:

Signature can be represented as $SIG_{identity}(\text{time}) = \text{sign}$

Verification can be represented as $SIG_{IDENTITY}^{-1}(\text{time}) = \text{sign}'$

The router configures CPK-card, to make it have digital signature and key exchange function. The contents of CPK-card are as follows: Assuming IP address of the router is alfa (Alfa can be real name such as China-Beijing-Haidian-Peking-University. Upon uniformly encoded, it becomes the codes that the machine can execute). Taking the ID-card of the router Alfa as an example, its contents are listed in Table 15. 1.

Table 15. 1　The contents of ID-card for router

1	Z1: verification parameter	16B	$E_{PWD}(R_1) = Z_1$
2	Z2: verification parameter	16B	$E_{R1}(R_1) \oplus R_1 = Z_2$
3	Identity definition	25B	AlfaID
4	Private key	32B	$E_{R1}(\text{alfa}) = Y_1$
5	Issue unit	25B	KMC
6	Signature of issue unit	48B	$SIG_{kmc}(MAC)$

15. 4　Origin Address Authentication

The router can be used in backbone network or enterprise network. When used in backbone network the connection will be router-to-router and when used in enterprise network the connection will be PC (user)-to router. The PC here stands for a group of users. The user may take user mane as its identity such as Alice@ tom. com. The routers take the IP address as its identity. Therefore the origin addresses will be the IP address in backbone network or the user name in enterprise network. In any case the connecting procedure and origin address authentication method is identical.

There may be some ways to authenticate the origin address:

Take the origin user name as origin address and all passing routers verify the user names.

Take the origin router IP as origin address and all passing outers verify the IP addresses.

Take router-to-router as an example, the connecting procedure is as follows:

1) Connection and data transmission

If the router does not support two-way protocol, then it executes one-way protocol.

Assuming the sending address is Alfa, the receiving address is Gamma, the public key of AlfaID is ALFA, and the private key is alfa. Application for connection is sent by Alfa. Its application form is as follows, e. g. , Msg1:

Msg1:Alfa→Gamma, { AlfaID, BetaID, time, $sign_1$ }

In which AlfaID is the sending address, BetaID is the destination address, $sign_1$ is the signature of the sender Alfa to the time, i. e. :

$$SIG_{alfa}(time) = sign_1$$

Wherein SIG is the signature function. The receiver Gamma is by-way address, to verify the signature of the sender:

$$SIG_{ALFA}^{-1}(time) = sign_1'$$

In which SIG^{-1} is verification function. If $sign_1 = sign_1'$, then Gamma believes that the sender is Alfa. If Alfa is a legal user (check the table), then a random number r is sent and signature to (time − 1) is:

$$SIG_{gamma}(time - 1) = sign_2$$

$Sign_2$ is sent to Alfa:

Msg2:Gamma→Alfa, { r, $sign_2$ }

Alfa verifies sign2:

$$SIG_{GAMMA}^{-1}(time - 1) = sign_2'$$

If $sign_2 = sign_2'$ then Alfa determines that the receiver is the by-way address Gamma. If the receiver is legal (check the table), then signature is made to r and (time + 1), and data is sent and signature to checksum is:

$$SIG_{alfa}(r) = sign_3$$
$$SIG_{alfa}(time + 1) = sign_4$$

$$SIG_{alfa}(\text{checksum}) = sign_5$$

Msg3 : Alfa→Gamma, $\{sign_3, data, sign_4, sign_5\}$

Gamma checks the signature:

$$SIG_{ALFA}^{-1}(r) = sign_3'$$
$$SIG_{ALFA}^{-1}(time+1) = sign_4',$$
$$SIG_{ALFA}^{-1}(\text{checksum}) = sign_5'$$

If $sign_3 = sign_3'$, then it is proved that the sender is Alfa, and this connection is allowed. If $sign_4 = sign_4'$, then it is proved that this data is from Alfa, receipt is errorless, and a message of acknowledgement is sent, i. e. signature of Gamma to the checksum:

$$SIG_{gamma}(\text{checksum}) = sign_6$$

Msg4 : Gamma→Alfa, $\{sign_6\}$

Alfa verifies $sign_6$:

$$SIG_{GAMMA}^{-1}(\text{checksum}) = sign_6'$$

If $sign_6 = sign_6'$, then it is proved that data has been sent to Gamma.

2) Delivery of segmented data

In many cases, data may be divided into a number of segments: data = $data_0//data_1//data_2//\ldots//data_n$. Delivery of segment data may occur in two situations: one is between two routers that have established connection, and the other one is between two routers that have not established connection. If data1 is via Alfa→Gamma, $data_2$ is via Alfa→Delta. However, the second situation may not happen, since no trusted connection has been established. If following the second route, trusted connection must be first established. Thus, all the issues go back to the first situation. That is, how to distribute segmented data under the situation of established connection.

When applying for connection, $data_1$ has been sent. How to send $data_2$? If treating the process of sending $data_2$ as an independent process, it can be done upon application process is over. However, the current situation is based on mutual recognition of Alfa and Gamma. Thus, except for the first segment, it only needs to repeat the above Msg3 and Msg4:

1st segment: Msg1 : Alfa→Gamma, $\{$ Alfa, Beta, time, $sign_1\}$

Msg2 : Gamma→Alfa, $\{r, sign_2\}$

$Msg3_1$: Alfa→Gamma, $\{sign_{3,1}, data_1, sign_{4,1}, sign_{5,1}\}$

$Msg4_1$: Gamma→Alfa, $\{sign_{6,1}\}$

2nd segment: $Msg3_2$: Alfa→Gamma, $\{data_2, sign_{4,2}\ sign_{5,2},\}$

$Msg4_2$: Gamma→Alfa, $\{sign_{6,2}\}$;

3rd segment: $Msg3_3$: Alfa→Gamma, $\{$ $data_3, sign_{4,3}, sign_{5,3}\}$

$Msg4_3$: Gamma→Alfa, $\{sign_{6,3}\}$;

...

In which, $sign4i = SIG_{alfa}(time + i)$, $(i = 1,2,\ldots)$, since $(time + i)$ is a factor in change, and Alfa & Gamma signed, to continue the connection status of mutual trust.

If this connection process is over, then it goes to the next connection process. The address Gamma becomes the sender, and the address Lambda becomes the receiver. Likewise, the routers conduct transmission one by one, which finally reaches to the terminal router. Thus, all the connections of each route have been proved. The destination address Beta finally handles data.

15.5　Encryption Function

Even though TSL protocol has encryption function to the data, the data encryption is the mission of the application layer, and the routers no longer undertake. If there are special needs, it can also provide encryption/decryption function.

The structure of the data is defined as follows:
$$data = \{ Alfa, Beta, time, sign, data \}$$
In which Alfa is the sender, Beta is the receiver
$$sign = SIG_{alfa}(time)$$
When the data is plain-text
$$data = \{ Alfa, Beta, time, sign, clear\text{-}text \}$$
When the data is cipher-text
$$data = \{ Alfa, Beta, time, sign, coded\text{-}key, coded\text{-}data \}$$
The destination router first authenticates authenticity of the sender:
$$SIG_{ALFA}^{-1}(time) = sign'$$
If $sign = sign'$, Beta believes that the sender is Alfa, then it goes to decryption process.

If the router provides encryption/decryption function, assuming Alfa is encrypted, Beta is decrypted, since the communication between Alfa and Beta is multi-hop communication, encryption can only be realized with CPK's Seperating Key, and the size of the key-pool is determined based on actual situation.

15.5.1　Encryption Process

If this data is a plain-data that needs to be encrypted:

1) Generating a random number r, Alfa calculates:
$$key = r(G)$$
In which G is the base point of the elliptic curve;

2) Using the other side's public key to encrypt the key:

$$ENC_{BETA}(key) = coded\text{-}key$$

3) The key adding to the user's role-key mod 2 to obtain new-key, in which role-key is provided by ID-card.

$$key \oplus role\text{-}key = new\text{-}key$$

4) Encrypting the data:

$$E_{new\text{-}key}(data) = coded\text{-}data$$

Sending cipher-text cipher = text and coded-key to Beta.

15. 5. 2　Decryption Process

Upon receiving Alfa's signal, Beta automatically enters into decryption process.

1) Beta calculates private key decryption:

$$DEC_{beta}(coded\text{-}key) = key$$

In which private key beta is provided by ID-card

2) Key adds to role-key mod 2 to obtain new-key:

$$key \oplus role\text{-}key = new\text{-}key$$

3) Data decryption:

$$D_{new\text{-}key}(coded\text{-}data) = data$$

15. 6　Requirement of Header Format

Newly added function requires to making new IP header format, in which the header at least includes sending address, identification code for receiving origin address, destination address, data, and checksum. Data encryption only affects data form, but not the IP header format.

Origin IP Addr
Destination IP Addr
Time
Signature by origin IP Addr
Passing IP Addr (option)
Signature by passing IP Addr (option)

15.7 Trusted Computing Environment

To ensure trustworthy of router operation, all the execution codes in the router must pass the manufacturer's authentication (level one authentication). That is, the manufacturer has signature to all the execution codes when the routers leave the factory. Each router has authentication function (provided by CPK-card). There are two ways to realize code authentication: one is to use Separating Key, and the other one is to use Accompanying Key. For convenience, Separating Key is used here as an example.

15.7.1 Evidence of Software Code

The manufacturer has CPK-card, to conduct manufacturer signature to all the system software in the router. All the executable software can be classified as Software-identity (CodeID) and Software-code (CodeBD), which are signed by the Manufacturer respectively:

$$SIG_{manufacturer}(CodeID) = sign_1$$
$$SIG_{manufacturer}(CodeBD) = sign_2$$

In which SIG is a signature function, CodeID is an execution code identity, CodeBD is a HASH value of the execution code. Any one execution code in the router has its own $sign_1$ and $sign_2$.

15.7.2 Authentication of Software Code

The router is inserted with an ID-card, to make it have CPK authentication function. There are two verification methods of the router: one is to uniformly verify when power-on, and uniformly delete the codes that fail to pass the verification, to ensure the system of the router return back to original state; and the other one is to verify first and then execute, when invoking the software codes.

To verify $sign_1$ and $sign_2$ respectively:

$$SIG_{MANUFACTURER}^{-1}(CodeID) = sign_1'$$
$$SIG_{MANUFACTURER}^{-1}(CodeBD) = sign_2'$$

If $sign_1 = sign_1'$ and $sign_2 = sign_2'$, then execution is allowed. Otherwise, execution is refused. In this way, it is ensured that the codes executed in this router are the codes all authenticated by the manufacturer, and other codes all will not be executed, to avoid attacks of virus, Trojan.

Conclusion

TCP/IP protocol cannot ensure trusted connection, and thus shall be modified. This disclosure proposed three key technologies of trusted connection based on geographical location addressing: adopting mechanism that the address can authenticate, to prevent illegal connection; adopting random Q&A mechanism, to prevent replay attacks; and, adopting mechanism that software code can authenticate, to prevent intrusion of virus and Trojan.

The above design fully suits for trusted connection of physical layer. There are two kinds of physical layers: one is the physical layer defined in information network 7-layer protocol, and the platform to support the information network is application program interface (API); the other one is the physical layer defined in telecommunication network, and the platform to support the telecommunication network is true reference point (TRP). In the information network, if the network layer can ensure trustworthy of transmission, the security of the physical layer can be replaced by network layer, without any work of the physical layer. However, with respect to the physical layer in the telecommunication network, without modification, it cannot realize trusted connection, and cannot prevent illegal access. Its modification method is completely same as that of the router.

Part Six

Trust e-Commerce

Chapter 16

e-Bank Authentication

16.1 Background

e-Banking refers to an electronic business that conducts depositing / withdrawing cash and transferring business via ATM and POS.

Up until now, the e-banking systems all adopt magnetic cards, which bring great convenience for making payments, and play a historic role. However, the security is also greatly challenged. Magnetic card verification system is implemented by using the method of symmetric key encryption, i. e. , the bank also has the customers' key or password. Otherwise, the bank cannot decrypt or verification. The method has the following two issues:

(1) Because the bank stores all the information of customers, especially the symmetric keys and passwords, if the bank loses its information, it also may involve loss of the customers' information: the banks in US and Hong Kong lost millions of customers' information is an example.

(2) Since the bank stores all the information of the customers, it would be very easy for its internal staffs in the bank to acquire the passwords, so as to steal the customers' deposit. Thus, if a theft case occurs, people will first suspect the possibility of the bank staff stealing the deposit, while the bank cannot provide evidence to show that its staff does not involve, so that the bank's reputation is greatly affected.

(3) The withdrawal slip is not kept after the customer withdrew the cash. If the customer, upon withdrawing the cash, claims that he did not withdraw the cash, the bank cannot provide evidence to show that the customer did withdraw the cash.

Currently, there is another approach, i. e. , adopting PKI signature technology with asymmetric keys to realize authentication of e-banking. Public key infrastructure (PKI) is an authentication system that is most widely used in China. In the system, encrypted keys and decrypted keys are different from each other. The sender uses the receiver's public key to encrypt the information, and the receiver uses his own specified private key to decrypt. Here comes a difficulty, i. e. , how the sender can obtain the receiver's public key. Typically, the sender accesses the bulky database system (LDAP) to obtain the receiver's public key. Each user's certificate is stored in LDAP. In general, one CA has one LDAP, and LDAP itself constitutes a bulky networking system. Since digital signature is initiated by the signer, the signer may send to the verifier the signature code with his own public key certificate, so that the verifier can avoid accessing LDAP to obtain the public key. Of course, this may cause the length of the signature code becomes longer, which is impossible to be used for e-banking.

Currently there is a novel cryptosystem, which is called as identity-based public key system. Identity-based public key directly uses identity of one entity as the entity's public key, and uses the inverse of the identity as the entity's private key. The inverse can only be calculated by the key management center, and distributed to the entity to use. In such a system, the key has the property of self-assured, i. e. , it can prove its own authenticity, without proof from a third party. Thus, the complicated authentication system becomes simple, and especially suits for e-business and e-banking system.

16.2　Counter Business

Counter system is composed of the head office, counter, and customer:

1) Head office refers to the portals in bank, such as PC portal, ATM portal, POS portal. Each portal has its own number as identity, inserted with ID-card, which is called portal card, and has CPK function and corresponding portal private key.

2) Counter refers to business devices such as PC, ATM, POS. Each device has its own number as identity, inserted with ID-card, which is called counter card and has CPK function and corresponding counter private key.

3) Customer refers to the card holder. The card holder holds ID-card, with account number as its identity, which is called customer card and has CPK function and account number private key.

The development trend of the current authentication network is a horizontal web network under one "trust root". Thus, all the customer terminals directly have relation with the bank terminals, i. e. , ATM is also one of the customer terminal.

If the customer does not have withdrawal machine, then he can only conduct the transaction over the counter. This is called counter customer. Some enterprises directly deal with the bank, which is called remote customer.

Fig. 16. 1 shows the links among ATMs and PORTALS

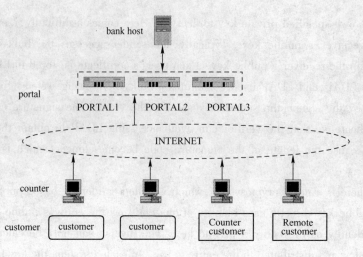

Fig. 16. 1   Links between ATMs and PORTALS

16. 3   Business Layer

The counter systems are all composed of communication layer, transaction layer, and calculation layer.

Transaction layer: The transaction between two users is conducted in the transaction layer. The transaction initiator A provides evidence related to the transaction, and the receiver verifies the evidence, to identify the authenticity of this transaction. Authentication includes user identity and transaction data authentication. The transaction data needs to be encrypted, to ensure trust worthy transaction and privacy.

Calculation layer: Contents of the transaction is running in the respective computers. Trust worthy calculation environment needs code authentication, to identity authenticity of the code, to prevent execution of illegal code (executive program), and to ensure reliability of the calculation environment.

Communication layer: Transaction data is exchanged by communication device. The sender S provides evidence associated with the communication, and the receiver R verifies the evidence, to identify the authenticity of this communication. Trusted communication needs communication identity authentication and encryption of communication data, to ensure trusted access and data privacy.

It can be seen that the trusted counter system includes trusted transacting, trusted connecting and trusted computing. Different tasks are completed in different layers, in which the trusted computing environment is provided by software identity authentication, which can be implemented separately. Each of the ATM and portal equipments is installed with executive software of grade 1 and grade 2 software identity authentications. Transaction layer and communication layer (device level) are the ones that often play a part in the transaction. The relationship between the customer and portal is transaction relationship, and the relationship between the teller and portal is communication relationship. Thus, the portal will take the tasks of communication authentication and transaction authentication. The business layers in transaction in shown in Fig. 16. 2.

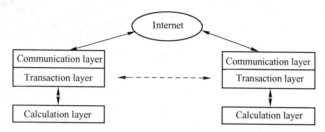

Fig. 16. 2 Business Layers in Transaction

16. 4   Basic Technology

The e-Bank authentication is realized by CPK Cryptosystem. CPK is a self-assured public key system in which an EntityID is mapped into a point ENTITY on the elliptic curve defined by $E: y^2 = x^3 + ax + b$ (modp) with the parameter $T = \{a, b, G, n, p\}$, if an integer *entity* satisfies ENTITY = (*entity*)G then ENTITY is public key and *entity* is private key. Because ENTITY = σ_1(EntityID) and σ_1 is open to public, the public key can be calculated by any one and the private key is provided by ID-card.

Signature is marked as

$$\text{SIG}_{entity}(\text{TAG}) = \text{sign}$$

Verification is marked as

$$\text{SIG}_{\text{ENTITY}}^{-1}(\text{TAG}) = \text{sign}'$$

Where SIG means signing, SIG^{-1} means verifying, TAG means time space. Key exchange: CPK key exchange protocol is based on Diffie-Helamam and AlGamal scheme can realize scalability and immediacy of key exchange without supports of LDAP.

Encryption is marked as

$$E_{\text{key}}(\text{data}) = \text{coded-data}$$
$$\text{ENC}_{\text{ENTITY}}(\text{key}) = \text{coded-key}$$

Decryption is marked as

$$DEC_{entity}(\text{coded-key}) = \text{key}$$
$$D_{key}(\text{coded-data}) = \text{data}$$

The functions mentioned above are realized by ID-card. The contents of ID-card are listed in Table 16.1:

Table 16.1   The contents of ID-card for account-no

1	Z1 : verification parameter	16B	$E_{PWD}(R_1) = Z_1$
2	Z2 verification parameter	16B	$E_{R1}(R_1) \oplus R_1 = Z_2$
3	Identity definition	25B	Account-no
4	Role level : customer	16B	5
5	Private key.	32B	$E_{R1}(\text{accoujnt-no}) = Y_1$
6	Role 5 key	48B	$E_{R1}(\text{key}_1) = Y_3$
7	Name of issuing unit	25B	KMC
8	Signature of issuing unit	48B	$Sig_{kmc}(\text{mac})$

Counter ID-card and Portal ID-card is the same as the above account-no card, only the identity definition and key variables are different each other.

16.5   Business at ATM

User operation may follow the existing procedure:

Enter password : xxxxxx

Select operation type : withdraw 1, deposit 2, transaction 3 : 1

Select amount : 2000(1), 1000(2), 500(3), 200(4), 100(5) : 1

Customer card : verifies user password, and receive information from ATM1

1. Customer input data to ATM1

$$data_1 = (\text{name} // \text{account-no.} // \text{amount})$$

2. ATM1 transfers the data into CPK-card, ATM1 and Card computes the hash code simultaneously :

$$mac_1 = \text{Hash}(data_1)$$

3. Sign to MAC$_1$ with account-no. :

$$SIG_{account-no}(MAC_1) = sign_1$$

ATM1 card : ATM1 handles the customer card information according to present procedure. The main task of the ATMs is to verify the account-no.

1. Verifies the signature:

$$SIG_{\text{ACCOUNT-NO}}^{-1}(MAC_1) = sign_1'$$

2. If $sign_1 = sign_1'$ then composes new data: $data_2 = (data_1//sign_1)$;
3. Computes:

$$mac_2 = Hash(data_2)$$

4. Signs to the data:

$$SIG_{atm1}(MAC_2) = sign_2$$

5. Encrypts the data:

$$E_{key}(data_2) = coded\text{-}data_2$$

16.6 Communication Between ATM and Portal

The communication between ATM and Portal is the main point of e-Banking. The authentication may be realized with Separating-key or Accompanying-Key. They work in the same way. But they have their own merits and demerits respectively, so it is recommended to select the key system according to actual application.

First ATM1 signs to time:

$$SIG_{atm1}(time) = sign_1$$

Sends time and $sign_1$ to portal:

Msg1 ATM1→Portal: $\{ATM1ID, time, sign_1\}$

Portal checks the sign:

$$SIG_{ATM1}^{-1}(time) = sign_1'$$

If $sign_1 = sign_1'$ then portal believes the request is coming form ATM1, and returns a random number r and a sign to time -1:

$$SIG_{portal}(time-1) = sign_2$$

Msg2 Portal→ATM1: $\{r, sign_2\}$

ATM1 checks the sign:

$$SIG_{PORTAL}^{-1}(time-1) = sign_2'$$

If $sign_2 = sign_2'$ then ATM1 believes the authenticity of the portal and sends a sign to r in response to the challenge and signs to time $+1$:

$$SIG_{atm1}(r) = sign_3$$
$$SIG_{atm1}(time+1) = sign_4$$

Msg3 ATM1→Portal: $\{sign_3, sign_4, coded\text{-}data_2\}$

The Portal checks the sign:

$$SIG_{ATM1}^{-1}(r) = sign_3'$$

$$SIG^{-1}ATM1(time+1) = sign_4'$$

If $sign_3 = sign_3'$ then Portal believes the authenticity of ATM1 and if $sign_4 = sign_4'$ then accepts the coded-data2 and go to the decryption process.

Data decryption:

$$D_{key}(coded\text{-}data_2) = data_2 = data_1 // sign_1$$

Computes:

$$MAC_1 = Hash(data_1)$$

Verification of transaction:

$$SIG_{ACCOUT\text{-}NO}^{-1}(MAC_1) = sign_1'$$

If $sign_1 = sign_1'$ then the business is submitted to the bank to handle, and enters into return receipt process. If $sign_1 \neq sign_1'$ then this transaction is canceled. Portal returns the receipt:

$$SIG_{portal}(MAC_1) = sign_4$$

Msg4 Portal→ATM1: $\{command, sign_5\}$

ATM1 verifies the receipt:

$$SIG_{PORTAL}^{-1}(MAC_1) = sign_5'$$

If $sign_5 = sign_5'$ then ATM1 allows the machine to pay out according to the command, and ends the withdrawal procedure. $Sign_1$ will be the evidence of withdraw.

Other procedures such as deposit and transfer are substantially identical.

16.7 The Advantages

The successful development of CPK cryptosystem and CPK-card, CPK-key provides feasibility for developing e-banking business. Comparing with e-banking accomplished by magnetic card, CPK e-Banking can greatly improve the security:

1. ID-card is IC-card, which is not easy to be copied.
2. ID-card has signature function, providing undeniable service.
3. ID-card has encryption function, providing privacy service.
4. The bank does not keep the sensitive information, such as the user password, user key.
5. The bank can provide evidence of user withdrawal; and the user cannot deny.
6. The bank staff also cannot commit crime.
7. There is no additional burden for system maintenance.
8. ID-card can be issued at the banking outlets, same as the existing rules.
9. ID-card can realize one card having multiple usages, and can realize inter-bank and trans-re-

gion use.

10. CPK authentication system can be securely running not only in specialized network but also in public network such as open Internet.

11. It can be applied for payment system of enterprises and digital homes.

The ID-card also has special advantages over other IC-card using non-CPK crypto-system.

1. The ATM machine can verify the authenticity of the account no. of the card. (option)

2. At the bank side the portal can verify the authenticity of all ATM and all account-no. of the cards. The authentication scale will be greater then thousands of millions, so far it can be done only with CPK-card.

In order to establish a secure e-banking system in Internet it is necessary to consider a method to resist middle-man's copying attack. The communication authentication between ATM and Portal must include challenge-response steps; therefore the network must be an on-line communication such as Client/Server type so that the challenge-response authentication can be implemented.

Chapter 17
e-Bill Authentication

17.1   Bill Authentication Network

Electronic bill is one core business of e-business. Most transactions are implemented in the form of bills, and thus security of the bills can present security of e-business. Bill system includes bank check, draft, invoices of tax system, tax receipt, and various electronic bills. Bank check system will be taken as a typical example in the below context, to describe the security of bill operation.

Bank check system is composed of the bank terminal (issuing check) and respective enterprise terminals which use the checks. The use of the check forms a circulation among respective enterprises, and the check finally returns to the issuing bank. (See Fig. 17.1) In the check circulation link or upon returning to the issuing bank, the common issue faced is how to identify the authenticity of the check. If a basis for identifying the authenticity of the check can be provided, then the acceptance process and handling process can be greatly eased.

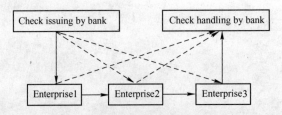

Fig. 17.1   Bill application and circulation

During check issuing and handling, the bank and the respective enterprises have authentication relationship. During circulation, respective enterprises have authentication relationship. Thus, the bank and the enterprises constitute horizontal authentication network.

17. 2　Main Technologies

The e-Bank authentication is realized by CPK Cryptosystem. CPK is a self-assured public key system in which an EntityID is mapped into a point ENTITY on the elliptic curve defined by $E : y^2 = x^3 + ax + b$ ($modp$) with the parameter $T = \{a, b, G, n, p\}$, if an integer $entity$ satisfies ENTITY = ($entity$)G then ENTITY is public key and $entity$ is private key. Because ENTITY = σ_1 (EntityID) and σ_1 is open to public, the public key can be calculated by any one and the private key is provided by ID-card.

In view that one enterprise owns multiple account numbers, in this example, the identity of a check is defined by the account number, and each account-noID can mapped into a point AC-COUNT-NO on the elliptic curve defined by E (a, b), if an integer ' $account\text{-}no$ ' satisfies AC-COUNT-NO = ($account\text{-}no$)G, then ACCOUT-NO is the public key and can be calculated by everyone and the integer is the private key that is provided by ID-card.

Bill authentication can be realized with Separating-key and also with Accompanying-Key of CPK, while they work in the same way. They have their own merits and demerits respectively, so it is recommended to select the key system according to actual application.

The Bill system needs account-no ID-card, bank ID-card, finance-section ID-card and corporation ID-card. The contents of the card are listed in Table 17. 1:

Table 17. 1　The contents of the card for accont-no

1	Z1 : verification parameter	16B	E_{PWD} (R_1) = Z_1
2	Z2 verification parameter	16B	E_{R1} (R_1) $\oplus$ R_1 = Z_2
3	Identity definition	25B	Account-no ID
4	Private key	32B	E_{R1} (account-no) = Y
5	Name of issuing unit	25B	KMC
6	Signature of issuing unit	48B	$Sig_{kmc\text{-}1}$ (mac)

17. 3　Application for Bills

Assuming that Enterprise A has an account number and applies to the issuing Bank for a check. The application form is as follows:

Enterprise signs to time with $account\text{-}no$:

$$SIG_{account\text{-}no}(\text{time}) = \text{sign}_1$$

Where SIG is signature protocol, *account-no* is the private key provided by ID-card. Then Enterprise sends time, Account-noID, sign_1 to the issuing Bank:

Msg1 Enterprise→XXbank: {time, Account-noID, sign_1}

The issuing Bank verifies the application:

$$SIG_{\text{ACCOUNT-NO}}^{-1}(\text{time}) = \text{sign}_1'$$

Where SIG^{-1} is verification protocol, ACCOUNT-N0 is the public key. If $\text{sign}_1 = \text{sign}_1'$, then the Bank will send a random number r and a sign to $(\text{time} - 1)$:

$$SIG_{xxbank}(\text{time} - 1) = \text{sign}_2$$

Msg2 XXbank→Enterprise: {r, sign_2}

The Enterprise verifies the signature:

$$SIG_{\text{XXBANK}}^{-1}(\text{time} - 1) = \text{sign}_2'$$

If $\text{sign}_2 = \text{sign}_2'$, the Enterprise believes that he is connecting with the correct Bank. Enterprise sends back the sign to r:

$$SIG_{account\text{-}no}(r) = \text{sign}_3$$

Msg3 Enterprise→XXbank: {sign_3}

The Bank verifies the signature:

$$SIG_{\text{ACCOUNT-NO}}^{-1}(r) = \text{sign}_3'$$

If $\text{sign}_3 = \text{sign}_3'$ then the Bank issues a blank check. The blank check has a digital signature of the issuing bank (with bank seal stamped) to the serial no. of the check, and sends it to Enterprise, to provide a basis for identifying the authenticity of the check. The authenticity of the check can be verified by the issuing Bank, other Banks, and any other Enterprises.

$$SIG_{xxbank}(\text{serial no.}) = \text{sign}_4$$

The bank check is shown as Fig. 17. 2:

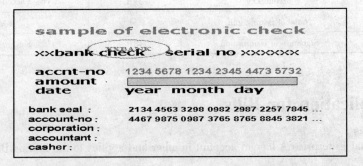

Fig. 17. 2　Blank check issued by the issuing bank

17. 4　Circulation of Bills

When the bills are in circulation, the legal person and financial section are responsible for the account number and the amount. First the amount and date of billing is filled in the check, and account number signature is conducted to the data:

$$data_1 = (\,account\ number//amount//date\,)$$

$$MAC_1 = Hash\ (\,data_1\,)$$

The accountant signs to MAC_1:

$$SIG_{accountant}(\,MAC_1\,) = sign_5$$

The corporation signs to MAC_1:

$$SIG_{corporation}(\,MAC_1\,) = sign_6$$

Finally casher forms a new data:

$$data_2 = (\,data_1 + sign_1 + sign_2\,)$$

$HASH(\,data_2\,) = MAC_2$,

Signs to MAC_2:

and

$$SIG_{casher}(\,MAC_2\,) = sign_7$$

The formal form of legal check is as Fig. 17. 3:

Fig. 17. 3　Form of legal Bill

17. 5　Verification of Check

1') acceptance/verification of check: A check issued by an enterprise is used in a store. The store first comes up with the issue whether the check can be accepted. Whether accepting the check or not can be identified by the bank's signature, because the bank's signature proves the legality of the check.

$$\text{SIG}_{\text{XXBANK}}^{-1}(\text{serial no.}) = \text{sign}_4'$$

If the verification result is $\text{sign}_4 = \text{sign}_4'$, then the check passes the verification, and can be accepted.

2) Authenticity of check: The accepted check will finally be back to the issuing bank for handling. Authenticity of the check can be verified through the signature of the accountant or corporation to the bill data:

$$\text{SIG}_{\text{ACCOUNTANT}}^{-1}(\text{MAC}_1) = \text{sign}_5' \text{ or}$$
$$\text{SIG}_{\text{CORPORATION}}^{-1}(\text{MAC}_1) = \text{sign}_6'$$

Where the AccountantID and CorporationID are stamped in front of the check, and MAC_1 is:

$$\text{data}_1 = (\text{account number}//\text{amount}//\text{date})$$

$$\text{MAC}_1 = \text{Hash}(\text{data}_1)$$

If passed, it can prove the authenticity of the check. If the amount is large, it is needed to check the corporation's signature.

Electronic bills together with digital signatures, can be stored in the database in the form of electronic documents, or be printed on the paper as paper bills. Both have same effects as the true bills. Leaving the legal basis aside, at least it can be guaranteed in the aspect of technology, because the technology used is universally acknowledged. Under current circumstances, the technology can be transferred to physical bill system, to improve the verification efficiency of physical bills. As far verification of physical bills mainly uses scanning ways to authenticate physical seal, which has very high misjudgment rate and very low speed. If the logic seal can be a supplement, misjudgment rate can be eliminated, while authentication efficiency can be greatly improved.

Part Seven

Trust Logistics

Chapter 18

e-Tag Authentication

18. 1　Background

Fake or inferior quality commodities not only seriously affect the economic development of the country, but also infringe upon the vital interests of enterprises and consumers and further disturb the social and economic order. In order to protect the benefits of enterprises and consumers as well as sound development of market economy, the state and enterprises put in numerous manpower and financial power to crack down on fake products every year. The common anti-counterfeit products and technologies in the domestic market includes: holographic patterns, color-changeable ink and concealed marks on products and packages. However, the existing technologies do not have uniqueness and exclusiveness, and are easy to copy; therefore, they are incapable to achieve effective anti-counterfeit function.

At present, electronic anti-counterfeit technology has become increasingly popular in the international anti-counterfeit field, in particular the application of radio frequency tags, and the advantages thereof have drawn great attention. Nevertheless, the key distribution technology in logic anti-counterfeit function is inflexible, the anti-counterfeit emphasis is still placed on the physical structure of radio frequency tag cards and logic anti-counterfeit function is inflexible and can only be signed by a publisher, therefore, different publishers require different verification devices, which is very inconvenient for the production and management of verification devices, that is to say, the anti-counterfeit verification devices are specialized rather than being generalized, therefore, their application scope is greatly limited.

How to develop a generalized anti-counterfeit technology with high safety for quick true or false identification has become a burning question to be solved.

This scheme is only used in a case that the signal copying attack is no significance.

18. 2 Main Technology

This scheme is an anti-counterfeit method for electronic tag relied on CPK system. The e-Tag authentication is realized by CPK Cryptosystem. CPK is a self-assured public key system in which an EntityID is mapped into a point ENTITY on the elliptic curve defined by $E: y^2 = x^3 + ax + b$ (mod p) with the parameter $T = \{a, b, G, n, p\}$, if an integer *entity* satisfies ENTITY = (*entity*) G then EN-TITY is public key and *entity* is private key. Because ENTITY = σ_1 (EntityID) and σ_1 is open to public, the public key can be calculated by any one and the private key is provided by ID-card.

The CPK electronic tag system is mainly composed of two parts, one is an electronic tag issuing system and the other is an electronic tag verification system.

The manufacturer defines TAG-ID, supplies the TAG to enterprises.

The enterprise defines the identity of article, signs to Article-ID with its private key, writes the signature into the electronic tag, bounds the tag and article, ensures that any attempt to separate the electronic tag from the article will lead to the damage to the electronic tag.

Only enterprise needs to have ID-card. The contents of the card are listed in Table 18. 1.

Table 18. 1 The contents of the card for enterprise

1	Z1 : verification parameter	16B	E_{PWD} (R1) = Z1
2	Z2 : verification parameter	16B	E_{R1} (R1) $\oplus$ R1 = Z2
3	Identity definition	25B	EnterpriseID
4	Private key1	32B	E_{R1} (enterprise) = Y1
5	Name of issuing unit	25B	KMC
6	Signature of issuing unit	48B	SIG_{KMC-1} (MAC)

The clients only verify the authenticity of articles and no need to have any private key or ID-card while had to hold a common Verification Device. The verification is in non-contact type, and verification results can be obtained at the spot.

The RFID technology is used for automatic collection of data and CPK technology is used for solving authenticity proof and logical counterfeit of data in the RFID; By combining RFID and CPK, every RFID can be internally equipped with an exclusive and unalterable ID number and article i-dentity number to ensure that the number can only be recognized by the verification device, but can not be copied and counterfeited.

A radio frequency identity (RFID) card is provided with unique TAG-ID defined by manufac-turer and different Article-ID defined by enterprises, and it can be verified at the same time; In a large-scale identity-based authentication system, the verification device is easy to generalize and popularize. Therefore, the technology can be widely applied to the counterfeiting prevention of various articles (such as containers, certificates and trademarks), bank notes, tickets, entrance tickets, and the like, and a uniform verifying device can be used for verification.

Verification function can be combined into hand-held appliances such as a cell phone and the like to endow the hand-held appliance with verification function, thus the verification function can become a kind of generalized activity which can be carried out by every one.

By integrating the electronic tag and the article into a whole, whether the article is true or false can be determined.

The generating flow of the CPK electronic tag is as shown in Fig. 18. 1.

The verification flow of the CPK electronic tag is as shown in Fig. 18. 2.

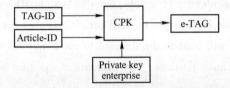

Fig. 18. 1   Generating flow of the electronic tag

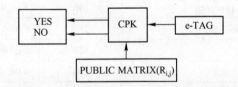

Fig. 18. 2   Verification flow of the electronic tag

Referring to the figures, some typical application of the CPK electronic tag is described in detail as follows.

18. 3   Embodiment (I)

The CPK electronic tag anti-counterfeit ticket includes venue entrance tickets, vehicle tickets, bank notes, etc. By adopting the RFID electronic tag, the ticket treatment is more efficient than that of traditional ticket. A reliable anti-counterfeit performance of tickets can be achieved by automatic verification.

A ticket anti-counterfeit system realized by RFID, includes a ticket issuing device and a ticket checking device.

(1) The ticket issuing module is composed of a ticket production part and issuing part and equipped with an issuing device.

The relevant data printed on the ticket is TAG-ID, issuer's name (EnterpriseID), match information (time, place), seat-no, etc. as:

$$Data = \{TAG\text{-}ID//Enterprise\text{-}ID//time\ of\ date//Seat\text{-}no\}$$

The Hash value is:

$$Hash(data) = mac$$

Enterprise signs to the MAC:

$$SIG_{enterprise}(MAC) = sign$$

Where, SIG is the signing protocol and 'enterprise' stand for the private key of issuer (Enterprise) provided by ID-card.

The data and sign are written into the RFID of the ticket.

(2) In the ticket checking process, the verification device reads and displays relevant data:

$$Data = \{TAG\text{-}ID//Enterprise\text{-}ID//Product\text{-}ID//time\ of\ date\}$$

First, calculates the Hash value:

$$Hash(data) = mac$$

Second, verifies signature:

$$SIG_{ENTERPRISE}^{-1}(MAC) = sign'$$

Where, SIG^{-1} is the verifying protocol and ENTERPRISE is public key can be calculated by every one.

If sign = sign' then the ticket holder is allowed to enter.

When the spectators holding the RFID entrance tickets enter a venue, once they pass through in front of a ticket checking device, the ticket checking device can judge whether the entrance ticket is true or false instantly, thus realizing quick automatic ticket checking.

(3) The RFID ticket checking device can unload ticket checking information to a server, the uploaded information is summarized and analyzed by data monitoring and analysis software operating on the server. If a network ticket checking system is adopted, the sponsor can carry out real-time monitoring to ticket checking state.

18. 4　Embodiment（Ⅱ）

The CPK electronic tag can be applied in tobacco management and counterfeit prevention; the

RFID technology can solve the problems of automatic collection and physical anti-counterfeiting of tags, and the CPK technology can solve the problems of authentication of the data in RFID. Moreover, the combination of the CPK technology and the RFID technology can effectively solve the anti-counterfeiting problem of tobacco.

The working process of the CPK electronic tag in the tobacco tag is as follows:

1) Writing in delivery information

Cigarettes factory (enterprise) makes up a data that is composed of Tag-ID, enterprise-ID, product-ID, Time of Data, prints it on the face of RFID and writes it into RFID.

$$data = \{TAG\text{-}ID//EnterpriseID//ProductID//time\ of\ date\}$$

Enterprise calculate Hash value of the data:

$$Hash(data) = mac$$

Enterprise signs to MAC:

$$SIG_{enterprise}(MAC) = sign$$

Enterprise writes mac and sign into RFID.

Where, SIG is signing protocol and 'enterprise' is the private key provided ID-card.

The signature in RFID only can be read, while can not be changed, thus effectively realizing counterfeit prevention.

2) Examination of the data in the circulation link

The RFID system can be checked by a verification device to confirm whether the product is false or true on the spot; the verification device can be exclusive or universal. Therefore, whether the cigarettes are false or true can be distinguished when a customer buys them.

The verification device reads and displays relevant data:

$$Data = \{TAG\text{-}ID//EnterpriseID//ProductID//time\ of\ date\}$$

First, calculates the Hash value:

$$Hash(data) = mac$$

Second, verifies signature:

$$SIG_{ENTERPRISE}^{-1}(MAC) = sign'$$

Where the public key is calculated by anyone of EnterpriseID.

If sign = sign' then the check is passed.

Chapter 19

The Design of Mywallet

In recently years, besides RFID, wireless smart card Mifare has also been developed. Besides storage function, the smart card also has simple calculation function, suitable for the fields such as public transportation card, e-purse.

No matter it is memory card or smart card, the security requirements are same, i. e. : ①anti-reproducing; ②anti-forgery. With respect to reproducing, it can only be solved with physical characteristics, and logic methods are helpless. With respect to anti-forgery, it can only be solved by logic characteristics, and physical methods are helpless. Thus, the whole world is seeking for a way that combines physical and logic characteristics. Preliminary analysis indicates that the static physical device cannot be reproduced, and dynamic physical device may not be able to prevent reproduction, just like Mifare.

19. 1 Two Kinds of Authentication Concept

The design characteristic of Mifare reflects different understanding to the authentication relationship. Among Writer, TAG, Reader, Mifare emphasizes on mutual authentication between Reader and TAG. (See Fig. 19. 1) Thus, it must offer TAG certain "intelligent" function. Accordingly, simple dynamic devices such as cipher machine and random number generator are set in TAG, to barely conduct interactive authentication with Reader. Such interactive authentication cannot be equal, because Reader is an active intelligent device, and TAG is a passive memory device. This causes irreconcilable fatal conflict. Practice proves that authentication and encryption of Mifare is not reliable. Recently, cracking of smart card Mifare and the appearance of simulated decipher ghost are the examples.

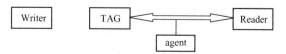

Fig. 19. 1   Relationship 1 among Writer, Reader and Tag

This concept requires to improve the intelligence of TAG. Low intelligence is easy to cause security issue.

The other authentication concept is to emphasize mutual authentication between Writer and Reader among the three (i. e. , Writer, TAG, and Reader), with TAG only as agent for Writer. Writer and Reader both are active intelligent device, and the mutual authentication can be equal. (See Fig. 19. 2) Thus, it greatly improves authentication security, and reduces strict requirements to TAG. CPK-based identity authentication technology can be directly applied to mutual authentication of Writer and Reader, to provide digital signature and verification, data encryption and decryption.

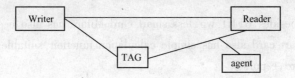

Fig. 19. 2   Relationship 2 among Writer, Reader, Tag

Thus, it can be seen that this concept is established on the basis of large scale mutual authentication technology. If this technology cannot solve, then this concept cannot be adopted. Authentication relationships are established between all Writer and Writer, all Reader and Reader, and all Writer and Reader, as shown in Fig. 19. 3.

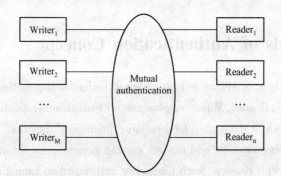

Fig. 19. 3   Verification relationship between Writer and Reader

19. 2   System Configuration

System configuration is as follows:

The system has 3 kinds of symetric Keys K_1, K_2 and K_3. The Keys are defined by KMC (or enterprise) and the configuration is skown as Fig. 19. 4.

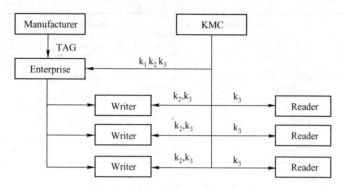

Fig. 19. 4   Configuration of authentication keys

Manufacturer: Define UID, supply to enterprises.

Enterprise: Hold CPK-card having key k_1, to sign on UID; supply to network operators.

Writer: Network operator holds CPK-card having key k_2, to sign on charging, and supply transportation card to the passengers.

Reader: The conductor on duty holds CPK-card having key k_3, to sign on the balance.

Enterprise ID-card contents are listed in Table 19. 1:

Table 19. 1   The ID-card for entenprise

1	Z1: Authentication Para	16B	$E_{PWD}(R_1) = Z_1$
2	Z2: Authentication Para	16B	$E_{R1}(R_1) \oplus R_1 = Z_2$
3	Identity definition	25B	EnterpriseID,
4	Private key	32B	$E_{R1}(\text{enterprise}) = Y$
5	Spare key K_1	48B	$E_{R1}(k_1) = W_1$ distribute to enterprise
6	Spare key K_2	48B	$E_{R1}(k_2) = W_2$ distribute to enterprise and Writer
7	Spare key K_3	48B	$E_{R1}(k_3) = W_3$ distribute to enterprise and Reader
8	Issue unit	25B	KMC
9	Signature of issue unit	48B	$SIG_{kmc}(MAC)$

19. 3   TAG Structure

19. 3. 1   Structure of Data Region

TAG is divided into control region and data region. Data region includes UID section, deposit section, and balance section. The structure is shown is Fig. 19. 5.

	1. UID section	2. Deposit section	3. Balance section
Item 1	UID(plain text)	Deposit (plain text)	Balance(plain text)
Item 2	$LFSR_1$	$LFSR_2$	$LFSR_3$
Item 3	$Signer_1$	$Signer_2$	$Signer_3$
Item 4	$Sign_1$	$Sign_2$	$Sign_3$
Item 5		n_2	n_3
Item 6		$Code_2$	$Code_3$

Fig. 19. 5   Division of regions in TAG

In which, Item 1, i. e. , UID, deposit, balance are stored in plain text; Item 2 $LFSR_i$' is the encryption of $LFSR_i$ with k_i; Item 3 signer is the identity of the signer; Item 4 sign is the signature of signer to data, different section has different definition to data, which will be explained below; Item 5 n_i is the encryption of control parameter mi with k_i (i = 1, 2, 3). Item 6 is codes where

$$code_2 = E_{k2} (LFSR_2) \quad code_3 = E_{k3} (LFSR_3)$$

19. 3. 2   Structure of Control Region

Control region is composed of parameters ma, mb, linear feedback shift register LFSR, and circulating shift register, as shown in Fig. 19. 6.

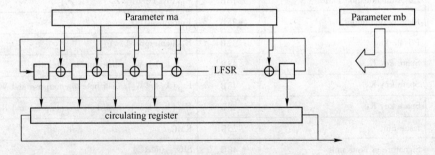

Fig. 19. 6   Structure of the controller

In which, LFSR is a 32-stage shift register; there are 31 mod 2 adders set between the stages; parameter ma is a 31-bit random number, each bit respectively controls the input line of the 31 mod 2 adders; mb is a 8-bit random parameter used to control the number of shifting steps of LFSR. The contents of ma and mb cannot be " all 0". m_i is directly changed into physical circuit in internal TAG, and n_i is stored in TAG as parameter for sending. At the Writer and Reader side, the decryption is first performed to obtain m_i,

$$D_{k_i}(n_i) = m_i (i = 2\cdots3)$$

19. 4 TAG Data Generation and Authentication

This anti-forgery authentication is realized with CPK public key system. In CPK public key system, Enterprise identity EnterpriseID is mapped to the point ENTERPRISE on the elliptic curve $E:y^2 = x^3 + ax + b \pmod{p}$ defined by parameter $T = \{a,b,G,n,p\}$. There are integers that satisfy ENTERPRISE = $(enterprise)G$, in which ENTERPRISE is a public key, and $enterprise$ is a private key. Because ENTERPRISE = σ_1(EnterpriseID) and σ_1 is open to public, the public key can be calculated by anyone, and the private key is provided by ID-card. In general, any IdentityID can be mapped to public/private key pair IDENTITY and identity. Thus, signature can be represented by

$$SIG_{identity}(\text{time}) = \text{sign}$$

and verification can be represented by

$$E_{k_3}(\text{time}) = \text{sign}'$$

19. 4. 1 KMC

(1) Write k_1, k_2, k_3 into CPK-card, and distribute to Enterprise.

(2) Write k_2, k_3 into CPK-card, and distribute to Writer operator.

(3) Write k_3 into CPK-card, and distribute to Reader operator.

19. 4. 2 Enterprise

(1) Enterprise defines 2 40-bit parameters mi for each TAG. Once mi is defined, it will be changed into physical circuit.

(2) Sign to UID:

$$SIG_{signer}(\text{UID}) = \text{sign}_1$$

Where sign_1 is written in laser holes. Encrypt m_i:

$$E_{ki}(m_i) = n_i \text{ and}$$

$$E_{ki}(LFSR_i) = code_i (i = 2,3)$$

Write signer, sign_1, n_i and $code_i (i = 2,3)$ into TAG.

19. 4. 3 Writer and Reader

Writer is mainly in charge of the deposit data:

(1) Signs on deposit data:

$$\text{SIG}_{signer}(\text{data}_2) = \text{sign}_2$$

(2) Verifies deposit data:

$$\text{SIG}_{\text{SIGNER}}^{-1}(\text{data}_2) = \text{sign}_2{}'$$

(3) Encryption/decryption function (optional):

$$\text{E}_{k_2}(\text{data}_2) = \text{encoded}_2$$

In which, data$_2$ is data$_2$ = UID + LFSR$_2$ + deposit

Reader is mainly in charge of the balance data:

(1) Signs on balance data:

$$\text{SIG}_{siger}(\text{data}_3) = \text{sign}_3$$

(2) Verifies balance data:

$$\text{SIG}_{\text{SIGNER}}^{-1}(\text{data}_3) = \text{sign}_3{}'$$

(3) Encryption/decryption function (option):

$$\text{E}_{k_3}(\text{data}_3) = \text{encoded}_3$$

In which, data$_3$ is data$_3$ = UID + LFSR$_2$ + balance

19.5　Protocol Design

With the restriction of use assigned to k_1, k_2, k_3, generally, only the Enterprise can decrypt the encoded data in UID section, deposit section and balance section; the Writer can decrypt the data in deposit section and balance section; the Reader can only decrypt the data in balance section. But to the plain data there is no restriction.

Here, deposit process will be taken as an example to describe the operation protocol.

1) Writer reads out UID, signer, sign1 and verifies

$$\text{SIG}_{\text{SIGNER}}^{-1}(\text{UID}) = \text{sign}_1{}'$$

2) Writer reads out code$_2$ and n$_2$, decrypt them with k$_2$:

$$\text{D}_{k2}(\text{code}_2) = \text{LFSR}_2$$

$$\text{D}_{k2}(\text{n}_2) = \text{m}_2$$

3) LFSRJ$_2$ of both sides moves mb$_2$ steps (status 2) on the basis of (status 1)

4) Writer sends out a random number $t_1(0\cdots31)$

5) TAG outputs consecutive 5 bits starting from t_1 of LFSR2

6) Writer checks and sends out $t_2(0\cdots31)$

7) TAG outputs consecutive 5 bits starting from t_2 of LFSR$_2$

8) If the check passed then Verifies the last signature sign$_2$ with signer when LFSR$_2$ is on status

2

$$SIG_{SIGNER}^{-1}(data_2) = sign_2 \text{'}$$

$$data_2 = deposit + UID + LFSR_2$$

9) Writer reads out the balance, to calculate new deposit value

10) $LFSR_2$ of Writer moves mb_2 steps (status 3) based on (status 2), encrypt status 3 contents with k_2

$$E_{k2}(LFSR_2) = code_2$$

11) $LFSR_2$ of Writer again moves mb_2 steps (status 4), to add up the new deposits to obtain data2

$$data_2 = deposit + UID + LFSR_2$$

12) Writer signs to $data_2$ on (status 4):

$$SIG_{writer_i}(data_2) = sign_2$$

Writer writes signer and $sign_2$ in TAG;

13) Shift register of TAG advances mb_2 steps (status 3) on the basis of (status 2), to keep consistency with $LFSR_2$ of Writer.

In the next round, TAG sends out signature of the shift register (status 3); Writer decrypts and moves a step to verify just right on (status 4). The whole process advances one round. The exposed ones are only the 10-bit information on (status 4). However, this does not affect security. Since it does not reduce the exhaustive volume, upon exhausting 2^{39}, there are still 2^{29} eligible possibilities left. These 2^{29} possibilities have to wait for next cumulative conditions. In other words, upon accumulating conditions to reach "decipher", it is only limited on knowing LFSR status of one chip, which cannot initiate to commit crimes, and affect security of other chips. This is due to without CPK support, even if a status of LFSR is obtained, it still cannot be encrypted, and is not able to communicate with Writer or Reader, and will be soon determined as counterfeits.

Thus, when there is any modification, displacement, or reproduction happened in UID field, deposit field, or balance field, which cause change to the signature contents, the reproduced signature will become invalid. Since illegal operator does not have the capability to re-sign, any counterfeiting or reproducing will be in vain.

19.6   Conclusion

This system closely connects CPK authentication system with Writer and Reader, to jointly protect TAG security. This solution directs the difficulties of dissection analysis and simulation analysis to the difficulties of cryptography analysis in CPK-card. With respect to TAG design, since it has 2^{39} different structures, and hardly to find same structured TAG, a card that can only copy one ID number is reproduced. Counterfeiting possibility is only $1/2^{16}$, and counterfeiting is very hard to succeed.

Thus, the decipher difficulty level of smart card and that of intelligent (with CPU) card are almost same. The difference is that the card itself does not have signature function.

In small-amount payment system, for example, public transportation card, does not need signature of the card itself, rather Reader can sign for it. Thus, smart card can be used. However, in big-amount credit card system, it needs signature of the card itself (or signature of the holder). Thus, in such circumstances, only intelligent card can be used, e. g. , available CPK-card. However, currently there is no non-contact CPK-card.

Annex:

Occupation of resource in TAG

field	data	signer	sign	LFSR	code	n
UID	6B	18B	18B			
DEP	6B	18B	18B	5B	8B	8B
BAL	6B	18B	18B	5B	8B	8B

Part Eight

File & Network Management

Chapter 20

e-Mail Authentication

20. 1　Main Technologies

Government, military and commercial office system needs to transmit official documents through E-mail communication.

In E-mail authentication system the E-mail address or user name is taken as the identity. E-mail communication is may originated from any E-mail address and terminated to any E-mail address via the Internet. E-mail authentication is implemented by ID-card. The typical structure of the network is a grid network, as shown in Fig. 20. 1.

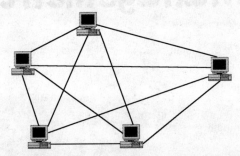

Fig. 20. 1　Web-like interlink of computer terminals

In the personalized secret communication, E-mail authentication system provides privacy for the communication content, i. e. , the content will not be read by any irrelevant personnel; and provides non-deniable service, with the required service defined in the ID-card.

The e-Mail authentication is realized by CPK Cryptosystem. CPK is a self-assured public key system in which an EntityID is mapped into a point ENTITY on the elliptic curve defined by $E:y^2 = x^3 + ax + b \pmod p$ with the parameter $T = \{a, b, G, n, p\}$, if an integer 'entity' satisfies ENTITY $=$ (entity) G then ENTITY is public key and the *entity* is private key. Because ENTITY $= \sigma_1$ (EntityID) and σ_1 is open to public, the public key can be calculated by any one and the private key is provided by ID-card.

Assuming: The communication parties have their own email address (or user name) and the addresses are known to other parties involved. Now Alice is sending data to Bob. Suppose that Alice's address is Alice@ tom. com, and her name is Alice, the address is used in communication and the name is used in digital signature. Bob's address is Bob@ jack. edu and his name is Bob. Then ALICE is the public key and 'alice' is private key. The ID-card for Alice is shown as Table 20. 1

Table 20. 1   ID-card for Alice

1	Z1 : verification parameter	16B	$E_{PWD}(R_1) = Z_1$
2	Z2 verification parameter	16B	$E_{R1}(R_1) \oplus R_1 = Z_2$
3	Identity definition1	25B	Alice@ tom. comID
4	Identity definition2	25B	AliceID
5	Role level : customer	16B	5
6	Identity1 's Private key 1.	32B	$E_{R1}(\text{alice@ tom. com} + ssk) = Y_1$
7	Identity2 's Private key 2.	32B	$E_{R1}(\text{alice}) = Y_2$
8	Role 5 key	48B	$E_{R1}(key_1) = Y_3$
9	Name of issuing unit	25B	KMC
10	Signature of issuing unit	48B	$SIG_{kmcc}(mac)$

This ID-card includes two identities, the email address and name of the user. Mail address is used to send and authenticate email, and the name of the user is used to sign document. In fact, there are two certificates in an ID-card.

E-mail network is of end to end communication, where the keys are horizontally distributed.

20. 2   Sending Process

1. The Sending Process of Alice

When converted to authentication state: {please insert the ID-card: }

Alice Inserts the ID-card,

Alice enters password: xxxxxx

Verification is implemented by the CPK password verification protocol.

Alice selects operation type and enters corresponding number: 1, 3

(1) signing (2) verifying (3) encrypting (4) decrypting

Alice enters file name: xxxxxxxxxxxx

Digital Signature Process

Digital signature protocol is implemented, with the following steps:

1) mac = Hash(file);

2) $SIG_{alice}(mac)$ = sign;

The sign is filled in the signature segment.

Encryption Process

1) Generates a random number r and calculates key = r(G);

2) Encrypts the key with Bob's public key:

$$ENC_{BOB}(key) = coded\text{-}key;$$

3) Key is modulo 2 added to the role key $role_n$: $key \oplus role_n$ = new-key;

4) The new-key is used to encrypt the file: $E_{new\text{-}key}(file)$ = cipher-text; and cipher-text is filled into the data segment.

Then, the signature segment, key segment and data segment are sent to Bob;

20.3 Receiving Process

Upon receiving the signature segment, key segment and data segment, Bob decodes the cipher-text with his own privacy key and checks signature with the public key of Alice. If the signature complies, a return receipt will be sent back to Alice. All the above processes are automatically implemented.

Data Decryption Process

1) Bob decrypts the coded-key:

$$DEC_{bob}(coded\text{-}key) = key$$

2) Key is modulo 2 added to role key $role_n$:

$$key \oplus role_n = new\text{-}key$$

3) Decrypt cipher-text with new-key:

$$D_{new\text{-}key}(cipher\text{-}text) = file_1$$

Signature Verification Process

1) Bob calculate MAC_1:

$$Hash(file_1) = MAC_1$$

2) Bob verifies the signature:

$$SIG_{ALICE}^{-1}(MAC_1) = sign'$$

3) If sign = sign', Bob sends a receipt to Alice.

The receipt is the sign to MAC_1:

$$SIG_{bob}(MAC_1) = sign_1$$

Chapter 21

Data Storage Authentication

21. 1   Security Requirements

Database system or various file storage system is developed with the development of network technique. Internet transaction cannot be implemented without data storage. Various transaction data storage has different security requirements. Upon many years of study, great achievements have been made in database security. However, since database operating system is not open, and the main authentication technology is poor, it is at a standstill on key issues.

Currently, database is developed from single intranet private database to public database on public network; and, database security technology is transferred from closed protection to open protection. Such a change requires us to re-examine database security.

There are various types of database. In summary, database can be classified as documental database and relational database, private database for private network and public database for public network. (See Fig. 21. 1) Below discussion will be focused on relational database and public database.

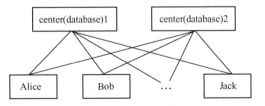

Fig. 21. 1   Connected relationship between center database and customers

Center database and users are connected via internet. The users can upload files or download files, and can access database 1 or database 2. Data center can uniformly manage the data, or can divide data to each user for user-self management (e. g. , mail box).

Assuming each center and each user are configured with CPK ID-card, and have CPK signature and encryption function, the following security requirements can be achieved.

1) Center database can authenticate authenticity of the visitor.

2) User can authenticate authenticity of the object database (Center).

3) Center database can prevent illegal access and DOS attacks.

4) Center database can prevent virus and Trojan(optional).

5) Center database can encrypt the stored file.

21.2　Basic Technology

File storage authentication is achieved with CPK public key system. In CPK public key system, entity ID (EntityID) is mapped to point ENTITY on the elliptic curve $E: y^2 = x^3 + ax + b \pmod{p}$ with $T = \{a, b, G, n, p\}$ as the parameter. If there is an integer *user* that satisfies ENTITY = (*entity*) G then ENTITY is public key and *entity* is private key. Because ENTITY = σ_1(EntityID) and σ_1 is open to public, the public key can be calculated by anyone, and the private key is provided by ID-card. Any IdentityID is mapped to public/private key pair (IDENTITY and identity). Thus, signature can be represented as $SIG_{identity}$(time) = sign, and verification can be represented as $SIG_{IDENTITY}^{-1}$ (time) = sign'.

Symbol E and D indicate encryption and decryption under symmetric key. ENC and DEC indicate encryption and decryption under asymmetric key.

Take Alice as an example, the contents of ID-card are listed in Table 21.1:

Table 21.1　ID-card for Alice

1	Z1: verification parameter	16B	$E_{PWD}(R_1) = Z_1$
2	Z2: verification parameter	16B	$E_{R1}(R_1) \oplus R_1 = Z_2$
3	Identity definition	25B	AliceID
4	Role level	16B	5
5	Private key	32B	$E_{R1}(alice) = Y_1$
6	Role 5 key	48B	$E_{R1}(role\text{-}key) = Y_3$
7	Issuing department	25B	KMC
8	Signature of issuing department	48B	$SIG_{kmc}(MAC)$

21.3　File Uploading Protocol

Assuming: Alice transfers file to Center:

Alice first sends out a connection request: request is the signature of Alice to time:

$$SIG_{alice}(time) = sign_1$$

In which SIG is a signature function, 'alice' is private key, provided by ID-card.

Msg1 Alice→Center: { AliceID, time, $sign_1$ }

Center checks the signature:

$$SIG_{ALICE}^{-1}(time) = sign_1'$$

In which SIG^{-1} is verification function. If $sign_1 = sign_1'$, then Center believes that the applicant is Alice, and sends a random number r to Alice while signing to (time − 1):

$$SIG_{center}(time - 1) = sign_2$$

Msg2 Center→Alice: { r, $sign_2$ }

Alice checks the signature:

$$SIG_{CENTER}^{-1}(time - 1) = sign_2'$$

If $sign_2 = sign_2'$, then Alice believes authenticity of Center, and sign to r. It enters into data transmission process. Data transmission includes the following steps: sign to time + 1, sign to file:

$$SIG_{alice}(r) = sign_3$$
$$SIG_{alice}(time + 1) = sign_4$$
$$SIG_{alice}(MAC) = sign_5$$

In which MAC = Hash(file).

Msg3 Alice→Center: { $sign_4$, file, $sign_5$ }

Center checks the signature:

$$SIG_{ALICE}^{-1}(r) = sign_3'$$
$$SIG_{ALICE}^{-1}(time + 1) = sign_4'$$
$$SIG_{ALICE}^{-1}(MAC) = sign_5'$$

If $sign_3 = sign_3'$, Center believes authenticity of Alice. If $sign_4 = sign_4'$, then Center receives file, calculates MAC and checks $sign_4$. If $sign_5 = sign_5'$, then Center sends acknowledgement message to Alice. Acknowledgement is the signature to MAC:

$$SIG_{center}(MAC) = sign_6$$

Msg4 Center→Alice: { $sign_6$ }

Alice checks signature:

$$SIG_{CENTER}^{-1}(MAC) = sign_6'$$

If $sign_6 = sign_6'$, Alice believes that this communication is correct, and the upload process ends.

21.4　File Downloading Protocol

User Alice applies to the Center for file:

Alice sends connection request: Alice signs to time:

$$SIG_{alice}(time) = sign_1$$

Sends time and $sign_1$ to Center:

Msg1 Alice→Center: { AliceID, time, $sign_1$ }

Center checks signature:

$$SIG_{ALICE}^{-1}(time) = sign_1{}'$$

If $sign_1 = sign_1{}'$, it proves the authenticity of Alice, and sends a random number r and sign to $(time - 1)$:

$$SIG_{CENTER}(time - 1) = sign_2$$

Msg2 Center→Alice: { r, $sign_2$ }

Alice checks signature:

$$SIG_{CENTER}^{-1}(time - 1) = sign_2{}'$$

If $sign_2 = sign_2{}'$, it proves the authenticity of this connection and Center, and enters into data application process.

Alice sign to r, time + 1 and the required file name:

$$SIG_{alice}(r) = sign_3$$
$$SIG_{alice}(time + 1) = sign_4$$
$$SIG_{alice}(FileID) = sign_5$$

Msg3 Alice→Center: { $sign_3$, FileID, $sign_4$, $sign_5$ }

Center checks signature:

$$SIG_{ALICE}^{-1}(r) = sign_3{}'$$
$$SIG_{ALICE}^{-1}(time + 1) = sign_4{}'$$
$$SIG_{ALICE}^{-1}(FileID) = sign_5{}'$$

If $sign_3 = sign_3{}'$, Center believes authenticity of Alice. If $sign_4 = sign_4{}'$, then Center receives the request, and sends the required file. Center sign to time + 1, fileID and MAC, respectively:

$$SIG_{center}(time + 1) = sign_6$$
$$SIG_{center}(FileID) = sign_7$$
$$SIG_{center}(MAC) = sign_8$$

Data and signature evidence are sent to the User.

Msg4 Center→Alice: { file, $sign_6$, $sign_7$, $sign_8$ }

21.5   Data Storing

Database is divided into two kinds: documental and relational. Documental database encryption adopts the way of user terminal encryption (outside database encryption), which uses self-storing, self-sending and self-receiving modal. Thus, its key does not need to re-define, and the online communication key can be used. The self-stored file, upon encrypted, can be stored in storage media such as hard disk, soft disk, or database.

Key management of the relational database adopts inside database centralized management, in which keys are dynamically generated in the database and dynamically distributed. All the keys are set in the database, and the definition, lifetime, and function need to be re-defined.

21.5.1   Establishment of Key File

Directory key: define each directory a key DK. Directory key is a 2-level key, and automatically stored in DK file under the encryption of database key. There are two types of directory key: directory established by the system generates DK file at the time of establishing the system; and, directory established by the user itself establishes corresponding DK file with establishment of the directory. DK is automatically generated by random key generation. DK is invoked with directory name.

File Key: define each file a key FK. File key is also called table key. According to the definition, table key sometimes appears in the form of recording key, and sometime appears in the form of field key. Table key is a 3-level key, for data encryption. FK file is established by the user. When the user establishes the file, he also establishes corresponding FS file. File key is automatically generated by random key generation. File key is invoked with file name.

Database key: define each database a database key BK. Database key is a protection key for directory key, and is a one-level key. Database key file is written in by authorized personnel when establishing the system, and can be modified anytime. Database key file is invoked with database name.

21.5.2   Storage of Key File

Database Key is under password encryption:
$$\text{Database key file} = E_{PWD}(BK)$$
Directory and subdirectory Key is under database key encryption:
$$\text{Directory key file} = E_{BK}(DK)$$
Subdirectory can be divided into multiple layers, called leveli subdirectory. The storage method

of subdirectory key is listed in Table 21. 2.

Table 21. 2 Gmcrypted subdirectory keys

Level 1 subdirectory	Level 2 subdirectory	Level 3 subdirectory
$E_{BK}(DK_1)$		
	$E_{BK}(DK_{11})$	
	$E_{BK}(DK_{12})$	
		$E_{BK}(DK_{121})$
		$E_{BK}(DK_{122})$
	$E_{BK}(DK_{13})$	
$E_{BK}(DK_2)$		
$E_{BK}(DK_3)$		
$E_{BK}(DK_4)$	$E_{BK}(DK_{41})$	
		$E_{BK}(DK_{411})$
	$E_{BK}(DK_{42})$	
		$E_{BK}(DK_{421})$

File Key is under subdirectory key encryption:

File key is stored under subdirectory key encryption where the file locates, e. g. , DK_1, the storage way of file key FK_1 is

$$E_{DK_1}(FK_1)$$

21. 5. 3 Documental Database Encryption

Encrypted data has two types: shared data and self-use data.

Encryption of shared data: shared data is encrypted with shared key. Shared data can be inquired in its definition field. In other words, inquiry of encrypted data does not have permission restriction in its definition field. Shared encryption data can be self-generated, or can be sent from other stations. When invocation and entry of encrypted data goes beyond its definition field, even though it does not affect security of the data itself much, to prevent destructive invocation and entry, typically operation beyond the definition field is not allowed.

Encryption of self-use data: self-use data is data that is encrypted with self-use key. Encrypted data can be self-generated, or can be transferred via key from encrypted data sent from other stations. The self-use data in the database either self-generated or transferred It can only be read by the key definer, and cannot directly be inquired by others. The key used is communication key, and is not the key specially defined by database system.

21. 5. 4　Relational Database Encryption

Encryption of relationship data is conducted in the database. Thus, keys for encryption of relational database table are all set in the database. Table is composed of record and segment. Encryption includes whole record or whole segment. Since the expense of encrypted system in the database is high, it is preferred not to use or seldom use full table encryption.

Table Key definition: table key is a mapping file of records or segment, including prompt table and variable table.

Table-level prompt table is stoun as Table 21. 3.

Table 21. 3　Table leval prompt table

name	
Confidential level	Level 1 ~ 256
Encryption method	Record or segment(10 for record, 01 for field)
Table key	8 bytes

If it is segment encryption, then segment-level prompt table shall be checked. If it is record encryption, then record-level prompt table shall be checked.

Segment-level prompt table:

Encryption method: 01, segment encryption

Segment 1	Segment 2	Segment 3		Segment n
0	1	0		0

Record-level prompt table:

Encryption method: 10, indicating record encryption

Record 1	Record 2	Record 3		Record n
0	0	1		0

Key variables: Each table has an 8-byte table key. The table key is not the functional key, and the true functional key is the compound key. The key variable of each compound key is composed of table key, record name, and segment name:

Compound Key ＝ table key + segment name + record name

File encryption (optional): the encrypting length is one block. In each block, the key shall be re-defined.

Encryption Procedure: select record encryption or segment encryption. First, FK is obtained:

$$D_{BK}(E_{BK}(DK)) = DK$$
$$D_{DK}(E_{DK}(FK)) = FK$$

With FK, each block can be calculated,

Block key BLK = table key + segment name + record name;

Encryption function ECPH:

$$ECPH[RN, data] \rightarrow E_{BLK}(data)$$

The function ECPH executes in three steps:

$$D_{DK}(RN) = FK$$

FK + record name + segment name = BLK

$$E_{BLK}(data)$$

File decryption: enter the file name to be decrypted. If it is a ciphered file, then check inside database encryption or outside database encryption. Before decrypting the file, first file key FK is obtained:

$$D_{BK}(E_{BK}(DK)) = DK$$
$$D_{DK}(E_{DK}(FK)) = FK$$

With FK, the key for each block can be calculated, to conduct decryption. The decryption function is named DCPH.

$$DCPH[RN, E_{BLK}(data)] \rightarrow data$$

This function is executed in two steps:

$$E_{KEY}(RN) = FK$$

FK + record name + segment name = BLK

$$D_{BLK}(E_{BLK}(data)) = data$$

Chapter 22

Secure File Box

22. 1　Background

With the development of e-government and e-business, information technology has entered into each section of the government and enterprise daily operation. No-paper office has become the development trend. The application of information technology greatly improves work efficiency. However, it also brings the safety risk. Hacker attack, Trojan steal, or loss/leakage of confidential documents, trade secrets and personal privacy due to improper safeguard of storage media, and transferred files in the network being stolen/modified happen frequently, which causes huge damage to the government, enterprises and users.

Threats are not only from outside, but also from inside. According to statistics issued by authorized organization, 80% of information leakage are from inside. Ordinary organizations and enterprises typically store interior confidential documents, core technology documents in servers and key staff's computers. Spies normally obtain special permission through means of attacks or tricks, to log on to the server, and download the documents; or, illegally steal information from key staff's computers via attacks, or even try to move the server and computers. Thus, adopting effective technical measures to ensure safety of important information and data stored in the servers and personal computers and solving the issue of safe storing and sharing the documents, become the issue that currently needs to be solved for the government, military, enterprises.

Achieving safe sharing of electronic files under networks is a complicated system project, and is also an international puzzle. There are two ways to solve file safety. One is to enhance control and management of use of the files. Starting from storage and usage environment of the electronic files, measures such as network physical isolation, control of illegal access, and strict authorized access control and audit to the file server are adopted, to prevent loss of files. The other one is to use cryptography to encrypt the file data. Even if data loses, there will be no breach of confidence. However, even though encrypting the file contents is the most effective and thorough solution, it also raises problem in use. In order to ensure information safety and ease information sharing, key management and dynamic exchange between client and server, and between client and client shall first be solved. CPK technology can perfectly solves this puzzle.

22. 2　System Framework

CPK is self-assured public key cryptosystem. CPK identity authentication system can directly calculate the public key with the identity. The calculation process itself can prove its authenticity, without the need of third party evidence and online database support, which greatly simplifies authentication and key exchange process, and creates conditions for achieving safe sharing of files.

To develop new generation of electronic file security system based on CPK identity authentication system, the two means of file control/management and file encryption can be closely combined, to constitute a confidential file management system that is from server to client end, covers each link from storing, transferring to using, integrated with file encryption, access control, authorization management, automatic key exchange, process audit, and dynamic tracking. Such a system not only can ensure file security under store status and during network transmission, but also can ensure authenticity, integrity and non-deniability of file and data through digital signature, so as to realize secure store, transfer and share of data and files. The system architecture is shown in Fig. 22. 1.

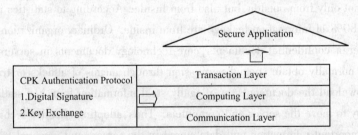

Fig. 22. 1　Structure of Secure File Service

22. 3　Features of the System

Identity-based digital signature and key exchange capability by using identity authentication system combines access control and file encryption together, to constitute strict security protection system from system to data, and achieve highly flexible secure sharing of data files.

Cryptography is used to encrypt all the data, and to ensure that each file has one key. Even if the file is stolen, it cannot be decrypted without the key.

The identity of the file user is used to generate keys, to encrypt the file with the receiver's public key, and the receiver decrypt the file with his private key, so as to effectively avoid spread of the file. Such an automatic key exchange may not encrypt/decrypt the file within the servers, so greatly reduce the burden of the servers, and ensure efficient running of the system.

The system uses digital signature based authentication login technology, to prevent illegal user access; conducts detailed record and secure audit of the login users and file downloading information with audit system, to timely detect and prohibit illegal operation; and performs management and audit to the user file uploading and downloading operation, which can track back once any problems occur.

File server configuration authorization management system can perform strict authorization management to each user's search, upload, download rights to each file, and provide functions such as tolerance and backup.

The identity-based key exchange technology provides file security at the user end and security information interaction among users, so as to constitute file security service system from server end to client end.

The server key and user key are both encrypted via user PIN code and then stored in CPK chip (CPK-key or card). Even if the chip is dissected, the user key still cannot be directly obtained. When starting the server or logging in the system, correct PIN code needs to be input. If successively inputting wrong PIN code for a number of times (which can be set), the system will be locked, to ensure security of the system.

Comparing with other current systems, this system not only has strong confidentiality and high efficiency, and can support large scale application, but also is simple in system structure (no need of third party evidence and online database support), easy and flexible to use, easy to manage, and can widely be applied in government, military and enterprise/public institution, to achieve secure store and sufficient share of internal confidential documents, which effectively solves the issue of missing confidential documents and vital data that is most concerned by each unit. In addition, this technology can also be expanded to apply in fields such as digital right management, video on demand, and has significant value to develop industries such as education and entertainment and protect IP rights.

22.4　System Implementation

Security file service system adopts the skillful combination of digital envelope technology and access control, to realize dynamic digital envelope technology, and solve the issue of key distribution and sharing. The system is mainly composed of three parts: CPK identity authentication system, security server and client end software (file box), with the following steps:

1) Arranging CPK identity authentication system, to use key management system to distribute keys (CPK key or CPK card) to specific users, and to provide basic digital signature and key exchange capability.

2) Assigning file box software (client end of the security file service system), to provide the users with encryption/decryption and security file interactive tools.

3) Deploying security file server in the information center, to provide system authorization management, secure file storage (file encryption), search (access control), and download (key exchange) services.

The detailed implementation process is shown in Fig. 22. 2.

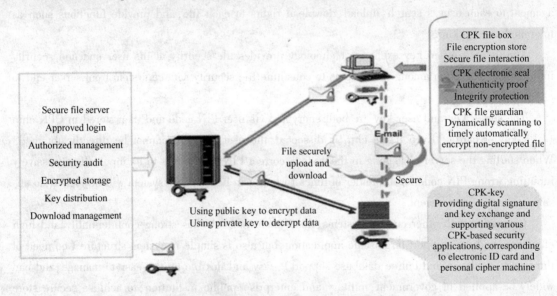

Fig. 22. 2　Constitution of File Security Service and Data Flow

1) When the user uploading the file, the system will generate a random number as session key, which is used to conduct symmetric encryption to the file (AES-256). Then the CPK key exchange technology is used to make the session key into digital envelope (using server identity as public key). Meanwhile, initial authorization is completed (designating which ones can access this file), and encrypted file is uploaded to the file server, digital envelope and authorized information are stored in the database.

2) Upon uploading the file, the administrator can change authorization of the file. The authorization adopts RBAC (Role Based Access Control) model.

3) When the user search or download the file, he first uses CPK Key to log in the server. The server first verifies and checks the user's identity and rights. Upon verification is passed, it displays the file directories within the authorized scope according to the user's rights. When the user selects certain specific file, the server will use its own private key to open the digital envelope and take out the session key, and use the user's identity to make a new digital envelope. Since the server does not need to conduct encryption/decryption to the file per se, essentially the server's efficiency will not be affected. In addition, the audit system inside the server will conduct detailed records to the operations such as user login and file invocation for future reference.

4) When downloading the file, the ciphered file and the digital envelope that the applied downloader has for this file are both downloaded, and new digital envelope is used to replace the old digital envelope in the file. With the private key the user can open the file. Other people are not able to decrypt.

5) Identity-based key exchange function is provided by file box, secure file exchange among users can also be realized. First, one can use the receiver's identity to encrypt the file, and then sends the file by means of email attachment. Thus, only the receiver who has corresponding identity key can decrypt. To facilitate operation, the file box can also support multi-users to open the same file with designated identity, to accommodate the need of centralized distribution of the file.

With such a system, one can establish secure and flexible information service system, which can realize sufficient sharing of information under the precondition of ensuring security and controllability.

Chapter 23

e-Seal of Classification

23. 1　Background Technology

The proposal relates to the field of security authentication of digital communications, in particular to an electronic seal security authentication system based on combined public key system (CPK) and a method thereof.

Thanks to the increasing popularization of e-government and e-business, numerous electronic documents such as official documents, securities, and the like, are transferred through the public Internet and gradually replace the traditional paper documents. In order to be in line with the advanced practices in the world, *the Electronic Signature Law of the People 's Republic of China*, which took effect on April 1, 2005, endowed electronic documents and electronic seals with legal validity, and provided legal basis for the network transmission of documents and vital information. Thanks to the law, the digital safety transmission of various documents in government and commercial activities can be realized.

However, the application of electronic seals has not been popularized, for the security of the current computer networks is commonly questioned.

The electronic seal authentication is composed of seal signature and seal verification. There are two key technologies in the electronic seal authentication: one is to solve the problem of large-scale electronic seal authentication, and the other is to achieve convenient verification technology which can direct output verification results.

However, the existing electronic seal authentication system does not have the two technologies mentioned above.

23. 2　Main Technologies

The proposal aims at overcoming the described defects and providing an electronic seal security authentication system based on CPK and a method thereof; it not only can solve the problem of large-scale electronic seals, but also can conveniently carry out security authentication to electronic seals.

The electronic seal authentication based on the CPK which is provided for realizing the purpose of the proposal includes a signature function and verification function. The system is shown in Fig. 23. 1.

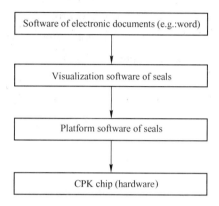

Fig. 23. 1   Architecture of The Signature System

An electronic seal security authentication method based on the CPK includes the following steps:

Step A. When sending electronic documents with electronic seal the signing party signs the document with seal identity and send the signature together with original data.

Step B. When receiving the electronic document with electronic seal the verifying party calculates the public key of the signing party with the public key matrix, checks digital signature and judges whether the signature is true or not. The verifying device may display the seal image showing the seal identity.

The beneficial effects of the proposal lie in that: the CPK-based electronic seal security authentication system and the method thereof in the invention have simple operation and convenient use, for example, they can be embedded in the office system in a form of office tool bars; users can fulfill sealing, verification, deleting, and other operations simply by clicking the corresponding buttons; with uniqueness and anti-counterfeiting capability, the system can realize the function of digital signature and guarantee the uniqueness of the seal; and the electronic seal is safer than a physical seal, thus effectively solving the trust problem of e-documents and e-bills; the integrity of the content of electronic official documents can be guaranteed, the specific security mechanism of the electronic signature can ensure that the document bearing a e-seal can not be altered at will and counterfeited, thus endowing the system with reliability and trustworthy; with economical, practical and waste-reducing performances, the electronic seal can be used for realizing no paper office, facilitate the protection of the society and environment, reduce the waste of natural resources and greatly save the cost of mailing and express mail service.

File has its classification and the classification is divided into four levels: top secret, confidential, secret, sensitive. Every classification level has its own public key and private key. And the holder of the classifying seal has his own public key and private key.

The e-Seal authentication is realized by CPK Cryptosystem. CPK is a self-assured public key system in which an EntityID is mapped into a point ENTITY on the elliptic curve defined by $E: y^2 = x^3 + ax + b \pmod{p}$ with the parameter $T = \{a, b, G, n, p\}$, if an integer "*entity*" satisfies ENTITY $=$ (*entity*) G then the point ENTITY is public key and *entity* is private key. Because ENTITY $= \sigma_1$ (EntityID) and σ_1 is open to public, the public key can be calculated by any one and the private key is provided by ID-card.

The ID-card contents are listed in Table 23. 1.

Table 23. 1　The ID-card for classification

1	Z1: verification parameter	16B	$E_{PWD}(R1) = Z1$
2	Z2: verification parameter	16B	$ER1(R1) \oplus R1 = Z2$
3	Identity 1	25B	**SecretID**
4	Identity2	25B	**SensitiveID**
5	Identity3	25B	**AliceID**
6	Role level	1B	**5**
7	Private key1	32B	$E_{R1}(\mathbf{secret}) = Y1$
8	Private key2	32B	$E_{R1}(\mathbf{sensitive}) = Y2$
9	Private key3	32B	$E_{R1}(\mathbf{alice}) = Y3$
10	Role level 5 key	48B	$E_{R1}(\mathbf{key1}) = Y3$
11	Name of issuing unit	25B	**KMC**
12	Signature of issuing unit	48B	$SIG_{kmc}(\mathbf{mac})$

23. 3　Working Flow

The working flows of CPK-based electronic seal signing and verification for electronic documents and electronic bills are shown in Fig. 23. 2.

1. The Stmping Procedure

Suppose Alice has a stamp identified by "secret" and data "file", Alice signs to the file with the stamp identified by "secret":

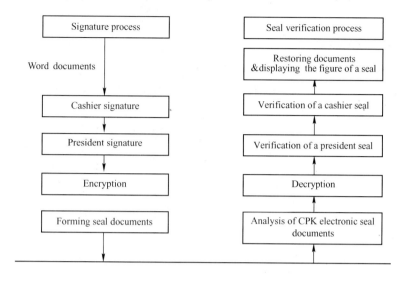

Fig. 23. 2　Processes of Signature and Seal Verification

$$SIG_{secret}(\text{fileID}) = \text{sign}_1$$

Here, SIG is signing protocol.

Alice signs to the seal identity and the time of sign

$$SIG_{alice}(\text{SecretID}//\text{time}) = \text{sign}_2$$

Here, the time is when the seal was stamped.

2. The verifying procedure

Everyone can check the seal

$$SIG_{SECRET}^{-1}(\text{FileID}) = \text{sign}_1'$$

If $\text{sign}_1 = \text{sign}_1'$ then it proves that the file classification is "secret".

$$SIG_{ALICE}^{-1}(\text{SecretID}//\text{time}) = \text{sign}_2'$$

If $\text{sign}_2 = \text{sign}_2'$ then it proves that this seal is stamped by Alice in that time.

When the verification passed may get into visualizing procedure, and generate the seal image according to the seal identity. The seal in shown as Fig. 23. 3.

Classified as	Confidential	Sign$_1$
Classified on	2010.3.31	
Declassify in	2020.3.20	
Classified by	Little Tom	Sign$_2$

Fig. 23. 3　Visualized Classification Seal

23. 4　Embodiment

As one realizing way of the embodiment of the proposal, the format of the electronic documents which are signed and encrypted by the signature system of the CPK electronic seal security authentication system in the proposal adopts ISO ASN. 1 Markup Language and is realized as follows: (the particular meanings and relevant operation thereof will be described below).

```
ContentInfo ::= SEQUENCE {
contentType      ContentType,
content          [0] EXPLICIT ANY DEFINED BY contentType
}        // format of the electronic documents in the CPK electronic signature system
SignedData ::= SEQUENCE {
    version                 Version,
    digestAlgorithms        DigestAlgorithmIdentifiers,
    encapContentInfo        EncapsulatedContentInfo,
    signerInfos             SignerInfos
    }           // description of the signed electronic document data
EncapsulatedContentInfo ::= SEQUENCE {
    eContentType            ContentType,
    eContent    [0] EXPLICIT OCTET STRING OPTIONAL
    }               //signed data
SignerInfo ::= SEQUENCE {
    version                 Version,
    sid                     SignerIdentifier,
    digestAlgorithm         DigestAlgorithmIdentifier,
    signatureAlgorithm   SignatureAlgorithmIdentifier,
    signature               SignatureValue,
    }           //a plurality of signatures of electronic document data by multiply signers
SignatureValue ::= OCTET STRING
EnvelopedData ::= SEQUENCE {
    version                 Version,
    recipientInfos          RecipientInfos,
    encryptedContentInfoEncryptedContentInfo,
    }               //description of the data generated by encrypting the CPK public key data
RecipientInfos ::= SET OF RecipientInfo
RecipientInfo ::= SEQUENCE {
```

```
            version                 Version,
            recipientId             CPKIdentifier,
        keyEncryptionAlgorithm   KeyEncryptionAlgorithmIdentifier,
            encryptedKey            EncryptedKey
        }                       //recipient information
EncryptedContentInfo ::= SEQUENCE {
            contentType             ContentType,
        contentEncryptionAlgorithm ContentEncryptionAlgorithmIdentifier,
        encryptedContent       [0] IMPLICIT EncryptedContent OPTIONAL
        }           // description of the electronic document data encrypted by symmetric algorithm
EncryptedContent ::= OCTET STRING
EncryptedKey ::= OCTET STRING
```

23. 5　Explanation

The process that the electronic document signature system adopts ISO ASN. 1 Markup Language to realize format is described in detail as follows:

Wherein:

1) ContentInfo ::= SEQUENCE {
　　contentType　　ContentType,
　　content　　　　　　[0] EXPLICIT ANY DEFINED BY contentType
　　}

The ContentInfo type describes the format of the electronic document of the CPK electronic signature system. Beginning from the identifier ContentType of the format, the particular type of the document is described. The particular type of the ContentType includes clear text data, signature data and encrypting signature data.

ContentType ::= OBJECT IDENTIFIER

The different types of ContentType must have an overall exclusive identifier and the value of the identifier is in accordance with corresponding standards issued by authority organizations.

2) SignedData ::= SEQUENCE {
　　　version　　　　　　　　　　Version,
　　　digestAlgorithms　　　　　DigestAlgorithmIdentifiers,
　　　encapContentInfo　　　　　EncapsulatedContentInfo,
　　　signerInfos　　　　　　　　SignerInfos

The data type of SignedData is used for describing the electronic document data with signature (security signature) or the digital signature containing no original data. The data type can support a plurality of signers to carry out a polarity of times of signature to the same original data by adopting the signature algorithm with different signature, that is, different Hash algorithms are adopted in different ECDSA signature algorithms.

SignedData. version is the version number of the data type.

SignedData. digestAlgorithms is the collection of the Hash algorithms used by a plurality of signers. A verification party can use these Hash algorithms to generate a plurality of Hash values of original data to be used in the following signature and verification process.

SignedData. encapContentInfo is the data to be signed, and the type of the data is EncapsulatedContentInfo; as the type of EncapsulatedContentInfo is flexible, original data can be a variety of forms and not limited to be clear text. The particular format and processing procedure should be agreed by both parties.

EncapsulatedContentInfo. eContentType is field consultation.

The OPTIONAL mark in the EncapsulatedContentInfo. eContetn field determines that the data can be blank; if it is blank, the SignedData only includes signature information.

```
EncapsulatedContentInfo ::= SEQUENCE {
    eContentType                  ContentType,
    eContent                      [0] EXPLICIT OCTET STRING OPTIONAL
}
```

3) The data type of SignerInfos contains a plurality of signatures of data signed by a plurality of signers; wherein every signer and the digital signature of original data signed by the signer are determined by SignerInfo type.

```
SignerInfos ::= SET OF SignerInfo
```

The data type of SignerInfo contains the version number of the data type (SignerInfo. version), the identity of the signer(SignerInfo. sid), Hash algorithm used in signature(SignerInfo. digestAlgorithm), signature algorithm (SignerInfo. signatureAlgorithm) and generated digital signature data (SignerInfo. signature).

```
SignerInfo ::= SEQUENCE {
    version                       Version,
    sid                           SignerIdentifier,
```

```
            digestAlgorithm                    DigestAlgorithmIdentifier,
            signatureAlgorithm                 SignatureAlgorithmIdentifier,
            signature                          SignatureValue,
            }
    SignatureValue  :: =  OCTET STRING
```

The better signature algorithm is ecdsa-SHA1, and the signature value, SignerInfo. signature, is ECDSA-Sig-Value. The two types are defined in the ISO (SEC1v1) and (SEC1v1.5) of elliptical curves which are entirely quoted in the embodiment and not mentioned here again.

4) The data type of EnvelopedData is used for describing the electronic document data generated by encrypting CPK public key data. If the encrypted electronic document data are signed data, that is, the data of SingerInfo type said above, the data of EnvelopedData type contain encryption and signature to form complete security information data.

The process of generating EnvelopedData is as follows:

① Preparing the clear text data to be encrypted.

② Generating a symmetric private key (e. g. 256bit AES encryption private key) at random, and using the private key and symmetric encryption algorithm (e. g. AES encryption algorithm) to encrypt the clear text data.

③ For every recipient receiving the data, using CPK public key encryption algorithm, the identity of a recipient and the public key matrix in the CPK security chip to work out the public key of the recipient which is adopted to encrypt the symmetric private key in the step 42.

④ Uniformly coding the mentioned data and relevant parameters into the EnvelopedData data type of encrypted signature electronic documents.

```
    EnvelopedData  :: =  SEQUENCE {
            version                    Version,
            recipientInfos             RecipientInfos,
            encryptedContentInfo       EncryptedContentInfo,
            }
    RecipientInfos  :: =  SET OF RecipientInfo
```

The EnvelopedData type contains the version number of the type (EnvelopedData. version), the information of a plurality of recipients receiving the encrypted data (EnvelopedData. recipientInfos) and the encrypted original data (EnvelopedData. encryptedContentInfo).

The information of every recipient includes the version of the data type and the identity of the recipient (recipientId), public key encryption algorithm used for encrypting the symmetric key (keyEncryptionAlgorithm) and the encrypted symmetric key.

```
RecipientInfo ::= SEQUENCE {
        version                     Version,
        recipientId                 CPKIdentifier,
        keyEncryptionAlgorithm      KeyEncryptionAlgorithmIdentifier,
        encryptedKey                EncryptedKey
}
```

Wherein RecipientInfo. keyEncryptionAlgorithm is the ECIES encryption algorithm used in CPK public key encryption and is defined in (SEC1v1.5) which is entirely quoted in the embodiment of the proposal, so it is not mentioned here again.

5) The data type of EncryptedContentInfo is used for describing the original data which are subject to symmetric encryption. The data type similarly uses a data type identifier (ContentType) to identify the type of the self-data. The contentEcnryptionAlgorithm refers to the encryption algorithm used for encrypting original data and relevant parameters (e. g. AES encryption algorithm and encryption parameters). The encrytedContent refers to the encrypted original data, and the type thereof is OPTIONAL; and if the encrypted data are optional, users can obtain encrypted data through other ways.

```
EncryptedContentInfo ::= SEQUENCE {
        ContentType                ContentType,
    ContentEncryptionAlgorithm ContentEncryptionAlgorithmIdentifier,
        EncryptedContent       [0] IMPLICIT EncryptedContent OPTIONAL
}
EncryptedContent ::= OCTET STRING
EncryptedKey ::= OCTET STRING
```

Step 0. After receiving the CPK encrypted signature electronic documents, the seal verification party uses the private key of the seal verification party to interpret the encrypted signature electronic document data to form the seal figures and electronic documents; and then every identity signed by the electronic seal and the public key matrix provided by the CPK security chip are used for calculating the public key of the identity, for directly working out a verification code and for judging whether the signature is true or false.

Step B1: one of the recipients of the electronic documents obtains the electronic document data through the Internet or other ways.

Step B2: The recipient checks whether the list of the recipient contain himself; if the recipient is contained, the RecipientInfo data of the corresponding recipient are extracted; if not, the process is ended.

Step B3: The recipient uses the CPK private key of the recipient to interpret the RecipientInfo data of the recipient of the electronic documents through the CPK security chip and adopts the CPK private key in the chip to decrypt the RecipientInfo data to obtain the symmetric encryption key in the electronic document data.

Step B4: The recipient uses the symmetric key obtained in the step B3 to interpret clear text from the encrypted signature data EncryptedContentInfo, that is, the signature data before being encrypted.

Step B5: The recipient sequentially reads the signature information data of the original data signed by every signer, and then every identity signed by the electronic seal and the public key matrix provided by the CPK security chip are used for calculating the public key of the identity, the CPK public key of the signer is used for verifying whether the signature is correct or not through the CPK signing algorithm; if the verification result is correct, the received data are confirmed to be correct.

One of the realizing ways of the embodiment in the proposal is as follows: the process for the decryption and seal verification of electronic documents by the seal verification system of the CPK electronic seal security authentication system adopts ISO ASN. 1 Markup Language realizing process which is in line with the signature process; however, the simple difference lies in that the signature process adopts the CPK system to sign and encrypt the electronic documents, while the seal verification system adopts the CPK system to decrypt and verify the electronic documents, and the processes are corresponding; those skilled in the field can easily realize the decryption and seal verification process of the seal verification system through the electronic document format adopted in the signature process, so the process is not mentioned in the embodiment of the proposal again.

A practical case of the embodiment of the proposal is as follows: a Word document is respectively signed by a president and a cashier, the identity of the president is "president seal, the electronic seal of a certain commercial bank in China," while the identity of the cashier is "cashier seal, the electronic seal of a certain commercial bank in China. " The document is respectively signed by the president and the cashier.

After receiving an electronic document with the CPK encrypted signature format, the recipient firstly uses a private key to interpret the recipient information data RecipientInfo in the electronic document, uses the data to decrypt the document and then verifies the identity-based digital signature in the document. If there are errors, the system can remind the users that the document has errors or has the possibility of counterfeiting in the form of a dialog box. If the signature is correct, the system can automatically generate a seal figure in a certain place of document browser through the identity in the signature, as two red seal figures shown in the attached drawing. One of the advantages of the electronic seal security authentication system lies in that the data of the binary digital signature which are difficult to be distinguished by users can be transformed into friendly visualization seal figures.

By directly transforming the identity into a graphic seal, the documents and bills with an electronic signature can achieve the visual effects similar to that of the documents with a paper signature.

Chapter 24

Water-wall for Intranet

24.1　Background

In Mid-1990s, with the introduction of Internet, firewall technology begun to enter into China from abroad. At that time, China proposed to construct a water-wall that can control access on the base of firewall, and developed the first-generation water-wall for the private network by Peking University in 1997 (Then we called it "secret-guarding gateway"). However, it encountered difficulties on binding of water-wall credential to files and on scaled authentication, thus it has been shelved. This issue has been the bottleneck and becomes the key issue on whether the water-wall can be put into application in practice. Until now, there has been no feasible desired product in the field.

Meanwhile, with development of network technology, network security has experienced a transition from passive defense of private network to a new era of cyber security based on active management of public network (e. g. : Internet). Comparing with private network, the public network is characterized by large scale, large number of user terminals up to tens of millions level or even hundreds of billions level, and widely spread across every corner of the world.

Generally, with more and more people use the public network, good and bad network resources gradually enter into the public network. Virus, Trojan, malicious codes like ROOTKIT and the like usually appear in the network resources used by the public users, or even interfere with the users. This is the main reason that prevents the users from normally using the network resources.

The basic security of the public network is the trustworthy of the network. When the terminal users use the network resources, the primary concern for the public use is how to authenticate the credibility of the network resources.

24.2　Working Principles

This solution intends to provide a water-wall based on CPK authentication technique to control the outgoing files and avoid the sensitive files to be stolen. The CPK-based water-wall device includes user applying unit, credential issuing unit and guarding unit.

The user applying unit is to prepare the documents or files to be sent. The user applying unit is inserted with ID-card and has all CPK functions. The preparation includes data encryption, digital signature to MAC. The prepared data sent to credential issuing unit.

The credential issuing unit is used to verify legality of the documents or files, and to determine whether to issue the water-wall credential. The issuing unit is inserted by ID-card and has all CPK functions.

The guarding unit is used to check legality of the water-wall credential, and controls documents to go out or to come in. It checks whether the user is a legal user and whether the user is responsible for the documents.

In order to achieve the objects of this solution, CPK-based water-wall methods include the following steps:

Step 1) the user applying unit prepares the documents, and sends the documents together with the application to the issuing unit.

Step 2) the issuing unit verifies legality of the user and the documents, and determines whether to issue the water-wall credential.

Step 3) water-wall checks legality of the water-wall credential, and controls documents in and out.

The above step 2) can include the following steps:

If the issuing unit verifies that the user and document are legal, then it will issue the water-wall credential. Otherwise, the application is rejected and the document is not allowed sent out.

The credential includes signature of the issuing unit to MAC of the document. In a simple way MAC may be a sample of the document because it mainly proves the unity of credential and document.

Water-wall checks only the credential, if it is legal then the document is allowed to be sent out. In receiving case water-wall checks the credential, if it is legal then the document is allowed to be received formally.

The functions of water wall above mentioned are realized by CPK authentication system. CPK is a self-assured public key system in which an EntityID is mapped into a point ENTITY on the elliptic curve defined by $E : y^2 = x^3 + ax + b \pmod{p}$ with the parameter $T = \{a, b, G, n, p\}$, if an integer "*entity*" satisfies $ENTITY = (entity)G$ then ENTITY is public key and *entity* is private key. Because $ENTITY = \sigma_1(EntityID)$ and σ_1 is open to public, the public key can be calculated by any one and the private key is provided by ID-card.

The user's ID-card used in water-wall is shown as Table 24.1.

Table 24. 1　The ID-card for Al:Ce

1	$Z1$: verification parameter	16 B	$E_{PWD}(R_1) = Z_1$
2	$Z2$: verification parameter	16 B	$E_{R1}(R_1) \oplus R_1 = Z_2$
3	Identity definition	25 B	AliceID
4	Role level : customer	16 B	5
5	Private key1	32 B	$E_{R1}(alice) = Y_1$
6	Role 5 key	48 B	$E_{R1}(key_1) = Y_2$
7	Name of issuing unit	25 B	KMC
8	Signature of issuing unit	48 B	$Sig_{kmc-1}(MAC)$

24. 3　The diagram of Intranet Water-wall

CPK-based water-wall techniques make the complicated scaled network-to-network trust problem easy. In the public network, setting water-wall between the internal network and public network, to achieve trust connection (trust access) in each internal network or between enterprise networks can realize authentication of any one water-wall to any other water-wall among tens of millions of internal networks via credentials, and constitute the infrastructure of trust connection (trust access). The CPK-based water-wall does not need to maintain the database having a large number of data. Because of using identity to generate the key pair, and making the public key open, the efficiency is very high during running, and the processing speed is very fast. Thus, it can be widely used in the network equipment such as the public network. In the construction of trust cyber world, it will constitute the basic technology that network technology influences the overall development, along with the trust code executing (code signing) and the feasible application.

Fig. 24. 1 is a flowchart of credential issuing procedure.

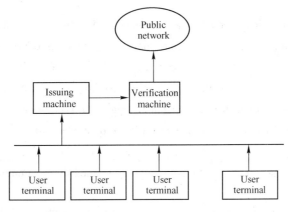

Fig. 24. 1　Flowchart of Credential Issuing When Leaving the Water-wall

Fig. 24. 2 is a flowchart of verificationprocedure.

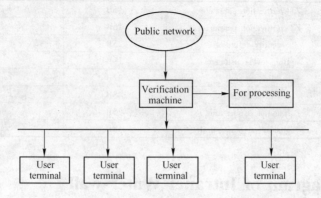

Fig. 24. 2   Flowchart of Verification When Entering the Water-wall

Water-wall is also as an inter-network connector, achieves network interconnection in the transmitting layer, and will be the most complicated network interconnection equipment. It only uses for network interconnection of two high levels having different protocols. The structure of water-wall is similar to that of a router. The difference is the interconnection layer. Water-wall can not only be used for interconnection of wide area network, but also be used for interconnection of local area network.

The CPK-based water-wall is composed of applying unit, issuing unit and guarding unit. The design of water-wall credential must be standardized. The credential must be mutually recognized in the network wide, and provides evidences such as integration of the document and the legality of the credential, and responsibility of the water-wall to the document.

Water-wall is only configured with the public matrix, with no private key, for checking the credential from other water-wall.

Water-wall adapts to various security policy, deals with various relationships, without affecting order of the current system. It applies to: the internal network with credential to the internal network with credential; the internal network with credential to the internal network or single machine without credential; the single machine to the water-wall with credential; in which the single machine is divided into having CPK authentication system and not having CPK authentication system.

Detailed description of CPK-based water-wall will be discussed below. The method includes the following steps.

Step 1: the applying User prepares the document, and sends the document and application to the credential Issuing-unit

The format of the application must be simple and self-assured, The content of the application includes the signs of the sender to the fileID and the MAC:

$$SIG_{user}(FileID) = sign1$$
$$SIG_{user}(MAC) = sign_2$$

Where SIG is signing function MAC is the sample integrity code of a specified location in the file. The location is decided by the length of the file. Assuming that the length of the file is n, the first location is n * (1/3), and taking a subgroup of codes; the second location of sample is n * (2/3), and taking another subgroup of codes, MAC is the Hashed value of this two subgroups (integrity code). MAC provides evidence for the integrity of the water-wall credential and the file.

It proves the legality of the owner User and to prove that the file is prepared and encrypted by user. The requesting message is:

Msg1 User→Issuing-unit: {userID, FileID, file, sign$_1$, sign$_2$}

Step 2: the Issuing-unit verifies the legality of sign$_1$:

$$SIG_{USER}^{-1}(FileID) = sign_1'$$
$$SIG_{USER}^{-1}(MAC) = sign_2'$$

If sign$_1$ = sign$_1'$, sign$_2$ = sign$_2'$ then issues the credential to the file or the request will be rejected. The core content of the water-wall credential is a sign to the FileID:

$$SIG_{issuing\text{-}unit}(FileID) = sign_3$$
$$SIG_{issuig\text{-}unit}(MAC) = sign_4$$

The Issuing-unit transfers the message to Verifying-unit.

Msg2 Issuing-unit→Verifying-unit: {Issuing-unitID, FileID, file, sign$_3$, sign$_4$}

Step 3: The Verifying-unit checks the legality of the credential, and controls the files in and out.

$$SIG_{ISSUING\text{-}UNIT}^{-1}(FileID) = sign_3'$$
$$SIG_{ISSUING\text{-}UNIT}^{-1}(MAC) = sign_4'$$

If sign$_3$ = sign$_3'$, sign$_4$ = sign$_4'$ then allows the file sent out. Because there is only one Issuing-unit in an intranet so the Verifying-unit is only needed to identify the signature whether signed by the Issuing-unit. All other signatures will be rejected.

Msg3 Verifying-unit→Internet: {issuing-unitID, FileID, file, sign$_3$, sign$_4$} or {FileID, file}. There are two sending ways: the document is sent with the credential and without the credential. Water-wall is only configured with the public key matrix, without the private key, to check the credential from any water-wall.

24. 4 Water-wall for Individual PC

The structure of individual water wall is shown in Fig. 24. 3.

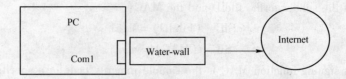

Fig. 24. 3   Structure of Individual Water-wall

The individual water wall is positioned the communication port of PC and take the roll of verifying unit. The credential is added by the user to the file. The form of credential is the user's sign to FileID and MAC:

$$SIG_{user}(FileID) = sign_1$$

$$SIG_{user}(MAC) = sign_2$$

Msg1 : User→Waterwall: $\{ FileID, file, sign_1, sign_2 \}$

The water-wall verifies the signs: $SIG_{USER}^{-1} FileID) = sign_1'$,

$$SIG_{USER}^{-1}(MAC) = sign_2'$$

If $sign_1 = sign_1'$, $sign_2 = sign_2'$ then the file to be sent out.

In individual water-wall the user is the only person to have the right to send files, so the task of water wall is to identify the signature whether signed by the user, all other signatures will be rejected. The sending form is:

Msg2 : Water-wall→internet: $\{ FileID, file, sign_1, sign_2 \}$ or $\{ FileID, file \}$

24. 5   Guarding Policy

Suppose all intranets have their credential issuing units then the issuing unit can stand for intranet. Therefore the connection among intranets may be taken as the connection among issuing units. There are different connection types in internet, and it will need different policy accords with the connection type.

1) Connection between intranet1 with waterwall and intranet2 with waterwall: when file passed the waterwall, it is allowed to send to intranet2 with the credential.

The credential of intranet1 :

$$SIG_{issuing\text{-}unit}(MAC) = sign_3$$

The Verifying- unit2 of intranet2 checks:

$$SIG_{ISSUING\text{-}UNIT}^{-1}(MAC) = sign_3'$$

If $sign_3 = sign_3'$ then waterwall2 confiscates the credential and allows the file to enter into intranet2.

2）Connection between intranet1 with water-wall and intranet2 without water wall：When file is passing waterwall1，it is allowed to send to intranet2 and at the same time confiscates the credential.

3）An intranet1 with water-wall is connected with any intranet，if it has a legal credential，it can normally enter the intranet；if it does not have a legal credential；it will be stored in a spare server for further processing.

Chapter 25

Digital Right Authentication

25. 1 Technical Background

This program deals with the digital rights protection method on the CPK-based public key system.

With the development of IPTV, the problem of digital rights authentication and protection has been increasingly involved in the playing of digital audio and video products. The key issue is how to protect the ownership of digital rights. The authentication methods in the current discussion of various programs are very complex, almost losing feasibility.

For example, the digital right authentication and protection system implemented by PKI can only provide authenticating function through data authentication but it cannot provide protection through data encryption.

Another example is digital watermark technology, and it is hard to provide an accepted authentication method for it.

In addition, in the situation that the application of digital rights have not reach ultra-large-scale, it seems that a variety of technical means is likely to be able to solve the protection of digital rights, but generally do not have adaptability for ultra-large-scale protection. Because of its failure to solve the large-scale management and identity authentication, some existing technologies can only solve the protection of rights without solution to the authentication of rights and some can only solve the authentication of rights but without solution to protection.

25. 2 Main Technologies

CPK-based digital rights authentication and protection methods, which cannot only solve large-scale management but also can easily authenticate the digital rights through identity authentication and protect data through encryption.

The system is composed of registrant, manufacturer, enterprise and client and All functions above mentioned are realized by CPK authentication system. CPK is of self-assured public key that the public key is derived from identity. An EntityID can be mapped into a point ENTITY on the elliptic curve $E: y^2 = x^3 + ax + b \pmod{p}$ defined by the parameter $T = \{a, b, G, n, p\}$, if there is an integer *entity* satisfies ENTITY = (*entity*)G, then ENTITY is the public key and *entity* is the private key. Because ENTITY = σ_1(EntityID) and σ_1 is open to public, the public key can be calculated by any one from the EntityID and the private key is provided by ID-card. Take manufacturer's ID-card for example. The ID-card is shown as Table 25.1.

Table 25.1　ID-card for manufacturer

1	Z1: verification parameter	16B	$E_{PWD}(R_1) = Z_1$
2	Z2: verification parameter	16B	$E_{R1}(R_1) \oplus R_1 = Z_2$
3	Identity definition	25B	ManufacturerID
4	Role level: customer	16B	5
5	Private key1	32B	$E_{R1}(manufacturer) = Y_1$
6	Role 5 key	48B	$E_{R1}(key_1) = Y_2$
7	Name of issuing unit	25B	KMC
8	Signature of issuing unit	48B	$Sig_{kmc-1}(MAC)$

The working process includes:

1) Manufacturer applies for the digital right to the registrant.

2) Enterprise applies for the operation right to manufacturer.

3) Client applies for the usage right to enterprise.

The beneficial effects of this program are: as the CPK technology is large-scale key management technology, and it is also identity-based key distribution technology (e. g.: identity authentication and system), therefore, the CPK-based digital rights protection and authentication method, can easily realize the non-gratuitous use of the rights in the ultra-large-scale fee system and its authentication of the ownership in the rights disputes, and its method is simple and convenient.

25.3　Manufacturer's Digital Right

The manufacturer applies for the right to registrant.

The manufacturer requests for the connection: signs to time:

$$SIG_{manufacturer}(time) = sign_1$$

Manufacturer sends time and $sign_1$ to the registrant:

Msg1   Manufacturer→Registrant: $\{ManufacturerID, time, sign_1\}$

The Registrant checks the sign:

$$SIG_{MANUFACTURER}^{-1}(time) = sign_1'$$

If $sign_1 = sign_1'$ then it proves the authenticity of the connection and sender.

Registrant sends a random number r as challenge and signs to $(time-1)$:

$$SIG_{registrant}(time-1) = sign_2$$

Registrant sends $sign_2$ to Manufacturer

Msg2   Registrant→Manufacturer: $\{r, sign_2\}$

Manufacturer checks the sign:

$$SIG_{REGISTRANT}^{-1}(time-1) = sign_2'$$

If $sign_2 = sign_2'$ then the Manufacturer believes the authentity of Registran and enters into data transmission procedure. first signs to r in response to the challenge signs to time + 1 and data. The data includes ProductID, product, MAC, where ProductID is the name of product and MAC is the integrity authentication code.

$$SIG_{manufacturer}(r) = sign_3$$
$$SIG_{manufacturer}(time+1) = sign_4$$
$$SIG_{manufacturer}(ProductID) = sign_5$$
$$SIG_{manufacturer}(MAC) = sign_6$$

Msg3   Manufacturer→Registrant: $\{data, sign_3, sign_4, sign_5, sign_6\}$

The Registrant checks the signs:

$$SIG_{MANUFACTURER}^{-1}(r) = sign_3'$$
$$SIG_{MANUFACTURER}^{-1}(time+1) = sign_4'$$
$$SIG_{MANUFACTURER}^{-1}(ProductID) = sign_5$$
$$SIG_{MANUFACTURER}^{-1}(MAC) = sign_6'$$

If $sign_3 = sign_3'$ then the Registrant believes the authenticity of Manufacturer, if $sign_4 = sign_4'$ then the Registrant registrates the IPR of the product, otherwise reject the connection and IPR request. The credential of IPR is the sign to time + 1, ProductID and MAC.

$$SIG_{registrant}(time+1) = sign_7$$
$$SIG_{registrant}(ProductID) = sign_8$$
$$SIG_{registrant}(MAC) = sign_9$$

Msg4   Registrant→Manufacturer: $\{product, sign_7, sign_8, sign_9\}$

So far manufacturer obtained the credential of IPR.

If it is needed to encrypt the product in transmission the Manufacturer randomly defines a data encrypting key and encrypts the product: E_{key} (product) = coded-data, where E is encrypting function with symmetric key. Manufacturer encrypts the key with receiver's public key:

$$ENC_{REGISTRANT} (key) = coded\text{-}key$$

Where ENC is encryption function with asymmetric key. The coded-data and coded-key is sent to registrant The Registrant decrypts the coded-key with his private key:

$$DEC_{registrant} (coded\text{-}key) = key$$

Decrypts the product with the key:

$$D_{key} (coded\text{-}data) = product$$

25.4　Enterprise's Right of Operation

The Enterprise requests for the connection: the equation is a sign to time:

$$SIG_{enterprise} (time) = sign_1$$

Enterprise sends time and $sign_1$ to the Manufacturer:

Msg1　Enterprise→Manufacturer: { EnterpriseID, time, $sign_1$ }

The Manufacturer checks the sign:

$$SIG_{ENTERPRISE}^{-1} (time) = sign_1'$$

If $sign_1 = sign_1'$ then it proves the authenticity of the connection and sender. The Manufacturer signs a random number r and a sign to (time − 1):

$$SIG_{manufacturer} (r, time - 1) = sign_2.$$

Msg2　Manufacturer→Enterprise: { r, $sign_2$ }

Enterprise checks the sign:

$$SIG_{MANUFACTURER}^{-1} (time - 1) = sign_2'$$

If $sign_2 = sign_2'$ then Enterprise believes the authentity of Manufacturer and enters into data transmission procedure. First Enterprise sign to r in response to the challenge of manufacturer. The request for product is composed of the signs to (time + 1) and productID:

$$SIG_{enterprise} (r) = sign_3$$
$$SIG_{enterprise} (time + 1) = sign_4,$$
$$SIG_{enterprise} (ProductID) = sign_5:$$

Msg3　Enterprise→Manufacturer: { $sign_3$, $sign_4$, $sign_5$ }

The Manufacturer checks the signs:

$$SIG_{ENTERPRISE}^{-1} (r) = sign_3'$$
$$SIG_{ENTERPRISE}^{-1} (time + 1) = sign_4'$$
$$SIG_{ENTERPRISE}^{-1} (ProductID) = sign_5'$$

If $sign_3 = sign_3'$ then the Manufacturer believes the authenticity of the Enterprise, and if $sign_4 = sign_4'$ then accepts the request of product, and sends signed data to Enterprise, the data is comprised of productID, product, MAC:

$$SIG_{manufacturer}(\text{time} + 1) = sign_6$$
$$SIG_{manufacturer}(\text{ProductID}) = sign_7$$
$$SIG_{manufacturer}(\text{MAC}) = sign_8$$

Msg4   Manufacturer→Enterprise: $\{\text{data}, sign_6, sign_7, sign_8\}$

If it is needed to encrypt the product in transmission the Manufacturer randomly defines a data encrypting key and encrypts the product:

$$E_{key}(\text{product}) = \text{coded-data}$$

Where E is encrypting function with symmetric key. Manufacturer encrypts the key with receiver's public key:

$$ENC_{ENTERPRISE}(\text{key}) = \text{coded-key}$$

Where ENC is encryption function with asymmetric key. The coded-data and coded-key is sent to Enterprise and the Enterprise decrypts the coded-key with his private key:

$$DEC_{enterprise}(\text{coded-key}) = \text{key}$$

Decrypts the product with the key:

$$D_{key}(\text{coded-data}) = \text{product}$$

25.5   Client's Right of Usage

The Client sends a request message to Enterprise for the connection: the request is a sign to time:

$$SIG_{client}(\text{time}) = sign_1$$

The Client sends time and $sign_1$ to the Enterprise:

Msg1   Client→Enterprise: $\{\text{ClientID}, \text{time}, sign_1\}$

The Enterprise checks the sign:

$$SIG_{CLIENT}^{-1}(\text{time}) = sign_1'$$

If $sign_1 = sign_1'$ then it proves the authenticity of the Client. The Enterprise sends a random number r and a sign to $(\text{time} - 1)$:

$$SIG_{enterprise}(\text{time} - 1) = sign_2$$

Msg2   Enterprise→Client: $\{r, sign_2\}$

Client checks the sign:

$$SIG_{ENTERPRISE}^{-1}(\text{time} - 1) = sign_2'$$

If $sign_2 = sign_2'$ then it proves the authenticity of the Enterprise and signs to r in response to the challenge. The request for product is composed of the signs to $(time + 1)$ and productID:

$$SIG_{client}(r) = sign_3$$
$$SIG_{client}(time + 1) = sign_4$$
$$SIG_{client}(ProductID) = sign_5$$

Msg3   Client→Enterprise: $\{sign_3, sign_4, sign_5\}$

The Enterprise checks the signs:

$$SIG_{ENTERPRISE}^{-1}(r) = sign_3'$$
$$SIG_{ENTERPRISE}^{-1}(time + 1) = sign_4'$$
$$SIG_{ENTERPRISE}^{-1}(ProductID) = sign_5'$$

If $sign_3 = sign_3'$ then the Enterprise believes the authenticity of the Client, if $sign_4 = sign_4'$ then Enterprise accepts the request and sends signed data to Client:

$$SIG_{enterprise}(time + 1) = sign_6$$
$$SIG_{enterprise}(ProductID) = sign_7$$
$$SIG_{enterprise}(MAC) = sign_8$$

Msg4   Enterprise→Client: $\{data, sign_6, sign_7, sign_8\}$

If it is needed to encrypt the product in transmission the Manufacturer randomly defines a data encrypting key and encrypts the product:

$$E_{key}(product) = coded\text{-}data$$

Where E is encryption function with symmetric key. Enterprise encrypts the key with receiver's public key:

$$ENC_{CLIENT}(key) = coded\text{-}key$$

Where ENC is encryption function with asymmetric key and CLIENT is the public key of the receiver. The coded-data and coded-key is sent to Client and the Client decrypts the coded-key with his private key:

$$DEC_{client}(coded\text{-}key) = key$$

Decrypts the product with the key:

$$D_{key}(coded\text{-}data) = product$$

So far the Manufacturer has Registrant's credential and Enterprise has Manufacturer's and Client has Enterprise's respectively.

Msg4   Registrat→Manufacurer: $\{data, sign_7, sign_8, sign_9\}$

Mas4   Manufacturer→Enterprise: $\{data, sign_6, sign_7, sign_8\}$

Mas4   Enterprise→Client: $\{data, sign_6, sign_7, sign_8\}$

Postscript

New Trend of Information Security

Evolved from the dedicated military network, information security has experienced two decades of development, and has made remarkable achievements. However, the problems existing in the information security strategy, technology route and management system also have been exposed. At present, information security is undergoing major changes. At this critical moment, every country is summing up experience, learning lessons and determining the efforts direction for the next step. This is embodied in the report *Cyber Security—a Crises of Prioritization* by President's Information Technology Advisory Committee (PITAC) in 2005.

Here the cyber space "Describes the world of connected computers and the society that gathers around them. Commonly known as the Internet". By this token, Internet is no longer a simple information network, but a world and a society. Only by really understanding the meaning of "cyber security", can we establish the correct concept of security.

1. History Review

Information security has gone through three important development stages: first, communications confidentiality in 1980s; second, network security in 1990s; third, cyber security in the 21st century. Every stage has its specific characteristic and corresponding technology route and strategy.

Private network stage: as private network (computer network) is close network, therefore the principal strategy is grading and mandatory protection. The characteristic of computer network is to get through (open) every terminal through nodes, realizing the exchange between the computer terminals for the first time. The main policy of this period is represented by the Orange Book by U. S. Department of Defense, in which the personnel is classified into authorization level in the exchange network, data classified into confidential level, and the traditional single-level management mode developed into a new type of multi-level control management mode. In late 1980s, this advanced management mode has been first implemented and applied in the military network of our country.

Internet stage: as Internet is open network, therefore, it gets through (open) the relation between networks, and gets through the relation between the users, realizing the personalized communication from user to user for the first time. The main policy of this period is represented by American Presidential Proclamation PDD63, which proposes the security awareness mainly based on vulnerability analysis and relying on all citizens, and implements assurance self-protection strategy, known as "deep-level defense strategy". Clinton's assurance strategy broke past (governmental) mandatory strategy and proposed independent strategy to adapt the interconnection of the individual communication system. This is a historic progress in the concept. But U. S. Department of Defense has published a book named *Information Self-protection Technology Framework*, which proposes the idea of "border protection" and "information enclave", and pulls open Internet back to close private network, seriously departing from the central idea of assurance (self-confidence) of Presidential Proclamation. We have to point out that this retrogressive idea of U. S. Department of Defense has brought a negative impact on our country.

Public network stage: information system is no longer a simple information system or a network system, but it is combined with other surrounding society to form new space, which is cyber space. It is proposed in the report *Cyber Security—a crisis of Prioritizations* by President's Information Technology Advisory Committee (PITAC) in 2005 that the main task of cyber security is "building the trusting system in the dangerous world" to provide trust services for the public. The space of information security has changed, and the main goal to be achieved has changed, therefore, 2005 marks a milestone of the transition from information security period to cyber security period.

2. Information Security

The definition of "information security" made by PITAC in its report *Cyber Security—A Crisis of Prioritization* is: "Information security refers to measures taken to protect or preserve information on a network as well as the network itself. " The report denied the defense strategy of information security mainly based on vulnerability analysis in Clinton's Presidential Direct PDD63 and some projects to implement this defense strategy. Denial is the necessity of the development of history. History is always carried on by correcting mistakes.

The PITAC report has proposed the conclusive views on information security and some significant opinions, which is worth referring and studying, for example:

1) Plugging the loopholes and patching is not the solution to information security.

2) The classification of external network and the internal network can only make the complex things more complex and will not help solve the problem.

3) The security classification of the military system is not applicable to the public network.

4) The basic idea of "border protection" and "information enclave" in the Department of Defense IATF (Information Assurance Technology Framework) departs from the self-assurance idea of the Presidential Direct.

5) The principle implemented by information security is "well-intentioned", while the principle implemented by cyber security is "mutual suspicion".

6) The trusting system is much complicated, there is no "silver bullet". silver bullet refers to a good solution. According to our study, the "silver bullet" exists, therefore, the accurate expression should be "we haven't found out 'silver bullet' yet".

3. Cyber Security

The PITAC report has proposed the new development trend in the future. The American research findings coincide with those of ours, but our understanding is more refined and more practical. However, the views of the United States are official, but those of our country stay in the civil awareness.

1) Main task: to build a trusting system, set up trusting network order, and provide trusting services for the public, from passive defense-oriented security to initiative management-oriented security. For this reason, PITAC has picked out ten research projects for priority development from hundreds of projects, in which the authentication technology is the first development project. The key of network order is to build authentication system, as in the physical world, the Ministry of Public Security presenting the "ID card" to every person, which provides a basis for the establishment of social order.

2) Main topic: scale authentication technology is the primary topic, from the topic based on the vulnerability analysis to the topic based on authenticity proof. The objective proposed by PITAC is to solve billions of authentications. The main technology is the digital signature and key exchange. The most prominent question in digital signature is to construct identity-based "short-signature", while the most problem in key exchange is the directness of encryption.

3) Main principle: the principle will be followed by the cyber security is "mutual suspicion", while the principle has been followed by information security is "good will". Cyber security will be based on identity authentication and trust logic, while information security theory has been based on object-based "belief logic".

4) Main application: in the cyber security age, the main application is not confined to the information system itself, but includes all the space interconnected with it. In addition to the transaction, it also includes communication protocol (preventing illegal receiving), software engineering (ensuring the code authentication of the computing environment), logistic network, holistic solution, network management and other fields relating to key national infrastructures, not only confined to the user level authentication, but also "any-to-any authentication", which may be called horizontal "A to A" authentication.

4. Technical Approach

To build a trusting system is the major change in the history. How to change from information security of passive defense to cyber security of initiative management is a major mission entrusted by history. Now the combat situation on the internet has changed, and the network has no national boundaries. The common "enemy" of all users is the malicious software, just as "terrorists" all over the world are the common enemies of the people.

In building a trusting system, our country has made, or the formed new technology, new theory, and new logic, and occupied a very advantageous position in the new round of international competition of cyber security, which is an excellent opportunity endowed with us by the history.

New technology: the development of authentication system brings about new technologies adapting to it. If the United States has solved the technology, then the scale authentication technology would not be proposed as the primary task in the future development. The system based on the authentication of the third parity does not meet the timeliness of authentication. Now a lot of identity-based public key systems are proposed, that is a new arithmetic which could prove the authenticity of it by itself. The CPK system of our country does not require the authentication of the third party and at the same time does not need the support of online databases, which can meet scale and timeliness property of authentication. After 10 years' improvement, currently CPK technology has been able to achieve the privacy protection mechanism of signature key that can be defined by the individual, which makes CPK technology more sophisticated, taking a big step in becoming the national and international standards.

New theory: the authentication technologies include subject authentication, object authentication, and behavior authentication, and the most core technology is the identity authentication, which has been a worldwide problem. In the past, as there was no authentication technology, and the authenticity of the subject can not be proved, only the "well-intentioned" principle can be used. Now, as the basic technology of the subject authentication, the theory of "identity authentication" is proposed. Identity authentication theory can authenticate the authenticity of subject prior to the incident, which makes the topic that cannot be solved before become easier to solve. Therefore, identity authentication technology is in fact the "silver bullet" that all over the world struggling to find. For example: illegal receiving in communication, you can rely on identity authentication to authenticate the authenticity of the transmitter before the data communication happens.

New logic: with identity authentication technology, you can build "trust logic". The past logic is the logic to prove the authenticity of the object, that is, to prove its authenticity on the condition that the subject is trusting, which is called "belief logic". Taking trust computing as an example, it is required to prove the authenticity of the subject, object and behavior separately. For example, if the subject is true, it can be loaded. After loading, prove the authenticity of the data, that is, to judge whether the loading is right. If it is right, then the authentication of behavior authenticity can be conducted, that is, whether the implementation is right. This "prior" authentication is more evident in the military confrontation and in the transaction process, that is, first to identify the "friend and enemy" or "true and false" before the confrontation or the transaction.

The establishment of trust logic mainly relies on the establishment of evidence-showing system. With evidence-showing system, the authenticity can be proved very quickly. The trust system a security system set up on the basis of authentication technology, so to speak. In the past, the disadvantage of information security lies in little attention to the building of the evidence-showing system. Trying to judge the authenticity with no evidence provided will make the things complicated in the end. In real life, our country has successful experience in building evidence showing, that is, every citizen has the ID card issued by the Ministry of Public Security, which provides convenience for travel, hotel, work and other things. The situation on the network is similar to that in the real society. The reason why the network is disordered is that this authentication system has not been set up yet. The identity authentication of CPK system has provided technical support for building this authentication system.

This shows that cyber security or trusting system is the information security based on the authentication system. CPK system, identity authentication and trust logic has set a good technical and theoretical foundation for the code authentication of software, the trust receiving of communication, trusting transaction on the internet and the building of trusting network order, and explored wider innovative fields. For example: the authentication of IPv4, IPv6, IPv9, wireless broadband mobile networks, sensor networks, mobile phone, ad hoc, cloud computing and other complex systems, can be solved by the advanced technology of horizontal (non-layering) management under a trust root.

Appendices

Appendix A

Cryptography applied in information security and cyber security needs innovation amid denials

Walk Out of Mysterious "Black Chamber"

—Interview with Professor Nan Xianghao, expert on Cryptography and information security

Reporter of *China Informationization*　　*Wei Jie*

March, 2006

As a common technology, cryptography has been extensively applied in information security field. With changing of the time, cryptography has been developed from mysteriousness to public. How to view cryptography under development? The dialogue between the reporter and Professor NAN allows us to understand the importance of cryptography in the information security.

Reporter:When talking about cryptology, people feel that it is mysterious and intangible; while cryptography especially is a profound science. Could you please tell us how cryptography has been developed?

Professor Nan:The mysteriousness of cryptology is a classical view on times of *Black Chamber*, i. e. , using confidential means to keep secrets. However, the view of the modern cryptography is to use open means to keep secrets.

"All the secrets lie on keys", cipher algorithm is not afraid to be open, especially nowadays that passwords has been prevailed among individuals. Cryptography has become an open science, a common sense, and shall not have any mysteriousness. Especially for cryptology applied in authentication logic, it not only can be open, but also has to be open, due to credibility of cryptology must be accepted by the public. For example, US Advance Encryption Standard AES was openly bid worldwide. Upon open appraisal, finally the Belgium scheme was chosen among 15 schemes.

From general aspect of view, cryptology can include cryptography and cryptanalysis. However, typically cryptology mainly refers to cryptography and key management. Cryptography is divided into classic, traditional and modern ones. The function of classic and traditional cryptography only concerns data encryption, wherein the encryption process and communication process are independent from each other. In the middle of last century, the appearance of electronic cipher machine marks the birth of communication security. Encryption and communication processes are taken place at the same time and the encryption process and communication process must be completed together. It means data encryption is changed into communication encryption.

The main task of encryption has been the main method to protect data from compromising, in another words the encryption function meets the new need of sending secrete data in the public network, because encryption can change secret data into public data, i. e. , wherein the cipher text can be open and it can be openly sent and stored. With the arrival of computer era, the comm-sec enters into info-sec. In the information system the main function of encryption still is data protection. However, the function of encryption expands to realize user classification, network division and entity authentication to prevent illegal access, etc.

Cipher is a kind of conversion from plaintext to cipher text. Cryptography is composed of encryption algorithm and key variables. The algorithm is a fixed factor, while key variables are active factors. The two just like rifle and bullets, in which algorithm is the rifle, and key variables are the bullets. Only when the bullets have been loaded, they have power. Algorithm is composed of logic structure, which is mainly used for encryption conversion to the data. In the era of information security the data was classified, thus the algorithm has typical confidentiality or specificity.

The 1970s is the era for cryptography development, and block cipher and public key were appeared for the first time. Block cipher makes cryptography more theoretical, and can allow the algorithm to be public. Thus, cryptology not only can be used in encryption of communication data and storage data, but also can be used in logic authentication. Accordingly, the application scope of cryptology has been greatly expanded, and cipher algorithm has become public.

Reporter: Only applying in practice can reflect its values. The greater value of cryptography lies on its application. From what I understand, e-signature, e-envelop and security authentication are all related to cryptology. I would like to know which aspects can we see the actual application of cryptology in information security?

Professor Nan: Various applications of cryptology are achieved by way of key changes. Thus, various applications in information security are related to key variables. The appearance of public key algorithm announced the foundation of a new cryptography different from traditional one. The function of the key is to achieve key exchange and digital signature while key exchange provides encryption and decryption. As a logic variable, the key can defines different domains, thus, the US military believes that key classification is the most economic and effective logic way to achieve network separation. The digital signature provides non-deniable evidence after event, which is no relation to the data grade, and thus having its public property. With the development of digital signature technology, hash function based on block cipher appeared, to provide compressed data for digital signature.

In general, cipher algorithm is used in data encryption; key algorithm is used in key exchange, digital signature and hash function is used in integrity code.

You are right, the value of cryptography lies on application. Cryptography is not a mathematical game, nor a vase. No matter how good the ciphers are, they are just a bunch of useless codes if not putting into use. In the Europe Cryptography Conference held in Italy in 1986, one expert said that ideal ciphers are not suitable for actual use, and the ciphers in use all have deficiencies, because ciphering unit is only a component of the system in use, rather than an isolated and independent part.

In the information security era, various private networks emphasize on confidentiality, and the main mission is to keep confidential. On the one hand, cipher mainly serves for data encryption, used in private network security field, such as cipher machine, encryption router, VPN encryption tunnel, and confidential gateway. On the other hand, cipher serves for digital signature, used in authentication systems in various private networks. In the era of cyber security, constructing a trust cyber world is the main purpose. Authentication service is the key point of constructing a pubic network. The ciphers can provide authenticity verification for trust computing, trust connecting and trust transaction.

With the development of anti-counterfeiting devices, ciphers will provide logic functions of anti-forgery, anti-counterfeiting verification for physical anti-counterfeiting systems.

Reporter: Currently, are there any gaps between theoretical studies and practice? If so, what aspects?

Professor Nan: During the last 50 years, cryptography broke through constrain of "Black Chamber" era, and has obtained great progress from theory to practice. However, development is not balanced, and big gaps still exist. Some countries and regions still remain in communication security era, while some other countries are in the transition from information security to cyber security. Theoretically, cipher can not only serve for pubic, but also serve for group interest, i. e. , with open and close requirements coexisting. Thus, different nations and regions have different opinion on ciphers, and accordingly will have different policies and strategies. For instance, in Germany and Switzerland, cipher products are viewed as common communication products, with no special limitation. In US, ciphers are classified into official ciphers and non-governmental ciphers, wherein the official ciphers are under top-secret control, and the non-governmental ciphers are loosely controlled but its exports are under control. In eastern Asia such as China, Japan, and South Korea, ciphers are still considered as sensitive field.

It is common in various countries that policies lag behind actual development. The U. S. Congress once criticized Department of Defense that the cipher policy still remained in computer security, and fell behind the actual needs of Internet development. Similarly, in China, the public needs for ciphers are already there for long time, but lacking of relevant policies. Especially some of the current rules and policies constrain the growth and development of independent innovation.

Reporter: How is the research situation of domestic cryptography? And how are the development perspectives?

Professor Nan: From global point of view, I agree with the conclusion made by an overseas scholar that the technology of traditional cipher with symmetric key is close to "saturate", because the security and complexity can be measured by modern cryptanalysis. In the new era information security based on passive defense is changing into cyber security based on active management. The closed private network is changing into open public network, so the key issue must deal with ultra-large scale key management. The scale is not counted by ten thousands or millions, but trillions. The currently popular systems PKI and IBE used in overseas cannot really settle this issue. Thus, last April, US raised the issue of authentication on the scale of billions as the priority mission in the emergency report submitted by PITAC(President Information Technology Advisory Committee).

We can say that we made breakthrough progress in analysis and explanation on hash function collision, CPK key algorithm, and trust authentication theory. These are our strong points and advantages in the world, and provide technical basis for constructing a trust network and credible society. Further, works such as CPK embedded chips that can manage ultra-large scale keys, CPK-based ID-card and electronic anti-forgery tags are under way.

Technology is developing, and new things are emerging constantly. This is the objective rule of social development. Opportunity always exists. The central government established development strategy of independent innovation, which is a great chance for us. However, whether we can grasp the opportunity depends on our understanding, concept and specific policy. Lagging behind the era to develop understanding, concept and policy is an obstacle to the development strategy of independent innovation. With the progress of technology, the connotation of information security and cryptology is under huge change. In the history of development of information security and cryptology, we have several glorious times. In the new era, we shall be "cautiously optimistic" on whether we can create new brilliant.

Reporter: As an expert on cryptography, you have studied in cryptography field for many years. Would you please tell us some of your own experience?

Professor Nan: From the design of the 1st generation cipher machine, computer network security and internet water-wall to research of cyber world trust authentication system, I have experienced several transitions. We can say that every transition is a generation process of new things, which surely brings collision of new and old things. Such collision is not mere collision of technology, it is also collision of understanding and concept, and sometimes relates to policy. Thus, we need innovation, and first of all we shall have the courage to say "no", dare to break through all kinds of resistance. I think this is the basic conscience and nature for a scientist. Without denial, there will be no innovation, no development. This is conspicuous. However, it is not easy to say "no". At the end, I would like to share a logion with all, "The meaning of life is not to do thing that you like to do, but to do things that you have to do".

China Informatization, March, 2006,

(This article was translated by Wang Feng)

Appendix B

Information security typically has the following characteristics: On the one hand, information security has a very high updating frequency. On the other hand, under current situation, the technology innovation trend faces a lot of confusion, especially the new technology and theory are enclosed by traditional forces, and are hard to find. Thus, challenging such revolutionary technology becomes a significant subject faced by information security.

Identity Authentication Opening a New Land for Information Security

—walking into Professor Nan's CPK world

Reporter of *Information and Communication Security*   Li Xue

September, 2006

With the development of network and application, the connotation and extension of ever-changing information security technology has also experienced great changes. Developing from closed computer network to open internet network, from simple data communication to online trading, makes information security technology as a whole to gradually develop from data security, network security to application security, and enters into a new stage, which is called cyber security in the field.

Such changes are fast, and the rapid changes make information security technology to update quickly. However, when viewing the trend of recent information security technology, people rarely see the emergence of revolutionary breakthrough technology. This is an issue that deserves consideration and attention.

Thus, when professor Nan proposed the concept of CPK(combined public key system), a lot of people did not truly recognize its values. Even for some professionals, they once indicated that professor Nan shall talk about CPK. What is CPK? What can CPK bring to information security? Whether CPK can bring revolutionary changes?

Recently, China Information Industry Trade Association(CIITA) Information Security Sub-Committee recommended to relevant state authorities in its innovation report, to establish CPK authentication engineering center and CPK authentication technology key laboratory. It can be seen that the theory has been widely recognized in the field.

Sitting with professor Nan face to face, and listening to his introduction of CPK, I felt that I am in a sea of identity authentication applications and was very encouraged.

"Information security theory and technology change so fast, you will fall behind the times if not updating in a timely basis. What CPK makes us proud is, we have the technology" The well-known cryptography expert Professor Nan Xianghao started our conversation in this way.

Authentication system resolving communication between two spaces

Safety practice tells us that the main safety requirement of information world is to ensure computing trust, connection trust and transaction trust. The ultimate purpose is to introduce the management means and methods in the real world such as " ID card" , " Residence Booklet" , " License plate" , " Household Registration System" , " Traffic Rules" into information space, to establish effective management that communicates two spaces and keep them well ordered. This will be a revolution driven by new technology; and only the government can lead this revolution. The basic weapon used is the new generation information security technology, with the authentication technology as the core. In the research of the new generation information security technology, there is a key technology, i. e. , authentication technology, especially identity authentication.

No matter whether it is the trust computing platform, trust accessed tag, agent event or transaction event, all need authentication technology. In the authentication system of information world, it typically uses logical parameters as the main basis of authentication. Currently there are the following three authentication technologies in the world:

1. authentication system realized by PKI-based(public key infrastructure) technology. Running of PKI relies on two basic parts, hierarchical CA mechanism and online certificate library. Because the system relies on database to run online, its running efficiency is relatively low, and the processing capability is limited. According to statistics, the processing capability of one certificate library does not exceed 1000.

2. Authentication system based on IBE algorithm(Identity Based Encryption). In 2001, Don Boneh and Matthew Franklin proposed identity-based IBE algorithm. Even though it canceled CA certificate that need to be proved by a third party, the key exchange still needs support from online key server. Even so, currently it still attracts a lot of attention, and tends to replace PKI.

3. Authentication system base on CPK algorithm (Combined Public Key). CPK system was proposed in 1999, and published in 2003. It is also an identity-based public key algorithm. Howev-

er, it does not need third party certification. In addition, it only needs to keep a few pubic parameters and does not need to keep users' data, so that it does not need support from online database. Thus, its running efficiency and processing capability is high, and accordingly largely expanding its application scope.

Comparing CPK with PKI, IBE, there are some similarities, but the technical routes are different. PKI is a system of indirect proof through a third party, while IBE and CPK are systems of direct proof by using identity as the public key. IBE is only used in key exchange while CPK can be used both signature and key exchange. Currently, only CPK can satisfy the needs of scalability of authentication, directness of proof and simplicity of management.

This is a brief summary of CPK from theoretically aspect of view.

Identity authentication is the core of information security

Professor Nan believes that, fundamentally CPK resolved the core issue of information security-identity authentication. Because of different translation, identity is apt to be considered as user in China. .

The traditional information security is in a much narrower level; while cyber security is a much broader field for information security. From technology aspect of view, the core technology of cyber security is: identity authentication.

Any entity (including object) has its identity. For example, each file has its own name, person has his/her name, user has username, equipment has its name (or serial number), software (process or procedure) has its name. The same user uses the e-mail address as his identity in e-mail communication, uses the cell phone number as his identity when calling, and uses the bank account number as his identity when depositing and withdrawing money, etc.

Professor Nan further explains: "Identity authentication is a technology that authenticates identity. The first issue that identity authentication encounters is scalability. The lowest requirement for authentication scale, taking the domestic cell phone for example, is to satisfy authentication of 10^{11} different phone number identities; for bank accounts, to satisfy authentication of 10^{22} different account numbers. Secondly, the issue is simplicity of verification. Identity authentication is composed of "prover" and "verifier". It is always easy to prove but difficult to verify. Thus, in an identity authentication system, it is not important whether it is simple to issue "certificate". It is more important whether it is simple to verify the "certificate". Taking an anti-forgery system for example, the seller provides evidence by way of pasting anti-forgery labels, which is easy to do. It is also very easy for PKI system to issue certificate, but how to verify its authenticity. If the verification procedure is very complicated, and can only use the way of phone enquiry or accessing database, instead of verifying on-the-spot, such authentication system is not the ideal system that we pursue. Finally, the issue is effectiveness of management. That is, the authentication activities must be under the effective supervision, management and control. "

The CPK system proposed by professor Nan satisfies all three requirements, that is, it includes very large scale, very simple operation and very effective management. These are the true value and soul of CPK technology.

Authentication technology is important because it can solve the authenticity issue, so as to totally change the preconditions to realize network security. In addition, the basis of authentication technology is key algorithm, which raises the attack technology threshold from ordinary hacker to professional code decryption, so that the security level increases dramatically. Thus, in the report "*Cyber Security-Crisis of Priority*" submitted to President Bush by PITAC, it lists the authentication technology, especially the authentication technology with scalability (ten of billions) as the No. 1 of 10 projects, which indicates that US realizes the importance of authentication technology, and that the authentication technology is not really solved. Professor Nan says: "This report reflects actuality of US information security. The ten projects were proposed after careful consideration, and all the ten projects are key issues of constructing trust system. However, the report has not seen through the inner relationship among the ten projects, and has not realized which one has the priority, and still puzzled by 'priority crisis'".

Professor Nan is very confident to solve the issue that has not been solved internationally. His study on trust transaction and identity authentication solved the international issue of identity authentication with a scale of $10^{48} - 10^{77}$. His research achievements are embodied in book *CPK Identity Authentication—Basis for Constructing a Trust System*, which will be published this month. The main achievements have filed CN and PCT applications. "All together 12 CN Invention applications and 11 CN Utility Model applications, 5 PCT applications have been filed. The drafting process is smoother and smoother. " When talking about CPK, Professor Nan is very excited, "Why? This is because that the key issue has been solved, and other issues become much easier to resolve. Identity Authentication is the core of whole information security. The issue is finally solved by our selves. " Professor Nan laughed when commented.

From this, it can be seen that CPK technology represents the development direction of authentication technology. This patent technology makes China to take the leading position on this key technology, and provides a solid base for developing self-innovated information security technology.

CPK: Develop with the latest information security concept

Previously when talking about information security; it was only limited within the information system field. To Professor Nan, application of anti-forgery technology actually also relates to Cyberworld.

Similar to the physical world, Cyber world is also divided into the world of order and the world without order. Experience of physical world and authentication theory studies indicate that the order of the world can only be built from top to bottom rather than from bottom to top; and, the order of the world without order can only be ensured by the world of order, rather than by the world without order itself(not partial guarantee but overall guarantee). In the physical world, the world of order uniformly prints banknotes, invoices, etc. , to provide to the world without order for use. Thus, the identity of each entity must also be under centralized management, i. e. , centralized and true-name system. Same, one has to take legal responsibility to one's own signature. This can regulate and restrict online behaviors, and provide a powerful technical means for handling junk mails and online evidence collection. In Professor Nan's eyes, cyber-world civilization brings human life from physical world to virtue world. The virtue world moves from the original world without order to a world of order, and finally one has to be responsible for his behavior and transaction. Such world is a trustworthy world, and then the whole society can live in harmony.

"Cyber is the truly 'information society', says Professor Nan, "" information society" is cyber-world. Here, "Cyber" not only refers to the virtue world but also refers to the physical world. The two are integral with each other. Our security involves both anti-counterfeits in logical and physical field. This reflects change of the times, and is broader. Thus, it is necessary to use the word " Cyber-world", which has a much broader meaning, to more accurately express.

He explains that development of *information security* undergoes an evolutionary process. The concept was first developed from private networks, which was called " military net" in China, and 'national defense net' in US, and adopted the strategy of Security(forceful guarantee). Another development process related to it is internet, which adopted the Assurance strategy(self-guarantee) proposed by Mr. Clinton. Up to the cyber times, Mr. Bush newly proposed the Trust strategy (trust guarantee), which made a big progress. The basis of trust is authenticity. From this point of view, identity authentication meets the current requirements of constructing a trust system.

Prosperous Future of Application of CPK Technology

CPK technology can not only be used in the applications that the current other authentication technology such as PKI involves, but also in other applications that other authentication technology such as PKI does not involve. " Currently the identity technology including the address system has basically formed, and we are in the process of developing various applications. Just like you need photo ID to take the plane, need driver's license to drive the car, such authentication will be gradually carried out in the internet. " Professor Nan says, "Thus, it is an inevitable trend that the more advanced CPK system will become part of the core technology in the new security field. " Since CPK does not need third-party authentication and support from online database, its application is more simple, flexible, effective, and less expensive, and the larger the scale of the system, the higher the effectiveness.

Because CPK is identity-based algorithm, another characteristic of CPK is that it can directly authenticate identity of any entity, i. e. , on-spot authentication, without support from external equipment. Thus, it can be used in authentication of communication address, to effectively prevent illegal access; in authentication of software identity, to effectively control access of illegal software; in authentication of anti-forgery tags, to effectively authenticate fake products; and, in trust transaction, to provide trustworthy certificate for users, data and seals, so as to realize authentication of every transaction link, and privacy of the whole process of the transaction.

Since CPK technology is an authentication system realized by chips, one ID certificate contains various keys, for various purposes, to realize one card pass. CPK technology can also divides the function domains with various parameters and key matrix, and can realize cross-domain authentication, so as to provide basis for complex authorized management. The basic form of CPK product is chip(such as U stick, IC card with built-in CPU, etc), which does not consume the host machine resource when conducting operations of encryption and decryption, and which establishes a confidential channel between the two parties under authentication, to achieve data encryption, storage, and transmission, while the cost may be only a fraction of the cipher machine.

With the limit time of interview, we may not be able to thoroughly understand the whole picture of CPK. However, one thing is clear. That is, CPK technology is a revolutionary and fundamental key technology. It solves the issue of identity authentication with scalability by way of chips, breaks through the traditional information security concept and development modes, produces new, great innovation space and business opportunities, and nurtures new research subjects and industry chain. If this achievement can be applied in all the fields it involves, for example a number of fields such as anti-forgery that has close relationship with common people's daily life, it will make our security products to have a great leap. In addition, proposal and completion of CPK technology can also give us a chance to take a leading position worldwide in this field, while such leading technology was rarely seen in the past.

It is known that a report with respect to CPK has been submitted to the state relevant authorities under normal procedure. It is hoped that under the state's guidance and management, CPK technology can prevail. This achievement also receives great supports from China Information Industry Trade Association(CIITA) Information Security Sub-Committee, and is on its way to actual application. However, there is still a long way to go to transfer the advanced theory, concept and technology to be realized, and hard working and enduring efforts are still needed.

When we wish technology like CPK serves for cyber world construction and public security, we also anticipate that more breakthrough security theories and technologies will appear. The contribution to MD5 by WANG Xiaoyun already shocked the world, the advanced technologies not familiar to people such as CPK will also astonish the world.

Information Security and Communication Confidentiality, September, 2006,

(This article was translated by Wang Feng)

Appendix C

Searching for Safe "Silver Bullet"

Reporter of CIO Insight   Wu Yisi

Nov. 2007

Whether "silver bullet" exists in cyber security? While scientists of various countries argue about its existence, Professor Nan proves the existence of "silver bullet" with facts.

In an international seminar on dealing with rogue software, one internationally well-known security expert made such comments: In the next 10 years, it is not possible that "silver bullet" will come out. The comments triggered discussion on "silver bullet", and a number of information security experts expressed their views about "silver bullet".

In the following 2005, PITAC (US President Information Technology Advisory Committee) submitted a report to President Bush, which confirmed the security expert's judgment. In this report entitled "Cyber Security-A crisis of prioritization", it explicitly proposed a new concept of building a trust system for the first time, and proposed ten scientific research projects that have top-priority, such as authentication technology, basic communication protocols, software security project, holistic security, web(CIO INSIGHT) criminology, etc. In addition, it made a conclusion on the then arguable issue of "silver bullet" in the information security field: Trusting system is very complicated, and there is no "silver bullet".

Is it just like the report said that no "silver bullet" exists? "In the report entitled" Cyber Security-A crisis of prioritization, "the report only paid attention to choose the ten new projects, with no further analysis on internal relation among the projects. Thus, they reached a wrong conclusion. In fact, President Bush's ten projects pointed out large scale authentication issue, which was only a step to 'silver bullet'. However, since there was no large scale authentication technology, it is natural that 'silver bullet' cannot be found", Professor Nan commented.

As an expert on military information security, Professor Nan has long term focused on research of cryptography. The CPK(combined public key) algorithm proposed by Professor Nan solved the technical puzzle of large scale authentication, and thus forming "silver bullet" theory of trusting system. Large scale authentication and "silver bullet" theory are indispensable core technology and basic theory for information infrastructure, such as trust transaction, trust connection, trust computing, trust logistics, and network management, etc. The proposal of large scale authentication technology and formation of "silver bullet" theory redefined the "base point" of information security theory, re-explained the information security development model, and brought revolutionary changes to the future development of information security.

The reporter of magazine CIO INSIGHT recently interviewed Professor Nan, and exchanged views with him on the relevant topics such as third-generation security technology, cyber security and trust system, etc.

CIOI: To most of CIOs, cyber security is still an unfamiliar concept. Can you give a brief introduction?

Professor Nan: With the network development and expansion/development of online business, the contents of information security also are changing and in expansion. Network is developed from closed computer network to open internet, and the business is also expanded from simple digital communication to online trading or transaction processing, which make the security technology enter into a new era of development. Before introducing cyber security, it is necessary to clarify three stages of information security technology development: data security, information security and cyber security. In addition, we will review the strategies, technology routes and management of the security protection for each era.

At the very beginning of computer network, especially in 1980s, each of the computer networks is closed network. Data security is the basic security requirement for era of closed computer network. The most basis security component is CIA, i. e. , C-confidentiality and privacy; I-integrity; and, A-access control and responsibility. Data security adopts compulsive confidentiality security policy, which classifies personnel and data into different grades. The grade classification is processed by manner of authorization, which is a system assured by authority.

Then, computer network entered into internet era, which mainly adopts self-protection. The most basic security component is PDR, i. e. , P-protection; D-detection; and, R-report and response. Network security mainly uses integrity strategy. The applied technology includes firewall, VPN encryption tunnel, IDS intrusion detection, anti-virus, etc. Thus, its basic technology is defense technology. Network belongs to public facility, which typically is not classified, and is only divided into " with protection measures" and "without protection measures". Now, it seems that the whole direction of network security measures of that era is totally wrong, and lasts until now. However, this kind of error is inevitable in the process of computer network development.

"If the internet likes the real physical world, and each person has his/her provable unique identity, the order on the internet is not hard to establish. Upon the order on the internet is established, all anonymous activities will be restricted, and the objects of law enforcement will be limited to the information that does not have legal identity"——Professor Nan Xianghao

We are in the era of pubic network, the report "Cyber Security-Crisis of Priority" submitted to President Bush by PITAC (Information Technology Advisory Committee) proposed the concept of cyber security. Cyber security is not strange to American CIOs. However, most Chinese CIOs do not quite understand. Cyber security requires to building trust system mainly by authentication technology. However, the previous information security was mainly based on vulnerability analysis and adopted defense strategy. Thus, the mission of computer network security protection is completely changed.

You mentioned that "the mission of the security protection in cyber security era is completely changed", what are the specific changes?

Cyber security is developed on the basis of information security. The two has strong continuity, but still has distinct differences. Generally speaking, the changes mainly include the followings:

The service objects of information security mainly are private networks such as military affairs, party and government; while the service objects of cyber security mainly are public networks. Of course, public network includes private network linked there with.

The service means of the information security are passive protection means such as patching and plugging; while the cyber security adopts active management means that provides trust services to the public.

The start point of all security protocols for information security is based on "good will". It always infers on the assumption that the subject is trustworthy (e. g. , BAN logic), to prove authenticity of the object. However, the start point of cyber security is "mutual suspicious" as the principle, which requires to first prove credibility of the subject (e. g. , trust logic), in order to establish trust system.

Here, the word "trust" shall use active verb "trusting" in English, instead of passive verb "trusted", which has a clear meaning. The report submitted by Information Technology Advisory Committee (PITAC) proposed that a trusting system can be composed of trusted or untrusted components. However, it is hard to distinguish active verb (trusting) and passive verb (trusted) in Chinese, which may cause confusion. Some people focus the research on trustworthy of the system itself. Trustworthy of the system itself certainly is very important, but it is more important whether trust services can be provided. In fact, providing trust services is the final goal.

The main purpose of the new generation information security is to construct a trust system, to provide trust services to the public. If the main activities in physical world and virtual world are all trustworthy, then the society can be stable, faithful and harmonious. If the society floods with cheating, imitating, fake commodities, and no honesty, the public will be unsatisfied, so as to trigger instability. Therefore, the report submitted by Information Technology Advisory Committee (PITAC) officially proposed a trust system with "mutual suspicious" as principle, which reflects the characteristic of the era of "peace and development is main stream".

· Why do you think network security is outdated and will be replaced by cyber security?

We all agree with such a trend, i. e. , the purpose of information development is openness. Internet is also a platform that gets more and more open. Even though point-to-point communication was used before, all the terminals of the current computer networks are open. Openness is the mainstream. What will happen as a result of self-defense persisted by information security? The information system will become to enclave. The Internet that shall be open turns out to be closed "small groups" by firewall, anti-virus software, etc. This completely violates the purpose of open trend, and is a set back. Of course, it cannot catch up with the development trend.

Network security pays attention to confrontation. However, with the development of computer network to today, no confrontation has been ever mentioned. Who was the enemy of the network confrontation, nobody knows. Now it is clear that the enemy is rogue software. However, this is not the relationship between nation and nation, it needs all of us to cooperate together to fight for rogue software. Thus, this cannot rely on confrontation. Rather, we need to use technology, to fight for this common enemy.

Whether such redefinition to the security means that all the current products in the computer security field will be phase out in the future, and may even result in the security companies to be reshuffled?

In the report "Cyber Security-a Crisis of Prioritization", it already totally denied the existing security products. This is the development trend that we have to face.

However, from the security concept and technology proposed by the internationally mainstream security products manufacturers, it is hard to see security moves towards cyber security. Is this because they are not aware of such a change?

We cannot say that they are not aware of such change; but there are more commercial interest concerns. If they admit the new trend of cyber security, then how can they handle the existing products? This also can explain why the concept of cyber security was resisted by various parties since it was appeared, because it involves interests of all parties.

Of course, some wise manufacturers are shifting towards cyber security. Any new things that comply with the development trend have very strong vitality, and are also irreversible.

Another important reason that restricts the acceptance of cyber security is the vagueness of the technology implementation route. Americans proposed the concept of " cyber security" , and claimed no " silver bullet" . How did you find the " silver bullet" , to allow cyber security to become reality from theory?

Cyber security is characterized by active management. The core requirement is to build a trust system. In the above-mentioned report "Cyber Security-A crisis of prioritization" , it proposed 10 prior missions that aim to establish a trust system, such as authentication technology, basic communication protocols, software security engineering, entire security and online criminology, etc. Listing authentication technology as the primary mission indicates that the Americans have recognized the importance of authentication technology. In addition, it also indicates that the authentication technology has not been resolved. Thus, they made the judgment that " trust system is very complicated and there is no silver bullet".

In order to fully understand "silver bullet" , it is necessary to first study identity and the nature of identity. Any entity has its own identity. For instance, a person has his/her name, a user has user name, equipment has equipment name(number or serial number) , data has data name, software(program) has software(program) name, etc. The same user uses the e-mail address as his own identity in e-mail communication, uses the cell phone number as his own identity when making phone calls, and uses the bank account number as his own identity when depositing/withdrawing money, etc. Entity identity is classified into user identity, communication tag identity, software tag identity, address identity, number identity, account number identity, seal identity, etc.

Identity has its uniqueness and independence. Each identity distinguishes from any other identity. Thus, when the entity is classified based on identity, independence is still kept among different classes. For instance, the address identity and phone number identity are independent from each other without penetrating into each other. Independence among identities and independence among various entities classified on the basis of identities provides a simple secure model for the entire security.

" Ten priority projects proposed by President Bush already pointed out super-scale authentication issue, which is only one step away from 'silver bullet'. However, since there is no super-scale authentication technology, it is natural that 'silver bullet' cannot be found".

—By Professor Nan Xianghao

Authenticity of any entity starts from identity authentication, and identity authentication is the simplest and most effective way for entity authentication. If authenticity proof technology of entity identity can be solved, other issues can be easily settled. Therefore, identity-based entity authentication technology is "key" or so-called "silver bullet". However, entity identity authentication technology is always a worldwide puzzle. Identity authentication needs two protocols to support: digital signature protocol and key exchange protocol. Digital signature protocol provides responsible service, and key exchange protocol provides privacy service. In modern authentication theory, key exchange also acts as a condition of subject authenticity proof: if A encrypts, whether B can decrypt. The digital signature protocol and key exchange protocol have already been there for a long time, but it is not easy to satisfy both scalability and immediacy. The sale of identity authentication must be super-scale, and authentication and exchange must be direct, without relying on support from any third party or external equipment.

CPK public key system was proposed in 1999. Upon several years of internal discussion and many times of modifications and perfection, it has been preliminarily completed, to realize identity-based digital signature protocol and key exchange protocol, and to satisfy scalability and immediacy. Settling the issue of super-scale identity authentication makes it easy to solve many technical problems that were hard to resolve in the past. The technical problems that have to use complicated process to resolve in the past can now be settled with simple proof. This will trigger chain reactions. The previously used authentication protocols(trust logic, belief logic), communication standards(including telecommunication network, information network), trust computing standard and the like need to be reconsidered and reformulated, and even the whole software industry will restart. Thus, many people believe that identity authentication theory will be revolutionary.

To cyber security, "silver bullet" has been found, and the core technology of "silver bullet" has been preliminarily resolved. "Silver bullet" links the space of physical world and logic world, and promotes security technology limited in narrow information system to a much broader information world. It indeed becomes one basic infrastructure.

You just mentioned two key words, i. e. , " scalability" and "immediacy". What are the specific requirements to scalability and immediacy?

The mission proposed by PITAC (Information Technology Advisory Committee) is to solve authentication in a scale of billions. If bank accounts authentication is conducted, the needed scale is at least 10^{22}. The phone number authentication needs a scale of at least 10^{11}. Thus, it can be seen that even if the object of the report "Cyber Security-A crisis of prioritization" can be realized, it still cannot satisfy such needs. With respect to CPK, its super-scale authentication capability has reached to 10^{148}.

Immediacy of authentication refers to "on the spot" verification, without support of external equipment such as phone, database. There are two kinds of authentication mechanisms: third party-based authentication and identity-based authentication. Third party-based authentication mechanism is represented by PGP, PEM, PKI. It cannot realize immediacy of authentication, or it is very hard to realize immediacy. Identity-based authentication is represented by IBC, IBE, CPK. It is very easy to realize immediacy of authentication. This is why identity-based authentication attracts more and more attention in recent years.

At present, what are the main applications of these new technologies related to "silver bullet"?

We found the "silver bullet", and settled super scale authentication. This can solve any entity identity authentication. For instance, user identity authentication and seal identity authentication are provided in trust transactions, such as e-bank, e-bill, e-seal, e-archives, to prevent fraud transaction. Trustworthy proof of communication tag is provided in trust connection such as telecommunication network, basic protocol of information network, cell phone, authentication gateway, to prevent illegal access. Trustworthy proof of software tag is provided in trust computing such as software, program tag verification, to guard against malicious software. Authenticity proof of article tag is provided in trust logistics such as nameplate, license plate, documents, bills, to prevent flood of fake products.

"Silver bullet" links the space of physical world and logic world, and promotes security technology limited in narrow information system to a much broader information world. It indeed becomes one of the basic infrastructures. —By Professor Nan Xianghao

"Silver bullet" is a technology that affects the overall situation, and will bring systematic revolution. The revolution will first be recognized by and receive active response from telecommunication experts, anti-forgery experts, computer specialists, and bank experts, because the long term puzzle can be smoothly settled. They may even feel inspired. However, "silver bullet" and super-scale authentication are both new concepts and new technologies, and it may take time to truly grasp their meaning and apply them in various fields.

Can you predict the application trend of "silver bullet" in era of cyber security?

Information security enters into a new era of cyber security. The subject of cyber security is to build a trust world, which is not a passive defense system but an active management world; which is not an information system separated from physical world, but an information world integrated with physical world. US president proposed to build a trust world, and our central party proposed to construct a harmonious society. Both reflect the pulse of the new era development, and represent the mainstream of development. The essence of a trust world or harmonious society lies on the "order" of the society. To build order, maintain order, and finally construct a trust or harmonious society is the main task of the new generation information security.

The basic requirement of trust world is to build order and maintain order. Only identity authentication technology can help to build order and maintain order. Since the founding of new China, after several decades of hard work, the order of physical world has been established. For instance, the "photo ID" issued by Ministry of Public Security indeed helps to establish the order of the physical world. The experience of physical world provides precious experience to the trust information society to be built. If the internet just likes the real physical world, that everyone has his provable unique identity, it is not difficult to build the order on the internet. Upon the online order is established, all anonymous activities will be restricted, the objects of law enforcement are limited to the information without legal identity. Right now, people gradually realize that online order affects existence of the internet.

Similar to physical world, cyber world is divided into the world of order and the world without order. Both experience of the physical world and research of authentication theory have shown that the order of a world without order can only be built from top to bottom but not from bottom to top; and, the order of a world without order can only be guaranteed by the world of order, rather than ensured by the world without order itself(not partial guarantee, but overall guarantee). In the physical world, the world of order uniformly prints banknotes, invoices, etc., to provide to the world without order for use. Thus, identity of each entity must also be under unified management, i. e., adopting centralized and real-name system. Therefore, one has to take legal responsibility to his own signature, so as to regulate and restrict online behavior, and provide powerful technological means for handling junk mails and taking evidence online.

(*CIO INSIGHT*) *November*, 2007

(this article was translated by Wang Feng)

Appendix D

"Electronic-ID card" Attracts International Attention

Reporter of Liao Wang   Yang Qingmin

March, 2007

News The innovative information security core technology—" Electronic-ID card" technology, i. e. , large scale identity authentication application technology, has conquered a universal puzzle. The executive chairman of America Cryptology Annual Conference paid a special trip, and praised it as an excellent solution. He also expressed the interest to work with us, to push it into an international standard. Experts believe that the technology provides a rare opportunity for us to seize future global IT construction, and deserves the nation's attention.

A universal puzzle not yet resolved in developed countries

According to experts'introduction, authentication technology is a branch of cryptography. It is realized through digital signature and key exchange. Modern cryptography believes that algorithm can be open, and "all the secrets lie in the keys". In physical world, authenticity is confirmed by authentication documents such as ID card. In cyber-world, authenticity must be performed through authentication technology.

Over the time, identity authentication is a universal puzzle. The difficulty lies on large scale authentication and direct verification. For example, bank account must satisfy 10^{22} different identity authentications; and mobile communication must satisfy 10^{11} different identity authentications. Both cannot depend on external equipment such as database to support.

Currently, there are mainly two kinds of authentication technologies; one is identity-based algorithm, such as IBC digital signature scheme invented by Shamir in 1984; and the other one is third party-based certificate system, such as PKI technology appeared in 1996, which is adopted by many countries, including China.

However, the third party-based proof system has significant deficiencies: 1. It can only be used in user level data authentication, and cannot be used in entity level identity authentication; 2. It must be supported by online certificate library, with limited processing capacity. Hierarchical management must be implemented to multiple libraries. When the users reach a million, it will experience blocking. 3. The construction and maintenance cost are high, with limited scope of application, low running efficiency, and high risks. Once the database experiences malfunction, the whole system will be paralyzed.

Our "Electronic-ID card" has unique technical principle

In 2003, after many years of research, Professor Nan Xianghao proposed CPK "combined public key algorithm" (CPK technology) from the concept of changing conventional key generation, to open up a new way to solve scalability by way of combination. CPK algorithm produces nearly unlimited keys with very small factor. It establishes identity and key corresponding with "mapping algorithm", so as to simplify the bulky database into small key generation matrix.

CPK technology uses combination manner, to put public keys in a chip (size of a rice grain). The chip can store personal characters and pictures, so as to make a read-only "Electronic-ID card", which can be made as a flash disk that is pluggable on the computer, or embedded in the bank card for use, without the need of internet support or third-party proof. Its authentication scalability can reach above 10^{48}, which can fully satisfy global needs.

Someone describes it as a music library. The overseas technology needs to store every piece of music. Since one music library cannot store all, multiple libraries have to be built. When calling a piece of music, one has to open all the libraries. With our technology, only musical notes that compose the music shall be stored. Based on the music name, musical notes are composed for calling.

Our technology provides authentication scalability and simplicity. Management only needs to store user certificates (private key) and corresponding management information into chips, distributes to users, so the users can establish authentication system of any scale and structure as desired, to implement effective supervision. Any users having the chip certificates can conduct direct authentication with other users having the same kind of chip certificates, without the support from authentication center and online database. The authentication process can be reduced to 2-step from the original 6-step. The trust connection process can be simplified to 1-step from the original 10-steps. This not only greatly reduces the cost, but also hardly need any daily maintenance, so as to make widespread application possible.

This kind of chip can be embedded in public's computers and cell phones, to authenticate information and articles having the information, at any time and anywhere. With respect to the currently popular PKI technology, it can authenticate millions of users at most. In addition, it needs hierarchical management and online support. Using our CPK for secret communication, the cryptographic synchronization takes less than one second. Using PKI for secret communication, the process lasts over 6 seconds, which can hardly stand.

In June of 2006, Beijing Science & Technology Committee invited 10 domestic well-known experts on information security, to evaluate this technology. All the experts believe that the technology is a significant innovation, and is worth spreading for use. Upon hearing the technology, the executive chairman of America Cryptology Annual Conference, James Hughes, paid a special trip to Beijing to meet with Professor Nan. He repeatedly commented: "excellent!", and praised it as an "excellent solution". He also expressed his sincere hope to work together, to make it an international standard, and indicated that he will recommend this in this year's EP cryptography annual conference in details.

"Electronic-ID card" has vital meaning to worldwide network construction

Over last two years, under the support from Beijing Science & Technology Committee, Professor Nan completed basic authentication system and CPK chip development, and extended to secure communication field. All reaches practical application requirements. CMBC (China Minsheng Bank) uses this technology to conduct e-bill signature and receives good results. They cooperated with relevant telecommunication department and developed high-end secure authentication sample cell phone for using in 3G system. The industrialization development has been taken off.

Currently, this technology has obtained invention patent. In addition, Professor Nan applied for 12 CN Patent applications in the fields such as trusted computing, trusted connection, e-bank, and anti-forgery tags. Under the support and financing aid from General Equipment Department, Professor Nan published his work "*CPK Identity Authentication*". Professor Nan has been working on new generation security theory and technology research for years, and published over 20 articles in professional press, which aroused repercussions in the information security community home and abroad. Experts in the field believe that CPK technology has significant technical meaning:

1. It benefits for global IT construction

In 1993, the then US president Clinton caught the historical opportunity and proposed the well-known "Information Highway" plan, which drove the global network construction, and gave US the opportunity to develop economy. Currently, building a trust network becomes the top event. To extend CPK technology to the world will bring us the economic benefits that internet transport protocols technology brought to US, and provide us rare opportunity to grab the opportunity for future global IT construction.

2. It benefits for global network construction

After formation of cyberworld, on the one side it creates wealth and provides convenience; and, on the other side it causes crimes and makes troubles. In February 2005, upon two years research and visiting hundreds of experts, the US President Information Technology Advisory Committee (PI-TAC) submitted a report "*Cyber Security-Crisis of Prioritization*" to President Bush. This report indicates that information security becomes worse and worse, lessons shall be drawn from boundary protection model, to build a trust system, and recommended to treat-authentication as priority mission. Pushing CPK technology and establishing "Electronic-ID card" can allow us to contribute to build a cyberworld with order.

3. It benefits for centralized network management

CPK technology provides us an effective technical guarantee for building centralized network management model. Because it has scalability of authentication and simplicity of verification, CPK can allow us to be the first one in the world to apply "Electronic-ID card" system. This helps to keep a stable political situation, a high speed economy development, and improve nation's spiritual civilization, so as to meet the requirements of well-building, well-use and well-managing cyberworld proposed by Mr. Hu Jingtao.

4. It benefits for reducing internet crime and computer virus

With the development of network, the global network crime and computer virus grow drastically, and the network security cost has accounted for 15% of the network economy. Information security enters into cyber security era. Views of strategic security have changed dramatically. Objectively, it requires cyberworld to move towards active management from passive defense. This universal puzzle can be solved by using super scaled identity authentication technology. Pursuing "Electronic-ID card" system worldwide can substantially reduce and frighten network crime and computer virus spreading.

5. It benefits for reducing fake and poor quality products worldwide

Fake and poor quality products are a hazard second to drugs. A research by UN indicates that worldwide the fake products transaction volume accounts over 5% of the world trade volume, and the legal companies lose as high as USD 13.8 billon annually because of this. For a long time, the fake and poor quality products in China remain incessant after repeated prohibition. Implementing "Electronic-ID card" system can deal with the stubborn problem from root, to purify the market environment.

According to the reporter's understanding, CPK technology is matured for use in practice, especially in sectors such as government, military, police, security, finance and insurance. It adapts for e-tickets, liquor & tobacco, vehicle, computer, military logistics management and authenticity, etc..

Facing invitation of international cooperation, Professor Nan commented: "we will not miss this historical opportunity".

Written in Mar. 2007 and revised in Feb. 2010

(This article was translated by Wang Feng)

Appendix E

CPK System Goes to the World

—Memo of Europe Cryptography Annual Conference in 2007

Information Science College, Information Security Lab. of Beijing University   Guanzhi

guanzhi@ infosec. pku. edu. cn

1. Overview of Europe Cryptography Annual Conference

Eurocrypt'07 is the 23rd Eurocrypt conference, which was held in Barcelona Hotel, located in Plaza de Espana in seashore city of Barcelona, Spain. Besides IACR (International Association for Cryptologic Research), the co-organizers of the conference include Applied Cryptography Research Team of Spain UPC college, and Information Security Research Team of UMA. The conference program chair is Moni Naor, and conference co-chairs are Javier López and Germán Sáez.

This conference attracted a large amount of people from academic and business community, and observers from government departments of a number of countries. There are 33 official reports, 2 special reports and 27 free reports. This is a grand gathering for cryptography community; and you can see many celebrities in academic and business community on security research. The registered participants are nearly 400. Besides the scholars who gave presentations during the meeting, any one who paid registration fees can attend. Besides the counterparts from China Academy of Sciences and two students of Professor Wang Xiaoyun, there are very few scholars and students from mainland China, and no one is from the domestic industry community. Professor Wei from Hong Kong Chinese University told us that their University was planning to apply for hosting Asia cryptography Annual Conference in 2008 or 2009.

The conference was officially opened in 21st, May. The conference totally recruited 33 papers. The main task of the conference was that author of each paper gave a 30 minutes presentation about his/her own paper, and the attendees can ask questions about the paper. According to different fields, 33 reports were divided into 11 Specials. Each special would choose a well-known scholar in that field as the chairman for that special.

Besides the papers recruited, there are two special reports: *Cryptology-from A to Z* by Jacques Stern and *Elliptic Curve & Cryptology: Invention and Influence* by Victor Miller. "*Cryptology-from A to Z*" looks back the history of the whole cryptology development in manner of alphabet. From A to Z, each letter is associated to one scholar or algorithm that relates to cryptology. For example, the letter S is used to introduce Shannon, founder of the information theory. Before the presentation, Stern specially chose 3 letters to ask the attendees. At the end of the presentation, he asked the attendees whether there are anybody guessed all the 3 letters, only Whitfield Diffie did. Over 20 attendees made 2 letters. Miller is one of the inventors of Elliptic Curve. With elliptic curve becomes more and more important in the cryptography field, it is just perfect for the inventor of elliptic curve himself to give a special presentation at the end of the cryptology annual conference. The presentation lasted for one hour, and it was excellent. During the presentation, he introduced the history of elliptic curve cryptology development and relevant scholars.

2. CPK Presentation

In last year's America Cryptology Annual Conference, James Hughes of Sun Microsystems learned from Professor ZHAI, Qibing who attended the conference about CPK system. At the end of last September, he made a special trip to Beijing to meet with Professor Nan, and expressed his intention to disclose CPK system in this year's Eurocrypt. Both Diffie and Hughes are Fellows at SUN, which is the highest technical position. In SUN, there are only 14 Fellows (about 100 vice presidents), who devote themselves to technology development and do not take any administrative work, and have great impact to the company's development. Hughes believes that CPK system would have significant effects on pushing operation system and Internet security, to greatly simplify the current application, and play an important role for company's future development.

Upon approval by Professor Nan, Hughes prepared relevant reports about CPK system in this year's Europe Cryptology Annual Conference, and discussed the algorithm and its application perspective with other cryptology experts attending the conference. I, both student of Professor Nan and visiting student of Hughes in SUN, attended this conference with Hughes. We brought along samples of CPK built-in USB token, to provide to relevant experts and scholars. During the conference, I was with James Hughes, to have dinner with celebrities, including Whitfield Diffie, Victor Miller, Greg Rose of Qualcomm, John M. Kelsey Jr. of NIST, Jean-Jacques Quisquater of UCL Crypto, and Susan of HP, etc.

In order to make the CPK report successful, Hughes did a lot of preparation before presentation. In addition to introduce the content of the report to each of the above mentioned well-known experts and scholars, Hughes also introduced and discussed relevant issues with Robert Granger, who presented to this conference with relevant article about elliptic curve cryptology, and other young scholars in elliptic curve field. Robert Granger indicated that there might be a paper similar to CPK, and helped us to find the paper, which finally is found not the same algorithm. Thus, it is essentially confirmed that CPK system is a new algorithm that differs from other IBE algorithms. In addition, the relevant experts/scholars did not raise doubts about security of CPK system. With respect to collusion issue, it needs specific qualitative and quantitative analysis. With respect to collision issue, experts who review the report believes that the security issue of Hashing Algorithm shall not be included in security of CPK system, especially the hashing functions or CBC-MAC functions that have not been breached still exist theoretically and practically.

Rump Session has 27 presentations. Rump Session is very active. Many new subjects/new ideas under research can be briefed here. Some upcoming academic conferences or events also announce here. Thus, Rump Session is a platform to understand cryptology development dynamics, and also a platform to issue new technology and new achievements. For instance, Professor Wang Xiaoyun issued her collision achievements on hashing function in the Rump Session of 2004 America Cryptology Annual Conference.

Hughes started his report about CPK system around 9:30pm. The report contents were affirmed by Chairman Brent Waters of Rump Session. Under his proposal, the title was finalized as "*CPK: Bounded Identity Encryption*", to make it more easy to distinguish from other IBE schemes. The report introduced CPK system, and once again raised the following two questions to the attendees: Is CPK system new? How to judge the security of CPK system? The report went very successfully, and attracted attention from the world cryptology scholars. On the second day, cryptology scholar of Stanford University further enquired details of CPK algorithm.

In addition, we discussed using chip to protect private keys with Professor Quisquater and his students. They did a lot of research on attacks to smart card chips; and enjoy high reputation in security community. Our two parties will continue cooperation on security analysis and security enhancement of chips.

Hughes believes our next urgent work is to publish a purified version of CPK system on the paper website maintained by IACR, to provide reference to the scholars who care about CPK system.

Information Security and Communication Security July, 2007

(This article was Translated by Wang Feng)

Appendix F

Identity Authentication Based on CPK System

—Interview with cryptography Scholar, Professor Nan Xianghao

Reporter of CNITSEC   Yang Guohui

Introduction

Recently I read a book of "CPK Identity Authentication" by professor Nan and relevant articles, and also discussed relevant issue of information security with the author. Professor Nan indicates that "CPK Identity Authentication" was published in 2005, and these couple of years there are new developments, such as: CPK system developed from identity-based single factor combined public key system(IB-CPK) to two-factor combined public key system(TF-CPK), and authentication logic developed from belief logic to trust logic. These new contents will be included in the revised edition, which was sent to the publisher, to be published in both Chinese and English. The readers will soon find the revised edition. Prior to the revised edition being published, from the discussion between the reporter and the author, it is believed that we have made great achievements on information security both theoretically and technically. Below is the preliminary understanding of the reporter, to share with the readers.

With the expansion of internet, public network and online business, the contents of information security also change and expand therewith. The network is developed from closed computer network to open internet, and the business is developed from simple data communication to online trading or transaction processing. This causes security technology to enter into a new development stage.

I. Basic contents of cyber security

1. Basic concepts

The development of information security technology has experienced three stages: data security, information security(including network security), and cyber security.

Data security is the basic security requirement of closed computer network age, and its basis components are CIA, i. e. , C—confidentiality and privacy, I—integrity, A—access control and responsibility. Data security adopts compulsive confidentiality security strategy that classifies personnel and data into different grades. The classification is conducted by way of authorization. This is an official guaranteed system. Data security strategy gives priority on confidentiality, and is based on modern cryptography technology.

Information security includes network security, which is a security technology produced and developed in the open internet age. The basic security construction is PDR, i. e. , P—protection, D—detection, R—report and response. The network security strategy gives priority on integrity, and the primary technology used includes firewall, VPN encryption tunnel, IDS invasion detection, antivirus, etc. , in which the basic technology is defense technology.

Cyber security corresponds to actual physical world or physical world. The basic requirement of cyber security relies on "order" established on the basis of trust. The basic components of cyber security include authentication, management, and supervision.

The property of cyber security goes beyond the scope of the previous data security, and thus being called "third generation security". Cyber security typically adopts individualized policy. Every entity is divided into different roles or responsibilities. The responsibility is not authorized by others, rather is applied by oneself. It is a self-assurance system at one's own risk.

Cyber security includes data security, and network security. Based on the circumstances, each one has its own security policy. The classification of components is not definite. That is, same component may have different functions, or same technology may constitute different components. Security technologies, due to different usage, can be divided into encrypting units and authenticating units

2. Main contents

The main task of cyber security is to construct "a trusting system in the dangerous world", to provide trusted services, including trusted computation, trusted communication, trusted transactions, etc. Thus, the trusting system is a new information security system built on the basis of authentication technology. In the trusting system, authenticity of each entity/event shall undergo corresponding proof or verification.

"Trusted" computing is developed from the original "authorized trust" to "behavior trust", and to code authentication according to the requirement of the trusting system, i. e. , authentication to the software tag, to determine whether to load or not, and to execute or not.

"Trusted" connection is realized by authentication technology or tag exchange technology. Tag exchange technology can designate route, and provide trusted proof for sending, forwarding, and receiving messages during communication.

"Trusted" transaction provides entity authenticity proof for online application. The theory for proving trust is called authentication theory. CPK authentication theory is based on "trust logic" in which subject trustworthy is verified through identity authentication without pre-assumption. It is different from traditional "belief logic", in which object trustworthy is verified through readability-rule, nonce-rule and jurisdiction-rule under the pre-assumption that subject is trusted.

3. Key Technology

(1). **Authentication technology.** No matter it is trusted computing platform, trusted connection tag, agent activity or transaction activity, all needs authentication technology. Therefore, authentication technology must satisfy authentication of users, equipment and processing. Such authentication will be super scaled. In some cases such authentication process cannot be online, and cannot rely on third party. Rather, it shall truly realize P-to-P (i. e. , authentication of any one entity to any other entity) in ultra-large scale. In authentication system, key is an important authentication parameter. Thus, key management technology is vital. It can say that authentication system is established on the key management system. US already took authentication technology as the top priority, and clearly stated that authentication in billion scale will be the top priority to solve in the future.

(2). **Tag authentication.** Authentication technology includes subject authentication, object authentication, and behavior authentication, in which subject authentication is the core technology, because trusting system first needs to prove authenticity of the subject. The most effective and simple way of subject authentication is "identity authentication", because identity is the only symbol to distinguish various entities.

Currently, there are three public key system used in authentication:

1. PKI third party-based authentication system. Running of PKI relies on two basic components, i. e. , layering CA mechanism and online running certificate library. Because the system relies on database online running, it has very low efficiency and weak handling capacity. The handling capability of one certificate library does not exceed 1000 users.

2. IBE(identity based encryption) key exchange mechanism. Shamir for the first time created a new system that take identity as public key and formed a signature scheme, but only proved the existence of identity-based key exchange system in 1984. Until 2001, Don Boneh and Matthew Franklin proposed identity-based IBE key exchange system that canceled support relied on third-party proof. However, the system relies on KGC online running. Its running efficiency is very low, and the handling capability also is not strong. Even so, it still attracts a lot of attention around the world and is likely to replace PKI key exchange system.

3. CPK(combined public key) authentication system. Like IBE, CPK is also an identity-based public key system. It supports digital signature, and key exchange, without the layering CA mecha-

nism chain of third party proof and support of database(LDAP). CPK can obtain the needed public key on the spot. It has high running efficiency, strong handling capability, and can greatly expand its applications. CPK has the characteristics of less occupied space(only occupy 25KB)and large scale (handling over 10^{48} public keys), and makes chip solution and agent solution of authentication system possible.

Thus, it can be seen that CPK can easily solve authentication puzzle that cannot be settled by PKI and IBE. This technology attracts high attention among the world authentication cycle. The function comparison of PKI, IBE and CPK is as follows:

Name	Published	CA	Key Exchange	signature	Sign-length	Cost
PKI	1996	Yes	No	Yes	256 Byte	100
IBE	2001	No	Yes	No		50
CPK	2003	No	Yes	Yes	30 Byte	5

Cyber security is breaking the restriction of information security framework. Security feature is changed from passive defense to active management. In order to build a trust cyber world it must have the capability of authenticity in the cyber and real world.

II. CPK System and Its Application

Now, information security is gradually developing to cyber security, and transforming from passive defense security to active management security. To build effective order in the cyber world, and to regulate cyber activities to provide the citizen with trusted services become the main task of cyber security. Cyber security is built on the trust logic principle of "mutual suspicion". It first needs to identify authenticity, and to identify friends or enemies, to build security on the basis of authenticity authentication. In the information security age, all protocols are built on the logic of "good will". As a result, it brought out enormous problems and loopholes, and always has not solved the key issue of security. Cyber security is established on logic of "mutual suspicion". It first needs to identify true or false, friends or enemies, and the security issue is established on the basis of authenticity authentication.

At the end of 1999, Professor Nan proposed the concept of CPK. In 2003, CPK system was internally discussed at Annual Meeting of the Committee of Information Secrecy. In 2004, when executive chairman James Hughes of America Cryptology Annual Meeting heard of it, he paid a special visit to Beijing. He praised it as a "simple and excellent solution", and expressed his hope to cooperate. In 2005, ten domestic well-known cryptographists and information security experts gave high evaluation on it, and believed that it is a "great independent innovation, with widespread application value". In 2007, in Euro Cryptology Annual Conference, CPK was recognized by world top cryptographists.

CPK system transforms the complex mapping of unbounded identity space to unbounded public key space to simple mapping of bounded identity to bounded public key space, which opened up a new idea of solving scalability by way of combination. It uses small generated matrix (a sheet) to combine and generate nearly infinite keys, to replace bulky database system. It automatically sets up identity and key correspondence through "mapping algorithm", without third-party proof. This is a novel authentication system built on the basis of new key systems. CPK technology stores personal information in tiny chips, to make non-editable "electronic ID card", to provide evidence of "who am I". Verification to the "electronic ID card" is automatically conducted; and authentication scale can reach to 10^{58}-10^{187}, to satisfy any scale needs and use globally. It is like a music library. The overseas technology needs to store every piece of music worldwide, and thus has to build a large number of music libraries. All the music libraries need to be opened when invoking. However, by adopting our innovative CPK technology, only musical notes that compose music shall be stored. Invoking is based on the music name to combine the musical notes.

Since 2005, professor Nan and his team completed development of basic system and CPK special chips after years of efforts and hard work, so that CPK is applicable to use. 12 invention applications have been filed in the application fields such as trusted connection (communication), trusted invocation (computer), bill exchange (transaction), tag authentication (anti-forgery), etc. From the running or testing results of Minsheng Bank bill authentication system and Guangdong code authentication system, CPK has very good feasibility.

Now, CPK has attracted high attention from relevant authorities and received support there from, and is widely recognized by the community. Such significant independently innovated new technology has rich contents and advanced technology, and is readily to be widely promoted. It has profound meaning:

1. It facilitates us to capture the opportunity of future global IT reconstruction. Currently, the top priority is to build a trust cyberworld. Promotion of CPK technology and international cooperation provide rare opportunity to make it an international standard. We also can gain great economic interests from CPK.

2. It facilitates our information security network construction. To build a trust system in a risky world, security authentication is the top priority. We push CPK technology and build "electronic-ID card", so that we can take the lead to contribute to build a harmonious cyberworld.

3. It facilitates reduction of network crimes and computer virus. Currently, network security cost already accounts for 15% of the network economy. If "electronic-ID card" system is implemen-

ted in the cyberworld, network crimes and computer virus spread can be greatly reduced.

4. It facilitates cutting down fake and poor quality products globally. Implementation of "electronic-ID card" system can cure this issue from the root, to build a healthy network environment and to purify market.

In conclusion, we take the lead with respect to identity-based CPK public key system and theory, which pushes our information security theory to the new stage of cyber security. As authenticity authentication technology and theory, CPK system and identity authentication will impact all the previous security protocols, communication protocols, and software engineering; can be used as anti-forgeable "Electronic-ID card", to play a vital role in constructing a trusting system; and hopefully will allow the cyberworld without order to become a trustworthy and harmonious society.

III. Identity authentication based on CPK

For a long time, identity authentication (i. e., identification authentication) of cyberworld has been a worldwide puzzle; because identity authentication system must meet new requirements of personalized authentication, to realize both digital signature and key exchange, to satisfy scalability of proof and immediacy of verification. CPK subject authentication theory realizes proof of "who am I" and verification of "who are you", i. e., identification of friends and enemies. The subject authentication relies on identity authentication technology to realize.

Each entity has its own identity. Authentication of identity is composed of "prover" and "verifier". However, it is easy to prove but hard to verify. Early in 1984 Shamir posed a new algorithm in which identity is taken as public key. With exploration of over 20 years, on the bases of identity-based public key system an identity authentication system was finally found. Currently there are two popular identity authentication systems: PKI and CPK. PKI itself is not an identity authentication system. However, with the help of third party proof, it can be used in user authentication. Usable identity authentication at least satisfies three conditions: ① Scalability of authentication. Taking domestic cell phone for example, it shall meet the needs of authentication for 10^{11} different identities. Taking bank account for example, it shall meet the needs of authentication for 10^{22} different identities. ② Simplicity of verification. Verification shall not rely on support of external equipments such as telephone or database. ③ Effectiveness of management. Authentication activities can be effectively supervised, managed and controlled by the nation. Using the above three criteria, PKI does not meet any of them, while CPK can meet all three.

Building order relies on identity authentication and maintaining order relies on identity management. From this point the core content of information security are in the two aspects: identity authentication and authorization control. Identity authentication is the basis of authorization control. If every one has a provable unique identity on the internet, then online order is not difficult to build.

In following session we will take e-transaction as example, to briefly demonstrate the role of identity authentication plays in the several main links. The main links in the transaction security that need to provide evidence are trusted transaction, trusted connection, trusted computing and trusted logistics, etc.

1. User identity authentication

In transactions, user to user business relation occurs first, which involves authentication of user identity and authentication of data. If data contains seals, then authentication of seal identity is also involved. For example, the bank ATM/POS system is an e-bank system using bank accounts as user identities. If the current magnetic stripe cards are changed to IC cards and account number authentication technology is adopted. The bank is always the verifier, who can directly verify authenticity of the account number. Because what the bank stores is only the public key, any suspect of internal crime can be ruled out. In addition, the loss of the bank information will not affect the interests of the customers. Evidence of withdrawal from this account number can also be obtained.

2. Communication identity authentication

The first issue encountered for the receiver in the communication is whether the data is sent by legal sender, and the second issue is whether the data is received correctly. As the first gateway of the trusted communication, the judgment of whether to receive or not is very important. This can be solved by authentication of communication identity. If it is an illegal identity, then it will be rejected, so as to effectively prevent illegal access. Such trust connection technology based on communication identity authentication will bring great changes to the basic protocol of communications. For instance, the original SSL, WLAN and other protocols need more than 10 steps of interaction in establishing secure connection. Now with the identity authentication, trust connection can be achieved only by 1 or two steps. In addition, the burden of authentication is scattered to each user terminals, and thus greatly alleviates the burden of exchange equipment, and achieves balance of load. This greatly facilitates authentication communication of cell phone, and full privacy can be realized technically.

3. Software identity authentication

Transactions between users are processed by a computer, and thus the demand of trusted computing occurs. The first issue encountered by trusted computing is whether the program shall be loaded; the second issue is whether the program is loaded correct; and the third issue is whether the program is running as expected. As the first gateway of trusted computing, the judgment of whether the program shall be loaded is very important. This can be solved by authentication of the program identity. All legal program identities have their own authentication codes, so that they can be identified easily. If a program identity has not authentication code it is an illegal identity, then the loading will be refused. Thus, malicious software such as virus can not work even if successfully invaded. To a banking system, if only the software approved by the bank is allowed to run in this system, and software that is not recognized is not allowed to run in the system, this is the true purpose pursued by trusted computing. The trust verification module (TVM) based on program identity authentication greatly differs from the traditional trust platform module (TPM) in design. The novel verifiable module only needs three components of identity authentication, integrity measurement agent and behavior-monitoring agent, to satisfy the trust computing environment. If encryption is needed to some software and data, key exchange and data encryption can solve it.

4. Electronic tag authentication

In the logistics aspect of transaction, if it is flooded with counterfeits, then there will be no trust transaction. Thus, there is a need against counterfeits. The FRID provides an excellent basis for electronic anti-forgery. Physical FRID can prevent imitation, and logical identity authentication can prevent impersonation. The combination of both can provide strong anti-forgery function. Anti-forgery based on identity authentication can authenticate millions of various articles with one verification machine, and each one can have one verification machine. For instance, authentication function can be applied into cell phone, to enable on-spot authentication to any FRID tags. Thus, a widespread net of anti-forgery will be built and can effectively restrain counterfeits.

Conclusion

From above, it can be seen that information security is undergoing significant changes, and information security is transformed from passive defense to active management cyber security. It can be seen that our independently innovated CPK system does not need third party proof, and does not need support of online database. It can satisfy scalability and immediacy of verification. It can also be seen that CPK and public key system provide excellent technical and theoretical basis for building trust cyber order and realizing identity-based entity authentication.

Identity authentication based on CPK system plays a key and fundamental role in trusted transaction (e. g. , e-bank, e-bill, e-seal, e-documents) , trusted connection (telecommunication network, information network basic protocols, cell phones, authentication gateway) , trusted computing (design of trust computing platform module) , tag anti-forgery (nameplates, license plates, admission tickets, certificates, bills, bank notes, etc) .

CPK system solves the puzzle of identity authentication. It is believed that with further research and expansion of application fields, the old information security concept and development model will be greatly impacted, and the new huge innovation space and business opportunities will be produced, which will generate new research subjects and industry chains. We believe that identity authentication based on CPK system will play a great role in constructing a trust system or building a harmonious society.

China Information Technology Security Evaluation Center(*CNITSEC*) 2008,

(This article was translated by Wang Feng)

Appendix G

CPK Cryptosystem

James Hughes

Sun Microsystems

James. Hughes@ Sun. com

December 2006

This document is an implementation of the CPK Cryptosystem as defined in the paper ***CPK Algorithm and ID Authentication*** , Prof. Nan Xianghao , CPK Inc , 2006.

This is intended as a didactic way of describing the cryptosystem.

This cryptosystem is considered the intellectual property of Beijing e-Henxen Authentication Technology Company Limited. Beijing , China. This notebook does not imply any license to use this IP for any purpose.

Setup

The system uses the Eliptic Curve notbook by José de Jesús Angel Angel , CINVESTAV-IPN , as modified by Jim Hughes.

In[1] : =<< **"DesktopêECDHS_english4. m"**

We seed the random number and print it just in case.

In[2] : = **IntegerPart** [**AbsoluteTime** [ ]]

SeedRandom [%]

Out[2] = 3374444114

CPK Cryptosystem Setup

Establish the parameters for this system. This is from **FIPS 186-2**, **Recommended Elliptic Curve Domain Parameters**:

In[4] : = **ECDomain** [**192**]

■ Construction of the Public and Private Matrices

The size of the matrix (in the paper is **m** and **h**) is **sx** by **sy**. The example here is 7×7, but the system parameters in the paper are 32×32.

In[5] : = **sx = sy = 7**;

We need to create the Secret matrix. These are simply random numbers between (1 , n-1).

In[6] : = **Secret = Table** [**PrivateKey** [ ] , {sx} , {sy}];

We then create the public matrix from the private matrix.

In[7] : = **Public = Table** [**kP** [**G** , **Secret** [[**i,j**]]] , { **i,sx** } , { **j,sy** }];

■ Check

In[8] : = **Assert** [**Public** [[**3,4**]] == **kP** [**G** , **Secret** [[**3,4**]]]]

Create a Private Key from from the Secret (Private) matrix

To make this w ork we first turn the identifier into a list of elements (using IdToElements). We can then use that information to select elements from the matrices. The elements from the Private matrix can be used to create a private key for the specific Id.

■ IdToElements

The IdToElements takes either a string or a number and creates a listof elements that will be used to create the private and public keys.

In[9] : = **IdToElements** [**x_**] : =
    (**IntegerDigits** [**Mod** [**Sha1** [**x**] , **sxsy**] , **sx**] / / . { {y____} } /;
    (**Length** [{ **y** }] < **sx**) - > { **0,y** } }) + **1**

■Check

In[10] : = **If** [**sx == sy == 7** , **TestVector** [
IdToElements [**159**] == {1,1,1,1,5,5,4} ,
IdToElements [**ToLowerCase** [<u>James. hughes@Sun. com</u>]] == {5,5,4,3,3,2,6}];
"Checked" , **"Not Checked"**]
Out[10] = Checked

In[11] := **Block** [{ **i = 0** },
While [**! MatchQ** [**IdToElements** [**++I**],{**1**,____ }]];
I]
Out[11] = 3

■ SelectElements

Using a list, it takes a specified entry from each row.

In[12] := **SelectElements** [**m_? ListQ,l_? ListQ**] /; (
    (**Length** [**l**] == **Length** [**m**] **&&**
    (**Depth**] > **2**)) :=
    Table [**m** [[**i,l**]]],{ **i,Length** [**l**] }]

■ Check

In[13] := **Partition** [**Range** [**49**],7];
Assert SelectElements [**%**, {**1,2,3,4,5,6,7** }] == {**1,9,17,25,33,41,49** },
"Select Elements is broken"]

■ IdToPrivateKey

This takes and identifier which is either a string in the form "name" or an integer. Both are hashed up and elements of the Secret matrix are choosen. To make different organizations, one can cat strings together with the organization like "ChinaMerchantBank,123-123-123" would be an account 123-123-123 of the China Merchant Bank. This string can be any character set as long as it is binary unique, specifically, case matters.

In this example, the Public and Secret matricies are just global variables, but the IdToPrivateKey function accesses the Secret matrix (The IdToPublicKey only accesses the Public matrix).

In[15] := **IdToPrivateKey** [**x_**] := **Mod** [**Plus @ @ SelectElements** [**Secret,IdToElements** [**x**]],**n**]

We then create a private key.

Create a Public Key from from the Public matrix

We then do the same thing with the ID to the Public Matrix.

In[16] : = **IdToPublicKey** [**x_**] : = **AddPoints** @ @ **SelectElements** [**Public** , **IdToEle-**
        ments [**x**]]

- -

Complete Example

In[17] : = **Pr = IdToPrivateKey** [**"James. HughesüSun. com"**]

Out[17] = 403754701701447563803169047868370451400232309286661318193 7

In[18] : = **Pu = IdToPublicKey** [**"James. HughesüSun. com"**]

Out[18] : = { 46 278813903488128093825530378840913646067183957937593463 93 ,
        412672125774816484308062906760412646682010943094042297658 3 }

That Simple. . .

■ Check

We now take the private key and the generator and show that it is indeed the same value.

In[19] : = **kP** [**G , Pr**]

        Assert [**% == Pu**]

Out[19] = { 4 627881390348812809382553037884091364606718395793759346393 ,
        412672125774816484308062906760412646682010943094042297658 3 }

For completeness , we now test 500 id' s

In[21] : = **TestVector** @ **Table** [**IdToPublicKey** [**i**] **== kP** [**G , IdToPrivateKey** [**i**]] ,
        { **i , 500** }]

References

[1] White Paper, The Clinton Administration's Policy on Critical Information Protection, President Decision Directive 63, May 1998

[2] NSA, Information Assurance Technical Framework, http://www. iatf. net, September 2000

[3] PITAC Report to the President, Cyber Security: Crisis of Prioritization, http://www. nitrd. gov, February 2005

[4] W. Diffie and M. E. Hellman, New Directions in Cryptography, IEEE Trans, Inform, Theory, IT-22 (1976), 644-
654

[5] Adi Shamir, Identity-Based Cryptosystems and Signature Schemes [C], Advances in Cryptology, CRYPT 84,
volume 196 of LNCS, Springer-Verlag, 1984: 47-53

[6] B. Schneier, Applied Cryptography, 2nd edition, Jphn Wiley & Sons Inc, 1996

[7] Standard for Efficient Cryptography, SET1: Elliptic Curve Cryptography, Certicom Research, version 1. 0,
Sep. 2000

[8] D. Boneh and M. Franklin, Identity-Based Encryption form the Weil Paring [C], Advances in Cryptology,
CRYPT 2001, VOLUME 2139 of LNCS, Springer-Verlag, 2001: 213-229

[9] M. Burrows, M. Abadi, R. Needham, "A Logic of Authentication, ACM Trans, on Computer Systems" 1990

[10] Li Gong, R. Needham, R. Yahalom, Reasoning about belief in cryptographic protocols, IEEE Computer Society
Press, May 1990

[11] Blaze M, Feigenbaum J, Lacy J, Decentralized trust management, IEEE Computer Society Press, 1996.

[12] R. Yahalom, B. Klein, and Th. Beth. , Trust relationships in secure systems—a distributed authentication perspective, IEEE Computer Society Press, 1993

[13] A. Jφsang. Prospectives for modeling trust in information security. NSW, Sydney, Australia, 1997

[14] TCPA, Design Philsophies and Concepts, version 1. 0, Jan. 2001

[15] TCPA, Main Specification, version 1. 1b, Feb. 2002

[16] Clay Wilson, Information Warfare and Cyberwaqr: Capabilities and Related Issues, Jun. 2004 (CRS reportfor
congress)

[17] PITAC, Cyber Security: a Crisis of Prioritization, Feb. 2005 (report to the president)

[18] Cyber Policy Review - Assuring Trusted and Regilient Information and communication infrastructure, http//:
www. usdoj. gov/criminal/cybercrime/cccriminal/01ccma. PDF

[19] Flavio D. Garcia, etc. Dismantling MIFARE Classic, www. sos. cs. n1/application/RFID/2008-esorics. pdf

［20］ S：WPSHR\LEGCNSL\XYWRITE\SCI09\CYBERSEC. 4 ［STAFF WORKING DRAFT］，Mar. 2009

［21］ 屈延文等．银行行为监管．北京：电子工业出版社，2004.11

［22］ 屈延文等．银行行为控制．北京：电子工业出版社，2004.11

［23］ 孙玉．电信网络总体概念讨论．北京：人民邮电出版社，2007.8

［24］ 孙玉．电信网络安全总体防卫讨论．北京：人民邮电出版社，2008.8

［25］ 王昭，袁春．信息安全原理与应用．北京：电子工业出版社，2010.1

反侵权盗版声明

电子工业出版社依法对本作品享有专有出版权。任何未经权利人书面许可，复制、销售或通过信息网络传播本作品的行为；歪曲、篡改、剽窃本作品的行为，均违反《中华人民共和国著作权法》，其行为人应承担相应的民事责任和行政责任，构成犯罪的，将被依法追究刑事责任。

为了维护市场秩序，保护权利人的合法权益，我社将依法查处和打击侵权盗版的单位和个人。欢迎社会各界人士积极举报侵权盗版行为，本社将奖励举报有功人员，并保证举报人的信息不被泄露。

举报电话：(010)88254396；(010)88258888

传　　真：(010)88254397

E-mail：dbqq@phei.com.cn

通信地址：北京市海淀区万寿路173信箱

　　　　　电子工业出版社总编办公室

邮　　编：100036